A PRISONER OF VERSAILLES

Golden Keyes Parsons

BOOK TWO IN THE
DARKNESS TO LIGHT SERIES

THOMAS NELSON
Since 1798

NASHVILLE DALLAS MEXICO CITY RIO DE JANEIRO BEIJING

Published in Nashville, Tennessee, by Thomas Nelson. Thomas Nelson is a registered trademark of Thomas Nelson, Inc.

Thomas Nelson, Inc., titles may be purchased in bulk for educational, business, fund-raising, or sales promotional use. For information, please e-mail SpecialMarkets@ThomasNelson.com.

Scripture references are taken from the King James Version of the Bible.

Publisher's Note: This novel is a work of fiction. Names, characters, places, and incidents are either products of the author's imagination or used fictitiously. All characters are fictional, and any similarity to people living or dead is purely coincidental.

Library of Congress Cataloging-in-Publication Data

Parsons, Golden Keyes, 1941–
    Prisoner of Versailles / Golden Keyes Parsons.
       p. cm. — (Darkness to light series ; bk. 2)
    ISBN 978-1-59554-627-2 (softcover)
    1. Huguenots—Fiction. 2. Louis XIV, King of France, 1638–1715—Fiction. 3. Persecution—France—History—17th century—Fiction. I. Title.
    PS3616.A7826P75 2009
    813'.6—dc22   2009021698

Printed in the United States of America

09 10 11 12 13 RRD 6 5 4 3 2 1

To our three daughers:
Amber, Andra, and Amanda,
who carry within them the rich heritage of
faith of our Huguenot ancestors.

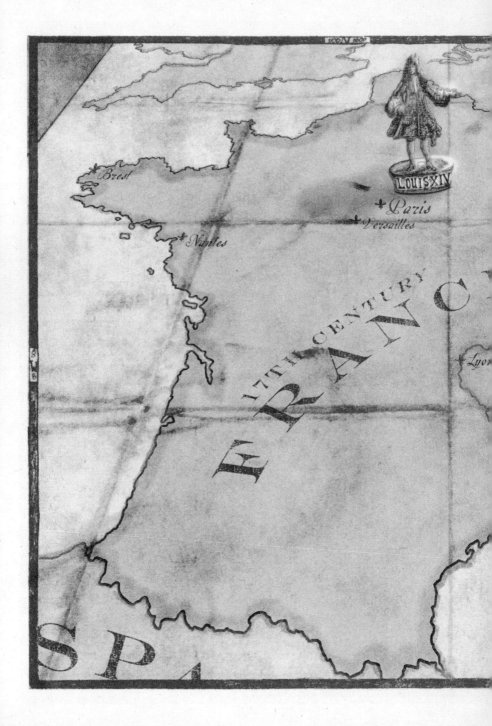

Brest

Paris
Versailles

Nantes

LOUIS XIV

17TH CENTURY
FRANCE

Lyon

SP

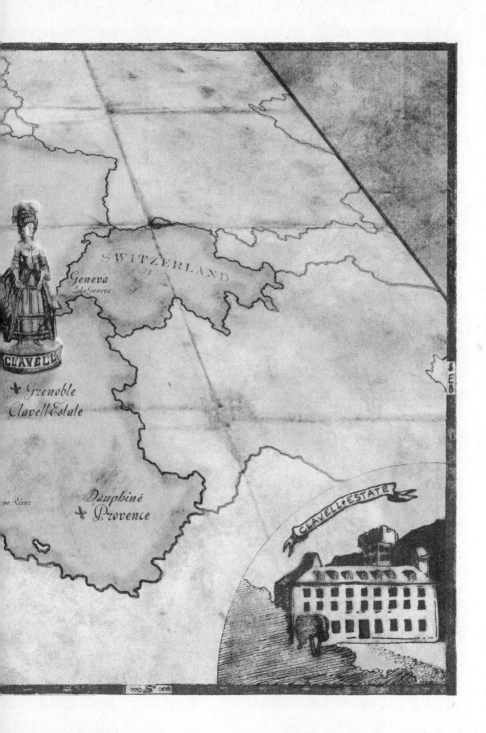

SWITZERLAND

Geneva
Lake Geneva

CLAVELL

★ Grenoble
Clavell Estate

ne River

Dauphiné
★ Provence

CLAVELL ESTATE

Glossary

Appartement—Literally an apartment, but was the name given the raucous gaming/gambling evenings at Versailles

Au revoir—Good-bye

Bastille—At this period in history, the king's prison in Paris

Bien—Fine, good

Bonjour—Hello, good morning, good afternoon

Bon—Good

Chéri (m), chérie (f)—Sweetheart

Consommation d'huile—Consumption, tuberculosis

Coucher—Evening ritual surrounding the king's retiring for the night

Coupé glissé—A gliding dance step

Cravate—Necktie

Cuisine de commune—Common kitchen

Fiacre—Carriage, hackney

Garde Suisse—An elite corps of palace bodyguards, known for their discipline and loyalty

Grand-mère—Grandmother

Grand-père—Grandfather

Hoitbois—Oboe

Incroyable—Incredible

Je t'aime—I love you

Je vous en prie—You are welcome

Justacorps a brevet—A blue garment worn by royalty and select courtiers

La Contredanse—A dance performed with couples facing each other, or in a circle

La Courante—A slow waltz

La Marelle Ronde—A children's game of hopscotch played in a circle

La Menuet—A dance in three-quarter time

La Sarabande—Slow dance in $3/2$ or $3/4$ time.

Lever—To get someone out of bed, i.e. the king's morning rising ceremony

Madame—Mrs., lady

Mademoiselle—Miss

Maîstresse—Mistress

Maîstresse en titre—Official, recognized mistress of the king

Maman—mommy

Méreau(x)—Tokens given to the faithful Huguenots upon
   entering worship, to be presented to elders before partaking of
   communion; used for identification as well

Merci—Thank you

Mère—Mother

Mesdames—Plural of Madame

Non—No

Oui—Yes

Pain mollet—Type of light bread roll made with milk

Papa—Daddy

Patron—Employer

Petite amie (f)—Term of endearment

Père—Father

Potage—Soup, stew

Pot-a-oie—Stuffed goose

Seigneur—Lord of an estate

S'il vous plaît—Please

Toilette—Washing up, grooming

Vraiment—Really

ONE

Go after her. Spare no expense. Do whatever you must, but bring Madeleine Clavell back to Versailles."

Captain Nicolas Maisson bowed to King Louis XIV. The musketeer's blue tunic brushed the floor as he swept his hat around in a flourish. "*Oui*, Your Majesty."

"I want her oldest son as well." The king rested against the front edge of his desk, his head lowered. The voluminous wig hid his eyes. He raised his head and stared past the soldier. He began to pace, then stopped to peer out a window. "Is Versailles not the most beautiful palace on earth?"

"Yes, Your Majesty. None more enchanting in all the world."

Visions of Madeleine strolling with him through the gardens when they and Versailles were all adolescents teased his mind. She

1

had grown up with him here. He would get her back. "Why would one not yearn to be here?"

The soldier did not answer. The king turned and with a wave of his hand dismissed the musketeer. "Be on your way. Take whomever you choose and whatever forces you need. I would begin in Geneva, John Calvin's bastion of Protestantism. That's where most of the Huguenots flee." The king's lips tightened, and he clipped his words. "If she is not there, find someone who knows where she is."

Captain Maisson bowed and prepared to take leave of the king.

"One more thing, Captain."

"Your Majesty?"

"You are not to use unnecessary force. Do not harm one hair of Madame Clavell's head, nor that of her son's."

JACOB VERON TIED HIS HORSE TO THE HITCHING RAIL IN front of the pub on the outskirts of Geneva and glanced around. The assistant to the pastor at the Cathedrale de St. Pierre pulled the brim of his soft hat down around his face and entered the noisy scene. A few men looked in his direction but didn't appear to pay him special attention. Thick, heavy smoke hung in the air, together with the odor of unwashed men, sweaty from work or travel. Jacob found a secluded table in the back and sat down.

A young barmaid approached. "What'll you have?"

"Just some ale."

"That's all?"

"That's all."

The barmaid chatted as she wiped down the table. "Don't believe I've seen you here before. New in town?"

He wished she would take her leave. "No . . . uh . . . well, actually, yes. That is, I haven't been here long."

She went to the bar and returned with a stein of ale. She bent over to place it in front of him, displaying a great deal of ample bosom over the top of her wide-cut bodice. "You wouldn't be in the market for some company tonight, now, would you?"

"Oh . . . uh, no," Jacob stammered. "I mean, you're very attractive, but I, uh, I'm here on business, or, uh, rather to meet a friend about a business, I mean . . ." His hand knocked into the stein, splattering drops of glistening liquor on the table before he caught it.

The barmaid swept the spill away with her towel and laughed. "Didn't mean to fluster you. If you change your mind, I'll be around, *chéri.*" She smiled at him again and left.

Jacob mopped his brow with his handkerchief and gulped down the ale.

Presently two musketeers entered, paused, and looked around the room. Jacob stood so they could see him in the crowd, and they shouldered their way toward him.

"Greetings, Monsieur Veron." The taller man with the bulbous nose and squinty eyes spoke first and sat on the opposite side of the table.

Jacob remembered his name to be Nicolas Maisson. The shorter man with the pockmarked face remained standing.

"Did you bring the money?" Jacob asked.

"No offer of drinks for your new . . . colleagues?"

"Of course. How rude of me." Jacob motioned to the barmaid as the shorter man pulled up a chair.

"Not nervous, are you, my friend?" Nicolas leaned across the table. "You are providing information valuable to the king of France. Surely you are not having second thoughts?"

"Not at all. I just need to get back to the Cathedrale."

"Back to your pastoral duties?" The tense atmosphere at the table exploded in coarse laughter. "Tell me, monsieur. Do all Huguenots exhibit such great loyalty as you?"

Jacob shifted in his chair. "My loyalty to King Louis, France's God-ordained sovereign, surpasses my loyalty to any other."

"That's what we like to hear. Give us the information we need, and then you get the money." Captain Maisson pulled a leather pouch from his tunic and threw it on the table.

Jacob reached for the bag, but Nicolas' huge paw clenched the pastor's skinny arm. "Not until you give us the information."

"How do I know the full amount is in the purse?"

"How do we know the information you have for us is accurate?"

"It is. I guarantee it is."

"*Bon!* I guarantee the money is all there." Nicolas leaned across the table again, his eyes boring into Jacob's and his hand still gripping Jacob's forearm. "I guess we are simply going to have to trust each other, *oui?*"

"Yes, I suppose so."

Nicolas released the pastor. Jacob kept his eye on the money bag as he talked.

"The king's hunch is correct. Madame Clavell and her children did come to Geneva from their estate in Grenoble to seek refuge at the Cathedrale de St. Pierre. They found a more permanent place to stay in a small village about an hour north of here with a Pastor Gérard Du Puy and his family."

"And her husband labors in the galleys."

"*Non.* The owner of the fleet to which François Clavell was sentenced, also a Huguenot, released him, and the Clavell family is now

4

reunited. However, you are in luck. Monsieur Clavell is ill, and from what I hear has only a few months left to live."

"Ah-h-h-h. This will be easier than we thought. And her son is with her?"

"She has two sons and a daughter."

"The older son."

"Yes, he is with her. Appears to be around fifteen years old."

"Hmmm. That would be about right."

"Excuse me?"

"Nothing. Nothing at all." Nicolas shoved the money bag toward Jacob. "I remember Madame Clavell from the early days at Versailles, when she and King Louis were inseparable. It's no surprise he can't get her out of his head." He paused. "Well, Pastor . . . enjoy your thirty pieces of silver."

Jacob cleared his throat and stuck the bag of coins in his belt. "Uh, there is one other thing that the king might like to know."

"What might that be?"

"One of King Louis' most trusted courtiers lent his able assistance to the reuniting of the Clavells. In fact, he escorted Monsieur Clavell from France to Geneva." Jacob's mouth settled in a grim slit. "The man has even embraced the Huguenot faith."

Nicolas pulled his gloves from his belt. "This information would certainly be of interest to the king. Who is it?"

Jacob Veron looked behind him and scanned the noisy barroom scene. "His name is Pierre Boveé."

Captain Maisson's eyebrows arched.

The smaller man spoke. "Let's get out of here. I don't like drinking with weasels."

But once Jacob started regurgitating information, he was like a

5

gossipy old woman. "I have reliable information that the Clavell family is planning to leave Switzerland in a few days and make their way to Amsterdam to book passage for the New World. If you plan to, uh, rescue her, that would be the time."

"Who will be with her? How many?"

"Well, her husband, her three children. Her brother-in-law. A couple of servants, probably."

"What about Boveé?"

"Maybe." Jacob jabbed the air with his bony finger. "But they won't be able to withstand your attack. They're not expecting trouble. I would stage it as a robbery. How many men do you have?"

The musketeer captain narrowed his already squinty eyes. "We don't need your advice on how to complete our mission. We will pick a time and place and use as little force as possible. The king does not want them harmed. He simply wants them back."

The two men pulled on their gloves.

"And he will get them back," Captain Maisson concluded. "King Louis always gets what he desires, and he desires Madeleine Clavell. As for Monsieur Boveé, I predict his days are numbered."

TWO

Madeleine Clavell and six-year-old Evangeline dawdled in front of the vendors and shops as they walked along the street. François had taken their two sons, Philippe and Charles, along with his brother, Jean, to the livery to secure repairs on some harnesses and bridles.

"*Maman*, where are we going?"

"I would like to go to a dress shop." She searched the street. "I wonder what is in fashion these days. I feel so out of touch with the civilized world." Madeleine looked at the coins in her hand. "It sounds like fun, just to be able to look."

"May I have a new bonnet?"

"Perhaps. I would like to purchase fabric to make some things for you and the boys. All of you are growing out of your clothes. And would you like to find something for Suzanne and Armond's little boy?"

Vangie bobbed her head up and down. "Yes, Maman! Could we get him a toy?" Vangie had grown attached to their former servants' toddler.

"We shall see. And then some fruit. Madame Du Puy asked me to see if we could find apples in the marketplace." She stopped in front of a small dress shop. "Let's go in here, *chérie*. We have some time before we're to meet your father and the boys."

"Why didn't they come with us?"

Madeleine laughed. "I think the men prefer to look at saddles and harnesses rather than dresses and bonnets, don't you?" She stuffed the coins into her drawstring bag and hurried inside.

The jingling of the bell on the door announced their entrance. Dark, highly polished wooden shelves reached to the ceiling on three sides of the shop. Hats and wigs rested on stands, and bolts of fabric lay stacked on tables.

Madeleine inhaled the odor of new fabric and dyes that recalled a more civilized time in her life. She touched the soft, silky fabrics and lifted the heavy brocades to look at the rich colors. She tried on a bonnet with a ridiculously tall tower of ribbons and looked in a wooden framed cheval mirror. Laughing at herself, she removed it and replaced her own bonnet, tucking her hair around her face beneath the ruffle and rearranging her mahogany curls around her shoulders.

The whispered words "French spies" and "Huguenots" halted Madeleine where she stood. Leaning into the mirror, she smoothed her dark eyebrows and pinched her cheeks.

The conversation was coming from two women trying on hats in the corner of the store, as the milliner, a wiry, elderly woman with thick, gray hair caught up under a lace cap, brought new wares from the back of the shop.

Madeleine sauntered through the store and picked up a parasol. She opened it and twirled it around. Perhaps she could afford that.

"Shhh." The milliner glanced over her shoulder.

Madeleine acted as if she hadn't heard and continued to walk back and forth between the bolts of material. Out of the corner of her eye, she saw the younger of the two women show the shopkeeper a *méreau*—the token of identification among Huguenots—and they continued their conversation in hushed tones. When the two women, with their new hats safely packed into boxes, exited the shop, the shopkeeper bustled toward Madeleine, a welcoming smile on her face.

"Does Madame wish to purchase the parasol?"

"Oh, why, yes, I believe I will." Madeleine had almost forgotten she was holding it.

"*Oui*, madame! It looks as if it were made for you. May I wrap it?"

"Yes, thank you." Madeleine shook some coins out of her bag. "How much will that be?"

The shopkeeper quoted her a price, and as Madeleine counted out the money, she included a méreau. The older woman looked at the coins in her hand, then shot a quick look at Madeleine. "I think you have given me too much."

"No, I don't think so." Madeleine picked up the new parasol along with the basket she had set on the counter. "Please, I'd like to inquire about the conversation I overheard with your two previous customers." Before continuing, she located Vangie, who sat in the corner of the shop with a kitten in her lap. In a whisper she asked, "French spies? In Geneva?"

The milliner fingered the méreau in her hand and lowered her voice. "I hear they are coming across the border and paying our citizenry to expel Huguenots from the cities. I understand the economy is suffering in France because so many of us . . . them . . . left to set up businesses in bordering countries. King Louis is livid and is reaching into other countries to try to lure the Huguenots back. But the French are not gaining many sympathizers here. As soon as the Huguenots are thrown out of a city through the front gate, the authorities usher them back into the town through the back."

She returned the méreau to Madeleine along with her change. "However, if those whom King Louis considers to be guilty of treason are caught, they are forced back into France and taken to the Bastille."

Madeleine took the coins and dropped them into her purse. "Thank you. Thank you very much. I will enjoy my new parasol, and I appreciate the information—more than you know."

The shopkeeper covered Madeleine's hand with her own and whispered, "God be with you."

"And with you. Come, Vangie." Madeleine took her daughter by the hand and walked out of the shop, her mind reeling. She looked into the faces of men on the street as they swiveled their heads to look at her. Were they French? Were there spies following her? A too-familiar sensation of panic began to overtake her. She picked up her skirt and ran into the street, dragging Vangie with her.

"Maman! Where are we going? You're hurting my arm!"

"Whoa there, madame!"

Madeleine whirled around to face a horse rearing over her and a buggy veering sharply to the curb. The skidding hooves narrowly missed her as the driver slung his whip in the air and struggled to bring the horse under control. Vangie screamed, and Madeleine scooped the child up in her arms and darted to the other side of the street.

"Madeleine!" François appeared from behind a vegetable cart and ran to her side.

"Where are the boys?" Madeleine grabbed the ruffled sleeve of her husband's shirt. "Where are my sons?" Her voice rose in alarm.

"They are right there, with Jean." He pointed to an ornate iron bench on the sidewalk next to a fruit and vegetable cart. Philippe and Charles sat there, chomping on bright-red apples, oblivious to their mother's narrow escape. "What's wrong? You nearly were run down."

Madeleine turned her back to Vangie and leaned in to whisper to her husband. "I just learned from the owner of the millinery shop that Louis is sending spies into Switzerland to flush out the Huguenots."

François took Madeleine's trembling hands. "Calm down. We are safe for now. Here, sit down." He led Madeleine to a bench and sat down with her. "We have known we cannot stay here indefinitely. We must make a new home for ourselves somewhere else—somewhere beyond Louis' reach."

"Where do you suggest? His arm is long indeed." Madeleine's bonnet had fallen off and hung loosely by the emerald green ribbons around her neck. A breeze blew down the street, whipping up tendrils of her hair that had come unpinned.

François reached toward her and twirled one of the curls around his finger. "We must go somewhere that he cannot find us or reach us. The New World. Our destiny has taken a strange turn, has it not?"

Vangie tugged at Madeleine's skirt. François took his daughter's hand. "Come with me, Vangie. Let's get the shopping done. Did you get a new bonnet?"

Vangie continued to sniffle. "No. Maman scared me."

11

"I'm sorry, *chérie*." Madeleine stood and kissed Vangie on the cheek. "Maman reacted foolishly. Forgive me?"

Vangie rubbed her eyes and nodded.

The small party finished their errands with haste—including the purchase of a bonnet for Vangie—and started back to the Du Puys' farm. The children sat in the bed of the wagon, comparing their new acquisitions. As usual, Charles kept up a running stream of comments and questions. The rocking of the wagon and steady clip-clopping of the horses' hooves finally lulled him and Vangie to sleep.

Silence engulfed the adults, till it was broken by François' coughing. Madeleine winced with each eruption.

"The coughing is getting worse."

François reached into a knapsack and removed a flask. He took a swig of the potion, and the coughing spasm eased. "I'm fine. No need to worry."

They lapsed once more into silence.

Jean maintained the team at a steady pace, glancing at Madeleine and François as they made their way home through the lengthening shadows.

Finally Madeleine spoke. "Jean, I overheard something in the milliner's shop." She glanced back at the sleeping children, then related what she had learned.

"I am not surprised." Jean chucked the reins to quicken the horses' gait. "What do you plan to do?"

François spoke up. "It becomes more apparent every day that we cannot remain here. The New World or Germany offers possibilities. It will be a challenge, but I'm sure Henri will go with us, and Philippe is maturing before our eyes."

Philippe's ears perked up at the mention of his name, and he leaned forward to hear the adults' conversation.

Madeleine smiled at her son. "We are discussing our future and your important part in it, but don't concern yourself with it right now. There will be plenty of time for making plans later." She reached back and patted his shoulder.

"I'm ready, Maman. Life on a pastor's farm is boring."

"Philippe! The Du Puys have been wonderful to us. We couldn't have made it this far without them."

"I know, but—"

"I'm afraid the high sense of danger and adventure in our lives the last two years has left its mark on you. You will never be content to live a sedentary life." Madeleine turned to François. "Perhaps he is more ready than I thought."

Her husband chuckled and nodded. "I understand his young man's heart. Consider all he has experienced: running for his life, protecting his brother from dragoons out to murder them, hiding out in a cave for weeks, ambushing a contingent of soldiers and having to kill a man in the process, fleeing to another country. He's been through more than most young men twice his age."

Young man? Philippe was Madeleine's little boy, but observing the fuzz beginning to appear on his upper lip, she realized he indeed had begun to mature into a man. And he had earned the title. He was tall, and muscular, and confident, and had proved himself not only physically strong but also hardy of soul. Charles was not far behind him, although Philippe still considered himself much superior to his younger brother.

Madeleine smiled. "You're right. Our sons are growing up."

Dusk was falling as they returned to the peaceful farm that had been their refuge for the past several months. Sitting between Jean and François on the wagon bench, Madeleine felt safe and secure.

Jean pulled the wagon around to the front of the house. "Let's unload your purchases, then I'll take care of the horses."

"Thank you, Jean." She reached back and shook Charles. His cap had fallen off, revealing his thick, red curls. She tousled his hair. "Wake up, Son."

Vangie sat up, rubbed her eyes, and whimpered. François helped Madeleine down and began to cough again.

Pierre Boveé, trusted courtier in King Louis' court, came out of the house. "Need any help?" He eyed the couple and approached the back of the wagon. "I'll get Vangie." He extended his arms. "Come here, Princess. I'll carry you."

The little girl willingly allowed herself to be taken into the courtier's strong arms. "I love you, Prince."

"I love you, too, Princess." Pierre had given the little girl the nickname when he and Jean rescued her from the convent where she'd been taken by dragoons acting under King Louis' orders. Vangie reciprocated with "Prince," and the nicknames had stuck. He kissed her forehead and carried her into the house.

François stood on the porch, bent over with his hands on his knees. Madeleine handed him a handkerchief. He covered his mouth and stood.

"A drink, please? Could you get me a drink?" Splotches of blood marred the white cloth when he pulled it away.

"Of course, dear." Madeleine ran into the house and returned with a tumbler of wine. "Here, this will help. Go on inside, *mon chéri*. I'll get the packages."

François' shoulders rose and his lips tightened as he drew in a labored breath.

Charles continued to snooze in the wagon bed, even amidst the jostling of packages being pulled out from around him. Madeleine reached over the side of the wagon and shook him again. "Charles! Wake up. We're home." She shoved the packages into his arms as he scooted out of the wagon and pointed him toward the house.

Home—not in reality. They had no place to call home. She knew now for certain that they would never return to France. France held danger for the Clavell family, and it appeared Switzerland did as well.

THREE

Death. Or life. Only a breath away. From a rocking chair on the porch, Madeleine watched her sons and their father play marbles in the late afternoon sunlight. Laughter and punches and slaps on the back punctuated the game as the male Clavells competed against one another. Then an unnatural, awkward split second of silence. François stood and clutched his chest.

Madeleine jumped to her feet, letting the rocking chair slam against the wall and rushed to catch her husband as he stumbled up the porch steps. He turned a tortured face toward her, his eyes laced with panic, and gasped, "I-I can't breathe."

He pulled Madeleine down with him as he dropped to his knees. She turned him over on the steps, face up. "Help! Somebody help me!"

Charles sprang from the game and ran inside, while Philippe knelt beside her and tried to hold his father upright.

"Relax, Papa. Breathe slowly. Breathe!" His voice rose in alarm. "Papa, breathe!"

Vangie ceased her game of *La Marelle Ronde* with the Du Puy daughters and ran onto the porch. "Papa! Papa! What's wrong with my daddy?"

Jean, Henri, and Pierre bounded across from the barn, the two younger men easily outrunning Henri, the Clavells' longtime servant and stable master.

Jean took charge. "Stand back, everybody. Give him air." He shooed the children away from the scene. "*S'il vous plaît*, we need room. Could someone get us a wet towel and some water?"

The Du Puys' oldest daughter, Rachel, turned and ran back inside. "I'll get them for you."

Jean scooped François, still struggling for each breath, into his arms and carried his gaunt frame upstairs to his bedroom. Rachel handed a damp towel and a tumbler of water to Madeleine as they passed by her on the stairs.

Pastor and Madame Du Puy hurried up to the bedroom. "What's wrong? What can we do?"

Jean answered, "A physician. Someone go for a doctor. Hurry!"

The gurgling in François' chest rattled throughout the room.

Madeleine's voice rose. "Somebody help him! He can't breathe!"

Pastor Du Puy turned on his heels and with surprising agility sped down the stairs. Jean placed his older brother on the bed, and Madeleine shoved pillows behind François' head. "Prop him up on these." She covered him with a comforter, although he was perspiring. It seemed the proper thing to do. With the towel she wiped his face and pushed his hair out of his eyes.

She looked around the room at her family. Philippe stood at the end of the bed, his eyes downcast. Charles knelt across the bed from her, his eyes wide with terror. Henri stood beside him with his hand on the boy's shoulder. She could hear Vangie crying behind her. Jean took the child by the hand and came beside Madeleine. Tears streamed down his cheeks.

Madeleine felt strangely calm.

Madame Du Puy gathered her daughters, who huddled at the doorway of the bedroom, and ushered them out. "I'll bring some broth."

And Pierre, the displaced courtier from Versailles, backed away from the intimate family scene and went out onto the porch. The only prayer he could utter was, "Oh, God, help him. Oh, God, help."

The family, speaking in guarded undertones, waited in the room until the doctor arrived. So young. Madeleine had expected an older man.

Henri and Claudine, the children's governess, stepped outside the room with the children. Madeleine and Jean sat on a bench in the corner of the bedroom. Madeleine stared out the window at the serene, stately peaks of the Swiss Alps in the distance, white with mountain snows.

After a bit, Jean stood and began to pace. The ticking of a large grandfather clock rose above the rustling of the doctor and the muffled sounds from downstairs and pierced Madeleine's awareness.

"I never noticed that clock being so loud before. Did you, Jean?"

"What? The clock?"

"Madame Clavell? Shall we step into the hallway?" The doctor stood at the foot of the bed.

Madeleine and Jean followed the doctor through the door.

"I'm sorry, Madame Clavell." He shook his head. "I'm afraid your husband is dying."

18

"Dying? But he seemed to be doing better, except for the coughing spells."

"I understand he spent some time in the king's galleys. That he got out alive at all is quite remarkable, but that is probably where he contracted *consommation d'huile*. The disease comes and goes, getting worse with each attack, until—until the end."

"How long does he have, doctor?"

"I predict a matter of hours, perhaps even less than that. Certainly no more than a day. He is suffocating from fluid collecting in his lungs, and he is not strong enough to expel it." The doctor took Madeleine's hand in his own. "Madame Clavell, if I were in your situation, I would pray that God, in his mercy, would take him quickly now. Your husband is suffering."

"Is there nothing you can do to ease his pain?"

"I will give you laudanum to mix with wine and spices, and you will need to help him drink it. Then he will fall into a dreamlike state. The only thing . . ." The doctor paused. "He will not be responsive to you after he has taken the laudanum. And if your religion involves taking last rites, confession of sins . . . he will not be able to do that."

"We are Huguenot. We believe the well-being of our souls is dictated by faith alone in Jesus' sacrificial death for us. My husband's eternal destiny is secure."

"As you say." The doctor waited.

Madeleine moved to Jean's side, and he put his arm around her shoulders. "Jean, are we in agreement?"

He stared at the emaciated frame of his brother. "I don't want him to suffer any longer."

"Nor do I."

Madeleine moved to the bed, sat next to her husband, and took his hand. It felt clammy.

François opened his once bright eyes, now sunken and hollow, and tried to sit up. He looked at his wife. Through the rattling in his throat, he managed to speak. "Madeleine, do what's best . . . for all of us." He closed his eyes and slumped back down on the pillow. His tormented breathing grated against Madeleine's heart with every heave of his chest.

She bent over and embraced him. His bony shoulders protruded through his shirt, and she could still feel the scars left by the galley master's lashes on his back. "My brave husband, don't worry. Jean and I will take care of everything." She stroked his hand. It felt cool, and the skin hung loose on his fingers. She loved his slender hands that had been so strong—the hands that had held a weapon and fought for their family; chopped wood and reined in a wild stallion; the hands that had cupped her chin and caressed her face. What would she do without François?

"Jean." François looked around for his brother.

"I'm right here."

"Take care of my family."

"I will. You know I will." Jean's throat caught, and he turned away.

The doctor approached the bedside with a wine goblet in his hand and gave it to Madeleine. The red liquid sloshed in the cup. She looked at her trembling hands and placed the vessel on the bedside table. The waning afternoon sun glinted through the window and sparkled on the surface of the potion.

"Jean, would you please go get the children? Summon Pastor Du Puy and the servants as well." When all had returned, François stirred, coughing and struggling for breath. "Help me to sit up, please."

The doctor put François' arms on his shoulders and, with an expert lift, raised him to a sitting position. Madeleine put extra pillows behind his head. François extended his hand and beckoned his children to gather around him. Vangie climbed on the bed beside her father and patted his hair.

François said, "I'm so proud of every one of you. Philippe, what a fine young man you have become. Come here, Son."

Philippe bent over, and François whispered something in his ear. Philippe nodded and embraced his father.

"Charles? What a joy you have been to us. A bright spot. Continue to bring that unbridled joy to your mother. *Oui?*"

"*Oui*, Papa." He sniffed and unashamedly wiped the tears away with the palm of his hand.

"And, Vangie . . ." François paused and started coughing again.

Vangie took his hand and caressed it. "Papa, does it hurt?"

"Yes, *ma petite*. It hurts a bit."

Vangie laid her head on his shoulder.

Madeleine motioned Pastor Du Puy to come closer. "Please pray for us, Pastor."

Gérard Du Puy began to pray softly over the family. "Heavenly Father, you are our hope in life. You are our hope in death. Whom have we in heaven but you? When we approach a moment like this, there's not much we can offer except our ceaseless praise and gratitude for your Son, Jesus, for his atoning blood to pay for our sins on the cross, and for his victory over death and the grave. So, we do that now. We simply praise you, and we thank you." He paused and wiped his eyes with his handkerchief. "We are your people, the sheep of your pasture. Into your hands we commit this precious soul." Pastor Du Puy looked around at his tiny assembled flock. "Amen and amen."

"Thank you," Madeleine whispered. She gathered Vangie in her arms. "Come, now. The doctor is going to give Papa something to take away the pain. Children, say good night to your papa."

"Thank you, Pastor." François reached to embrace Gérard. The pastor wept openly as he held François' frail frame in his arms. Then François repeated his request. "Jean, Henri, Claudine. You will take care of my family? You will take good care of them?"

Henri straightened himself up as tall as he could in his old age. "I shall consider it an honor to continue to serve your family."

François smiled and lay back down. "Loyal Henri. I knew I could count on you."

Madeleine leaned over François with Vangie, and the little girl kissed him on the cheek. "Good night, Papa."

François smiled and held on to her hand for a moment, then he let her go.

Charles and Philippe started out the door. Philippe's eyes filled with unshed tears, and he grabbed hold of Charles' arm. Charles turned back toward his father, broke from Philippe's grip, and dashed to his father's bedside, flinging himself into François' arms. "Oh, Papa! Don't go. Don't leave us!"

"I will always be with you, Son. God is with you, and I will be with God. So I will always be there."

Jean gently pulled the boy away from his father and took him out. Madeleine could hear him sobbing even as they moved down the stairs. Claudine took Vangie with her and closed the door.

Left alone now, Madeleine sat down on the bed and took François' hand between her own, caressing and kissing it over and over. He struggled to smile at her.

"*Mon amor*, I have been the luckiest man alive to have you for my wife."

"And I have been the luckiest—no, the most blessed, woman alive to have you for my husband."

"I have given Jean and Philippe instructions. You have no need to worry." François heaved a labored inhalation. "And . . . Madeleine, let Pierre help you."

Madeleine startled at her husband's words.

"Don't fret over this. He loves you. Let him help you any way he can." He paused, breathing heavily. "You must go to the New World as we planned. God will provide."

"The New World? I cannot, François—not without you!"

"Listen to me. You must get out of Europe. I have a sense that you don't have much time. You must go quickly."

Madeleine shook her head. "We will be fine. We can make that decision later."

François hesitated, and his breathing calmed. "I told you once that *je t'aime* was not enough to express how much I love you. I still feel that way. But that is what I want to leave you with—*je t'aime. Je t'aime.*"

"I love you, too, my dearest. Oh, how I love you." She brushed his hair away from his damp forehead and held him in her arms.

François rested his head on her shoulder. Then he reached for the wine goblet. Madeleine held it as he drank the mixture. The flame in the lantern flickered in its feeble attempt to stay the descending darkness. Madeleine raised the wick. She lay beside her husband of sixteen years for the last time. It seemed to her that the shadows in the room pulsated with the spirits of Huguenots gone before.

When he took his last breath, Madeleine buried her face in the comforter and muffled her sobs of grief. The room grew dark and cool. How long she stayed curled up beside François, she did not know. At length she stood, brushed his hair back, and placed a kiss on his forehead. Her lips brushed across the distinctive scar, inflicted by the dragoon's sword so long ago when they first met. She caressed his cheek.

"Oh, my beloved. It's too soon, too soon. Our children, our . . . grand . . . chil . . . dren . . ." She took a deep, broken breath. "How can I go on without you? Where do we go now?"

Rivulets of hot tears flowed down her cheeks and fell off her chin, and she didn't bother to wipe them away. Madeleine held on to his hand and stared at his face, memorizing every wrinkle, every detail. "I think I've not seen such peace on your face, my husband, in a very long time." Presently, she folded both his hands on his chest. "Farewell, my brave François. Until we meet on the other side."

FOUR

"You've heard of the man in the iron mask?" Pierre looked about the circle gathered around the fireplace.

They all nodded. With François' funeral only two days past, a somber mood still hung in the air, but the laughter of children filtered through the room from the kitchen.

"That is not fantasy. He truly exists. No one knows who he is for sure, but the rumor is that he is Louis' twin brother. The twin, allegedly carried away at birth to be raised in obscurity, opened the way for Louis alone to claim the throne when his father died. When they became young men, they say Louis had him confined in the mask so no one could identify him."

Philippe, sitting on the floor beside his mother, looked up and gulped.

"I've heard those rumors, Pierre, but I never believed them. I never saw that side of Louis." Madeleine's voice grew taut.

An awkward hush followed. Jean and Gérard Du Puy leaned forward in their chairs. The light from the fire flickered across the faces gathered around the hearth.

Pierre lowered his head. "Forgive me, madame, if I have insulted you. I mean no offense." His voice softened. "The rumor about the prisoner being Louis' twin may not be true, but there is indeed such a man that has been held captive these many years. I have seen the man in the iron mask for myself."

Jean spoke up. "You have seen him with your own eyes?"

"*Oui*, with my own eyes."

Madeleine sat back into her chair. "Well, I certainly want to hear this. Forgive me, Pierre. I did not mean to question your word. Tell us, when did you see him and . . . how?"

"Two musketeers are assigned to guard him at all times. Late one night, when I was returning to the palace, I observed them taking him into the Bastille. The court gossip is that he has been confined to the island of Sainte-Marguerite for most of his life. He continually wears a mask; however, it is not always an iron one. The one I saw was iron, making his appearance hideous. But those who attend him say that while in his cell, he wears a black velvet mask."

Madeleine's curiosity spurred her on. "Could you tell anything else about his appearance?"

"Only that he does seem to be about the same size as Louis. But to be perfectly honest, I couldn't see all that well in the darkness."

Madeleine exhaled slowly. "I had always discounted those stories as fanciful rumor. It seems I may have been mistaken. Obviously the

Louis who rules France at this time is not the Louis I knew as a girl."

Madame Du Puy puttered around the kitchen, finishing the evening chores. Claudine, still taking her responsibilities as governess to the Clavell children seriously, had taken Vangie and Charles upstairs to bed.

The conversation in the parlor turned to the possibility of the Clavells traveling to the New World.

"I am sure you are aware of the dangers of that venture. The voyage is long and arduous. Many never make it across the ocean. And then the rigors of homesteading in an unfamiliar country—much planning and prayer should accompany a decision such as this." Pastor Du Puy slapped his knees for emphasis.

"What other choice do we have?" Madeleine leaned forward in her chair. "Louis' influence is too far-reaching in Europe. We cannot escape from him anyplace we go in this part of the world."

"I must agree with Madeleine." Pierre sighed. "Having been in court at Versailles for many years, I have firsthand knowledge of how far the king will go to satisfy his whims. One walk through the gardens at Versailles will confirm that he will go to any expense to get precisely what he wants."

Henri nodded. "I've seen that for myself. The gardens are magnificent—fountains and pools at every turn. Just the water supply has to cost the government untold expenditures. And the flowers, the orange trees . . . incredible."

Pierre spoke again. "King Louis has a soft, compassionate side, but he also has a troubling dark side. He will do whatever is necessary to get what he wants." He looked at Madeleine. "Even to the extent of sending spies into Switzerland."

MADELEINE AWOKE THE NEXT MORNING TO THE CLATTER of pots and pans in the kitchen. She glanced over at Vangie, who had insisted on sleeping with her mother since François' death. It was just dawn. As Madeleine reached for her dressing gown, she noticed that Philippe and Charles were gone from their pallet beside her bed. She hurried to the door and opened it.

Madeleine dressed quickly. She breathed in the heavy aroma of bread baking as she opened the door and glanced back at Vangie. The child had not stirred.

As she entered the kitchen, the men around the table glanced up and greeted her. Lanterns lit the kitchen, along with the fireplace. Pastor Du Puy motioned for her to join them. "Come, dear. Pierre is taking leave of us today."

"No! Why so soon?" The words were out of her mouth before she could censor them.

"Madame, the king is going to become suspicious if I stay away much longer." Pierre's characteristic wide Boveé smile spread across his face. "He would be certain that I had found a beautiful lady and escaped to a far country, never to return. Then he would send out another courtier to find you and your family." He stood and put a round of cheese and a loaf of rye bread in his pack. "If I return to court now, I believe I can delay Louis' pursuit of you at least a few months. By then, we can hope, he will grow weary of the chase and turn his attention to other things."

"What will you report to him?" Madeleine allowed herself to look directly into Pierre's dusky gray eyes—the eyes that she saw the first time hidden behind a mask at a court ball and that now hid behind a mask of concealed emotion.

"I will tell him that I was able to find the owner of the ship to which François was assigned in Brest, which is the truth—well, almost the truth. I did find the grandson of the owner. I will tell him that he was no longer listed. He will assume from that information that François died at sea—which, of course, is now no longer an issue . . ." Pierre hesitated and looked down. "Due to the fact that I have been gone so long, I will tell him that I went to the estate to try to trace Madame Clavell, but could not find anything at all."

Pierre looked at Madeleine. "I will tell Louis that we can assume you have left the country, but I have no idea where you have gone. By that time, I genuinely will not know where you are." He closed his pack and hoisted it onto his shoulder. "I prefer not to know at this point. A strange occurrence—since I've come to faith, I'm finding it more difficult to lie. It used to be so easy."

Pastor De Puy chuckled.

Pierre shifted his pack. "Well, be that as it may, I can always contact you, Pastor, if I need to find the Clavells. Can I not?"

"Indeed! You are welcome here anytime."

"*Merci*. You have been most kind . . ." Pierre looked around the table, his eyes bright with unshed tears. "How can I ever . . . ?" He faltered. "I don't know how to thank you for what your family has done for me. I have come to know God. You have shown me the way of faith. You have shown me the way to have true life."

The group gathered around, and Pastor Du Puy began to pray over Pierre. Pierre could not speak as the men bade him farewell.

Madeleine stood apart from the others, holding a handkerchief to her eyes. Of course Pierre must return to Versailles, but she didn't feel she could bear another loss so soon. She turned her head away.

"Maman, what's wrong?" Vangie had come down the stairs, unnoticed during the prayer, and stood by her mother's side, rubbing her eyes.

"Oh, I didn't hear you, chérie." Madeleine blew her nose and took a deep breath. "Pierre has decided to return to France."

"No! I don't want you to go, Prince!" Vangie ran and threw herself into Pierre's arms.

"Ah, Princess. I will see you again someday."

Vangie began to sob. "No, you can't go. You can't leave us again. Please don't go. Don't let him leave. Maman, stop him!"

Jean tried to pull the distraught child from Pierre's arms, but she refused to let go. "Come on, Vangie. Pierre must return to court for now."

"But why? Why can't he stay with us?"

Madeleine stepped in. "Listen to me, chérie. He is going to go back and report to King Louis that we have fled the country so that the king will cease looking for us. Pierre's going to continue to help us, but he has to return to France to do that."

Vangie began to loosen her hold. Madeleine looked at Pierre. Her heart thudded in her chest, and she found herself short of breath. "Anyway, he may be joining us again after a while. Right, Pierre?"

His eyes softened. "We shall see. But for now, I must finish my assignment." He tickled Vangie underneath her chin. "Besides that, don't you remember that you promised to marry me when you grow up? I'll need to see you again to collect on my promise."

Vangie nodded and let her mother take her. Madeleine shook her head at Pierre. Promises made to a little girl were not easily forgotten. He walked toward the door amidst much backslapping and good wishes. He turned and looked at his newfound family once more, then stepped out the door. They all watched from the porch as the sun sliced over the rugged peaks of the Alps. Pierre put on his gloves and mounted his horse. The black Percheron, anxious to be on his way, pranced sideways, waiting for Pierre's command to go.

"*Au revoir*, dear friends. Until we meet again." He tipped his hat, spurred his horse, and rode off to the east toward France.

The family waved at the young man who had become an integral part of their family in the mysterious way only God can work. The others went back into the house, but Madeleine leaned against a post on the porch and watched Pierre ride out of her life once more. She squinted against the sun and shaded her eyes with her hand. Without warning, Pierre stopped, turned, and touched his hand to his heart, then whirled the stallion around and galloped away.

MADELEINE WENT THROUGH THE DAY AUTOMATICALLY performing her chores, unmindful of the bustle of activities around her. She responded with unconscious smiles at the antics of her children and gave mindless answers to their questions.

After supper she ascended the stairs to her empty room and pulled a small, dark chest from under her bed. She placed it on the vanity and got the key from her trunk. A slight smile creased her face as she thought how enraged Commander Paul Boveé would be to know that he and his soldiers had overlooked the box in their plundering of the chateau. In one small way, at least, they had outwitted their nemesis. She imagined his glistening black eyes and his set jaw grinding in consternation. It was hard to believe that he was Pierre's father. The two were a study in startling contrasts.

It had been François who thought to look for the chest in

the rubble of their family chateau and brought it with him to Switzerland—so like her husband to quietly provide for his family and offset her impetuousness.

Madeleine opened the chest and sighed. Jewelry that belonged to another life lay atop the coins—her own pieces as well as those inherited from her mother and grandmother. She pulled an enamel and ruby necklace from the chest and fingered the cold stones.

She remembered her mother wearing the exquisite piece in the early days of Versailles. How she as a child had begged her mother to let her wear it. Maman would laugh and always give her the same answer: "When you grow up."

Madeleine picked up another heavy necklace encrusted with emeralds and diamonds. *I am grown up now, and what am I to do with all of this? I have no need of it anymore.*

She laid the lavish adornment on the table. She removed the other gems and gently arranged them by matching sets—earrings, bracelets, brooches, necklaces, and rings. Memories flooded over her as she recalled her mother and grandmother wearing the glittering jewels.

She found her mother's favorite pearl brooch, placed it beside a long multi-strand pearl necklace. Her breath caught as she saw the glittering jet of her mother's mourning brooch lying among the fanciful pieces. She pulled it out of the box and put it on. Tears that came so quickly now filled her eyes as she looked in the mirror. Now she was a widow.

She fingered the pin and looked at the display of sparkling stones. *I'm not ready to part with them. They are all I have left of Maman.*

She removed a bag of coins and dumped it out on the table. Small pieces of silver clanked onto the wooden surface along with the coins—ornate serving spoons, carving knives, a small cloisonné box.

She opened the box and emptied out a pair of petite pearl earrings . . . Louis' gift to her on her fourteenth birthday. It was the beginning of their young fascination with each other. How long ago it seemed now.

She surveyed the contents of the chest. They were in better shape to purchase passage to the New World than she realized.

A sinking sensation pulled at Madeleine's emotions. Another country. Another language. An arduous, if not perilous, ocean voyage. How could she subject her children to such a dangerous journey? How could she leave Europe?

But how could she stay? How much more could the Clavell family endure?

I will be with you. I will never leave you or forsake you.

Madeleine had her answer. She would do whatever was necessary to save her family. She would go wherever she needed to go. God would be with her.

FIVE

Pierre dismounted and groaned. The odor of leather and horse sweat in the outer yard of the stables, together with the fragrance of the flowers in the gardens and the dusty smell of the perpetual construction, wrapped familiar arms around him.

A stableboy jumped to catch hold of the reins. "Welcome back to Versailles, Monsieur Boveé. I trust your trip was successful."

Pierre stared at the young man. *What is he asking? Does he know where I've been? But how could he know that?* Then Pierre realized his imagination was playing tricks on him. It was simply a casual remark. "*Oui*, but terribly long and draining. I am eager to get back into my apartment and bathe." He tugged at his pack.

"Shall I call someone to assist you?"

"That's not necessary." Pierre started to go, then turned back. "Can you tell me, is the king in residence?"

"He returned just this morning. The king has been in Paris for a few weeks, conferring with his generals."

"What does the court gossip say about that?"

The stableboy looked around. "That the king plans continued penetration into Holland and the Rhineland."

Pierre shook his head. Would Louis never be satisfied? "Thank you." He gave the young man a pat on the shoulder. "Take good care of my steed—he's a special one."

"*Oui*, monsieur. You can count on me. A black Percheron—unusual."

"Yes, and a more even-tempered and dependable horse you'd be hard-pressed to find."

"What's his name?"

"*Tonnerre.*"

"Thunder—that is a fitting name for him?"

Pierre chuckled. "*Oui.* He is a bit more high-spirited than most Percherons, but he has a quiet strength and courage. His power rather rumbles beneath the surface. And what is *your* name?"

"Gabriel, monsieur."

"Ummm, Gabriel. Is that a fitting name for *you?*"

The young lad laughed. "Well, I'm no angel, if that's what you mean."

Something about the lad reminded Pierre of Philippe. His eyes were lighter, but the age and his smile—Pierre couldn't quite put his finger on it. "You remind me of a young man I care very much about."

The boy's countenance brightened. "Your son?"

Pierre laughed. "No, I have no children. I'm not married. But he's much like family to me." Pierre started to say that the boy they were discussing lived in Switzerland, but he caught himself. "He lives in . . . he lives out of the country."

Tonnerre began to paw the ground.

"Better fetch him some feed and water, Gabriel, and get that saddle off. He really enjoys being curried down. He will be your friend forever."

"*Oui*, monsieur. Right away."

"Perhaps I shall see you again soon."

"I hope so." The eyes of the underling reflected his admiration for the striking courtier.

Pierre dug in his tunic and pulled out a coin. "Here, son. Thank you for the extra good care you're going to see that my horse receives."

"*Oui*, monsieur. You can count on me." Gabriel turned and led the horse toward the stable. "*Au revoir*. I shall give Tonnerre the finest attention of any steed in the stables."

Pierre chuckled and trudged through the dispersing crowd in the courtyard as shadows of the approaching evening began to engulf the chateau. He waved to a group of fellow courtiers huddled together in a cluster.

The young men tossed greetings his way.

"Ahhh, it's Pierre! Welcome back."

"Hasn't been the same without you."

"We had best warn the ladies of the court. Their virtue is no longer safe."

Pierre shifted his pack and kept walking, dismissing their crude comments with a gesture of his head.

The spectral images of darkness spreading across the cobblestones spelled the end of another day at Versailles. Pierre sensed a finality of his tenure at the opulent court of King Louis XIV. Not that he was surprised. Ever since the Lord God of heaven had reached through the trees of the forest that day and breathed life into his soul, Pierre knew that his future did not lie in the posturing and politics of the government of France.

Now that he had converted and was a Huguenot—*a Huguenot!* Pierre stopped in his progress to his apartment, one foot on a highly polished marble step. He looked down at his boots, dirty and scuffed from his travels. His knees trembled beneath him, and he leaned against the banister for balance. This unspeakable notion, which had been forming in the mists of his mind, now floated to the forefront. Although still Catholic, he had been privy to what it meant to be Huguenot. He had identified closely with the Clavells and their beliefs. He was confused and didn't know what he was now. Snide remarks, guffaws of derision, jeers, and judgments of the persecuted Protestants, whom he had come to love, echoed in his memory. He hung his head.

Oh, God, I have slandered your children, my brothers. How can you ever forgive me?

He shook his head, walked around the ever-present scaffoldings, and climbed the stairs. How long would he be able to maintain a façade of conformity to the court system? He knew he must give the Clavells time to flee. But he also knew that he could not remain at court much beyond that. Either he would be discovered, thus perhaps leading to the discovery of Madeleine and her family's whereabouts, or he would be sucked back into the subtle seduction of the immoral and conniving court life. Remembrances of his former life sickened him. He let himself into his tiny, sparsely furnished apartment, dropped his gear, and sat on the edge of his bed.

He rang for a servant and scrawled a message for the lad to deliver to the king's quarters, informing Louis of his return. Perhaps he could see the king tomorrow evening during gaming at *appartement*, tie things up swiftly, and leave. He washed and climbed into bed. The meeting with King Louis dominated his thoughts. Pierre wanted nothing more than to complete his "mission" and be on his way.

How strange was this life. He had spent his entire career learning the nuances of double-talk in the politics of court life, and now his newfound faith disallowed him to use the cunning half-truths. When tempted to lapse into it, something alive and moving deep within him jabbed at his spirit. It was more than simply wounded feelings; it was a physical searing in his soul. He had never experienced anything like it before.

In spite of their troubled history together, Pierre hoped to find his father at Versailles and not off on some long-extended assignment. The seeds of bewilderment had been sown into the soft soil of Pierre's innocent heart as a three-year-old boy when his father abandoned him and his mother had matured into a bitter crop of resentment. Upon his mother's death several years later, his father had brought him to Versailles to be a stableboy, leaving his care entirely to the stable master.

Commander Boveé had made overtures toward his son in the last few months, inviting him to accompany him places, introducing him loudly as "my son." Why did he want to claim Pierre now, when he had wanted nothing to do with him as a boy? Pierre resented his father's recent intrusion into his life. And yet he knew he could not carry that burden of resentment any longer. He wanted to attempt some sort of reconciliation and express a veiled good-bye.

Pierre tossed to the right, then to the left in his dark, dreary room. The mere slit of a window allowed only a minute view of the sky, but Pierre was grateful to even have a cubicle at the chateau. Many of his fellow courtiers slept wherever they could or resided in matchboard cabins in town, hot in summer and cold in the winter, with the ever-present stench of neighboring latrines lingering in the air.

As weary as he was from his long trip, slumber escaped him. He played out his conversation with Louis over and over in his head, until finally he floated into a restless sleep.

A loud crash startled Pierre awake. He bolted up, the thumping in his chest threatening to suffocate him. He leapt from his bed and grabbed the sword hanging from the bedpost. Glancing wildly around the room, he noticed a streak of sunlight gleaming through the window.

He breathed a sigh of relief and began to chuckle. Broken shards of the basin and water pitcher lay scattered on the floor at the base of the washstand. He must have hit it with his foot. He grabbed the towel and swabbed the water. He must gain control of himself. Louis would see right through him.

His knees trembled beneath him, and he sat on his bed. What would he say to the king? How would he skirt the truth that he had indeed found the Clavells and that they were planning a way of escape—without telling a blatant lie? And wouldn't God forgive him if he had to lie in order to protect them?

Pierre sheathed his sword and lay back down on his bed. No hurry this morning. Only a few people knew he had returned. He had all day to rest and plan his approach to the king this evening at appartement. He closed his eyes.

Then suddenly Pierre slipped to his knees. "Heavenly Father, I'm such a novice at this. I didn't even think to pray." He bowed his head.

"Will I ever learn to seek your direction first, instead of making my own plans and then asking you to bless them? Will I ever learn how to hear your voice above my own? Forgive me of my pride and arrogance. Cleanse my mind from my selfish thinking. Place your thoughts in me. Protect me as I talk to the king, and protect Madeleine and her family as they make preparations to flee. Work out the timing. Give them a way of escape." Pierre couldn't think of anything else to say. "Uh, amen."

A habit of a lifetime, he made the sign of the cross and arose. Was it still acceptable to make that gesture? He seemed to sense a smile from the Lord.

"Very well, I guess I'm—uh—we're ready. Oh, one more thing." Pierre knelt again quickly. "I would like to see my father before I leave. Would you make a way for that to happen?" Was it permissible to ask God to do something like that? "Uh . . . if it is your will, that is." He had heard Pastor Du Puy end his prayers in that manner.

Pierre took the time to give his goatee an overdue trim, dressed, and went to breakfast with the other courtiers and staff to catch up on the latest court gossip. Only in the company of fellow courtiers could one speak freely of politics. Cleverly disguised language, however, abounded even in the attendants' dining area. He sighted familiar faces and joined with his colleagues.

"*Bonjour!*"

"Look who has returned from his countryside wanderings."

"Good to see you. Are you back for a while?"

"What clandestine mission took you away this time?" Pierre's closest acquaintance, Robert Devereaux, climbed over the bench and sat beside Pierre with a jab to his side. "You left quite suddenly, didn't you? Your patron has latched onto me—working me doubly hard."

Robert grinned, and Pierre noticed that his friend had chipped one of his front teeth.

"Work's good for you." Pierre slapped him on the back. "I've been on one of the king's wild goose chases to satisfy his curiosity about a spurned lost love."

The young men guffawed at Pierre's joke.

"What mischief have *you* been in, my friend? Looks like you found yourself on the wrong end of a fist."

Robert touched his mouth. He was known among the courtiers, and the ladies of the court, for his blond good looks. He and Pierre presented a dashing picture of contrasts. Robert's perfect, white teeth now bore the battle scars of a confrontation. However, Pierre noted, the disfigurement didn't hinder his friend's handsomeness. In fact, it seemed to add some needed character.

Robert looked around the table with his sky blue eyes. "Nothing really. Simply a disagreement concerning a lady's honor."

Pierre laughed. "Since when have you worried about a lady's honor?"

The young men around the table snickered as they dug into their morning meal. The initial bantering over with, Pierre worked his way through the conversational maze and found that things appeared to be quiet, except for Colbert, the king's minister of finance, who was ranting as usual that the king was bankrupting the country with his continual raising of taxes, expansion of the French military, and never-ending construction at Versailles.

"Will you be going to gaming tonight, Robert?" On the one hand, Pierre would welcome his friend with him as he reported to the king. On the other, the less that everyone knew about his latest mission, the better—fewer questions to answer.

Pierre felt pressed on every side by hypocrisy and duplicity. Nothing bore the mark of authenticity. He searched the faces of those around him—faces he had grown up with and knew—or thought he knew—well. But it seemed now that the Spirit of God had opened his eyes to see the loneliness and the hearts behind the smiling faces, which ached for recognition. No wonder Jesus called this phenomenon being born again. It was as if Pierre were seeing the court of France from the perspective of a different person—a new person entirely.

"Of course."

Robert's reply interrupted Pierre's thoughts. "What?"

"Of course I will be going to appartement tonight. I don't want the king wondering if I've trounced off to Paris." Robert stared at Pierre. "You asked if I was going to gaming tonight."

"Oh, sorry. I was lost in my thoughts." Pierre turned and smiled at his friend. "Wonderful. It will be like old times."

PIERRE MADE HIS WAY WITH THE OTHER COURTIERS, ladies, and nobility of the court through the continuing construction of the Hercules Drawing Room, along the east wall of the chateau, past the sumptuous buffet tables piled high with pyramids of fruit, lemons, oranges, and flowers, and into the Diana Drawing Room. He tugged at his lace *cravate* and adjusted his *justaucorps*. The tight-fitting waistcoat flattered Pierre's slim body, but he had gotten out of the habit of wearing the confining, frivolous court attire. He slung one side of his brocade cape over his shoulder and glanced up at the sculpture of King Louis in the alcove as he passed through the Venus Drawing Room.

He executed a mock bow at the unseeing figure. "I hope you are in a good mood tonight."

Pierre enjoyed the relative informality that existed during these gaming evenings. The concert was already underway. He found Robert, and they hurried to find a seat. At precisely the moment they were being seated, the king turned and made eye contact with Pierre and nodded to him. Pierre knew by that slight nod that he had permission to approach the king later in the evening.

Pierre and Robert chose a gaming table after the concert. Hoots of challenges and conquests at the various games permeated the festive atmosphere. Courtesans and courtiers gambled freely. The king stood at one end of a billiards table, making expert shots to the accolades of his subjects. The evening grew late, but the gambling continued and didn't promise to subside anytime soon. Pierre was anxious to get this unpleasant task of reporting to the king over with.

Eventually Robert nudged him. "The king is beckoning to you."

Pierre turned and acknowledged the king's invitation. Rising, he bowed to the group of ladies flocked around the table. "Excuse me, mademoiselles. Your company is most charming, but it appears I am being summoned by His Majesty."

"O-o-o-o, Pierre. Please return after you speak with the king. We have missed you."

The ladies held their fans and peered over them at the popular courtier.

One young lady with curly blonde hair moved closer to Pierre and placed a bejeweled hand on his arm. Her intense green eyes peered into his, and she stood on tiptoe to whisper in his ear, "I have truly missed you, chéri."

Pierre sighed and put his hand over hers. "I will see you later, Lisette, but not tonight." He smiled and brought her hand to his lips and kissed it. The scent of rose water on her perfumed gloves brought back a flood of memories of trysts in the moonlight and rides in the gardens. It occurred to him that he had more ties at court than he realized, and he would have to deal with them, one way or another. Or perhaps it would be best simply to disappear, never to be heard from again. What would his friends think? Could he do that to lifelong colleagues? He didn't know.

What he did know at this moment was that he needed to focus on his conversation with the king. Pierre approached and bowed. "Your Majesty."

"Come now. We can speak informally here. Let us have a seat." The king indicated a small table with two chairs. "I am glad you are back at court. Were you successful in your mission?"

Pierre followed the king's lead and sat down. He could feel beads of sweat beginning to form on his brow. Whether one agreed with the king's policies or not, the grandeur of his persona was intimidating. The Sun King he truly was.

"Well?"

"Please forgive me, Your Majesty. I returned only last night, and I am a bit overwhelmed at the grandeur of your presence and at being back in court. Being on horseback for these weeks has dulled my tongue, I fear."

The king smiled. "Put yourself at ease. What news do you have for me?"

Pierre breathed a silent prayer to heaven for wisdom and words, and began. "I went to the Bastille as you instructed me to do, and found that Monsieur Clavell had been sentenced to the galleys aboard *La Fidelle*, which was anchored at Brest. I proceeded to Brest and found his name indeed was on the galley list of slaves, but it had been crossed off. I assumed that meant he had died at sea. I spoke with the owner of the fleet . . ." Pierre hesitated.

"Go on."

"Well, I didn't actually speak with the elderly gentleman who owns the fleet. He had fallen ill, and I dealt with the grandson who had taken over the business." Pierre tiptoed through the account, meticulously choosing his words. "He assured me that when one's name was crossed off a galley list, it usually meant that the man had died at sea."

"Usually?"

Pierre nodded. "Nearly always." He hurried on with his story. "So I decided to travel to Dauphiné Province to the Clavell estate to see if I could find any trace of Madame Clavell or her family. That journey took me several weeks."

"Excellent!" Louis slapped his knee. "Excellent! Did you travel alone?"

Pierre's heart began to pound. Was the king suspicious? Pierre decided to be as honest as he possibly could be without arousing suspicion. He could not tell the king that one of his traveling companions had been François Clavell himself, but perhaps he could avoid answering directly.

Oh, God, protect me. "Part of the way. I picked up a couple of traveling companions at an inn in Nantes who were also journeying in the same direction. It made the trip more pleasant."

An outbreak of applause and laughter from a neighboring table interrupted their conversation. The king clapped and joined in the mirth. "*Bien*, my man! Good play!"

He turned back to Pierre. "Now, where were we?"

Pierre jumped ahead, hoping the king wouldn't ask about the identity of his traveling companions. "I found the Clavell estate in ruins, and no sign of Madame Clavell or her family. I went into Grenoble and asked around the village concerning the family. The word among the villagers was that the Clavells had fled to Switzerland."

"I see. Do you know where in Switzerland?"

"No one seemed to know."

"Don't the Huguenots usually flee to Geneva, the refuge of Calvin's disciples?" Louis narrowed his eyes.

"I'm sure that's true, but whether the Clavells are in Geneva . . ." Pierre shrugged his shoulders. "I regret that I don't have more definitive answers for you."

Louis rubbed his chin, speaking almost to himself. "I have been known to send emissaries into Switzerland to ferret out French citizens who have fled." He looked at Pierre. "I could send a contingent to Switzerland to look specifically for Madeleine."

"That is one option, Your Majesty. However, the evening I escorted Madame Clavell to the Trianon, she also mentioned that they had relatives in Spain. That is also a possibility." Pierre would be willing to go look for the Clavells in Switzerland. If he got there in time, his dilemma would be solved. He could accompany them to the New World.

The regent shook his head and glared at Pierre. "That is probably a wild goose chase." His mood darkened, and he stroked his moustache. "There is something different about you."

"I . . . I have just traveled from one end of France to another, Your Majesty. I am exhausted."

"No, it is not weariness that I am seeing. There is something in your eyes. You were not at Mass this morning."

"Please forgive me, sire. As I said, I am exhausted."

"No excuse. You shall not miss again."

"Yes, Your Majesty."

"Are you sure you explored every avenue, turned over every stone in Dauphiné? The estate is completely destroyed?"

"All but the barn. And that is where I slept. I searched it thoroughly."

Louis leaned back in his chair. "Very well. At least we know Monsieur Clavell is dead." Louis looked at Pierre. "Don't we?"

Pierre did not answer.

"And Madeleine—Madame Clavell—is nowhere to be found in France."

"*Oui,* Your Majesty."

Louis continued to stare at Pierre. He leaned forward and began tapping his fingers on the top of the table. Then he leaned back once more in his chair, not releasing Pierre from his gaze. "I am discharging you from this assignment. Thank you for your service." He paused for what seemed an eternity. "If you ever encounter any of the Clavell family again, particularly Madame Clavell, you are to report it to me immediately."

Again Pierre remained silent.

"Is that order perfectly clear?"

"Yes, Your Majesty, perfectly clear."

Louis waved his hand. "Return to your table. And again, I thank you for your service to the crown. You are dismissed—for now."

"*Oui,* Your Majesty." Pierre rose, bowed, and backed away. He made his way through the noisy gamblers, past the buffets, and down the stairs. The opulence that greeted him at every turn—the gold ornate filigree lining the trim over the doors and along the moldings, the ostentatious murals on the ceilings and walls, statues looming in alcove after alcove—all seemed to close in on him.

Yes, perfectly clear, Your Majesty. However, I will not be around to report to you, O glorious Sun King. My days in the court of King Louis will soon be nothing but a distant memory.

SIX

Madeleine opened her eyes and smiled at Philippe, who had pushed her bedroom door open and stuck his head in. The wick of a candle sputtered in melted wax around the base of the candle stand.

"Were you already asleep, Maman? It's not late."

"No, Son, I was just lying here thinking." Madeleine sat up and looked over at Vangie sleeping on the pillow beside her. She pulled a light quilt over her daughter's shoulders. "Vangie went to sleep right away, but I was restless."

"Uncle Jean asked if you would come down to his room for a moment."

"Is something wrong?" Madeleine stood and pulled her robe around her shoulders.

"*Non.* I think he wants to talk about our plans."

Madeleine sighed. "Can it not wait until morning? Is Charles asleep?"

"No, he's awake." Philippe shuffled his feet. "*Mère,* we need you to come to our room."

So formal. This must be serious. Madeleine started for the door, which Philippe held open for her. She hesitated and looked back at Vangie.

"She'll be fine."

"I don't want her to awaken and be frightened. The nightmares . . . since Papa died."

"We can send Claudine to stay with her. This won't take long."

Philippe's changing voice took on a tone of gentle authority, so like François'.

"Very well. I'll leave the candle burning."

Philippe swung the door almost closed, leaving a crack. They stopped at Claudine's room, and Madeleine knocked on the door softly. The governess answered, her sewing in her hands. "Claudine, would you mind watching Vangie?"

"*Oui,* madame."

Madeleine watched Claudine's figure disappear into the room. *How faithful she has been to our family, and how much she must love my children. I've taken her for granted.*

Henri and Jean sat at the table in their room. Charles played with his marbles on the hearth. A small fire crackled in the fireplace.

"That fire feels good. Mine has gone out."

Henri and Jean stood. "Here, madame, sit here." Henri scooted his chair toward Madeleine. "I'll go restart it for you."

"Thank you, Henri. What is this all about?" Madeleine sat down and looked around at the faces of the men in her life. Charles ceased his play, and his marbles clicked as he dropped them into a leather bag.

Philippe pulled an unopened envelope from his tunic. "Papa left a letter for us. He told me that he placed it in his trunk, and we were to read it with all of us together a few days after he . . . left." He paused, tears shimmering unshed in his dark eyes. "Here."

Madeleine took the envelope from him, then grasped her son's hand and held it to her cheek as he stood over her. "Oh, Philippe." She held on to his hand. "What are we to do?"

"Read the letter, Maman."

Madeleine released his hand, and Philippe stood behind her with his hands on her shoulders. Jean leaned forward in his chair. Madeleine broke open the seal on the envelope and pulled the letter from its sheath. The letter quaked in her hand as she read aloud.

> *My Dearest Family,*
>
> *Oh, how I love you, and how I have treasured these last few months God allowed us to be together. Although I do not know how much longer I have left with you on this earth, I sense that my time to go to the Father is near.*
>
> *Jean will take leadership of the family. Philippe, as the oldest son, you will be next in line. You have matured into a fine young man. You are ready to assume that role. Charles, Philippe will need your complete support and encouragement. You are ready too. Vangie, you need to be a big girl for your maman now. I know you will be. I am so proud of all three of my children. You have been the joy of my life.*
>
> *And, of course, our loyal servants, Henri and Claudine, will*

51

*be with you as well. What would we have done through the years
without them?*

*I want you, my dear family, to proceed with plans to go to
the New World. The situation in Germany is too tenuous with
King Louis' persistent invasions into the Rhineland. If he should
gain knowledge that you, Madeleine, were still in Europe, I have
no doubt that he would come after you.*

Madeleine looked at Jean and shook her head. "I cannot. I just
could not bear the hardships of a voyage right now. Not so soon after
I . . ." She looked back down at the letter in her hand that carried her
husband's voice to her from the grave.

*Madeleine, I know you are not going to want to leave Europe at
this point, but my last wish is for you to do so. I'm convinced that
our family will not be safe until you do. If God wills it, perhaps
he will prolong my life, in order for me to see you safely situated
out of harm's way. If not, please continue with our plans. Go to
the New World. There should be enough money left to buy land
and start anew.*

*It won't be easy, but God will be with you. Carry on our
heritage; carry it on in a place that is free. I shall be waiting for
you on the other side of the veil. Until then, my love is always
with you.*

He did not sign his name. Madeleine sobbed and crumpled the
letter in her hand. Then she moaned and tried to straighten it out. She
rocked back and forth, clutching the letter in her lap. When she finally
looked up at her loved ones around her, Jean was wiping tears from

his cheeks. Charles cried openly and embraced his mother. Philippe stood silently by as the tears fell from his eyes. Henri hesitated at the doorway.

Madeleine stood with the epistle still in one hand and gathered Charles to her with her other arm as she rose. "Please forgive me. How selfish I've been. You—all of you—are also mourning François. I've been so focused on my own grief that I've been insensitive to yours." She shook her head. "I don't understand why God allowed him to be taken from us in the first place. But then to return him, and take him away again . . . that seems more than one should be asked to bear."

Madeleine struggled to find words to express emotions that were larger than her ability to explain. "I feel as if there is a hole in my heart that has a thousand sharp edges. They cut and irritate as I try to make sense of it and smooth it out." She pressed over and over on her gown as if trying to iron out the wrinkles. "But nothing makes it go away. Nothing fits. Not yet anyway. I don't know that it ever will." She hesitated again, still holding Charles close. "One's personal grief cannot be explained." She looked around the circle of her family one at a time. "Yours, and yours, and mine. It has to be felt."

Murmurs of agreement echoed her sentiments. The minutes ticked by, and the only sound in the room was Charles sniffling. Madeleine sighed. She kissed Charles on the cheek and walked to the table beside the window, which held a ewer and washbasin. She picked up a towel and wiped her face.

"So, François has made it very clear that we are to go on with our plans to voyage to the New World—right away, even so soon after his passing. He has given us instructions, and I will do my best to honor them." She folded the towel and put it back on the table. "It's time for bed. We shall begin preparations tomorrow."

SEVEN

Pierre leaned on his elbows against the marble banister on the balcony outside the ballroom and breathed in the crisp night air. The splashing fountains in the tranquil courtyard created a welcome respite from the suffocating press of the court attendants, diplomats, and assorted royal parasites.

It was in this same ballroom over two years ago that Pierre had flirted with and held Madeleine Clavell in his arms for the first time. Who could have known the twists and turns his life would take because of that serendipitous meeting? Not exactly serendipitous, however. King Louis had instructed him to dance with the beautiful woman and find out all he could about why she had appeared at the *bal masque* that night. Pierre didn't mind complying with the king's wishes with a woman as gorgeous as Madeleine.

"You are certainly deep in thought." The soft, familiar voice transported him back into the present.

"Lisette. I didn't hear you." Pierre straightened up, then bowed and kissed her hand.

"If I didn't know better, I would accuse you of avoiding me."

"Why would I ever avoid such a lovely mademoiselle?" He ushered her to a stone bench. "Come. Let's talk."

Pierre sat down next to this beautiful girl whose presence had been so comfortable to him in the past, yet seemed a stranger to him now. Shafts of light from the ballroom and the moonlight illuminated her porcelain skin. She had been his constant companion and dance partner at court, and he genuinely cared for her.

Lisette fingered her cameo necklace. "I think of you every time I wear this." She laughed. "And I finally found earrings to match."

Pierre chuckled. "I am sorry I didn't think to get the earrings when I purchased the necklace. Men can be incredibly dull at times." He touched one of the long, dangling earrings. "They match perfectly." Pierre hesitated. "And you're wearing my favorite dress."

"I hoped you'd notice." Lisette smoothed the skirt of the pink silk dress that brought out the color in her skin.

Pierre studied her face. Lisette's delicate bone structure, fair skin, and blonde hair combined to give her an aura of fragility. She seemed to almost float in and out of scenes unobtrusively. Yet, when one did take note of her, one found her soft beauty captivating.

Madeleine's dark beauty, on the other hand, stood in stunning contrast. She carried a commanding presence about her. Her voluminous dark-brown hair framed her angular and dramatic face and blue-green eyes, and every head turned when she entered a room.

Here I am with a gorgeous woman who is in love with me, and I am thinking about a woman I can never claim. This woman is here now, for the taking.

"Why are you trembling?" Pierre took Lisette's hand.

"I don't know. I suppose I'm excited to see you again." She sounded like a child, her voice soft and unsure. She looked directly into Pierre's eyes. "I am afraid . . . I am sensing . . ."

Pierre didn't respond to her timid probing, and silence fell between them. He let go of her hands and sat with his awkwardly in his lap. He knew he needed to be cautious.

Lisette broke the silence. "Pierre, have you returned for good? Do you still . . . do you want to pick up where we left off?"

"Lisette, you are beautiful, and I do care very much for you. But . . ."

"But what?"

"Things don't always stay the same. Things change."

"Things? What kind of 'things'?"

"Don't make this harder than it has to be." Pierre touched her hair with his hand.

"I need to know, Pierre. Things like your professed love for me? Things like our plans for the future? Things like our . . . nights together? Those kinds of 'things'?"

Pierre hung his head and whispered. "*Oui.*"

"Is there someone else?"

"*I* have changed, Lisette. It's not you." Pierre reached for her hands again, but she pulled away. "If I had returned the same man I was when I left, things between us would be the same."

"You've fallen in love with someone else."

"Listen to me, Lisette. It's more than that."

"Whom have you fallen in love with? Someone you met on your mission?"

Pierre hesitated. "She was married and committed to her husband. That is not something that I will pursue, nor will I discuss it." He knelt in front of her and pleaded with his eyes. "I beg you. Please listen to me. Hear my heart."

How much should I tell her? Can I trust her?

"The king sent me on a mission to find a Huguenot family. The husband and father of the family had been sentenced to the galleys, so my first destination was to go to Paris and locate his records in the Bastille."

Lisette took a lace handkerchief from her small drawstring bag and dabbed at her eyes, but she listened. "Why had he been sentenced to the galleys?"

"He was Huguenot, but more than that, he—" Pierre didn't know how to explain the entanglement of Madeleine and the king. "Have you ever heard the stories about the king's first love many years ago, and how she left court never to return?"

"*Oui,* I've heard gossip."

"That's the family I was sent to find."

"And did you find them?"

Oh, God, help me. Pierre decided once more that telling the truth would be the best option. "I found the husband's name removed from the galley list, which usually means the man died onboard ship. And upon going to their estate, I found it destroyed and abandoned."

"What do you think happened to them?"

"I think they fled to another country."

"And this changed you?"

"Indirectly."

Pierre stood. He walked toward the lights of the ballroom, then turned and came back to stand in front of Lisette. "Do you ever think about God?"

The shadows, interspersed with the beams of moonlight, illuminated her face. She looked almost angelic. "God? What does God have to do with this?"

"The king's vendetta against this family got me to thinking about why there has to be such animosity between the Catholics and the Huguenots. Haven't you ever wondered about that? Whether there is more to knowing God than just going to Mass and performing rituals? Haven't you ever longed for more reality in your religion?" Pierre sat back down beside her.

Lisette sat with her head lowered at first, then she stared at Pierre as he told her about his encounter with God. "What does this mean?" she asked, her eyes wide. "Are you going to be a priest?"

"*Non!* Absolutely not!" Pierre laughed, and the tension between the two lessened.

Lisette giggled. "I can't imagine you being celibate."

"Yes, well . . ."

"Well? Then what *does* it mean?"

"Honestly, I don't know what much of it means. But this I do know: the essentials of life, such as relationships—with my father, with you—are more meaningful, not less so. And I want to make them right. I cannot demean you or anyone else by carrying on surface relationships any longer and pretending—"

"Surface relationships? Pretending? That's what it was with me? Pretense?"

"Not at the time, it wasn't. It's simply that I see things differently now. I see more clearly." Pierre put his arms around Lisette and pulled her to him. "Please try to understand. I am not rejecting you. I ... I ..."

He didn't know how to say it without hurting her. He sat back and looked into her eyes. "I don't want to use you anymore for a moment's pleasure." He saw the pain flicker across her eyes and hated himself for having to inflict that wound. "I am simply trying to be as honest with you as I know how to be. I have caused you pain, and I am heartsick for it."

Lisette lowered her head, and tears fell freely onto her skirt. She didn't bother to use her handkerchief, which she twisted back and forth in her hands. "I am completely bewildered. You are right; you have changed." She looked up and inhaled sharply. "Have you converted to Huguenot?"

"*Non*, chérie, I'm still Catholic. This I have learned—God is neither Catholic nor Huguenot. He is God—above all religion."

"Who talked you into this ... this new religion?"

"Nobody talked me into it. I had much time to think as I was traveling from one end of France to the other. I had been sent to hunt a man down, a family, simply because their belief in the same God we believe in took a different form. It didn't make sense to me."

Pierre didn't tell Lisette about his firsthand observations of the Huguenots he had come to know and the love and forgiveness and joy that characterized their lives. He continued, "One day I stopped to rest in the forest, and God came to me. I can't explain it. One moment God was far away and untouchable, and the next moment he became reality in my life. He is more real to me than ... than ..."

"Than I am? That simple? He 'came' to you?"

"Yes."

"No one else was around?"

"Not a soul." Pierre paused. "Later, I did run into Joost Fourié at an inn in Nantes. Do you remember him?"

"*Oui*, the redheaded courier?"

"Yes, and studying to be clergy in his faith. He helped me understand that what had happened was the Spirit of God drawing me to himself. But my meeting with Joost was after the fact."

Long moments passed, and the two sat in silence. The strains of a *menuet* drifted into the night air.

Pierre stood and executed an exaggerated court bow. "May I have the honor of this dance?"

Lisette sniffled, wiped her nose with her handkerchief, and stuffed the wadded cloth back into her bag. She hung it on her wrist with her fan and stood. She looked up at Pierre and smiled. "Of course."

Pierre held her hand, and they walked toward the entrance of the ballroom. To have her by his side once again felt surprisingly good to him. "*Merci*, chérie."

Lisette looked up at Pierre, and a smile tweaked the edges of her rosebud mouth. "The pleasure is all mine."

The striking couple, Pierre with his dark good looks and Lisette with her delicate, fair beauty, joined the rotating couples on the dance floor. Pierre saw King Louis look toward them and smile.

EIGHT

Madeleine slung her cloak around her shoulders and picked up the folded quilt that had been her mother's. She ran her hand over the soft squares and brought the blanket up to her face. The scent of her mother still resided in the weave of the fabric. With her hand on the latch, Madeleine lingered at the door of the bedroom, then closed it. The floor creaked beneath her steps as she descended the stairs and walked toward the kitchen.

The Clavell clan were gathered around the table and fireplace to say their good-byes to the pastor and his wife. Jean held Vangie in his arms, although she had grown almost too large for him to hold for very long. Her legs dangled at an awkward angle as she grasped his neck. Charles stood by his uncle's side.

"Chérie, get down," Madeleine scolded.

61

Philippe burst into the kitchen. "All is ready. Let's go."

Henri waited outside with a modest black coach and a wagon, which Jean had purchased in Geneva.

Madeleine's heart jumped as it came time for good-byes. Pastor Du Puy interspersed his farewells with prayer as he petitioned the heavenly Father to protect and guide the Clavells.

Madame Du Puy dabbed at her eyes and engulfed Madeleine in a bosomy hug. Armond and Suzanne stood at the edge of the group, holding their toddler by the hands.

Madeleine approached her former servant. "Oh, Suzanne. I can hardly bear to leave you. You have been by my side since you were a young girl."

Armond took the child from Suzanne, and the two women embraced, stifling the sobs that threatened to erupt.

Philippe stood at the door, eager to get started. "Come on. Henri is waiting for us."

The little entourage moved onto the porch. Henri climbed onto the seat of the coach and took the reins. He held his head proud and sat upright on the driver's seat as if they were traveling once again in their grand carriage.

Pastor Du Puy began to sing a psalm, and the others joined in as his strong voice took the lead. "May God arise and his enemies be scattered; may his foes flee before him."

Jean, now the official head of the Clavell family, pulled Madeleine to him, his arm around her shoulder. He bellowed his praise to God, although somewhat off-key, and Madeleine's mellow voice filled in harmony. The children watched, looking a little embarrassed and eager to start on their journey. Vangie hid her face in Claudine's shoulder.

The psalm died away, and a holy hush fell over the group. Madeleine turned and shooed Claudine and Vangie into the cab of the coach. She looked back at Philippe and Jean as they climbed onto the driver's bench of the wagon, which carried their luggage and few remaining earthly possessions. Charles rode in the bed of the wagon with the baggage.

Jean nodded and smiled—a smile that spoke volumes to his sister-in-law. *We're going to make it*, it said. *This is the right choice. Our family will be safe.*

Madeleine returned the nod and stepped up into the coach. "Let's go, Henri."

The old man snapped the reins, and the coach lurched forward. Madeleine turned and peered behind her through the opening in the back of the coach. Charles and Philippe waved to the Du Puys and the servants. Madeleine knew this was the last time she would see these loved ones who had been a major part of her life. She faced forward and did not allow herself to look back again.

NICOLAS WATCHED AS THE GUARD ASSIGNED TO OBSERVE the Du Puys' house scrambled up the ledge to their campsite. The guard leaned his musket against a pine tree and stood doubled over with his hands on his knees, catching his breath. "L-looks like they are pulling out."

"How many?"

"A small coach with Madame Clavell and her daughter, with probably a governess. And a wagon driven by a man in his thirties, I'd say, and two boys."

"Who's driving the coach, and who is in the lead?"

"Coach is in the lead, and an old man is driving it."

The man with the pockmarked face stood at the edge of the campfire along with four others. "This is going to be easier than we thought."

"Take your places as we planned. I don't want them to get too far. The quicker we can get back over the border into France, the better." Nicolas hoisted his saddle and started toward the horses. "And I, for one, will be glad to get home. It's getting colder every night."

The soldiers kicked dirt into the campfire and readied their horses.

"One more thing, men." Nicolas mounted, turned in his saddle, and faced his men. "Upon strict orders from King Louis himself—no one in this party is to be harmed. Is that understood?"

The small party of musketeers headed out, followed by an elegant coach driven by one of the younger soldiers dressed in footman's attire.

VANGIE FELL ASLEEP WITH HER HEAD IN HER MOTHER'S lap as the coach settled into a rhythmic sway. The somber black of Madeleine's mourning attire contrasted with her daughter's fair skin. She stroked her daughter's hair. The occasional lurch from a rut or hole in the road did not seem to threaten the deep, innocent sleep of the child. Claudine, too, began to nod. The after-lunch, early afternoon doldrums settled on them all. The gentle fragrance of occasional sprinkles of rain floated through the cab. Madeleine watched the landscape slide by as they headed north toward Holland.

Madeleine turned and peered once again out the back window. Jean and Philippe, in the wagon behind, seemed unaware of the intermittent sprinkles sparkling in the sun. Jean punctuated the air with his hand, emphasizing a point as he talked. Madeleine faced forward, smoothed Vangie's hair, and laid her head back. A sudden joggle from the carriage jolted them all.

Vangie sat up, rubbing her eyes. "I was dreaming."

"What were you dreaming, chérie?"

"I was dreaming about Prince."

"Oh, I see. What about Pri—Pierre?"

"I dreamed he was with us. He was riding right alongside us on Tonnerre." Vangie bounced up and stuck her head out of the window. The wind caught her hair and tossed it awry. She waved to her brother and uncle. "But he's not really there."

"Vangie, get your head back in here!"

The little girl pulled herself into the coach, wiped raindrops off her nose, and snuggled beneath Madeleine's arm. She sat quietly for a few moments, twirling a piece of her hair round and round.

"Maman, why didn't Prince come with us? Does he not love us anymore?"

Madeleine sighed. "Of course he does, but his life is in France. He had to go back."

"Why?"

"If he hadn't, King Louis would be very angry at him. We don't want that, do we?"

"No, but if he came with us, when *we* escape from King Louis, then King Louis couldn't find him either, could he? He could hide with us." Vangie looked up at her mother in wide-eyed naïveté.

Madeleine hesitated. "Yes, I suppose he could. But Pierre's father is at Versailles, and he wanted to see him again."

Vangie sniffled. "I will miss him."

"I will too."

65

Vangie pulled a small doll out of a bag at her feet and began to play.

Madeleine patted her daughter's shoulder, leaned her head on the back of the coach, and closed her eyes. Her thoughts returned to a scene she had struggled to dismiss from her memory, but the image of Pierre holding her hand, his eyes brimming with love for her, refused to vanish. The unbidden emotions still flooded over her when she recalled her refusal of his advances, his gallant declaration that he would never speak of love again to her as long as François was alive, the way he tapped his hat and then his heart as he rode off. Then the image of François' last frail moments flashed through her memory. She looked down at Vangie, cooing and playing with her doll, and blinked the tears away.

"I know he'll come back, Maman. Prince will find us and come help us."

"Why do you say that?"

"He always does. Like when he rescued me from the con-con—"

"Convent."

"The place with the ladies with the black and white robes on, and then like he found Papa."

"This is different. We are going a long way from France."

"It doesn't matter. He will find us. I know he will." The little girl returned to her play.

Madeleine stared at her daughter. Did such brusque boldness sprout through the soul of a child at random? Or was she discerning something out of Madeleine's reach? Was she hearing the supernatural voice of God?

Madeleine did not have any answers. She only knew that with every stride of the horses pulling the coaches northeast across the

Swiss countryside, they were moving away from their homeland. She fidgeted with the jet brooch at her collar and tried not to think of their former, content life in France.

The future before them was unknown and untried. Did the Clavell family have what it took to settle in a foreign country with no prior history, influence, or acquaintances? They had no place to live. What would they do for income?

Madeleine couldn't think that far ahead. All she knew to do at this point was try to trust God with their future. What other option did she have? Only the God of heaven knew the future.

Although she had her children and brother-in-law, Madeleine felt alone. The image of François on his deathbed haunted her. *My beautiful François—emaciated and scarred.* A tear trickled down her cheek. She ducked her head, pulled out a handkerchief with a wide lace hem, and wiped the telltale tear away before Vangie could see it. Silently she petitioned her heavenly Father.

Lord of heaven and earth, I implore you to guide our every step as we seek safety for our family—safety from the tyranny of a vindictive king and government that will not allow us to worship you in freedom. Make a way for us.

Her thoughts settled for a moment on her childhood friend who had betrayed her, and she felt her jaw tighten. She pulled herself back to her prayer.

God in heaven, I choose to forgive Louis, but I will not remain where he can harm us.

NINE

Madeleine heard shouts and a blast from a musket. The carriage accelerated, then stopped almost as quickly. She looked out the window to see French musketeers surrounding the carriage. Tan traveling tunics covered their blue coats, but they were unmistakably musketeers. Ammunition hung from their buff bandoliers, as well as heavy swords.

"Halt! Whoa there, old man!" Captain Maisson shouted. "Do not attempt to escape. We mean no harm to anyone, but we have come for Madame Clavell upon the direct orders of King Louis."

Jean shouted to the officer from the wagon bench. "You have no jurisdiction here. Get out of our way!"

"What is the meaning of this?" Madeleine descended from her carriage. The horses snorted and stomped the ground.

Nicolas dismounted, whipped off his hat, and bowed to Madeleine. "Madame Clavell. Let me reiterate, we mean no harm to anyone. We have detained your party to take you to the king, at his personal request."

"His personal request! You have come into a foreign country to kidnap me, after burning our estate, sentencing my husband to the galleys, and hunting us down like animals, to return to court at Louis' 'personal request'?" Madeleine turned to Jean. "Let us proceed on our way." She turned to step back into her coach.

Nicolas drew his sword. "I said we mean no harm. I didn't say we would not use force." The other soldiers followed his lead, one of them aiming his musket toward Madeleine.

Madeleine glared at the soldiers, then at Jean and Philippe. Charles peered over the side of the wagon. Claudine clutched Vangie in her arms inside the coach. Henri still sat on the perch of the coach holding the reins.

Jean jumped off the wagon bench, his knife drawn, his muscles twitching underneath his shirt.

"Jean!" Madeleine grabbed his arm. "Don't!" She turned toward him and whispered, "We are no match for them. I know this officer. Let me appeal to him." She walked toward Captain Maisson. "I know you—you were in training at Versailles years ago. We both were much younger."

"*Oui*, madame. Nicolas Maisson, at your service. I am flattered you remembered."

"Still seeing that Louis' every wish is carried out, I see."

Nicolas nodded. "His wishes are my command." He motioned toward a grove of trees off the road, and the carriage they had brought with them bounced over the rough terrain toward the halted entourage.

Madeleine turned and motioned for Jean and Henri to come to the back of their coach with her. She was trembling. "Jean, what are we to do?"

Claudine and Vangie stepped cautiously out of the coach. Vangie began to cry and pull on her governess' hand. "I want my mommy!"

Jean leaned with his arms outstretched against the back of the wagon. "We can either fight them and all die here in the road, or . . ."

"Or I can go with them."

"I'm afraid so."

"But the children. They are wrenching me away from my children." A sob escaped from her throat. "How can I do that? They've just lost their father. I cannot leave them." She covered her mouth with her handkerchief.

"God will show us how to rescue you later, Madeleine. We must trust him. I'll see that the children are cared for."

Madeleine took a deep breath. "Of course, you are right. We have no choice." She tucked her handkerchief into her sleeve.

Captain Maisson stepped toward the family. "Madame?"

"Give us a moment, Captain." She turned to Henri and began to give terse instructions. "Henri, would you untie my small trunk, please?" Madeleine paused. "Hand me the jewelry chest as well, please. Leave the rest."

Nicolas stepped toward Jean with one hand on his sword and the other outstretched. "I'll take care of that knife for you."

Jean glowered at him, but unsheathed the weapon and handed it over. The captain walked back to his men, turning Jean's knife over and over in his hands.

Grumbling underneath his breath, Jean helped Henri loosen Madeleine's luggage. She motioned to Jean as he pulled the jewelry chest from the back of the coach. She opened it and removed a bag of coins. "Take this."

"No, Madeleine. You may need it."

"I have more. You will need it to see to the children's needs."

Madeleine closed the chest and gave it back to Jean, who began loading her luggage into the coach the musketeers had brought alongside their own. She walked toward Nicolas. "Very well. You've won this round, but it is only temporary."

"I'm glad you decided to cooperate." He nodded toward the wagon where Charles had clambered onto the bench with his brother. "Is that your son?"

"Yes, both of them."

"Instruct the older one to come with us."

"What? Why? This is no affair of his." Panic rose in her voice.

"Interesting choice of words." The musketeer looked to the sky at the gathering clouds. "Looks like the skies are going to open up any minute. Let's get on with this." He motioned toward the carriage. "King Louis is adamant to see your son. I think you know why."

Madeleine frowned at the officer. "I'm sure I have no idea what you are talking about."

"No matter. My orders were to deliver you two to the king, and that is exactly what I intend to do."

"Please allow me to speak to Philippe alone." Madeleine turned her back on the soldiers and walked to Philippe, who was still seated on the wagon bench. "I need you to come with me."

"Me? Why?"

"Don't ask any questions now. I will explain later. Just get down—slowly—and get your baggage."

Eyeing the soldiers, the young man handed the reins to Charles and stepped down. Jean, standing by Madeleine's side, nodded toward the back of the wagon. "Henri, help Master Philippe with his things, please." Henri and Philippe moved to the wagon bed.

"Do whatever your mother instructs you to do, without question, without hesitation." Henri kept his voice low, so the soldiers could not hear. As he handed Philippe's single piece of baggage to him, he slipped him a knife. "Keep it hidden until you need it." Philippe slid the knife into his boot as he bent down to pick up his case.

"Good boy." Henri patted him on his back.

Vangie continued to pull on her governess and whine for her mother.

"Now, as for the rest of you, I am far too much of a gentleman to tie up a lady and a little girl." Nicolas laughed and looked around at his men. "I am going to leave two of my men here to keep you company long enough for us to get over the border into France. You know where we are going, so there's no need for a chase. Madame Clavell and her son will be well taken care of—elegantly taken care of. Sometime tomorrow my men will release you and let you go wherever you wish to go—back to your friend's place or to Geneva to the Cathedrale."

Madeleine startled at the mention of the Cathedrale and looked at Jean. How did they know of their connection at the church of John Calvin? Or was he simply assuming their association there because they were Huguenots?

Vangie finally broke away from Claudine and ran to her mother, screaming hysterically. "Maman! Don't let them take me! Not again!"

Madeleine bent down and gathered her little girl in her arms. "There, there, chérie. Everything will be fine." She found it hard to believe her own words. She pleaded with Nicolas. "Please, sir. May I take her with us?" Standing, she held the weeping child in her arms. "Nearly three years ago she was kidnapped by a dragoon commander and taken to a convent. She spent several months there before . . . before we got her out." Her voice caught. "Please, if you have any compassion, allow her to come with us."

The soldier hesitated, looked at the child, and stroked his goatee. "I'm sorry, madame. My orders were to bring you and your oldest son to Versailles. Nothing was said about a little girl."

Madeleine closed her eyes and sighed. She put Vangie down and stooped to look the child in her eyes. "Chérie, Maman is just going on a trip into France for a few days. Philippe is going with me. Charles, Jean, and Claudine are going to stay with you. And Henri as well. I need you to be a brave, grown-up girl for mommy. Can you do that for me?"

Vangie rubbed her eyes and looked around. "B-but the mean soldiers are taking you away, like they took me away to the con-con—"

"Convent, ma petite. But it's different this time. They are not kidnapping us. They are simply escorting us to see the king."

"B-but I thought we were . . . were trying to get away from the k-king." The child sniffled.

"That's right, but he's an old friend, and I need to see him anyway to clear up a misunderstanding. And since these nice men—" Madeleine looked around the circle of soldiers, who averted their gaze. "These nice men are traveling in that same direction, they have graciously offered to see that we get there safely."

She motioned for Jean to come and get Vangie. "Uncle Jean will take good care of you." Madeleine wound her arms around her daughter and hugged her tightly and kissed her. "Now give Philippe a kiss, and we will see you soon."

Philippe picked up his little sister and kissed her on the forehead. "We'll be back soon, little sister."

Vangie, tears still running down her blotchy cheeks, looked around at the scene. For the sake of the children, the adults maintained their composure. Charles began to cry as he told his mother and brother good-bye.

Philippe held his younger brother's shoulders at arm's length. "None of that. You need to be a grown-up for Vangie."

Charles wiped his nose on his sleeve and nodded. "I will. I promise."

"Where's your handkerchief? Clavell men are gentlemen."

Charles pulled his handkerchief out of his tunic. "Right here."

"Good. Now be brave." The two brothers embraced.

The soldiers had loaded Madeleine's and Philippe's luggage onto the luxurious coach. Nicolas opened the carriage door while executing a courtly bow. "If you please, madame."

"No, I do not please, but it looks as if I must." Madeleine stepped into the carriage, followed by Philippe. They sat across from each other, tight-lipped and solemn.

After all she had been through the last three years to escape from France; to be reunited with François; then to lose him in death; now attempting to flee to another country to escape the infiltration of King Louis into Switzerland; only to be apprehended in flight and taken back to the person who was the cause of it all—it was more than she could handle.

She swallowed hard and leaned out of one window to wave good-bye to her forlorn little family standing in the grove of trees, guarded by the two musketeers. Jean had put Vangie down, and as the carriage pulled out of sight, the child began to run toward it. Madeleine could hear her anguished cries.

"Maman! Maman! Come back! Don't go—don't leave us! Maman!"

The carriage went around a bend in the road, and Madeleine could no longer see them. Lightning crackled nearby, and a roll of thunder enveloped them. Rain began to pelt the roof of the carriage, drowning out her weeping. She rocked back and forth on the seat of the carriage, her face hidden in her hands. "Will this never end? Will it never end?"

TEN

After Mass Pierre wove his way from the chateau across the busy courtyard and headed for the soldiers' quarters. He threw his cloak behind his shoulders. The long, hot days of summer were dwindling, and the nights had begun to cool off, but today felt like midsummer again. He thought about the Clavells and wondered where they were by now, and if they would attempt a voyage across the ocean during the stormy, winter months.

Diplomats and ambassadors from foreign countries in plumed hats and colorful jackets trimmed in gold braid, and mademoiselles with their delicate parasols, gathered in clusters in the courtyard as the sun rose in the sky. A few horses, belonging to the higher nobility, pranced through the crowd, the clicking of their hooves on the cobblestone punctuating the chaos of the daily gathering.

Just beyond, through the first set of gates, the enormous semicircle of stables on either side of the entrance to the grounds appeared to enfold the property like a hovering mother hen. Horses and carriages streamed in and out of the gigantic enclosures. Pierre reminded himself that he needed to check on his horse before returning to the chateau.

Pierre nodded to his colleagues as he hurried past them, with no desire to become involved in a lengthy tête-à-tête. He noticed Robert Devereaux coming toward him and groaned.

"Wait up, friend! Where are you headed in such a rush?"

"*Bonjour*, Robert. I am on my way to the soldiers' quarters to inquire after my father." Trusting it would give him an excuse to hasten on, Pierre added, "If he is on his way out on an assignment, I might catch him before he leaves."

"Since when do you bother yourself with where your father goes?" Robert grinned. "Let's go talk to the ladies." He motioned to a group of the ladies-in-waiting. Lisette stood in the middle of the circle of chattering women. "That sounds much more enticing, don't you think? Besides, I think Lisette has missed you sorely." Robert looked at the object of his comment. "Not a bad welcome-home gift."

Pierre glanced at the young woman, and guilt washed over him. "Not right now. I need to check on my horse as well."

"You prefer your horse to these lovely ladies?"

"No, of course not. But I'm in a hurry at the moment."

"Well, I suppose you do need to ready your horse, since you are assigned to the hunt this afternoon."

"I am?"

"You didn't check your orders for the day? You and your patron, whom I am gratefully giving back to you, are to go with the king on his hunt."

Pierre hit the side of his thigh with his gloves. "Arrghh! The king doesn't waste his time getting me back in the harness, does he?"

Robert sidled up close to Pierre. The two had arrived on the other side of the courtyard and were entering the soldiers' training field. "I think it would be wise to watch what you say. At least lower your voice. One never knows."

"Of course, Robert, you are right. I had hoped for a day or so to rest, but it's back to work, isn't it?" Pierre would have to play a part and play it well. He had been careless.

The vast training grounds loomed in front of them. Soldiers lined up, rifles at attention, responding to officers' commands to aim or present their arms for inspection. The diverse colors of the coats from various companies and battalions designated their stations and assignments. Flags slapped in the breeze from each company. Shouts of correction flew through the air, and coarse laughter directed at the new recruits humiliated them into conformity.

Pierre slowed his pace and searched the training grounds for his father. Not spotting any dragoon regiments, he continued toward the billeting quarters. Forcing a laugh, he clapped his friend on his back. "Will you be enjoying the hunt with us today?"

"Not today. I must report back to my patron. I have neglected him somewhat since you've been gone." Robert chuckled and covered his mouth.

Pierre teased his friend. "Perhaps if you had been more industrious about being on duty, you wouldn't have gotten in the altercation that cost you your tooth." They moved on past the soldiers practicing their battle stances.

"It wasn't as glamorous as it sounds. The uncouth coward insulted my lady friend, and I challenged him. He swung a bottle at me and missed. Then I ran at him. He ducked, and I hit the top of his head with my mouth. It was over in a matter of seconds." Robert bared his teeth at Pierre. "Does it look too terribly bad?"

"Not at all, my narcissistic friend. In fact, I think it adds some character to that too-handsome face."

Robert took a swat at Pierre. "You're just jealous."

"Not on your life."

Robert became serious. "I've missed you. You've been gone too much on . . . God knows what kind of missions. It's all been very mys-. terious. Come, man, you can tell me. Was it the man in the iron mask? Have you been to the Bastille?"

Pierre paused and selected his words carefully. "I was sent to the Bastille, but it wasn't about the man in the iron mask." He lowered his voice. "It was to find the whereabouts of a galley slave."

"A galley slave? Why should the king care about a galley slave?"

"I told you yesterday, I was chasing down one of the king's lady friends who fled from his amorous intentions. Louis sentenced her husband to the galleys, and—it's much too long to go into now. I'll tell you the whole story when we have more time."

"Very well." Robert stared at his longtime friend. "I'm glad you are back, but you seem—I don't know—so serious."

Pierre waved his friend off. "I'm just tired. I'll be back to normal after I get rested up. It was a long journey."

"Then it'll be like old times again, *oui?*"

"Like old times." Pierre knew he was not telling the truth. It would never again be like old times between the two of them, but he didn't care to explain at the moment.

How much do I tell him? Can I trust him completely? Pierre wondered. They had been friends since coming to Versailles as young stableboys. They had experienced most of their "firsts" together—their first fights, their first loves, their first days in court.

They were much alike, except that Robert was a true orphan. His patron had raised him until he was nine years old, and then brought him to Versailles about the same time that Commander Boveé dumped his son off at the newly burgeoning headquarters of the king. Robert and Pierre were the same age, birthdays even in the same month. They always claimed each other as brothers, rather than best friends, but nobody ever mistook them for natural brothers. Robert's tall stature, blond hair, blue eyes, and slender build contrasted sharply with Pierre's dark hair, olive skin, and muscular physique.

Neither Pierre nor Robert had ever served at court in Paris. While they had been sent there on short-term assignments, Versailles was home to them.

Pierre had to admit he had missed Robert, too, more than he realized. He put his arm around his friend as they walked to the stark soldiers' billet.

"I'll wait out here for you." Robert leaned against the stone wall. "I enjoy watching the drills."

Pierre went inside the cool enclosure. Several soldiers lounged on their bunks, and some played card games. A low hum of deep voices simmered throughout the large, dank room, punctuated by the occasional outburst of laughter.

Pierre spotted an older soldier reclining on his bed near the door. "My name is Pierre Boveé. I'm looking for my father, Commander Paul Boveé."

The grizzly combatant sat up and spat in a cup he held close to his mouth. "I know who you are." The soldier looked Pierre over from head to toe. "In spite of your court finery, you look like him."

Pierre winced. "Can you tell me where I might find him?"

The soldier lay back on his bunk, setting the cup on the floor. "He and some of his dragoons just went over to the stables a few minutes ago."

"Are they on their way out?"

"How should I know? The dragoons don't check in with me."

"Uh, *oui*, of course." Pierre backed toward the door. "Thank you." He found Robert where he had left him.

"That didn't take long."

"My father is at the stables."

"*Bien!* We were going there anyway."

"We?"

Robert's face registered his disappointment. "Do you not want me to go with you?"

Pierre looked at his friend. He had wanted to speak to his father privately, but he probably wouldn't be able to do so at this point anyway. "Of course I do. I simply didn't know if you preferred to get back to the ladies—and your patron."

"I'd rather spend some time with you. And I haven't seen your father in a while either." Robert smiled. "Not that I've missed him. What is this sudden interest in a renewed relationship?"

"Just getting older, I suppose."

"All of thirty."

"We are thirty-two this year." Pierre chuckled at Robert's habit of shaving a couple of years off his age. "And neither of us is married or has a family."

Robert shrugged. "True, but we have an exciting life, *non?* How can we be encumbered with a family and enjoy the—ummm—benefits of court life that we do?" He grinned.

Pierre ignored Robert's licentious insinuation. The two comrades walked through the massive gates of Versailles toward the stables. Pierre decided to test the waters. "Robert, you are my dearest friend in the world."

"Like a brother."

"You know almost everything there is to know about me, all my secrets, and you still love me."

"Yes, and the reverse is true."

Pierre hesitated as they walked. "Absolutely." He pulled his cloak off and carried it in his arms. "May I be completely honest with you?"

"Haven't we always been so with each other?"

"I am becoming weary of court life. There is a longing deep inside of me for—for . . . I don't know . . . for something more."

"Something more? More than the privilege of being a courtier in King Louis' court at Versailles?"

Pierre stopped and looked directly at Robert. "Yes. Something more substantial. Something that will sustain our souls as we grow older. Do you not ever feel that way? Am I being foolish?"

Robert's eyebrows pulled up in a characteristic wrinkle that meant he didn't understand. He looked around as if to be sure nobody could overhear them. "Something that will 'sustain our souls'? What in the world are you talking about?"

Pierre proceeded, trusting that his friend could hear his heart. "It's honest talk. Not the innuendoes and double-talk that have become second nature to us in flirting with relationships and advancement. Always looking around to be sure nobody is lurking in the shadows, spying on us—like you did just now. I'm weary of it. I want to be free."

Robert looked down at his feet and lowered his voice. "Free? That is dangerous talk. This is not the appropriate place to be baring your heart and soul."

Pierre shifted his weight and started again toward the stables. "You're right." He shook his head and with a wave of his hand dismissed the conversation. "Never mind. I'm rambling. I've just come off a long mission, and I need to get reoriented to the court. Forget everything I've said."

"Not likely."

Fingers of fear clamped down around Pierre's heart, and his palms began to sweat. He forced a smile. "Come now, Robert. Give me a few days, and I'll be as good as new."

"Yes, as good as new." Robert looked askance at his friend and shook his head as they walked.

They reached the yawning entrance of the stable where the horses for the military units were kept. Walking inside, they began their search for Commander Boveé, but Pierre was aware of Robert's sideward glances.

The smell of the animals, horse sweat mixed with straw, excrement, and leather, filled their nostrils as they entered the enclosure. They passed carriage after carriage being readied for nobility by busy footmen and grooms. Horses nickering and snorting, stableboys barking commands to the horses and poking fun at each other filled the dense air.

Robert covered his nose with his handkerchief, but Pierre breathed in the scents of the stables. He preferred the prancing of the horses in the stables to the prancing at the court balls. Although he executed the court dances with skill, he favored executing expert moves with his horse. King Louis demanded both of his courtiers. That was one reason Pierre was the king's frequent companion on the daily hunts. The courtier knew what he was doing and enjoyed a bois-terous hunt, as did Louis.

Robert, on the other hand, preferred to do his prancing indoors. He was an adequate horseman, but he excelled at the intricate steps of the court dances. The ladies of the court vied for his attention and competed for his invitation to accompany him on the dance floor.

"I do hope we find your father quickly. I spent enough time in the stables growing up."

"You may go back to the ladies in the courtyard anytime you choose."

Robert shook his head and tucked his handkerchief back in his sleeve. "No, I'll stay. It simply takes me a minute to get used to the . . . uh . . . fragrance."

Pierre spied the red and blue colors of his father's dragoon regi-ment toward the rear of the first section. He heard the deep, resonant voice of his father's commands before he saw him. "Come. This way."

Robert tiptoed through the straw. Pierre laughed under his breath at his friend trying to protect his white leather shoes with the red leather soles and heels and the newly fashionable oval buckles.

"Hurry up. It's going to take us all day at this rate."

Robert threw a dirty look at Pierre. "I'm going to ruin my new shoes. Look at that!" He leaned against a wooden gate and lifted one foot. Picking up a piece of wood from the floor, he began to scrape the mud and horse droppings off the soles of his shoes. "Maybe I should have stayed in the courtyard." He continued to grumble as Pierre went on without him.

Pierre found his father checking the ankle of a dappled Boulonnais. He was not in uniform, though some of his men were. His head was down, intent on his work, and he did not notice Pierre approaching.

"Bonjour, Père."

Paul Boveé's head snapped around and he straightened up, still holding the horse's leg in his hand. Upon seeing his son, he dropped the hoof and started toward Pierre. *"Bonjour!"*

Pierre thought his father meant to embrace him, but the commander stopped short.

"When did you get back?" The characteristic wide Boveé smile spread across his father's leathered face.

In spite of himself, Pierre found himself glad to see the man. "A couple of days ago." Pierre shuffled his feet. "That's a nice Boulonnais."

"Yes, isn't he?" He patted the horse on his rump. "Good temperament, too, although he's pretty lively. But I like that in a military horse. Always ready to get to work."

An uneasy silence interjected itself into the space between the two men—father and son who had never learned to converse or stand side by side in that comfortable relationship that should exist between parent and child, whether words are spoken or not. "I . . . I'm glad to see you, Son."

That was new. "I'm glad to see you, too, Father."

Robert stole into the stall, picking his way through the straw. "Commander Boveé." He executed a perfect courtly bow. "It's been a long time."

The commander returned the bow. "It certainly has been, Robert. Are you still following Pierre around?"

"I suppose I would, if he would stay in one place."

Commander Boveé threw his head back and bellowed a laugh too loud for the comment.

Is he nervous? Pierre stared at his father.

"What brings you to the stables today?"

"I came looking for you. And I need to get Tonnerre ready for the hunt this afternoon."

"In that order? As I remember, your horses always came first."

"Actually, yes."

"Yes, what?"

"My first priority was to find you. I didn't even know I'd been assigned to the hunt until my faithful friend here informed me. So I thought I would take care of both at the same time."

"*Bon.* What can I do for you?"

Pierre found himself feeling like a little boy again, intimidated by a father whom he never really knew. A dashing, stern commander. A father who didn't want to be bothered by his son.

Pierre willed his voice to remain steady and firm. "I hoped you weren't out on assignment. I'd like us to have dinner sometime soon. I'd like to talk . . . just the two of us."

"Sounds serious. Have you found a lady who has captured your heart? Perhaps you are planning to marry?"

His father's comment sent Pierre's thoughts plummeting back to Madeleine. *Yes, I've found a lady who has captured my heart, but, no, I'm not planning to marry. She is desperately out of my reach.*

"No, nothing like that. I wanted us to catch up on . . . I . . ." Pierre didn't know how to finish.

"I will be leaving on an assignment in three days," Commander Boveé said. "How about if we meet in town tonight at the tavern. Eight o'clock?"

"I'll be there."

Pierre left his father to check on his horse. Dinner with his father—unbelievably, a first for the courtier. He felt like a child again, excited at the possibility of seeing his papa.

IN SPITE OF PIERRE'S INITIAL NEGATIVE REACTION TO having been assigned to the daily hunt, he enjoyed the devil-may-care diversion of riding the hounds, the boisterous camaraderie of the hunt, and the satisfaction of completing the kill.

King Louis engaged him briefly in conversation as they dismounted at the stables. "I see you have not lost your affinity for the hunt. Well done."

"Thank you, Your Majesty. It was an enjoyable afternoon." And then Pierre added, hoping to defray any more doubt on the part of the king, "It's good to be back."

Louis smiled. "It's good to have you back. Stay close. I intend to keep you busy." With that the king handed his horse over to a stableboy, turned his back, and walked away.

What did that mean? Is he warning me not to leave? Possibly—no, probably. I will have to play my cards skillfully for as long as I remain at Versailles.

ELEVEN

"It's time that you knew the history between the king and me."
Madeleine moved over onto the cushioned seat beside her son.

He put his hands on the edge of the carriage seat as they jostled along the road headed toward France and turned to look at his mother. "I know that you and the king were childhood friends when Grand-père and Grand-mère were at court."

Madeleine nodded. "That's right."

"I am no longer a child, Mère. There is more to it than simply friends, isn't there?"

"*Oui*, there is much more."

Philippe's mouth constricted into a tight slit, and he looked down. He removed his cap, and his dark hair fell across his forehead, just the way François' always did. Then he raised his head and leaned back in the seat, fidgeting with his cap in his hands. "I'm ready to hear what you have to say. The reason King Louis wants you back at Versailles has something to do with me, does it not?" His changing voice, most of the time deep and resonant, crackled at the end of his question.

"Yes, it does." Madeleine took a deep breath and began to unfold the story of her relationship with the king. "When Louis and I were young, as was Versailles, we were friends. He was already king, crowned at the age of five, as you know. He was a very lonely young child, under the care of governesses and servants most of the time. One day, because he was left unattended, he narrowly escaped drowning in a pond."

She paused and stared into space, trying to snatch the memories from the recesses of her mind and put them into a sensible order so Philippe could understand. "As he grew into his teen years, he began to assert his authority more and more, and he gathered a group of friends around to amuse him and keep him company. He threw lavish parties at Versailles. He married at fifteen, but that didn't stop his flirtations with the ladies of the court."

"Were you one of those ladies?"

"Yes, among many others."

"But he had special feelings for you—more than just flirtations?"

Madeleine's breath quickened, and her stomach felt uneasy. "He taught me the court dances. We rode together. But it was more than that. He felt he could trust me and that I loved him for himself, not just because he was the king."

"Loved him?"

"Oui."

"Did you love him?"

"Yes, Philippe, I did. And the strange thing was he . . . he trusted

89

me because I was Huguenot. Several of his court ministers at the time were Huguenot, and that was the very reason he had appointed them. He knew they were honest and trustworthy."

"Wasn't his wife jealous of you?"

"Most probably. She adored him and hung on his every word. But he never was in love with her. I think as he has gotten older, however, he has developed a certain fondness for her, even though he has a *maîtresse en titre*."

"Were you one of those 'official mistresses'?"

Madeleine hesitated again before answering her son. She watched the trees rush by in a blur, just as her life had rushed by her the past three years since being expelled from their estate by the dragoons. She looked back at her son's innocent face awaiting her answer.

"It would serve no purpose to lie to you." She took his hands in hers. "Please try to understand. I was very young and besotted with the king. He pledged his undying love to me—assured me that there was no other for whom he truly cared. I was not one of his official mistresses, but . . ."

Philippe waited.

"But we were lovers. King Louis was my first love."

Philippe pulled his hands from hers and looked away. The plodding of the horses' hooves and the turning wheels of the carriage pervaded the afternoon stillness. The rain had stopped, and a moisture-laden breeze blew through the windows and tousled Philippe's hair. "I'm not really shocked, I suppose. I guessed as much."

Tears hung on Madeleine's thick, dark eyelashes and then spilled down her cheeks. "When Grand-père and Grand-mère realized what was occurring between us, they moved me at once back to the estate, away from court, away from Louis. They knew what would be ahead

90

for me if the relationship continued. He tried to contact me, but your grandparents protected me from his letters. Eventually he got buried in the affairs of state, instead of the affairs of the heart, and gave up his attempts to coax me back to court."

"Why has he begun pursuing you again? Why does it matter now?"

"He is under a false assumption concerning us." She struggled to find the right words. "He is convinced that . . . that you might . . ." She wiped her eyes as she looked at her son. "Philippe, Louis thinks there is a possibility that you are his son."

Philippe's eyes reflected his shock. "Th-the king's son?" He shook his head. "What about Papa? You were married when I was born, *non*?"

"Yes, we were married. Soon after I got home from court I met your father, and we married quickly. And you were born soon after that."

"How soon?"

"Philippe, you are a Clavell. You are François Clavell's son."

"How soon?"

"Seven months."

"So, there *is* a possibility?"

"*Non*, my son. I don't think so. I was too young and not capable of carrying a baby the full nine months. You were so tiny, we feared for your life. Your papa could hold you in the palm of his hand."

"But the king believes I might be his son."

"*Oui*, he does. That's why we have been kidnapped. He wants to see you."

"Do I look like him?"

"Not at all! You are much taller than he is. Your nose is like your father's, and your hair—your hair is exactly like your father's."

"That's true." Philippe pushed his hair out of his eyes and replaced his cap. "Did the king ever meet Papa?"

"Not that I know of."

"Am I older than his oldest son?"

"By about ten months."

"So I . . . we are in a dangerous position because the king *thinks* that I may be his firstborn son."

Madeleine nodded and marveled at the maturity of her firstborn. "I am so proud of you, as was your father."

"Did Papa know?"

"Of course. And I assured him the night he returned that you are indeed a Clavell. He had never questioned me about it before then."

"How do you intend to convince the king?"

"I don't know yet. I'm hoping when he sees you that he will see the truth for himself."

"What if you cannot convince him? What will happen to us then?"

"Don't borrow trouble, Son. He has legitimized his children born from his mistresses. He has great affection for them. That would be the most he would do. But I will convince him." Madeleine put her arm around her son's shoulders. "You are going to have to trust me implicitly. You may see me in situations while we are at Versailles that may trouble you, but they will be because I am designing a scheme to get us out of this. The world of the French court appears to be one thing on the surface, but beneath that glittering façade an entirely different agenda boils. Covert meanings hide beneath the words spoken—another language has to be learned and perfected."

She took her arm away and patted his hands. "I used to be good at it, but after my trip to Versailles when the dragoons invaded, I realized my 'skills' had grown more than a little rusty. I will help you, but I wish there were a man who could take you under his wing." The thought hit her like a shot. "Pierre! Pierre is at Versailles. He will help us. Perhaps once again, he will be the one to come to our rescue."

They rode for several miles in silence, mother and son lost in their own thoughts. Finally Philippe broke the silence.

"Where will we stay? Will we be there for very long?"

"I don't know the answer to either of those questions." She looked out at the soldiers riding alongside the coach. Pictures of Charles and Vangie's twisted faces crying as they were torn away from her tortured her. "I feel completely powerless—out of control." She looked up, then closed her eyes and sighed. "Our situation is out of our control for now, but it is never out of God's control. We are his children. Nothing comes to us but by his permission. Therefore, we will not be afraid. No matter what comes our way, we shall trust him!" Her voice rose until the last phrase came out in a shout.

"Whoa!" The driver brought the carriage to a halt.

Nicolas rode up beside the carriage door, dismounted, and stuck his head in the window. "Is there anything wrong, madame? Did you need something?"

"Why, how kind of you, sir. We don't need a thing. We were simply talking about how excited we are to be going to Versailles."

"Excited? Humph . . . well, glad to see you have changed your mind. It will make your trip much easier."

"This is a small misunderstanding that can be cleared up quickly, but in the meantime, yes . . . I am excited to show my son the place I grew up, the wonders of Versailles."

"Very well." The captain looked around. A small stream wound its lazy way through a stand of trees to the side. "We shall water the horses at that stream as long as we are stopped. And then on to—as you say—the wonders of Versailles." The musketeer opened the door for Madeleine and helped her out, then went back to his horse and ordered his men to dismount.

Philippe emerged behind her.

"See what I mean, Son? The tongue can express one thing and mean another. Grand-mère warned me when we went to Versailles last time to be 'as wise as a serpent, but innocent as a dove.' That is still good advice. Heed it, my son, heed it well."

TWELVE

Pierre arrived late at the tavern, a favorite spot for off-duty soldiers and guards. He spotted his father's dappled Boulonnais to the side in an alley and brought his black Percheron stallion alongside.

He summoned a boy who seemed to be watching over his father's steed. "The Boulonnais belongs to my father. Has he commissioned you to watch over him?"

"*Oui*, monsieur."

"Tend to mine as well, and I will double what he offered you."

"I shall be honored, sir!" The lad, who looked to be about eleven or twelve, jumped from the stone fence on which he was perched to take the reins from Pierre.

"Very well. I'll be right inside." Pierre looked back at the trio, the two horses and the boy, as he turned the corner to the front of the inn. The lad gave him a slight wave and then reached up to pet the Percheron.

Pierre entered the raucous room. Not a very good place to talk, but he would not pass up the opportunity. His father sat huddled over a table in front of the fireplace, talking to two other dragoon officers, and a large woman stood beside the table. The woman held a tray of beer steins in one hand and with the other, waved in wide gestures as they conversed.

Commander Boveé glanced toward the entrance, stood as soon as he spotted Pierre, and beckoned to him. Pierre wound his way through the crowded area, recognizing court acquaintances scattered throughout the room at rustic, wooden tables. A pig roasted on an iron rotisserie in the fireplace, sending an enticing aroma around the room. The woman left his father's table and checked the roasting pig before returning to the bar.

Approaching his father, Pierre found himself wary. The man could be cruel and unbending; that Pierre knew from experience. He was completely loyal to the crown and devoted to his regiment. And in carrying out his military responsibilities, he had been the vindictive hammer of the king to bring down destruction on Madeleine's family. A tug-of-war put Pierre's heart in upheaval. Paul Boveé had given Pierre natural birth, but the Clavells had shown him the way to spiritual birth.

His father stood. "Ah! Here he is. I had begun to wonder if you were going to make it."

"Sorry, the hunt ran late."

"No matter. You know Officers Du Buisson and Martineau?"

The two dragoons pushed the heavy chairs back in which they had been sitting and gathered their gloves. They nodded to the courtier.

"I believe we've met. Please, be seated. Won't you join us for dinner?" Pierre secretly hoped they would decline. He wanted his father to himself this evening.

"*Merci,* but we'll be joining our party over by the window." The two soldiers excused themselves and made their way to a long trestle table filled with bantering soldiers.

"Are you hungry?" Pierre's father offered him a stein of ale, while motioning to the barmaid at the same time.

"Famished. I hadn't realized how hungry I was until I smelled that pig roasting."

The barmaid approached, and Paul Boveé wrapped his arm around her waist. "My dear Johanna, this is my son, Pierre."

"As if one couldn't tell." She belted out a hearty laugh. "Why have you kept him a secret all these years?"

"No secret. Our paths of duty have simply taken us in different directions. Pierre is a courtier in the king's court. And I . . . well, you know what I do."

"I certainly do. And that very well." Johanna laughed again and gave him a kiss on his cheek.

Pierre laughed with them, but he felt uncomfortable. But why should he? His father's womanizing was no surprise.

"Well, gentlemen, what can I serve you tonight? The hog is about ready."

"It smells wonderful." Pierre's mouth began to water.

"Bring the usual. Is it too late in the season for strawberries?"

"I think Monsieur Lombard picked the last of them yesterday. I'll see if there are any left in the back."

"*Bien.* I'd like some with cheese for dessert if there are. And bring us some wine."

Johanna shouted orders to the cooks, and eventually she returned with a platter of meat and vegetables, a dish of herbal salad, a marinated cucumber and asparagus salad, and a basket of baguettes.

"Who would have known such a gourmet meal awaited one here?"

"Have you never been here before? You must get out more."

"My responsibilities are more confining to the chateau than are yours."

"True. But you've been away for quite a few weeks. What was that about?" His father fingered his wine goblet and leaned back in his chair.

Pierre hesitated. Was he fishing for information? "As a matter of coincidence, I was sent to find out what had happened to François Clavell and his family."

"I could have told the king the condition of their estate. My men and I took care of that item of business ourselves."

"I think the king was more interested in what happened to Madame Clavell, if you know what I mean."

"Ah, yes. The king is not accustomed to being the jilted lover." His laughter rang. "Why did he send you on that mission? That's not the usual assignment for a courtier."

"I suppose because he had assigned me to escort her to the Trianon one night, and I know what she looks like. But that wasn't the whole assignment. I was also sent to find out what had happened to François Clavell himself."

His father seemed to accept Pierre's story.

Pierre continued, "The king sent me to the Bastille to search the galley records, which in turn propelled me to the port of Brest. Clavell had been crossed off the galley slave list, so I assume he died at sea." Pierre tore off a piece of the baguette and sopped up juice from the roast pig. "Then I traveled to the Clavell estate in Dauphiné Provence to see if I could find any lingering Clavells. I found the estate destroyed. No one was around."

Paul Boveé smiled and took another swig of wine.

"And then I came back and reported to the king. That little excursion took several weeks."

"Indeed. From one end of France to the other. Where do you think Madame Clavell and her family are now?"

"It's hard to tell. Many Huguenots are fleeing to Switzerland, but I know the Clavells have relatives in Spain. Perhaps they have gone there."

Paul raised his eyebrows. "How do you know that?"

Pierre's heart began to pound. "She mentioned them the night we were at the Trianon."

"Hmmm, I see." Pierre's father searched his son's face. "You are not the same since you've returned. Perhaps you are just maturing." He poured more wine into both of their goblets. "But I perceive that it's more than that."

Pierre smirked. "We haven't been around each other enough to know whether there have been changes in either one of us or not, have we?"

Paul sighed and set his wine on the table. "You are probably right." He fidgeted with the goblet and looked around the room. "Well, what is it that you wanted to talk to me about?"

Pierre leaned forward. His heart hammered in his chest. He took a deep breath. "Père, I have begun to realize as I've matured that some things in life are important, and other things that seemed to be important at the time are fleeting." He searched his father's eyes. "I have come to realize that I've been an ungrateful son."

The commander began to shake his head. "I probably was not the best father in the world either."

"True, you weren't."

The two fell silent for a moment, staring at each other. Paul scooted back in his chair and picked up his gloves.

"No. Wait. Don't leave. Listen to what I have to say."

"I didn't come here to get a lecture from my son." His voice rose. Soldiers and patrons at surrounding tables cut their eyes in the direction of the two men.

"I don't intend to lecture you. Please, Père, lower your voice and sit down and hear me out."

Paul turned to the fireplace next to their table and put his foot up on the hearth. "Go on."

Pierre remained seated and set his elbows on the table. He looked up at his father. "As I was saying, even though you may not have been the best father in the world, I certainly have not been the best son either."

Commander Boveé took his foot off the hearth and pulled his chair around, but remained standing.

Pierre continued, "I've not made a real effort to see you or include you in my life. In fact, I've done just the opposite. I've tried to . . . cut you out of my life."

Paul laid his gloves on the table and sat in the chair. He picked up his wine goblet and took a sip. "Go on."

"I . . . I felt I didn't need you, that I could make it on my own at court without you. And I suppose I've done pretty well."

Paul frowned and nodded.

"But in recent days I've come to understand that family is important, and . . . and you're all the family I have—we only have each other."

Tears brightened Pierre's eyes. "What I want to say is . . . I want to ask you to forgive me for not being the son I should have been." He paused and leaned forward. "I want you in my life, Père. I need you in my life."

The hardened commander cocked his head and pursed his lips. "I . . . I don't know what to say." He looked around the room and continued to swirl the wine in the goblet. "You've been a fine son." He coughed. "I admit I've not been a good father to you. I can't even rightfully claim the title. The fact that I abandoned you and your mother is something that I will always regret. Then when she died . . . I . . . she was a good woman and incredibly beautiful. I . . ." His voice trailed off.

"I never found anyone to truly take her place. I was too busy training dragoons and fighting King Louis' skirmishes rather than training my own son and fighting the battles for his well-being. We had no other family, so I did the only thing I knew to do, and that was to bring you here to Versailles. At the very least you would be fed and would have shelter. At least . . . at least I did that." The commander looked down. "I had good intentions of seeing you more often, of taking you with me when I could, but my good intentions never seemed to materialize. I was so proud when you started courtier training, even though I would have preferred you to be a soldier." He smiled and looked back at Pierre. "But those were not your mother's wishes. She would have loved seeing you in the court. She . . ."

Pierre stared at his father. He had never seen this human side of the man. "Can you forgive me for being an ungrateful son?"

The noise of the tavern seemed to fade into a wordless hum. As his father hesitated, Pierre said, "I would understand if you cannot find it in your heart to forgive me."

Visions of his father riding out of the stables, leading a regiment of dragoons past him as the boy stood holding the reins of a horse, desperately hoping his father would nod in his direction, ran through his mind. But time after time his father never even looked his way. The few times his father visited him in his stable quarters with the promise of returning soon, he never did. Occasionally a bundle of clothes tied up in a burlap bag with twine would arrive, but Pierre never knew if they were from his father or not.

"Did you care for my mother at all?"

"I'm sure you find this hard to believe, but I've thought about that much through the years . . . when I allowed myself to think at all." Paul cut off another piece of meat and bit into it. "I did love her, but I suppose if I had genuinely cared for her—and you—I wouldn't have left."

A growing knot of anger began to arise in Pierre's gut—resentment that Pierre had pushed down time after time that he attempted to cover up by his societal climb out of the stables and into the opulence of the court. "Mère was a wonderful woman. The loss was yours."

"I know that now." Paul Bovee's voice grew uncharacteristically soft. "But you have not fared so ill, have you? You are a courtier in King Louis' court, well thought of and respected, can have any woman you desire, hunts with the king—many young men would be envious of you."

Years of buried rage threatened to bubble to the surface. Pierre leaned across the table and spoke through clenched teeth. "Socializing, fine horses and hunts, women, wine, and banqueting can never substitute for the security and love of a father." Pierre doubled up his fist and pounded the table, emphasizing each point.

Pierre leaned back in his chair and took a deep breath. He saw a look in his father's eyes he had never seen before—astonishment, hurt, awareness, understanding. Pierre didn't know for sure, but it seemed there was a vulnerability in his expression that Paul Boveé seldom exposed.

Pierre threw up his hands. "I'm sorry. I came to ask your forgiveness, and instead I accuse you. I'm sorry."

"It needed to be said."

"Perhaps." Pierre looked down and tore off a piece of bread. "I . . . I would like for us to try to rescue whatever relationship we have left and build on it from this point. Could we do that?"

Pierre looked into his father's face, astonished to see his father's eyes redden.

"Well?" Pierre raised his eyebrows and waited. "Father?"

Paul shook his head, and a slight upturn of his mouth began to surface. "I am shocked. But, of course." He stuck his hand out across the table. He grabbed Pierre's forearm and came around the table to embrace his son.

Pierre stepped back. "I have one question. Did you ever bring clothes wrapped in burlap to the stable for me when I was a boy?"

Paul looked at his son, and his eye twitched. He nodded, ever so slightly. Pierre laughed and embraced his father once more.

"Thank you. I never thanked you."

The two rode back to Versailles that night, united in heart for the first time as father and son. It was a turn of events Pierre had hoped for all of his life.

THIRTEEN

Captain Maisson whistled the party to a halt and opened the door to the carriage. It was their fourth night on the road. He stuck his head inside the cab. "We shall stop here for the night. Remain in the carriage, and I'll see to rooms." The door snapped shut and latched as the captain shouted orders to one of his men to stand guard.

Madeleine peered out of the window on the other side at the carved sign of a rustic inn. The sign swung in the wind, Inn of the Stag, proclaiming a creaky invitation to the reluctant guests in the carriage. Madeleine twisted her gloves in her hand, much as her thoughts twisted in her head. Echoes of Vangie's screams tore at her heart and kept her from sleep. Tears surfaced unbidden for the first two days as the carriage sped toward Versailles. She could not seem to control them. Then her countenance settled in grim determination.

Every evening Captain Maisson went through the same routine.

They approached an inn frequented by the king's soldiers; he bid Madeleine and Philippe wait while he secured a room; a guard escorted them directly to their quarters; and a servant of the inn brought them supper. But tonight Madeleine saw what she had been waiting for—a large inn with many guests and a stable of considerable size. Almost a dozen horses stood tied to the hitching posts outside. Soldiers and civilians alike bustled in and out of the heavy wooden doors.

She heard boisterous laughter from within, and when Captain Maisson opened the door for them, she sighted several women in the crowd. A long, dark wooden bar ran along the left side of the room, with tables filling a large room adjacent. Dragoons, musketeers, and soldiers from different companies stood at the bar, drinking and exchanging jokes. Women moved from table to table, serving large tureens and platters of food and drink.

The captain motioned Madeleine and Philippe, carrying his mother's jewelry chest, to a staircase on the right.

Madeleine inhaled. "Ummmm, smells like the *potage* Thèrése used to prepare at our estate. There's some spice that she—"

"I'll have a kettle sent to your room right away, madame."

"Thank you. You have been surprisingly kind, Captain, given the difficult situation."

Captain Maisson cleared his throat and adjusted his sword. "Just following orders."

Madeleine looked at the musketeer officer and felt a moment of compassion for him. He was but another puppet in Louis' schemes. He led them to a room on the second floor, with more amenities than the previous inns. Philippe would sleep in a bed tonight instead of on the floor. Two four-poster canopied beds awaited them, as well as a vanity holding a washbasin, ewer, and towels. A chaise and screen sat in the corner of the room. Madeleine peeked behind the screen and saw a porcelain bathing tub, along with lavender salts and pumice stones.

"These are the king's quarters when he travels this way." The captain smiled. "Enjoy your evening."

"Yes, thank you. We will."

The captain turned and left, latching the door behind him. Madeleine put her finger to her mouth and cautioned Philippe with a nod of her head. Lowering her voice, she said, "This is our chance. There are so many people here and horses outside that we won't be as conspicuous. The guards will be lulled into complacency by the accommodations and food. If we are lucky, they will have too much to drink. We've not caused them any problems so far. They won't be suspicious."

Philippe nodded. "What do you propose?"

"When the servants bring our supper, I'll distract them, and you stuff this piece of leather into the latch." Madeleine pulled the leather drawstring from her coin purse and handed it to her son. "Then later tonight or early morning, when the guard is asleep, we'll slip out and find the horses and ride out of here."

"But they'll know exactly where to look for us."

Madeleine walked to the window and closed the shutters. She watched her own hand tremble on the wooden slats and steadied it. "That's true. We'll have to go someplace else and get word to Uncle Jean to bring the others and meet us in ... in ..."

"Where, Maman? Where can we go?"

Madeleine looked at her son—not yet a man, but no longer a boy. Her heart broke for what her children had endured, and a knot formed in her throat. How much more could the family tolerate? She sat down beside him again and brushed his hair out of his eyes. "I'm thinking Germany. Perhaps they will be sympathetic toward us."

"Germany? Can we make it? Just the two of us? What about our things?"

"We are Clavells. We can make it." Her voice wavered. "We . . . we must make it. As for our things—we'll have to leave everything, except the jewelry chest."

A scratching at the door alerted them that their dinner had arrived. The musketeer guard pushed open the door, and a plump domestic hustled into the room with a kettle of stew, a basket of bread, and two bottles of wine. Her rosy cheeks were covered in perspiration. She set the bread and wine on a table and hung the kettle over the low fire in the fireplace.

Madeleine peered out the door as the musketeer guard took up his seat once again in a heavy wooden chair, his musket in his lap. A covey of women from down the hall called to him.

"Hey, what's one so debonair doing sitting in our hallway? Why don't you come down here and visit us?"

The guard stood and rearranged his bandoliers, but didn't leave his assigned position.

"Does Madame need anything else?" The servant wiped her face with her apron.

Philippe ambled toward the door.

"Please, would you help me with these shutters?" Madeleine indicated the window in the farthest corner of the room from the door. "They seem to be stuck."

"Certainly, madame. Ach, these old things. They give us problems all the time." She waddled toward the window.

Madeleine placed herself between the servant and her son.

Philippe stood at the door and slipped the strip of leather into the space between the door and the latch. If all went well, the door would latch partway, but wouldn't lock.

The servant closed the shutters with ease. "These seem to be fine."

"Oh well, I guess you have the magic touch. *Merci.*"

"You are welcome. Enjoy your supper. You may leave the dishes on the table, and I'll retrieve them in the morning." The servant went out the door, pulling it shut behind her.

Madeleine held her breath. They watched the latch wiggle as the servant struggled with it from outside in the hall. When it wouldn't latch securely, a pudgy hand with stubby fingers wrapped around the latch apparatus.

"Hmmm, seems to be stuck." The maid jiggled it, and the strip of leather fell unnoticed onto the floor in the hallway. She locked the door and left.

"Ah, no." Madeleine plopped down on the chaise, her shoulders sagging.

Philippe shook his head and stood by the door. In a few moments, he quietly tried the latch. Locked. In tandem, the two looked at the windows.

"Philippe, blow out the candle."

In the glow of the fireplace, they went to the far window and opened the shutters. Madeleine tried the window lever on the right side, then the left—both locked.

"Here, Maman. I can open that." Philippe took his knife out of his boot.

"Where did you get *that?*"

"Henri gave it to me while we were unloading my things." He grinned at his mother. "I knew it would come in handy." After a few tries, he pried the lock on the right side open. "That's all we need. We can get through this side."

"Good work, Son. Look, we are in luck." The window opened onto a rising overhang behind the inn. The stable stood to the side. "We can easily jump to the ground here." She closed the window and shutters and went to the table to relight the candle. "Let's eat something, then wait until the inn settles down and the guards are asleep. Leave your clothes on." She cast a longing glance toward the tub and sighed.

MADELEINE SAT ON THE CHAISE WITH HER JEWELRY chest on the floor beside her. Philippe slept the deep sleep of the young, curled up on the bed, fully clothed, his jacket over him, cap on the table beside his bed. They had stuffed the beds with pillows to make it appear as if they were asleep. The inn was quiet.

Madeleine stood and walked to Philippe's bed and shook him. "Philippe, wake up." Her voice was barely a whisper.

His eyes popped open. "Is it time?"

"Yes, Son. Let's go."

Philippe put on his jacket and cap and went to the window.

Madeleine swung her cloak around her shoulders and put on her bonnet. "You go out first, and I'll hand you the chest."

He nodded and grabbed hold of the vertical bar of the window. He slid through the opening and jumped to the ground. "Ow!"

"Philippe! What happened? Are you hurt?"

"There are loose rocks here on the ground. I twisted my ankle." The boy flexed his foot and groaned. "It hurts, but I will be fine. Here, give me the chest."

Leaning out of the window, Madeleine lowered the chest as far as she could, then released it into Philippe's arms. He set it down beside him.

"Got it. Now, lower yourself as far as you can before you jump. It's really not that far to the ground. I'll break your fall. Be prepared for the ground to crumble a bit beneath your feet."

Madeleine turned around and eased herself out of the window, her feet dangling as she hung on to the windowsill.

"You're not far from the ground. Now, Maman, let go."

Her fingers scraped against the stone as she let go and tumbled to the ground. She fell into Philippe's arms, and they both rolled back down the incline into the wall of the inn. They paused in a heap, listening. Nothing.

Philippe hobbled up and gave his mother his hand. "Are you all right?"

Madeleine brushed her skirt and straightened her bonnet. "I'm fine. But what about your foot?"

"Never mind. Won't slow me down."

"Let us get the horses and get out of here."

"Let me get the chest." Philippe scrambled up the incline, limping on one foot, and retrieved the chest. The two started to the stable.

"Uh!" A guttural cough spewed from a mound of drunken human flesh lying in the shadows on the side of the stable as Madeleine stumbled into him. She jumped back and grabbed Philippe's arm. The drunk looked up at her with bleary eyes, turned over, and returned to his snoring.

Madeleine's knees melted like water into ground that felt like it would give way any moment. She buried her head in Philippe's shoulder.

"Keep going. We cannot stop now." Philippe took his mother's arm as they slipped through the partially open door of the barn. The sounds of animals rustling in the hay and the snoring of soldiers and stable attendants punctuated the night air.

Madeleine whispered, "There are the horses, in the back, by the coach."

The pair tiptoed through the straw around sleeping bodies, tools, and buckets to their coach. Philippe patted a black gelding's white face and got the matching horse from the back of the stall. They bridled the horses quickly and started through the maze to the door—around a bale of hay, past the stalls. The horse's hooves clanked against the floor.

Philippe turned and motioned to Madeleine. "We're almost to the door." He pushed on the door and recoiled as the hinges creaked through the still night air. They stopped and held their breath. A low nicker from a horse was all they heard. "Come, we're clear." They led the horses out and began to mount.

"Going somewhere?" From out of the shadows the familiar voice of Captain Maisson stopped them short.

SEVERAL DAYS LATER, THE MUSKETEERS LED THE CARRIAGE into the immense stable area at the palace of Versailles. The darkness of the late hour folded its velvet mantle about them.

Madeleine shook Philippe's shoulder. "Wake up, Son, we have arrived at the palace."

The boy awoke from a sound sleep, put on his cap, and touched the knife in his boot to be sure it was still in place. His sprained ankle had healed.

Officer Maisson dismounted, opened the door of the coach, and assisted the former lady of the court in her descent.

"*Merci*, Officer Maisson."

"*Je vous en prie.*" He took off his hat and bowed to her. "Madame Clavell, although the circumstances have been somewhat unpleasant, it has been a pleasure to see you again."

She looked at the officer. "Even though we tried to escape from your clutches?" She tightened the ribbon on her bonnet.

"Sometimes the duties of one's office require one to perform unpleasant tasks."

"I understand. Thank you for your kindness."

Officer Maisson replaced his hat and barked orders to his men. "I shall escort you myself to your apartment."

Madeleine swung on her cloak. She realized as they walked through the grand chateau that they were approaching the area where she and her mother had been quartered on her previous visit. Tall, brilliant candelabras flickered above them and lit their path. The magnificence of the décor reached out and caressed them as they progressed through the confusing network of rooms. Nobody spoke.

Officer Maisson stopped in front of the same apartment as before. Louis was toying with her. A Swiss Guard stood at attention in front of the door. The servants set the luggage in the anteroom and left, save one young girl who went about lighting candles and the fire in the fireplace.

"Thank you, Officer Maisson. You have been most . . . helpful."

He bowed once again. "Do you need anything else, madame? Elise will stay and assist you. She has been instructed to supply anything you need." He motioned to a diminutive servant girl standing in the

112

shadows. A long, dark braid hung over her shoulder from beneath the domestic's cap.

"That will be beneficial. But other than that, no, thank you. We don't need a thing."

"Madame . . ." He hesitated.

"Yes?"

"The *Garde Suisse* has been assigned twenty-four-hour duty to attend you."

"So I noticed."

"You may walk in the gardens, go to the balls, whatever you wish, but the guard will accompany you at all times."

"I see."

"And one other thing. You will be required to attend daily Mass."

"We are Huguenot."

"At the king's command."

In the split second of the moment, Madeleine decided to cooperate. She didn't need to antagonize Louis unnecessarily. "Yes, very well. We shall be happy to attend the king's Mass." She took off her gloves and bonnet and laid them on the table. "Anything else? I am very tired and wish to retire."

"*Non*, madame. I take my leave of you. Sleep well."

"Good night, Captain Maisson."

The musketeer tipped his hat, bowed, and left. The servant girl awaited further instructions.

Philippe gazed out the window upon the dark grounds. He pulled the tall, ornately fashioned shutters together and turned to face his mother. "So this is Versailles."

"This is Versailles, but you've seen nothing yet."

"I've seen enough to know that I don't like it."

"Hmmm, yes . . . well, I would prefer you didn't like it rather than be sucked into its sticky grasp." Madeleine motioned to her former bedroom. "Elise, please put my things in there. Philippe will take the front room. Philippe, let's get some sleep. Tomorrow we wake upon a whole new world."

FOURTEEN

"Madame, it's time to arise." Elise opened the shutters, letting the early morning sunlight flood the room.

Madeleine groaned and laid the back of her hand over her eyes. "*Non*, Suzanne, I'm not ready to get up."

"Madame?"

"Oh. I forgot where I was." For a moment, Madeleine had been back at their estate, and her girlhood domestic was performing her regular duties.

"*Oui*, madame. You must ready yourself for Mass. What would Madame like to wear?" The servant had put Madeleine's gowns in a large armoire beside the window.

"Mass?" Then she remembered. "Yes, Mass. The black silk, my pearl necklace and earrings, and the black mourning brooch."

Madeleine went to Philippe's room. She caught her breath. He was not in the bed, nor was he anywhere in the room or apartment. "Philippe!"

No answer. She threw open the door from the anteroom and found him sitting across the foyer from the Swiss Guard, staring at the imposing figure in the red and blue uniform.

"Does he ever move?" Philippe walked around the stoic guard.

"Of course, but not when he's on guard or when you're looking." She ushered him back into their apartment. "Come, now. We must hurry to get to Mass on time. The king will be looking for us. Put on your best clothes, and see to it that your hair is brushed. And your hat . . . you don't have a proper hat, do you?"

"I have my cap."

"That will not do. Go on and get dressed."

Philippe went into his room and closed the door.

Madeleine turned to the young chambermaid and hesitated. She didn't know how much liberty she had to make requests of the servant. "Elise, do you think you could find a more suitable hat for my son?"

"*Oui*, madame. I think so."

"And I need to send a message to the king. Are there writing quills and paper in the room?"

The maid blinked and pointed to the desk.

"*Bien!* I'll have the letter ready to go when you get back with the hat."

Elise curtsied and scurried out the door.

Madeleine sat down at the desk in the corner of the room and dipped the quill in the ink bottle.

> *Louis,*
>
> *I am shocked and appalled that you would revert to such*

measures to bring me to Versailles. Let me assure you that your
assumption regarding Philippe is unfounded

She crossed out *unfounded* and inserted *is not true.*
I demand . . . Ummm, *demand* would not set well with the king.

I request an audience with you immediately, without delay.
Yours, Madeleine

She didn't like *Yours* either. She wadded up the sheet and got another.

Louis,
    I am shocked that you would revert to such measures to
bring me to Versailles. Let me assure you that your assumption
that Philippe is your son is untrue. I respectfully request an audi-
ence with you immediately, without delay.
—Madeleine

She read it over and then sealed it. Elise returned shortly with a hat for Philippe, then took the letter and disappeared to find a messenger.

MADELEINE AND PHILIPPE WALKED OUT OF THE DOOR OF the apartment toward the chapel. The Swiss Guard snapped to attention and followed them, and a replacement took his place at the entry of the apartment. The two of them, followed at a discreet distance by the guard, approached the entrance to the chapel and awaited the

117

arrival of the king. Philippe kept pushing the hat down to keep it on his head.

"When the king walks by, execute your finest bow. He may not acknowledge us, but he'll see us. Louis misses nothing." Madeleine felt conspicuously drab in her mourning black. The rainbow of the elegant gowns of the ladies of the court and the gaudy costumes of the men blended together in a beautiful painting—the black dress a muddy spot on the canvas. She wanted Louis to see her in it. She wanted him to know that François indeed was dead. But she would not wear the black again. The enormity of the situation left no time for proper mourning. She would do what was necessary to free them from being prisoners at Versailles.

The unmistakable rustle among the worshippers alerted Madeleine that the king was progressing their way. The crowd parted in front of them as the king and his party strode toward the entrance of the chapel. The wave of curtsies and bows undulated in front of his entourage and then filled in behind him.

Although the rituals of the Mass were unfamiliar to Philippe, Madeleine found the service strangely comforting. *Why can we all not resolve to worship the same God in tolerance and peace? Why must we run for our lives simply because we choose to worship the same God differently?*

Philippe looked from side to side as they knelt and stood and then sat. Madeleine reassured him with her hand on his knee.

The king, upon exiting down the aisle of the edifice, caught Madeleine's eye and with an almost imperceptible nod acknowledged her presence. She smiled and curtsied. His gaze darted to Philippe, but he kept moving.

"He's seen us. We shall receive a summons soon."

Madeleine scanned the crowd. "See if you can spot Pierre. He should be here."

Philippe, now taller than his mother, stood on tiptoe to try to find the courtier. "*Non*, I do not see him. But everybody has on big, plumed hats. I could be looking right at him and not see him."

"Very well. Would you like to see some of the gardens?"

"What I'd really like to do right now is get something to eat."

Madeleine chuckled at her continually hungry son, who seemed to grow inches every week. She eyed the Swiss Guard, who stood at a respectable distance from them, but she knew he was ready to move with them. "Perhaps we could eat in the *cuisine de commune*."

"What is that?"

"The king's dining hall for everybody at court. Pierre might be there as well."

Philippe's eyes widened as they entered the noisy room. "How many people eat here?"

"About five hundred, I think."

"Every day?"

"Yes, every day."

"Who pays for it?"

"The king."

"And just anybody can come here and eat?"

"Pretty much." Madeleine glanced over at the guard. "I don't think we are going to have any trouble getting in." They found a place at the far end of the room. Huge platters of fruits and vegetables, as well as roasted fowl and rabbits, sat ready for the taking, along with tureens of the *oille*.

Philippe grinned and filled his plate that was set before him. "Maybe Versailles isn't so bad after all."

"SUMMON MY TAILORS." HAVING RETURNED FROM THE chapel, the king disappeared into his private room with his inner circle to dispense orders for the day. He sat at the head of a table in an armchair, an immense window that reached from the floor to the ceiling to his right. "Commence your reading."

The foreign secretary began his reading to the king from a Dutch newspaper. Ushered in by a courtier, the Delobel brothers, one old and bent, the other a younger carbon copy of the older man, scurried into the room.

"Ah, excellent!" The king arose and walked toward them. "It is fortunate I brought you with the court from Paris this time." He strode to the window and looked out. Tapping his walking stick, he sat back down in his chair. "I have a task for you that shall take precedence over any other garments you are working on."

The two men nodded.

"There is a Madame Clavell who is my special guest at the chateau, along with her son. She is an old and very dear friend from the early days here at Versailles. Her husband has passed away, and she has no suitable court gowns. She is here in her mourning black. I want you to make a dozen new gowns for her. Anything she wants. Shoes to match. And an ermine cape for the winter, with a muff to go with it."

The tailors' eyes widened. "Ermine, sire?"

"Yes, ermine, jewels . . . whatever she desires. And one of the gowns is to be red. I always liked her in red." Louis visualized Madeleine's dark hair set off by the brilliance of a red gown she wore the last time he danced with her at court years ago.

"Now the boy. He needs appropriate court clothes as well. Outfit him and . . . and make sure you sew him a suitable hat—one that fits properly."

"Yes, Your Majesty. And when is all this to be completed?" The older tailor took the lead.

"As soon as possible. Begin immediately. If you need materials from Paris, send for them. Spare no expense. You are dismissed."

The Delobels bowed and exited the room. Louis stood and again went to the window.

The foreign secretary waited, newspaper in hand. "Shall I continue?"

"Do you like red gowns?"

"Sire?"

"Do you like red ball gowns? In your opinion, are they the most outstanding at a ball? Red gowns?"

"They indeed are beautiful. I would say it depends on the lady wearing the gown."

"Yes, that would be true." The king continued to stare out the window. "This lady exceeds them all. She truly exceeds them all."

FIFTEEN

The next morning Madeleine and Philippe awoke to the fragrance of potage being brought into the room. Elise attended the fire and served breakfast, delivered by a kitchen domestic.

"Mmmm, that smells good. Don't you think so, Maman?"

Madeleine didn't answer. She simply nodded and broke off a piece of the bread. "I've missed this yeast bread. Delicious." Madeleine spread red jam on her slice. "Do you remember Thèrése's *pain mollet*? Nobody made better."

"I remember now. I like it better than the Swiss rye bread."

"I do too."

Despite the conditions under which they had been brought to Versailles, Madeleine found herself sliding into the comfortable familiarity of her growing-up years. After the past three years of running and hiding, fearing for their lives, and then losing François, she welcomed the security and luxury that surrounded her at the moment.

Wise as a serpent, innocent as a dove.

She shook her head. What was she thinking? The memory of Vangie's tortured face loomed before her. They were in a lions' den— the lions simply had not yet been loosed.

"We must keep alert, Son. It is easy to be lulled into complacency. We shall go along with King Louis to a certain degree, but we will not fall for his schemes."

A soft scratching came from the front door. Elise answered, and two men, with two female servants, entered. Madeleine pulled her robe about her and stood.

The older gentleman spoke. "Madame Clavell?"

"*Oui.*"

He looked at Madeleine, with her thick, dark hair cascading around her shoulders, and took the lead. "Ach! You are not exactly what we . . . uh . . . we expected a much older lady. No wonder the king . . . well!" The tailor drew himself up, almost standing at attention. "We are the brothers Delobel, the king's tailors and dressmakers. We have been commissioned by King Louis to construct garments suitable for you and your son to wear in the royal court."

Madeleine motioned for Philippe to come to her side. "I have gowns suitable for the short time we are to be here. However, my son could use a hat . . . and shoes, perhaps."

Philippe whipped his head around to look at his mother. "*Non, Mère!* My boots are fine."

"Trust me. You need suitable clothes while we are here."

"Please, madame. The king has given explicit instructions, even to the specific color of at least one of your gowns. We must follow our orders."

"Red?"

"*Oui*, madame." The tailors bowed slightly.

Madeleine sighed. "Very well. Proceed with your work."

The brothers and assistants measured, pinned, and poked until Madeleine could stand still no longer. She stepped down from the footstool on which she had been instructed to stand. "That's enough. You have all the measurements you need. You may leave now."

Philippe, standing on a chair, appeared to be most miserable. He waved off the women, who were buzzing around him like bees gathering pollen, and sat down in the chair.

"But, madame, the king will be furious if we don't get the garments fitted exactly right."

"Do you have enough to get started?"

"Possibly. But we need Monsieur Philippe's foot measurements and head circumference . . . for a hat."

"Very well. Get those, then you are excused. You can come back another day when you have the dummies pinned and basted."

Philippe stood once more and allowed the final measurements. The tailors gathered their paraphernalia and left in a flurry of activity.

"We shall return next week to do final fittings. The hat and shoes, for sure, for the young monsieur."

Elise let the tailors out and smiled as she returned to the main room of the apartment.

Madeleine sat back in a chair, exhausted. "Elise, would you get the jade-colored gown out of the armoire, please? And there are shoes to match."

The maid curtsied and went into Madeleine's bedroom.

Madeleine lowered her voice. "I don't plan on being here long enough for these garments to be completed."

"How are we going to leave with a guard watching our every move?"

"I must secure an audience with the king. He won't stop until he's convinced you are not his son." Madeleine walked to the window. "We need to get ready for Mass."

"Again this morning?"

"We will need to go every morning, or the king will become suspicious. Then we shall explore the gardens. I'm quite astonished at the changes just since Grand-mère and I were here, after the dragoons . . ." Her thoughts drifted off to another day, another time.

"Mère?"

"Memories flood my head every time I come here. Go on, now, and dress, or we shall be late."

Madeleine instructed Elise on how to arrange her thick hair. Although she enjoyed following the fashion of the day, Madeleine always had preferred letting her hair fall more naturally rather than putting it up in the stiff curls. Suzanne had learned the knack of making Madeleine's hair follow certain lines of fashion while retaining her own style. She emerged now in her favorite jade silk gown.

"Maman, you look beautiful."

Madeleine gave her son a slight curtsy. "Merci. I guess you had better wear that ridiculous hat, although it doesn't fit you."

"Look, I tore the seam open enough for it to come down on my head. See?" Philippe donned the too-small headgear and beamed at his mother.

"Well, that is some better. Come here; let me pull the plume over the tear." She reached up to fix the hat and realized she had to stand on tiptoe to get hold of it. "You are getting too tall." She succeeded in making the hat more presentable. "Now, give me your arm. We shall walk into the chapel as if we were noble members of the court."

FOLLOWING MASS, MADELEINE AND PHILIPPE WANDERED through the gardens and beside the splashing fountains. She pointed out the Latona Fountain and the Royal Avenue lined with statues and vases. She named the varieties of flowers and ornately pruned hedges.

Philippe stared at the expanse and design of the gardens. "I thought the gardens at our estate were beautiful, but they pale in comparison with this. These go on forever. It would take us a week to walk through the entire grounds."

They watched couples stroll by arm in arm in their court dress—the diplomats and courtiers in their beribboned breeches, fitted brocade jackets, and plumed hats; the courtesans in their low-cut gowns, voluminous skirts, and flowing trains. Philippe seemed most fascinated by the men's shoes, with their high-stacked heels and bows. "Do they dress like this every day?"

"*Oui*, fashion is part of the politics here. One's status can be determined by the way one is clad."

A trio of young women walked by, giggling behind their fans, and stopped a few feet away. They chattered and tittered, glancing at Madeleine and Philippe from time to time.

"See what I mean? They are measuring us by our dress, or lack thereof."

Philippe glowered at the women, but Madeleine grabbed his hand. "They mean no harm."

Two courtiers—one tall, blond, and striking; the other, not quite as tall, but muscular and darkly handsome—approached the three women and began to talk. Madeleine stared at the courtiers. Her fan tumbled to the ground. "Pierre!"

The courtier's head whipped around. His dark eyes flashed in recognition, and his charming, wide smile spread across his face. "Madeleine!" He left his group of friends and rushed to her side.

"What are you doing here?" He executed a perfect court bow and kissed her hand. "And, Philippe, what . . . ? What a shock"—he looked back at his friends—"to see you at Versailles once again."

Madeleine curtsied and smiled. "It's a long story."

Pierre lapsed into his court vernacular. "Of course, madame. The absence of your incomparable beauty created a vacant spot when you left so suddenly." He called his friends over. "May I introduce Mademoiselle Lisette Lereau."

A delicately beautiful young woman curtsied, moved close to Pierre's side, and took his arm.

The blond man stepped forward.

"And my oldest and dearest friend in the world, Robert Devereaux. This is Madame Madeleine Clavell."

The other two women moved on.

Monsieur Devereaux bowed low, sweeping his plumed hat in a wide circle and taking Madeleine's hand at the same time, kissing it. "And the young man?"

"My oldest son, Philippe."

Robert and Pierre bowed slightly to him, and Philippe returned the courtesy. Madeleine ducked her head and smiled. Perhaps her son could learn court manners more easily than she thought.

"So, my friend, how do you know these good people?" Robert seemed curious.

Pierre hesitated, but only for a moment. "I met Madame Clavell here at Versailles a few years ago when she came to visit her old friend, the king."

Robert and Lisette were visibly impressed.

"I was here in the early days of Versailles, and we were very close," Madeleine said. "The king has summoned me for another visit—since the death of my husband."

"Our condolences, madame." Robert nodded slightly, as did the other two.

Pierre glanced at the Swiss Guard hovering nearby. "Very nice to see you, Madame Clavell. Perhaps we shall run into each other again during your visit." They began to walk away.

"Oh, you dropped your fan, madame." Pierre broke away from his friends and retrieved the item for Madeleine.

She took the fan from him, snapped it open, and whispered to him, "We need to talk. Same apartment."

Pierre tipped his hat and then his heart. "Until we meet again."

A scratching at the door of Madeleine and Philippe's apartment late in the evening sent Elise, already in her nightclothes, scurrying to the door.

Pierre's voice announced, "Pierre Boveé, here to see Madame Clavell as per order of the king."

The servant girl curtsied and let Pierre in. Madeleine looked up from where she sat on a chaise.

"Pierre . . ."

Pierre inclined his head toward the servant.

"Thank you, Elise," Madeleine said. "It's late. I won't require your services anymore tonight. You may retire."

Elise curtsied and went to a small cubicle adjoining Madeleine's bedroom. Madeleine followed her and closed the door.

"I'm so glad you came, Pierre. I prayed we could find you."

"My patron has left Versailles for a diplomat position in Spain. I am between assignments. Is Philippe asleep?"

"*Oui.*"

Pierre stepped closer and lowered his voice. "I had to persuade the guard that I am here on official business."

"Please, sit down."

Madeleine allowed Pierre to take both her hands in his, and they sat on the chaise.

"Tell me what happened. How did he find you?"

"Spies in Switzerland. Someone informed a band of musketeers of our departure for Holland, and they overtook us before we even reached the Swiss border. I suspect the informant to be Pastor Veron."

Pierre shook his head. "I never did trust that man."

"And I think Louis believes Philippe to be his son."

Pierre searched Madeleine's eyes. "Is that possible?"

"If you are asking if Louis and I were lovers, then, yes, it would be possible. If you are asking if Philippe *is* Louis' son, then no. François and I married shortly after—"

Pierre held up his hand. "You owe me no explanation. If you say Philippe is not Louis' son, that is good enough for me."

"When one looks at him, it's obvious. He has François' nose and hair, and he's going to be so tall."

"And he has your smile." Pierre caressed the back of Madeleine's cheek with his fingers and then held his arms open. "The smile I want to see. Come here, chérie. My arms are yearning to embrace you."

Madeleine allowed Pierre to encircle her in his arms—this man whom she had fallen in love with during the two years her husband was missing; this man who stepped back because of her love for François and her commitment to their marriage. Her shoulders began to heave, and she grieved in his arms the loss of the years, for her children, over the death of her husband, over being kidnapped and held against her will. Finally she pulled back from his embrace, shaking her head and sniffling. "Ah, Pierre, what am I going to do?"

"We will have to go along with the king for now. Let's see if he is going to be reasonable about Philippe. Perhaps when he sees the boy, he will realize he has made a mistake."

"And then let us leave? I don't think Louis is that magnanimous."

"Perhaps not. We will just have to wait and see, won't we?"

"Yes, I suppose so."

"What of the others?"

"As far as I know, the musketeers let them return to the Du Puys.' I shall never forget Vangie's screams as we drove off. She tried to catch up with the carriage. Jean ran after her. It was awful." Madeleine's voice broke. "I can't stand this, being torn from her once again, and separated from Jean and Charles. It's too much." She covered her mouth with her handkerchief and caught her breath.

Pierre frowned and shook his head.

"I begged the officer in charge to let Vangie come with us, but he refused. I thought he might be persuaded to have mercy on us, but . . ."

"Do you know his name?"

"Nicolas Maisson."

"Yes, I know him. He has the king's ear."

"You must be careful as well, Pierre. If Jacob Veron told them about us, I'm certain he has disclosed your participation. You may not be safe here any longer. Your aligning yourself with our family has put you in danger."

"No need for worry. I hadn't intended to stay much longer. My father and I have reconciled."

Madeleine smiled. "That's wonderful news. And did you tell your father about your faith? Are you still trusting God?"

"More than ever. I haven't told my father, but he senses a change in me. All my friends do. I did tell Lisette about my encounter with God. Upon returning to Versailles, I see things much more clearly than before—the deceit, the unhappiness, the shallowness. It screams at me on every turn. I cannot stay." Pierre looked into Madeleine's eyes. "But now that you are here, I cannot leave. I told you once that I would never speak of love to you again as long as François was alive. But now that he is gone . . . I . . . it may be too soon, but I . . . Madeleine, I am so in love with you. My heart aches to be with you." He kissed her hand again and again. "I will wait as long as you need me to. Just tell me there is a chance for us. I'll go wherever, do whatever it takes for us to be together."

Madeleine's eyes brimmed. She cupped his face in her hands. "Oh, Pierre, I . . . I do . . ."

Philippe's door creaked open, and the boy came into the room. "Pierre! I thought I heard voices."

Pierre walked to the boy and embraced him. "I came under the guise of orders from the king to see what had happened."

Philippe looked at Madeleine and then Pierre. His face registered no surprise at finding them together. "It seems the king believes me to be his son, and wants to see for himself." He walked to the fireplace and stoked the fire. "It is rather embarrassing . . . to be accused of being a bastard son of the king."

"Philippe!"

"I'm sorry, but that's the truth, isn't it?" He blinked his eyes.

Nobody spoke for a moment, then Madeleine stood. "I told you that you are not Louis' son. Do you doubt me now? I would tell you if you were his child."

"I don't know what to think."

"François Clavell was your father. I did not deny that I was involved with the king prior to marrying your father. I have been truthful with you. Why are you doubting me now?"

Philippe shuffled his feet. "I don't know."

"I'll tell you why. It's Versailles. It will woo you and intoxicate you. It will capture you. Beware of its charms."

"Have *you* fallen captive to its charms once again, Maman?"

The courtier stepped forward. "There is much to tell you, Philippe, but your mother has been nothing but honorable and truthful."

"We must be united before the king summons us, Son. Divided, he will confuse us." She pulled Philippe by the shoulders, forcing him to face her. "I swear to you that you are my son from my union with François Clavell, not from my dalliance with King Louis. I swear to you."

Philippe lowered his head onto his mother's shoulder and returned her embrace. "I-I'm sorry. I just started thinking and . . . and . . . I-I'm sorry I doubted you."

Madeleine handed him a handkerchief. "Clavell men use handkerchiefs."

Philippe smiled and blew his nose. "I could tell there were feelings between you and Pierre."

"But we never . . . ," Madeleine protested. "I didn't allow . . ."

"Perhaps not, but the affection between the two of you was evident to anyone who cared to be observant."

"I am grieved, Son, that you were concerned. Our feelings for each other developed during the time your father was in the galleys, and we didn't know whether he was dead or alive."

Pierre put his hand on the young man's shoulder. "I did tell your mother how I felt at the Cathedrale before I went to look for your father. But she told me she loved her husband and was committed to him. I vowed never to speak of love again to her as long as your father was alive, and I kept my word."

Philippe held up his hand. "You owe me no explanation. I am glad you are here with us."

"Thank you. As am I." He embraced Philippe again. Then he began to pace between the mother, the son, and the door. "We need to form a strategy, but I don't know that we can do anything until the king sends for you. You are being constantly guarded."

"And measured."

"What?"

Madeleine chuckled. "Louis sent his personal tailors today to measure us for suitable court clothes."

"That hat *was* pretty bad, Philippe."

Nervous laughter eased the taut emotions strung out in the elegant room that served as a prison cell—imprisoned as certain as if they were in the Bastille.

"I must go. I will keep an eye on you from a distance. If you need to talk to me, come to the Latone Parterre where you were today after Mass. We walk by there nearly every day after chapel."

"Tell me about the young woman, Pierre. She is beautiful."

"She is, but your beauty far surpasses hers."

"Stop it, Pierre. Who is she?"

"A former . . ." Pierre looked at Philippe. "We are an accepted couple at court, but no formal ties. She is not happy with the change in me. I'm surprised she continues to be interested."

"You underestimate yourself. Do I have reason to be jealous?"

Pierre reached for his hat and put it on. "None whatsoever." He turned to Philippe. "Your mother stole my heart the first time I saw her." He took the boy by the shoulder. "Would you approve of that? Could you accept . . . ?"

Philippe ducked his head. "It is not for me to say."

"But it is. You are the oldest son."

"I guess so. Yet it is strange to see my mother with another man."

"I understand."

Madeleine moved to the desk and picked up a piece of paper and a quill pen. "Pierre, can you find some way to get a letter to the family for me?"

"A courier goes to Geneva periodically. Write a letter and give it to me tomorrow after Mass, and I'll see that it is sent."

"Very well."

Pierre bowed, turned to Madeleine, and kissed her hand. "Until tomorrow." He lingered but a moment, holding her hand. Then he touched his heart and went out the door into the labyrinth of Versailles.

SIXTEEN

Nicolas Maisson stood in the crowd of courtiers, gentlemen servitors, and government officials surrounding the king's dressing room. Even having served the Sun King for most of his life, he still quaked at the prospect of a face-to-face audience.

The king entered and made his way through his loyal subjects, acknowledging those on both sides of his path. A servitor ushered those desiring an audience into the presence of the king.

King Louis stopped at a table and picked up some papers, shuffled through them, then turned and faced his subjects. One by one the petitioners stepped forward, and one by one their requests were granted or denied. Finally it was Nicolas' turn.

"Yes? Have you something additional to report, other than the arrival of Madame Clavell?"

Nicolas bowed. "*Oui,* Your Majesty. And I fear it will be an unpleasant message."

"Go ahead."

"I have the grievous duty to report that a traitor has been discovered among your courtiers."

A shadow crossed the king's countenance. His dark eyes bored into Nicolas' squinty ones. "Impossible!"

"*Non,* sire. I am afraid I have reliable testimony of his deeds."

"Name him!"

"Could we speak in private, Your Majesty?"

Louis shooed his fawning ministers and servants away and motioned for the musketeer to follow him to a corner of the room. He turned toward the officer, smoothing his moustache with his thumb and forefinger. "Continue."

"The name I have to give you is one of your favorite courtiers: Pierre Boveé."

"You must be mistaken. Monsieur Boveé has recently returned from a successful mission. He reported back to me just a few weeks ago."

"And did that mission happen to involve the Clavell family?"

"It did."

"Forgive me, Your Majesty." Nicolas bowed to his sovereign again. "You have been deceived."

A roar arose from the king. "Deceived? Who dares to deceive his king?" He stomped to his desk, picked up his walking stick, and began waving it about. "Out! Everybody out!"

The flabbergasted assembly backed out the door, leaving only his minister of finance and chief advisor, Jean Baptiste Colbert. Louis motioned for him to remain. "You stay. I want you to hear this." He gestured to Nicolas. "Officer Maisson, where did you get your information?"

"The information came from an assistant to the Huguenot pastor in Geneva who had given the Clavells refuge at the Cathedrale de St. Pierre. It seems Monsieur Boveé has acted as a liaison between the Clavells and France for these past several months."

"This cannot be. Monsieur Boveé reported to me that François Clavell died in the galleys and that Madame Clavell had fled the country."

"François Clavell is indeed dead, but he didn't die in the galleys. As Monsieur Boveé headed for Brest to find him, a chance meeting occurred with Monsieur Clavell at an inn in Nantes. Your fine courtier actually accompanied him across the border to meet his wife. What happened to persuade Monsieur Boveé to aid the Clavells, I do not know. But he used his privileged position as one of Your Majesty's courtiers to cover his deeds. Clavell succumbed to consumption before Pierre Boveé returned to Versailles."

"Why would he participate in this web of deception? What does he hope to gain?" The monarch paced back and forth, the red heels of his shoes clicking on the wooden floor. "Of course. It's obvious. It is Madeleine Clavell. She has bewitched him. He has fallen in love with her." He stopped his pacing. "I asked him to escort her to the Trianon that night when she appealed to me on behalf of her family. That's when it all started." He turned to the informant. "Arrest Pierre Boveé—tomorrow morning. You shall be rewarded for your allegiance to the crown. You are dismissed."

"Yes, Your Majesty. Thank you, Your Majesty." The officer bowed and backed out of the room.

THE KING SAT AT HIS DESK, FLICKING HIS THUMBNAIL against the edge of the table. He seethed beneath his cool exterior. Pierre Boveé, a traitor? *Incroyable!* Louis knew he should feel munificent toward his musketeer officer and be furious with his courtier. But his emotions waged a battle inside of him. He liked Pierre Boveé. He had believed the courtier to be a loyal servant of the crown. And he did not like sniveling members of his musketeers lowering themselves to expose other members of the court. He got up and moved toward his room.

"I will take dinner privately now," he said to Colbert. "Then I shall go hunting. I need to get some fresh air. It reeks of rottenness in here."

"WHAT . . . WHAT'S GOING ON HERE? UNHAND ME!"

Two musketeers grabbed Pierre as he left his apartment the next morning. Their muscular hands held his arms in a steely grasp and pulled the courtier's sword from its sheath.

Nicolas Maisson stepped out of the shadows and poked Pierre's chest with his sword. "I wouldn't resist, if I were you. These are orders from the king." The other two musketeers tied his hands behind his back.

"Summoned . . . or arrested?"

"Both."

The staircase held not one courtier or courtesan at this early hour. "What is this about?"

Nicolas growled. "Don't act so innocent. The king doesn't take kindly to traitors."

The musketeers pushed and shoved the courtier down the stairs and into a room.

"Where are you taking me?"

"You'll see soon enough." Nicolas proceeded to the far end of the room, where a gilded bookcase reached to the ceiling. He parted the books on one of the shelves, reached behind them, and pushed a button. The bookcase swung open. "Come, my friend. This will be a safer, less public way to go."

"I'm not your friend."

"No, I guess you are not. Traitors are not friends of the king or of his loyal subjects."

A dank odor rushed from the opening. Nicolas lit a torch and entered the yawning passageway. The second musketeer pushed Pierre into a narrow tunnel, which eventually opened onto steep steps leading to another underground passageway. The floor appeared to be sand. Large slabs of stone lined the walls. Pierre glanced behind him and watched the third musketeer struggle to light another torch.

Pierre knew where they were taking him. When he and Robert were stableboys, they had explored the mysterious, winding, off-limits tunnels as they were being built. But they had come in through the outside.

In the beginning they used the entrance of the passage as a place to escape and share growing-up secrets. Then they began to venture farther and farther, exploring passages that led to rooms in the palace. Sometimes they even cracked the secret doorways back into the chateau ajar and listened to conversations between statesmen or clandestine lovers who thought they were beyond eavesdroppers. Then one day they discovered the rooms with the bars, and a coffin with a decomposed body in it.

"Cells!" Robert had exclaimed. Pierre could still hear his friend's changing voice crack. "The king's prison! And people die here!"

"N-no, it's too small for a prison. Maybe holding cells before they take prisoners to Paris to the Bastille."

The boys had stared at the enclosures, frozen in their footsteps.

A rat had skittered across Robert's foot, and he screamed, "Let's get out of here!" They scrambled back the way they had come and never went back.

The trio of musketeers and Pierre rounded the stone corner and approached the cells—the very cells that Pierre and Robert had stumbled upon years ago. Nothing much about them had changed. Two small cells on one side of the tunnel faced a larger one on the opposite side. They were all empty. The same stone slabs that lined the walls paved the floor in the cell area. A slight stirring of a breeze freshened the air. They must be close to the back entrance. Pierre could see light coming in from the left around a bend.

"Which accommodations would you like—the larger cell or a smaller one?" Nicolas mocked his prisoner.

"I don't seem to be making the decisions here."

"Throw him in the smallest one. Tomorrow we take him to the Bastille."

"Without an audience before the king?"

"He is convinced of your treachery. You will never see the face of your king again."

"I demand to see the king!"

"You are in no position to demand anything. I assure you that I am carrying out direct orders from the king himself."

The musketeer clenching Pierre's arm let go and removed the binding from his wrists while Nicolas opened the cell door. The rusty hinges groaned, and the heavy door swung open. Pierre felt a boot on his backside shove him into the cell. He fell face-first onto a damp, slimy surface. His cape twisted around him, and his hat tumbled into the corner.

"You lost something, Monsieur Boveé. However, you won't be needing your fine hat in the Bastille."

Pierre scrambled to his feet and picked up his hat, now covered in slime.

Nicolas grabbed one of the bars with his gloved hand and leaned in. "We will bring you some water and stew. It will do until tomorrow." He lit a candle and handed it to Pierre.

The grating of a gate announced the arrival of the third soldier, who had disappeared and now returned with a bowl and a crude metal pitcher of water. He set the meager fare on a rough wooden bench in the corner of the cell.

Nicolas locked the cell as the musketeer exited. "We shall take our leave of you now. *Au revoir.*"

"Wait! Would you take my father a message—let him know what has happened?"

"Commander Boveé? Do you think me a fool? Of all people, we would not tell him. He would have you broken out of here in no time. I have orders to tell no one where you are."

"What about . . . ?" Pierre hesitated. "Surely you would not deny informing my . . . my lover of what has occurred." *God forgive me. She was my lover at one time.*

"Ah, yes. Mademoiselle Lereau. A beautiful young lady." Nicolas smiled. "Why should I concern myself with informing her of your whereabouts?"

"Ahhh, Captain Maisson, you know how women are. She will fret herself sick not knowing where I am. At least let her know I have not deserted her willingly."

"I shall consider it, but not right away. You will be safely tucked away in the Bastille before I speak with her."

"*Merci.* I would be grateful."

Nicolas picked up a torch and set it in a holder anchored in the stone area between the cells. "This will burn for a few hours. Then it will go out, and you won't be able to see the other side of the cell until daylight, at which time a meager bit of light will make its way around the bend in the cave." Nicolas turned to go. "By the way, I would recommend that you eat your stew promptly. You will have visitors during the night. They will help themselves to your dinner." His laughter echoed down the corridor as he left.

Pierre could hear their footsteps on the stone pavement as the gloom closed in behind them, then the crunching of the sand as they left the holding area. After a few moments, he heard muffled voices and the closing of a door. Then the quiet—deafening quiet.

The candle flickered on the edge of the bench, along with the pitcher and bowl of potage. No spoon. No cup. No chair. No bed. No chamber pot. He began to pace back and forth in front of the cell door. One-two-three-four. Four steps across. One-two-three-four-five-six. Six steps front to back.

He still had his hat in his hand. He touched the wall and drew his hand back in disgust. Slimy and wet like the floor. No place to hang or put his hat. He plopped it back on his head.

A rat scampered along the edge of the cell, then stopped and turned his beady eyes toward Pierre.

"Oh no, you don't. I'm not sharing my breakfast with you." The courtier picked up the bowl and began to drink the watery stew. "Ugh, that's disgusting! You may get this after all." He peered into the bowl of a few chunks of turnips floating around in dark water. "But not yet . . ."

He thought about what was going on at the chateau—Mass, then their usual walk in the gardens. Madeleine would be at the Latona Fountain, waiting to give him her letter for the Switzerland courier. He stood. The bowl of watery concoction rocked on the bench and fell over, spilling the contents on the floor. The rat poked its head out of a crack in the corner.

Pierre sighed. "I guess you will get it now after all."

He looked toward the ceiling. *Oh, God, I'm in a mess. What am I to do? I've been discovered, and . . . and I'm frightened. I'll admit it. Nobody knows where I am.* He went to the door of the cell and gripped the bars, rattling them back and forth. "Help! Somebody help me! Help!"

His voice bounced off the walls and echoed through the silent passageway. The walls in his cell seemed to mock him with the silent screams of those incarcerated before him. Panic darted in and out of his brain like a dagger, slicing and then retreating, then back again.

How many have died in here? What if they just leave me here to waste away? How do I pray? God, help me! Rescue me, protect me? What if they plan to torture me? What did François do? Or what would Joost do? Or Pastor Du Puy? Or Madeleine?

The thought of Madeleine stopped the progression of panic.

I must get word to her somehow. That's what I need to pray. Father, warn her that the king is aware of our collusion. Make her aware that something is wrong. Madeleine is in danger, God. Warn her!

SEVENTEEN

Madeleine and Philippe walked along the crescent of the Latona Parterre leading to the Royal Avenue. She was furious with the king. He had not answered her request for an audience. He was ignoring her intentionally and making her wait. In addition, she had not seen Pierre at Mass. Perhaps he would be with his friends around the fountain. The Swiss Guard lurked nearby.

Madeleine opened her parasol to shield her face from the climbing sun and looked down the Royal Avenue toward the canal. "Let's walk to the Apollo Fountain. Perhaps we will see Pierre along the way."

The sunlight glinted and danced on the surface of the Grand Canal. Memories of the night Pierre escorted her on the gondola to meet Louis in the Porcelain Trianon wove in and out of her thinking—the same night that ended in her fleeing Versailles in the midnight hours in a desperate attempt to beat the dragoons to their estate. She had been on the run ever since.

A shroud of weariness wound around her. Her emotions spun from calm to terror. "I need to stop for a moment." She clutched Philippe's arm.

"Maman? What's wrong? Are you ill?"

"No, I . . . I . . . let me rest a minute."

Philippe steered her to one of the statues and looked around for a place for his mother to sit. "There are no benches."

Madeleine chuckled. "*Non*, no benches. Louis wants to keep everyone active." She fanned herself. "I think the trauma of the past few weeks—actually the past three years—is catching up with me. I miss your father terribly, and I cannot stop thinking of the others, especially little Vangie."

She looked around at the trees, urns, fountains and statues, and the court personnel walking throughout the gardens. "Being back at Versailles has given me a fresh understanding of Louis' desperation to maintain control. Look at the ordered pruning of the trees, the dictated costuming of his court, even the funneling of the water in the fountains. What he cannot control, he destroys." Madeleine leaned against the base of the statue. "Life at Versailles is a shallow, pretentious façade that everyone plays along with, pretending that all is well."

"Let's walk back to the Latona Fountain, Maman. There is a place to rest there." Philippe cradled her elbow, and they retraced their steps.

As they approached the fountain, Madeleine saw Pierre's friend Robert chatting with a group of courtiers. "There's the friend Pierre introduced us to. Maybe he knows where Pierre is."

Robert headed toward Madeleine and Philippe before they could call to him and executed a flawless court bow. "Madame Clavell, so nice to encounter your exquisite beauty today." He kissed her hand, and then turned to Philippe and nodded. "Monsieur Clavell."

Philippe nodded in return. "Monsieur Devereaux."

Madeleine curtsied and closed her parasol. "I was looking for Pierre. Have you seen him this morning?"

"*Non*, I was about to ask you the same question. Nobody seems to know where he is." Robert looked around. "There's Lisette. Perhaps she has seen him."

The courtier approached the young woman. She turned and looked at Madeleine with a glance that only two women in love with the same man would recognize. Then she shook her head. Robert came back to Madeleine and Philippe.

"Nobody knows where he is, which is very strange. Unless he is out on assignment, we always eat breakfast together and then go to Mass. When he didn't show this morning, I just assumed he had been sent out on another assignment or was with . . ." He hesitated. ". . . was with you or Lisette."

"Where might he be?" Madeleine struggled to keep her voice under control. She reached into her bag and pulled out the letter. "He was going to get this to the Swiss courier for me."

Robert reached toward the letter. "I can do that for you."

Madeleine hesitated. She looked at the address: *Pastor Etienne LeSeuer, Cathedrale de St. Pierre, Geneva, Switzerland*. And in bold letters scrawled across the bottom, *Personal*. "Well, I suppose that would be fine." She handed the message to Robert. "Tell the courier that he is to hand this directly to Pastor LeSeuer. Absolutely no one else."

"Yes, of course."

"You don't think anything has happened to Pierre, do you?"

"Oh, *non*. Not Pierre. Let me check down at the stables to see if his horse is there. I'm sure there is a logical explanation for his absence. Where can I find you?"

Madeleine checked her rising alarm. "We will remain in the gardens for a bit. If it gets close to dinnertime, we will go to the cuisine de commune. Tell Pierre to meet us there."

"Any message for him?"

Madeleine laughed, attempting to make light of the situation. "Oh no, Robert. I just had that letter for him to take care of, and I wanted to ... to, uh ... to see if he could help me find a horse for Philippe. My son is missing riding."

"Pierre is the one who can help you; that is a fact. If not he, his father would know of horses available. I will get back to you later." He patted the letter. "Never fear. I'll take good care of this."

"It's simply a letter to my family, and I wanted to make sure they receive it." Madeleine extended her hand to the charming courtier. "*Merci*, Robert. You and Pierre are very close, *non?*"

"Like brothers. And we fight like brothers at times as well." He laughed, then his countenance turned serious. "We had only each other growing up. Commander Boveé was stationed here at Versailles, but he was never around. Pierre hardly knew him. And I was an orphan, no brothers or sisters. I would give my life for him. And he for me." He smiled. "*Au revoir*. I will let you know something within the hour."

"Thank you. I'm sure he is fine. We shall await word from you."

PIERRE HEARD A DOOR SLIDING OPEN FROM DEEP WITHIN the tunnel, then footsteps and the sound of men's voices. He stood and peered out from between the bars. The glimmer of a torch came into view. He recognized the king's personal guards. *The king!* He put on his hat, tried to wipe the grime from his jacket, and stepped back from the cell door.

The king, dressed in his hunting attire, strode into the holding area and stopped in front of Pierre's cell. He folded his arms and stared at Pierre as the courtier bowed. The king unfolded his arms and walked closer to the cell. "Come here, Pierre. Let me look into your face."

Pierre stepped to the bars. Even in this gloomy setting, the magnificent Sun King bore himself with a commanding presence—his posture erect and chiseled determination in his face.

Louis searched the courtier's eyes. Then he stepped back. "Gentlemen, this—this is what treason looks like."

The king's guards remained silent.

"On the surface, it appears to be the face of a loyal subject, but in reality it is the face of a conspirator against your king."

Pierre said nothing.

"Well? Do you have nothing to say for yourself?"

"*Non*, Your Majesty."

"*Non?* You haven't even asked why you are being imprisoned. But you know, don't you? You already know."

Pierre hung his head. "Your Majesty, I never intended . . ."

"You 'never intended'? You *never intended?*" The monarch's ire filled the tunnel. "You orchestrate the escape of the very man I send you after, and you *never intended?*" He turned his back and walked to the other side of the holding area, shaking visibly. Then he walked to Pierre's cell door again. His voice rumbled in low tones as he whispered to his courtier, "I trusted you. You've been a loyal servant for years. You grew up at Versailles. Is this the thanks I get for the wonderful life I gave to you?" He paused. "It's Madeleine, is it not? You have fallen in love with her, haven't you?"

Pierre's silence was answer enough.

"Never mind. It will amount to nothing. My plans for her will exclude any other man in her life from now on. So much for your scheme to have her for yourself."

At this Pierre finally spoke. "*Non,* Your Majesty. I never thought I would see her again. My affection was never acted upon. She was committed to her marriage and family, and I had returned to Versailles. God would not let me—"

"God? Since when has God dictated your behavior?" The king glowered at Pierre. "Have you become a Huguenot? Has Madeleine's influence over you lured you into the web of deceit so far that you have *converted?*" His voice rose to a shout.

Pierre fell to his knees. "Oh no, sire. I am still Catholic. I-I have simply become more aware of God and his love for all of us."

"Be very glad of that. If you had become a Huguenot, you would have paid with your life." The king turned to his guards. "Take him immediately to Paris. I never want to see his traitor's face again."

Without another word the king turned and with two of his guards returned through the tunnel. The other two guards unlocked the cell and took Pierre out of the darkness in the opposite direction toward the light.

MADELEINE SENSED THAT PIERRE WAS IN DANGER. Something must have happened to him. However, she could do nothing but wait. She and Philippe went to the communal dining hall for dinner, but Pierre was not there.

Back in their apartment, Philippe paced from his bedroom to the living room of the suite, then back again, tossing his cap in the air and catching it. He sat down and twirled the cap on one finger. "We cannot simply lock ourselves in our apartment and sit. What is there to do?"

Madeleine looked at her handsome young son. He needed companionship. He needed activity. "Would you like to see the stables? Perhaps we could ride this afternoon."

He jumped up, and his eyes brightened. "*Oui!* I would like that very much."

"Very well. Elise!"

The young domestic hurried from Madeleine's bedroom.

"Send for a messenger to summon Monsieur Devereaux. We need someone to escort us to the stables."

MADELEINE SWUNG UP ON THE ROUSSIN RED ROAN AND hooked her knee over the pommel between her legs. She preferred not to ride sidesaddle, but court etiquette required it.

Robert led a bay from the interior of the stable for Philippe. "A wonderful horse. I think you will enjoy riding him."

"Thank you, Robert." Madeleine arranged her riding skirt. "You will continue to try to ascertain Pierre's whereabouts?"

"*Oui.* It is not unusual that Commander Boveé doesn't know where he is." Robert chuckled. "They don't exactly ask permission of one another to leave."

"Is Pierre's horse here? I—"

Madeleine's attention was diverted by the king's hunting party entering the stable grounds. All activity stopped as the king, with the Dauphin at his side, rode through the stable grounds. Louis sat astride his magnificent chestnut Breton, the hunting hounds baying at the excitement of the day's hunt.

He stopped in front of Madeleine and tipped his hat. "Good to see you at Versailles once again, Madame Clavell."

Madeleine bowed her head in acknowledgment. "Thank you, Your Majesty. I see you still love the hunt."

"Always. It stimulates the mind as well as the body."

She checked her horse as the mare started to skitter backward. "I didn't plan to visit here again so soon."

The king smiled at her for what seemed an eternity and stroked his moustache. "You will have to join us one day soon."

"As you wish, sire. Your Majesty, I would respectfully request an audience with you . . . soon. As soon as possible."

The king ignored Madeleine's request and turned his attention to Philippe. He scrutinized him from head to toe. "And this is . . . ?"

"This is my elder son, Philippe Clavell."

Philippe stared at the king. Louis was so much more handsome close up and his presence intimidating. Philippe, not having yet mounted, held the reins of his horse and bowed in front of the king.

"A handsome young man. Do you hunt, Philippe *Clavell?*"

"Yes, Your Majesty."

"I would like you and your mother to join me one afternoon soon."

"Yes, Your Majesty."

"Louis, please . . ."

The king ignored Madeleine. He motioned to his party, and they rode into the surrounding woods. The howling of the hounds echoed through the woods and back to the stables as the chase began.

Philippe mounted his horse and looked at his mother with unspoken questions on his lips.

Madeleine held up her hand. "We will talk later."

"Would you like me to ride with you?" Robert stepped up to Madeleine's horse. "I would be happy to escort such a gorgeous lady."

"No, thank you, Robert. We already have an escort." She nodded toward the guard on his own mount close by. "We will be fine. You find Pierre."

"I will keep you informed." He patted her horse's neck. "We will find him."

Madeleine looked down into Robert's face and saw concern in his eyes. "You are worried, too, aren't you?"

"Just a bit concerned. He will turn up, though. You'll see."

"I asked you if his horse was here in the stable, and you didn't answer me. Is he?"

"He is. He has not been ridden for a couple of days."

"Is that unusual?"

"It is." Robert stepped back. "Go on, now, and enjoy your ride. I'll have information for you when you return. Pierre may even be here to meet you when you get back." He gave Madeleine's horse a gentle swat, and mother and son rode off in the opposite direction from the king's hunting party.

They rode through the woods at a gentle canter, then galloped the horses when they hit a large open space of meadow. It felt good to be riding. They slowed down, and Madeleine pointed out points of interest to her son—places where she and Louis rode as young people; spots that had been forest but now were planted with crops or where buildings had mushroomed. The landscape had changed considerably, but the gazebo where she had once waited for Louis many years ago remained. They dismounted and rested on the benches in the gazebo. The Swiss Guard let the horses graze at a discreet distance.

"We need to walk a tightrope while we are here, Son," Madeleine said. "I will have to play along with the king's games of cat and mouse. It may seem at times that I am not simply playing along, but actually enjoying it." She took his hand. "Please believe me, I will not be enjoying it. You are going to have to trust me to get us out of this by any means I can."

"I get confused, Maman, especially in the presence of the king. He is so . . . so . . ."

"Magnificent?"

"I suppose that is the word."

"Why do you think they call him the Sun King?"

"I am beginning to see what you meant when you said that the charms of Versailles can seduce one."

Madeleine looked in her son's eyes—eyes that were not exactly the color of François', but so like his father's in expression. She sensed the familiar rising of emotion as waves of grief for François began to wash over her.

Philippe placed his arm around her in an awkward hug. "Maman, don't cry. We're going to be fine."

"I-I miss your father more than you can imagine. I miss his quiet strength." She pulled out her handkerchief. "He always knew what to do. And now he-he's g-gone." She tried to catch her breath and shook her head. "I feel so alone."

"I'm here."

She smiled through her tears at her son, who'd had to grow up too soon. "And I am grateful for that."

"I know I'm no substitute for Papa."

"You shouldn't have to be. You are my son. That's all you have to be." She stood and walked to the outside of the gazebo and watched the horses. The Swiss Guard looked away. After a bit, Madeleine walked back into the gazebo. She looked at her son, who sat on the bench and waited for her—his long, gangly legs crossed and stretched out in front of him. "Philippe, tell me that you trust me. No matter what it may look like, you must trust me."

Philippe untangled his legs, stood, and faced his mother. "I do trust you, Maman. No matter what it looks like, I will trust you."

"And you, too, must learn to play the game. Our lives may depend on it."

"I understand. I will do my best."

Madeleine threw her arms around her son in a firm embrace. She dried her eyes, and they mounted up and rode back to Versailles.

The late afternoon sun beamed in the remaining warmth of the day as Madeleine and Philippe rode into the stable area. They dismounted and gave their horses to a stableboy. "Do you know the courtier, Robert Devereaux?"

The stableboy pointed toward one of the huge openings into the stables. Robert was walking out with another courtier. He spotted Madeleine and Philippe and came immediately toward them.

"Have you any news?"

Robert shook his head. "Nothing. Nobody has seen him or heard from him all day. I checked his apartment, and it appears as if he left this morning as usual, but hasn't been back. He didn't go to breakfast or Mass. He was not at dinner. He has not been to the stables. Lisette has not seen him." He sighed. "Now I am worried, Madame Clavell. I am very worried."

EIGHTEEN

Pierre's legs ached from gripping the sides of his mount. His bound wrists gave him little leverage for balance. The two musketeers and their prisoner reached Paris by nightfall and proceeded straight to the Bastille.

Pierre remembered the last time he rode across the drawbridges and entered the ominous gates at the imposing prison. That time he came as a messenger of the king. This time he entered as a prisoner.

Four guards approached them. Captain Maisson handed over the *letter de cache*, along with Pierre's sword, to a head guard, who peered at the courtier through tangled, bushy eyebrows. The musketeer's raspy voice seemed to fit the surroundings—harsh, cutting, cold. "Pierre Boveé—treason against King Louis XIV."

"Empty your pockets." The guard set about his business.

Pierre handed over a few coins, a handkerchief, and a méreau.

The guard picked up the méreau. "Hummpff. Huguenot?"

"*Non*, just a keepsake—from a friend."

"Dangerous keepsake. Is that all?"

Pierre nodded.

"Take off your ring, your cape, and your shoes."

"My shoes?" Pierre removed a gold ring and put it on the table.

The guard glared at the courtier. "Is my speech not clear?" He indicated a chair beside a table. "Sit there."

Pierre took off his shoes and handed them to the guard, who proceeded to cut off the buckles, then handed them back to him. "Read this form and sign."

This day Monsieur Pierre Boveé entered the Bastille, brought by the king's musketeers by order of the king. Monsieur Boveé had on him gold coins, a méreau, a gold ring, and a handkerchief. We have put them in an envelope, sealed with the castle's seal, which package he has signed with his hand. In regards to his sword, it is a normal carved sword carried by a courtier. Having no other effects on him, Monsieur Boveé has signed the said entry.

"When, or perhaps I should say *if* you leave, you will receive a standard exit or liberty form to sign. All your belongings will be returned to you. We shall soon be taking you to your room, whose number, along with the name of the tower you are housed in, will become your name during your stay here. Surprisingly, the food is fairly tasty. King Louis treats his prisoners well. You will have enough firewood to keep warm. You will be allowed an hour of exercise a day. The castle has a library for your convenience." The guard paused in his rehearsed recitation and drew a breath. "Any questions?"

"Are visitors allowed?"

The guard looked through the papers. "I don't see anything here that says you cannot have them."

Pierre didn't know why he asked. Nobody knew where he was—at least for the time being.

"Take him to his cell. South Tower 110. We will bring you something to eat shortly."

One guard grabbed his arm, and the other led the way into the bowels of the castle. When they reached his cell, the guard handed him his cape and shoved him into the dank room. "Supper will be arriving soon." He laughed. "Make yourself at home."

Pierre surveyed his quarters. The cell appeared to be about twelve feet by ten feet, with a table and chair on one wall and a bed and chamber pot on the other. The arched ceiling must have ascended for twenty feet, at the top of which he noticed two small windows. He pulled wood from a stack beside a small fireplace at the end of the room and removed a tinderbox from the mantel. Outcroppings in the stone offered places to stack books or personal items. Pierre chuckled. *King Louis thinks of everything, even for "traitors."* The fire caught and soon crackled a bit of warmth into the cell.

He draped his cape over the chair and put his hat on one of the outcroppings. Then he sat in the chair and drummed his fingers on the table. He could hear noises around him, but could not make out exactly what they were. Was it conversations? He listened. It was. The cells were isolated and distant, but he could hear men talking.

His cell door sprang open, and two servants entered—one with a coarse, white tablecloth and the other with a tray of food. Pierre stood and allowed the servant to drape the table with the cloth and place an earthenware dish, a fork and spoon, and a goblet on the table. Then they sat a platter of sliced beef, a bowl of broth, a salad, bread, and wine before him.

Pierre stared at the jailors in disbelief. "Is this the usual fare for a prisoner?"

"*Oui,* monsieur. But no dessert."

Pierre shook his head. "*Merci.* I am grateful."

The jailors left, and Pierre stared at the food. He no longer felt hungry, but he ate the bread with the broth and drank some wine. He lay down on the bed.

God, what do I do now? How long will the king leave me imprisoned in a tolerable cell until my mind accepts and conforms to being locked up? This will be a creeping, oozing death—more pleasant than many, to be certain—but one that will overtake me inch by inch. I won't even realize it until the tentacles wrap around me and suck the life out, just as certain as torture. It will eventually destroy me. Oh, God, let somebody know where I am. Rescue me!

He fell asleep and slept the slumber of exhaustion, dreaming the fitful dreams of the ill-fated.

MADELEINE COULD NOT GO TO SLEEP. SHE KEPT HEARING Robert's words, *Now I am worried.*

She put on her robe and went into the dark front room. She curled up on the chaise and pulled a shawl around her shoulders. The air was chilly, but she didn't want to wake Philippe banging the wood around to start a fire. She felt like a puppet on a string. She hated having to wait for Louis to pull those strings to tell them what to do each day. Why didn't he summon them for a private audience?

I know I could convince him that Philippe is not his. But will he let us leave, even if I do?

Madeleine tossed and turned on the chaise. Finally she fell into a restless sleep and awoke the next morning to Elise opening the shutters.

"What time is it, Elise?"

"Nearly nine o'clock, madame."

"I-I couldn't sleep last night, so I came out here. Philippe?"

"He's still asleep."

"Very well. Would you see if our breakfast has arrived, please?"

The young servant girl curtsied and went into the anteroom and returned with a large tray. "Your breakfast arrived some time ago. I'll heat it up." She stirred the fire and set a pot of water and an iron kettle of porridge over the flame. Two loaves of bread, fruit, and jam sat on the tray as well.

Madeleine heard scratching on the door. She clutched her robe about her and went to answer it herself. Perhaps it was Robert with news of Pierre. But when she opened the door, the brothers Delobel descended upon her, amidst voluminous gowns, hats, shoes, boots, and a host of swarming servants.

"We are ready for the final fitting for the first of your clothes ordered by the king. Please accommodate us quickly."

The crew set about rearranging chairs and stools and laying out the new garments. Madeleine threw up her hands and went to wake Philippe.

She had to admit that, except for one, she loved each garment the king's tailors had made for her, especially the red gown. The pearl-encrusted bodice clung to her form with expert crafting. The pearls cascaded around the neckline and down the front of the dress to the waistline, where bows pulled back the red velvet overskirt to reveal an underpinning of rich brocade fabric in ivory. White ermine, the choice of royalty, trimmed the edges of the hem. Layers of ivory lace peeked out from under the ermine-trimmed sleeves. A red velvet cape trimmed in ermine, a matching ermine muff, and red brocade shoes completed the ensemble.

The tailors brought other garments: an emerald green silk, a royal blue ball gown, an ecru ball gown with exquisite lace trim, and a gold gown trimmed in brown fur with a huge bustle. Madeleine turned up her nose at that one. She didn't like yellow and never wore it.

Finally Monsieur Delobel brought out a half-finished black and red—plaid riding outfit for Madeleine, complete with boots. "The king just commissioned the riding outfits day before yesterday," he said, his exasperation evident. "We've stayed up for two nights working on one for you, madame, plus two for Monsieur Clavell." The royal tailor spread out a brown hunting ensemble and a black one, trimmed in red.

"What's the rush?"

"I wish I could tell you. Evidently the king is most anxious for you to be integrated into the court." He and his brother crisscrossed from Madeleine to Philippe in trying the garments on them, pinning and basting. "And he wants the two of you to join him soon for the hunt." The tailor swiveled a hat back and forth on Philippe's head. "There, perfect!"

The black hat sported red and white feathers, accenting his black breeches and waistcoat with red trim. The young man kept pushing down the huge lace cravate. He looked up with a crooked grin on his face. "What does it look like, Mère?" He pulled at the lace. "This really bothers me."

"You look very handsome. Just like your father." She fussed with the cravate and tried to press it down. "Monsieur Delobel, would you cut some of this lace out, please? It's bothersome to him. And you may take the gold gown back and fit it for somebody else."

"Madame?"

"I don't wear gold or yellow, and the king knows that."

"But he commissioned it."

"Then he is toying with me. I'll not wear it. Take it back."

The tailor's jaw dropped open. "But, madame—"

"I said, take it back."

"*Oui*, madame. As you wish."

Philippe pulled the coat and shirt off. "I never saw my father wear outfits like this."

"You just don't remember. He wore them only when he had to."

The entourage of tailors and seamstresses made their adjustments and left, leaving two of the finished gowns and Philippe's black and red outfit.

The door opened, and Monsieur Delobel rushed in once more. "I almost forgot." He placed on the table an envelope with the king's seal. Then he left, his head bobbing above the gowns he carried.

Madeleine went back to her breakfast tray and covered a piece of bread with jam.

"Aren't you going to open the king's letter?" Philippe spooned out a bowl of porridge and sat down with his mother.

Madeleine eyed the dispatch and poured herself some hot water to make tea. "I think I know what it is."

"What?" Philippe's impatience revealed his curiosity. "Is he summoning us to come see him?"

"No, I recognize this. It is an invitation to a ball." She munched on the bread and picked up the piece of parchment. She stood and walked to the window. This all seemed much too déjà vu, a replay of her stay here with her mother three years ago. They would walk the same halls to the ballroom; dance the same waltzes and minuets; play the court games with the courtiers and then the king. But this time the king had summoned her.

She opened the invitation.

Madame and Monsieur Clavell,

    You are hereby invited to attend the king's ball tonight.

    The Swiss Guard assigned to you will escort you to the ballroom.

    Wear the red gown.

As ever, Louis

How dare he order her what to wear. She would not. It was bad enough that the king had kidnapped her and was holding her prisoner. And, in addition, would not give her an audience. She would not be told what gown to wear to a ball.

NINETEEN

Commander Boveé handed his horse over to a stableboy and walked through the massive stables toward the soldiers' quarters. He noticed Pierre's horse munching on his feed in the stall and paused to pat the Percheron's neck. The stallion didn't appear to have been ridden lately. Pierre must be busy courting the ladies. *Takes after his father.* The officer laughed to himself and proceeded to his billet.

The lights in the chateau flickered on one by one as dusk fingered its way across the courtyard. Paul's rumbling stomach let him know that he needed to eat something. He wanted to clean off the road dust first, then he would either go into town to the tavern or to the communal dining hall.

"Commander Boveé!"

Paul recognized the voice and saw the young courtier coming

163

toward him in the shadows. "Robert, what brings you down here with us mere peasants?" He flipped the voluminous lace up on the sleeves of the courtier's jacket.

Robert straightened his sleeve and frowned. "I have something important to discuss with you."

"Where's your constant companion?"

"That's what I've come about."

A cold shiver shot down Paul Boveé's spine. The officer put on a façade of indifference, perfected by years as a calloused soldier, but his knees turned to jelly and seemed disconnected from his feet. "Where is my son?"

"I cannot find him. Nobody has seen him. His horse has been in the stable for two days. And he has not been to his apartment."

"Lisette?"

"She has not seen him either."

Two men who loved Pierre—one, more than he would care to admit, and the other unashamedly as a brother—continued to walk toward the chateau. They stopped in the soldiers' yard, and Commander Boveé looked around at the vacating personnel making their way to their quarters or to the chateau for the evening. "Any chance he simply went out on an assignment?"

"Without Tonnerre?"

"You are right. He would not go anywhere without that horse." Paul took off his riding gloves and gripped his sword, strumming his fingers on the carved handle. "I will see what I can find out, but you are in a better position to do that. Ask around. What are your duties this evening?"

"I am to be at the king's ball."

"Good. Make inquiries. Report back to me afterward."

"It will be late."

"Very well. Meet me for breakfast in the morning."

"Hopefully Pierre will be with me." Robert bent down and straightened the decorative buckle on his shoe, then he stood and looked Paul directly in the eyes. "I'm concerned, Monsieur Boveé. This is not like Pierre—to vanish without letting someone know."

"Oh, I'm sure he is fine. He will turn up soon." Paul's words conveyed assurance, but his countenance did not. He grabbed the younger man's forearm in an unusual gesture of affection. "We will find him."

Paul watched Robert walk away until the lights of the palace closed in around him. He had not realized how much Robert loved his son. If he had not been such an indifferent father during the boys' growing-up years, he would have thought about the fact that this orphan boy had nobody else.

He turned back toward the soldiers' quarters. Pierre had never found it necessary to let his father know where he was going; their relationship hadn't demanded that kind of accountability. But Robert was a different matter. He always knew where Pierre was, or at least that he had gone out on assignment.

The commander walked through the heavy door leading to the soldiers' dormitory and bumped shoulders with a musketeer. "Good evening, Captain Maisson."

The musketeer tipped his hat and exited.

ROBERT STOOD AT THE ENTRANCE OF THE BALLROOM AS the ladies of the court in their bouffant gowns and the bowing courtiers and officials moved around him. He reveled in the glittering scene of the king's ball. He stepped inside the archway and searched the corner where he and his friends usually congregated, but no Pierre.

The king had arrived and conversed with Colbert and several ladies of the court in front of the dais. The musicians struck up the strains of *La Contredanse*, and most of the crowd moved onto the ballroom floor to participate in the popular dance. Robert watched as the king walked toward a stunning brunette in an emerald green gown and led her onto the dance floor. Robert blinked his eyes and looked again. It was Madame Clavell.

Although the king no longer performed solo, he prided himself in his proficiency of the dance and enjoyed himself at a ball. All his subjects knew that and looked forward to his participation. The couple executed the lively dance expertly—as if they had been dancing together for years. Robert remembered Madame Clavell's comment that they were old friends. It was obvious from the way they danced together. And Robert noticed something else apparent to anyone who was looking: the obvious affection the king showed toward the lady. *Old friend* may have been an understatement.

"YOU ARE RAVISHING TONIGHT, MY DEAR, BUT . . ."

The conversation came in bits and pieces according to the rise and fall of the music, as the couples came together, then parted as per the musical cues.

". . . you did not wear the gown I requested."

"*Non*, Your Majesty, I . . ."

". . . preferred to wear this one tonight."

He smiled at her and took her hand as they danced down the floor.

"... Same old Madeleine. Nobody..."

They turned and came back together.

"... not even the king..."

"... is going to tell you what to do."

Madeleine twirled away from him. She smiled as they dipped and caught hands once again. "I see you still dance as well as ever..."

"... the best partner in the room."

The king nodded and executed a perfect *coupé glissé* and moved toward her.

The music ended. They bowed, and Madeleine opened her fan. She laughed as she caught her breath. "I'm out of practice."

"You were dazzling." The king took her hand. "You belong here. You know that, don't you?"

"I know nothing of the sort. After all, I am not here of my own volition."

"I simply provided a little encouragement."

The musicians began another piece.

"Dance *La Sarabande* with me?"

"Oh, Louis. I haven't danced that since I left court."

"You'll remember. Come." The king extended his hand, and they moved onto the dance floor. The slow music began.

Louis was right. The steps came back to her. Soon the other couples moved to the side and watched the king and Madeleine. She felt herself slipping into the seduction of the music, the king, and the surroundings. They finished, and a hush fell over the court. Then the observers burst into applause.

"See? You were magnificent."

"Thank you, Your Majesty." Madeleine curtsied and waited for Louis to cue her.

"Now, I must pay attention to my other subjects, although I would prefer to be with you . . . alone."

Madeleine looked down and nodded. "Louis, I must speak with you—"

The king cut her off. "I will send for you soon . . . and your son."

PHILIPPE WATCHED HIS MOTHER DANCING WITH LOUIS and was shocked at the way his mother flirted with the king. They dipped and swayed together as a couple, familiar with each other's moves. Their affection for each other was apparent to the boy, and he did not like what he was seeing. First Pierre, now the king.

His jaw drew tight, and he tugged on the heavy brocade jacket. It didn't feel right. Uncomfortable, both in body and in presence, he waited for his mother to rejoin him along the side of the ballroom. The king did not escort her. She made her own way through the crowd, nodding and greeting different members of the court along the way. She smiled at Philippe, but he stared at her. He did not know this woman.

Madeleine lowered her voice as she approached her son and hid her lips behind her fan. "Stop glaring at me and smile. Eyes are watching us." She took him by the arm. "Remember, you are going to have to trust me." She closed her fan and laughed out loud.

Philippe managed a weak smile, then put his hand over hers on his arm. His smile widened. "*Oui*, Mère. I . . . I . . . this is all new to me."

"I know. Come, dance with me."

"Oh no! I can't . . . I don't know how."

Madeleine pulled her son onto the dance floor as the musicians

began *La Menuet.* "This one is easy. We need another couple to complete the circle." She looked around and saw Robert, motioning him
to join them.

Robert acknowledged her invitation and grabbed a reluctant
Lisette. She blushed, her porcelain skin almost matching her pink
gown.

"You will need to be patient with my son. I am afraid we have
neglected his education in the area of dance, but he will learn quickly."

The four took their places facing each other. Philippe looked at
his mother. She laughed. "I don't think I have ever seen sheer terror
on your face before. This dance is mostly walking back and forth. Just
dip up and down as you go. We will help you."

Philippe stumbled through the opening strains of the music and
then began to fall into step. He seemed to have a natural rhythm.
Robert coached him through the switch of partners. Lisette took hold
of his hand and guided him. Her skin felt soft and cool. The young
boy flushed as she flirted with him in the context of the dance. He
had never touched the hand of another woman. He hoped the others
would think he was simply breathless from the exertion of the dance.
In spite of himself, he found he enjoyed learning to execute the steps,
but he was glad when the music ended. His three partners applauded
him as they finished.

"Well done!" Robert clapped him on the back.

Lisette curtsied. "What a pleasure to dance with such a handsome
young man."

Philippe bowed and blushed. "The pleasure was mine, to be sure.
Thank you for your patience and instruction."

Robert whispered to Madeleine, "We need to talk. Let's sit over
here."

The ladies fanned themselves vigorously and sat on a gold fili-greed, padded couch in a small alcove while Robert and Philippe stood in front of them. Philippe did not know exactly what to do, but his mother reached up and held his hand.

"Make small talk for the moment." They chatted and laughed until they made sure no one had ears for their conversation.

Robert turned his back to the main crowd. "I spoke with Commander Boveé earlier this evening. He has not seen nor heard from Pierre either. Madame Clavell, do you have any idea where he might be?"

"*Non*, but I have an idea what might have happened. I think the king has found out about Pierre's . . . involvement . . . with"—Lisette turned her head and looked at Madeleine—"with us, our family. He helped my husband escape from France after Louis had sentenced him to the galleys. If Louis does indeed know that, after he specifi-cally sent him on a mission to make sure François was dead, he would be furious. That would constitute treason."

"How would the king know about that? Who knew, and who would tell the king?" Robert seemed confused.

"Captain Nicolas Maisson, the musketeer officer who kidnapped us and brought us here. He knew." Madeleine tapped her fan on the palm of her hand. "A pastor we thought was a friend betrayed us. I am sure he must have told Captain Maisson about Pierre."

The group fell silent.

Lisette spoke up. "How can we find out for certain? Neither Captain Maisson nor the king will reveal his whereabouts to us. They know of our . . . close associations with Pierre." Her slender fingers fidgeted with the cameo at her throat.

Robert extended his hand toward Lisette and pulled her up

toward him. "I think this beautiful lady is our best bet. Any inquiries she makes will be accepted as those of a lover who feels she has been abandoned. Now let us dance the night away as if we have not a care in the world."

PIERRE OPENED HIS EYES. HE COULD SEE ENOUGH FROM a small ray of light struggling through the window high on the wall behind his bed to remind him where he was. Dankness hovered around his head like a damp cloth. The rope bed creaked underneath his weight. It must be dawn.

He groaned and rubbed his wrists, raw from being tied up yesterday, then stood and groped his way to the fireplace, where he found the tinderbox and lit a candle. No cinders left in the fireplace. He retrieved kindling and firewood from the stock in a copper tub and started a fire.

He lay back down on his bed. What was he to do—languish here until somebody discovered his whereabouts? Even at that, how could anybody get him out, aside from a pardon from the king? And that was not likely. Pierre sat up again, his heart pounding. Maybe Louis had sentenced him to the Bastille until he decided whether or not to execute him. He *was* guilty of treason, after all. Whether he agreed with the king's policies or not, he had betrayed him. Pierre stood and walked to the table.

I will never leave you nor forsake you.

The voice—whether audible or not he could not tell—was the voice he had come to recognize.

When you pass through the waters, I will be with you.

Pierre sat down at the table. *Many are being martyred for their faith*

171

in France. And I am so young in the faith. I don't know what to do. I am unschooled and unworthy to be a testimony for the faith. And what about prison, Father God? Are you here with me in prison?

I will never leave you nor forsake you.

Pierre sat at the table for a long time, thinking and praying. A peace that he could not explain resonated and settled in the core of his soul.

The clanking of keys alerted him that the prison servants were delivering breakfast. He went to the cell door and peered out. The guards and servants were headed his way, and he stepped back to let them enter his cell. The guards stood at the entrance while the servants once again spread a cloth on the table and set before him a bowl of porridge, a round of cheese and bread, and some kind of hot drink.

A slender man, with beady eyes that reminded Pierre of the rats cohabitating with him, set a kettle by the fireplace. "In case you'd like to reheat your potage later on."

The breakfast brigade picked up the leftovers from the night before and left. Pierre lifted the lid on the drink. "Chocolate!" He laughed and shook his head. "If one has to be in prison, I suppose this is the ideal one to inhabit."

He dug into the porridge and drank the chocolate with relish. Then he remembered to thank the Lord for his food and his "good fortune."

The reality of his situation, however, and the awareness that Madeleine and Philippe were in danger, clamped onto his heart like a vise. Unless Madeleine agreed to Louis' plans for her, she and her son would be subject to the wrath of the king as well. There was nothing

Pierre could do. He himself needed rescuing, and he did not know who that rescuer would be.

ROBERT DEVEREAUX LOOKED OVER THE CHAOTIC COM-motion in the dining hall. Soldiers, courtiers, diplomats, patrons, and ladies of the court all mingled, exchanging cordialities and stories of romances and battles lost and conquered. He didn't spot Commander Boveé until the officer stood and motioned for the courtier to join him. He sat next to the officer and proceeded to fill his bowl from the large tureen of stew, but he did not begin to eat.

Commander Boveé searched Robert's face for a clue. "Any word?"

"Not a thing. It's as if the earth opened up and swallowed him. Nobody has seen him or knows where he is."

Paul Boveé worked his jaw back and forth. "This is not like Pierre. Something has happened to him, and that against his will. I'm sure of it." He stood, his sword clanking against the wooden bench. "Whoever has harmed my son will rue the day."

TWENTY

Several days passed and still no word from Pierre. Madeleine and Philippe sat in their apartment, dressed in their new hunting attire, awaiting an escort from the king. Perhaps Louis would grant her an audience today.

Madeleine went to the window and surveyed the gardens. The summer flowers still bloomed and filled the air with their fragrance. But fall was only a month away. The longer they were kept captive at Versailles, the less chance they had of getting back to their family and booking passage to the New World this year. It was probably already too late in the season. She sighed and hooked the heavy burgundy drapery on the brass ornamentation on the window frame.

"Maman?" Philippe sat on the chaise, with a riding whip in his hand. "I . . . I'm looking forward to riding on the hunt today . . . with the king." He looked down and tapped his foot with the whip. Then he looked up at his mother. "Is that wrong? I mean, since we are being held against our will—prisoners—is it wrong to enjoy . . ." His voice trailed off.

Madeleine turned to her son. "Is it wrong?" She sat down beside him. "No, it's not wrong. We will enjoy some of the activities. It is not a matter of what's right and what's wrong. It is a matter of our convictions being compromised, and if we are not careful . . ." She paused. "Louis is clever. He knows the longer we stay, the more at home we will begin to feel. Especially me."

"Why especially you?"

"Because I grew up here. It was my home. I hate to admit that it has been tempting already for me to slip back into old roles. When I was dancing with Louis the other evening, it was like putting on a pair of old shoes—still beautiful, but broken in and comfortable. In spite of everything, I find myself believing that the kind and compassionate Louis I knew as a boy is underneath the politics and sometimes cruel behavior." She stood and put on the red riding jacket. "They should be here soon for us."

"You look really sporting." Philippe stood and grinned at his mother.

"And may I return the compliment?"

Philippe put on a brown hat that matched the hunting outfit the king had tailored for the boy. He tapped his boots again with the riding whip. "I really like these boots. I think I shall keep them when we leave."

Madeleine smiled. "*Absolutement*! A small price for the king to pay for our internment." She hesitated. "What did you do with the knife?"

"It is in my trunk."

Madeleine nodded.

The door opened, and the Swiss Guard entered with another of the king's personal bodyguards. "Madame Clavell? I've come to escort you to the stables."

"Thank you. Philippe? Shall we go?"

The party proceeded through the chateau and out into the courtyard. The escort obtained a *fiacre* to take Madeleine and Philippe to the stables. As Madeleine climbed into the hackney, she sighted Lisette talking to a musketeer. She looked closer. It was Nicolas Maisson.

LISETTE HAD READ AND REREAD THE NOTE DELIVERED TO her earlier that morning.

> *Mademoiselle Lereau,*
>
> *I have word for you from Pierre Boveé. Please meet me in the courtyard this afternoon following dinner. Say nothing to anyone else if you value Monsieur Boveé's life.*
>
> *Captain Nicolas Maisson*

She had hurried to Mass and found Robert before going into the chapel.

"You look dazzling this morning, as usual." Robert kissed her hand.

She smiled and acknowledged his flattery. "*Merci.* You are always so kind, but looks can sometimes mask the forebodings of the heart."

"Forebodings of the heart? What misgivings could possibly be brewing behind that beautiful face?" A slight frown crossed Robert's countenance. He lowered his voice. "You've heard something about Pierre?"

"I cannot say." She reached a trembling hand out to his. "Please hold my hand and don't ask any more questions. I have been warned to say nothing if I value Pierre's life."

They found their places for the Mass.

Lisette watched the king kneel at the altar and take the Eucharist. *What does the king pray about? Does he pray about personal matters or for national issues? Does God place more importance on a king's prayers than those of his subjects?* She was sure that the prayers of the king of France were much more important to God than hers.

Lisette followed along with the rest of the congregation in the kneeling and rituals, but her mind was far from the chapel. She looked at the sea of bowed heads around her and wondered if everybody around her felt as empty inside as she.

Lisette had always possessed a heart for God, even as a child. She smiled as she remembered the exemplary life of goodness and uprightness and devotion her parents had lived and had in turn raised her and her siblings to do. But since being at court, she seemed to be unable to grab hold of that commitment. This morning she could not concentrate on the priest's words. Her appointment with Captain Maisson was uppermost in her mind.

She hurried through the noon meal and then made her way to the courtyard. A blustery wind greeted her as she opened the heavy door. She threw her cape around her shoulders and stepped outside. She walked across the square, and the warmth of the sun encouraged her to loosen the cord around the neck. She opened her parasol against the sun's insistent rays, and a gust of wind whipped around her and tugged the parasol out of her hands.

A musketeer bent down to pick it up. "I think you lost something, Mademoiselle Lereau."

"Captain Maisson. I was just looking for you." She extended her hand.

The captain's eyes squeezed almost shut when he smiled. He bowed and swept his hat around, took her hand, and kissed it. "I wish I could say that I am flattered, but of course I know why you would be seeking a rendezvous with me today." He hung on to the parasol a bit too long before releasing it to her.

Lisette tucked the parasol under her arm and brushed his comment aside. "You have word of Pierre?"

"You might say that." Nicolas offered his arm. "Come, let's walk. It is a beautiful day."

Lisette had no interest in taking a walk with the musketeer, but she had no choice. "It would be my pleasure."

"I'm sure."

Instead of going to the gardens, the pair walked through the courtyard toward the stables. The musketeer rambled on about nothing, and Lisette grew impatient.

"Please, Captain Maisson. I have been sick with worry about Pierre. Will you not tell me what has happened to him?"

"Ah, yes. That *was* the reason for our meeting, wasn't it?" He chuckled. "It seems that your lover got caught up in the emotional saga of a Huguenot family." He paused as if waiting for a response. Lisette gave him none.

"Our king was once in love with a Madeleine Clavell—de Vaudois, in those days—when she was at court in her younger years. Her parents moved her back to their estate in southern France when she was an adolescent, and the king never saw her again, despite his messages to her to return. After dragoons were ordered to seize the Clavell estate two or three years ago, Madame Clavell came to Versailles and appealed to Louis for mercy based on their past relationship. The king was not interested in mercy, but in Madame Clavell herself. Evidently she refused him, and so the king sentenced her husband to the galleys."

Lisette shook her head. "What does all of this have to do with Pierre?"

"When Madame Clavell was here at Versailles, the king assigned Pierre to be her escort. Because of that slight connection, the king sent him on a trek to determine if François Clavell had died in the galleys and where Madeleine had fled."

"I see."

"Pierre simply got caught up in the drama and made some foolish choices."

"Where is he, Captain?"

"Let me say that he is alive. But he will . . . um . . . be detained for quite some time."

"Won't you tell me where he is? Is he well?"

Captain Maisson kissed Lisette's hand again. "I cannot tell you where he is, but I might be persuaded to take you to him—for a price."

Lisette shuddered and withdrew her hand. "You are insufferably bold—and coarse."

Nicolas' countenance clouded. "Forgive me. Monsieur Boveé is as well as can be expected, and he was most anxious that you know he had not stolen away with another woman."

Tears filled her eyes. "Not physically, perhaps, but I fear his heart has been captured by another."

A fiacre clattered by. Lisette turned and saw Madeleine Clavell and her son headed for the stables.

PHILIPPE STEPPED FROM THE HACKNEY AND HELPED HIS mother descend. A stableboy moved forward toward them. "Madame, monsieur? May I assist you?"

"*Oui*, we are to be in the king's hunting party today—Clavell, Madeleine and Philippe Clavell."

"Ah, yes. The king sent word that you would be coming. You may wait here. I'll fetch your horses."

"I'll help you." Philippe stepped toward the young man.

"Oh, no, monsieur. That's my job."

"I would like to help you. I'm bored." Philippe bowed slightly. "And please call me Philippe."

"I'm Gabriel."

Philippe looked to his mother, and she nodded. "Go ahead, son. I'll wait here."

The two young men, who appeared to be about the same age, went into the stable and proceeded down the aisle, passing stall after stall of beautifully bred and groomed horses.

Philippe stopped in front of the gate of a stall containing a large black Percheron. He stared into the darkness. "Tonnerre?"

The horse nickered and moved to the front of the stall, where it nuzzled against Philippe's outstretched palm.

"Good boy. Do you know where Pierre is?" He patted Tonnerre's neck.

Gabriel moved to the gate. "You know this horse and his master?"

"Yes, a good friend. Do you know Pierre Boveé?"

"I have met him. He comes in nearly every day to check on his horse and often goes with the king on the hunt. He has not been around, however, for several days. Most unusual." Gabriel reached out and patted the Percheron as well. "Wonderful horse." He stepped back and looked at Philippe. "Where are you from?"

"Our home was in southern France, around Grenoble." Philippe hesitated. "But we have been living in another country . . . for a while."

"Ach! You are the one Monsieur Boveé told me about! He said I reminded him of a young man who was much like family to him but lived in another country."

"He did? When was that?"

"Oh, that was several weeks ago."

Philippe fell silent as Gabriel guided him farther into the interior of the stable. They stopped in front of a stall, and Gabriel led out a pair of chestnut Bretons. The two boys saddled and bridled them.

"These are some of our best steeds. You must be special guests of the king."

"You could say that. He and my mother were friends when they were young." Philippe looked at Gabriel. Could he perhaps kindle a friendship with this stableboy? He kicked at a rock as they came out into the holding area. "Listen, I don't know how long we are going to be . . . be visiting here at Versailles, but I need a friend—someone to ride with, go fishing. Would you like to . . . would you be interested in doing some things with me? Mère is great, but . . ."

"You want to be friends with me? Monsieur, I'm just a stableboy." Gabriel looked at Philippe's fine garments.

"And I'm just a boy who needs a friend. Don't let the clothes fool you. King Louis had these made for us after we got here. Believe me, I wouldn't be wearing them if I didn't have to. Besides, if Pierre likes you, then I know I will too."

"I have duties here at the stables, but when I'm free, I would be happy to accompany you. If you are certain."

"I'm sure. I shall see you soon." Philippe took both horses, led them to his mother, and left a startled Gabriel gaping at his new friend.

"MAMAN! I MADE A FRIEND. HIS NAME IS GABRIEL, AND he knows Pierre. I saw Tonnerre in his stall, and it's obvious he hasn't been ridden in days. Gabriel said Pierre is usually down here every day, but he hasn't seen him in days, and—"

"Whoa, whoa! You sound like Charles now, running your sentences together. Catch your breath, Son."

Philippe grinned as he handed the reins of Madeleine's horse to her. "And Pierre had told him about me." He took his hat off and brushed his hair out of his eyes. "I'm going to come down here sometimes and help him. Now I have a friend to talk to and do things with."

"That is very well, but don't allow yourself to become too attached. We are not going to be here much longer."

"At least for now I'll have a friend. Besides, how do we know how long it's going to be?"

The king's party entered the stable arena then, and Louis rode directly over to Madeleine and Philippe. "Ah, very good. I see you are ready to go."

The Dauphin rode beside his father and at first paid little attention to the Clavells.

Louis turned to Philippe. "I wish you to ride up front with me, Monsieur Clavell—with me and my son."

The Dauphin whipped his head around and looked at Philippe. He slowly viewed him from the top of his new brown hat, sliding down the brown jacket, hugging his broad shoulders and trim waist-line down to the handsome boots. Then he smiled at Philippe and nodded. The boy's rosy, round face and blond hair stood in bold con-trast to Philippe's slender face, with his olive complexion and dark hair.

Madeleine leaned forward in her saddle. "Your Majesty, did you get my message?"

"I did."

She paused. The horses stamped their feet and pulled on their bits. "I must talk with you—immediately."

"I shall decide when it is time." He motioned for the hunt to begin.

"But, Louis . . ."

"When I decide it's time." He chucked his reins and trotted away from her toward his party.

Madeleine started to rein in behind them when Louis turned. "You might like to ride with the other ladies."

She inhaled sharply. "But I've always ridden—"

"Today, Madeleine, I wish you to ride with the other women." He smiled at her. "I would like to get to know your son—man to man." He whirled his horse around and motioned for his party to follow.

Philippe looked at his mother for confirmation, his eyes full of questions. She smiled to reassure him, but inside she seethed. Her thoughts scampered through her head like squirrels jumping from one tree to another, and she clenched her fists around her saddle horn.

You are a tyrant, Louis. You play with my heart. You cannot take my son! He is my son, not yours!

Play the game, Philippe. You must play the game. Ride hard, my son, and shoot well. Don't be intimidated by the king or his party. Remember who you are.

TWENTY-ONE

Jean leaned against a rough wooden post on the porch of the Du Puys' and gazed at the orange glow over the mountains.

"Staring into the west is not going to bring Madeleine and Philippe back."

Jean jerked his head around at the sound of Henri's deep bass voice.

"I know." He sat down on a chair. "I try to formulate a plan in my mind to rescue them, but nothing seems feasible. We cannot go storming into Versailles and ride away with them. But to just sit here and wait, and with Vangie ill . . ." Jean leaned his elbows on his knees and clasped his hands.

"After Dina and the baby died, I thought all ability to love had left me. Then came the incidents with the dragoons. I killed a man. I

185

committed murder—twice. Each new trauma pierced my heart like a knife, and I seemed to grow more callused with each thrust. I felt I had descended to the depths of humanity. Certainly I cared for our family, but my emotions seemed to be rubbed out." He looked up at Henri.

"But watching Madeleine and Philippe be carried off by the musketeers . . . I don't know . . . it stirred the embers. I'm not a monster, Henri. I'm just a man—a weak man, to be sure—but a man who wants to protect what is left of our family." He scoffed. "Some head of the family."

The old stable master put a gnarly hand on Jean's muscular shoulder. "I've watched you grow from a boy into a man, Jean Clavell, and I tell you that you are a good man—a man to whom heartache has come, that's true. Not only are you a good man; you are a brave man. You had to make hard choices along the way, and you made them. Any man would be proud to call you his son—or his brother." Henri paused and wiped his eyes with his handkerchief. "Surely you know how proud François was of you."

Flashes of all that Jean had seen and endured through the years flitted through his mind—his mother and sisters raped and killed by the king's soldiers; the faces of his dead wife and baby; the pleading eyes of the young dragoon soldier whose throat he slit—a mere boy himself; the Huguenot family he rescued in the forest after ambushing their captors; Vangie running and screaming after her mother and brother as the musketeers rode away with them. A groan forced its way up through Jean's gut and out his throat, and he began to weep. He stumbled from the porch toward the barn, barely able to see where he was going.

He sat on a bale of hay outside the corral until the heaving stopped. The moon had risen, and Jean lifted his face toward the heavens. *Father God, what kind of man have I become? I feel completely helpless just waiting here. What am I to do?*

Several minutes passed in silence. Jean sensed nothing from the Lord. Then a scripture came to him: *Be still and know that I am God.*

Jean waited. Again silence.

Is that what I am to do? Simply be still . . . and acknowledge that you are God? I'm not to try to rescue Madeleine and Philippe? What about Vangie? What's wrong with her? Is she going to get well? Her little body is so frail.

A few more moments passed. Then as Jean started to get up and go into the house, another scripture came to him: *They that wait upon the Lord shall renew their strength. They shall mount up with wings like eagles. They shall run and not be weary. They shall walk and not faint.*

And then another: *No weapon formed against you shall prosper.*

Jean stopped. *Thank you, Lord. I shall wait and rest in you. Renew my strength. I am weary. Prepare me for what lies ahead and . . .*

Whatever your hand finds to do, do it heartily as unto the Lord.

Am I making all this up? All these Scriptures that are coming to me, are they instructions from you, Lord, or am I playing games here?

Be still and know that I am God.

Slow, resounding, silent moments passed. Jean wiped his face with his handkerchief and trudged back to the house. *Very well. I shall work and work hard and wait for further instructions.*

Henri sat in the rocking chair on the porch, slowly swaying back and forth. Smoke from a rough pipe hovered over his head like a ghostly halo. "Did you and the Lord work things out, Son?"

"How did you know . . . ?"

Henri chuckled. "The Father speaks to me as well."

"UNCLE JEAN, WHEN ARE MAMAN AND PHILIPPE COMING back? Are we still going to the New World? What if they never come back?" Charles paused in his shoveling out the stall in the Du Puys' barn. His rust-colored eyes, touched with flecks of amber, welled up with tears. He wiped them away on his sleeve. "Vangie cries all the time and is sick. I miss them."

"I do too." Jean put his arm around Charles' shoulders and gave him a squeeze. "And I don't know the answers to your questions."

"Do you think they are safe and well?"

Jean picked up a harness off a bale of hay. What should he tell the boy? He had no idea whether they were safe and well. However, he didn't want to worry Charles unduly. "I don't think King Louis means for them to be harmed. He just wants . . ."

"What? What does he want with Maman and Philippe?" The boy waited. His eyes bored into his uncle's.

Jean sighed. "It's hard to explain. You know your mother and the king were friends a long time ago when she and your grandparents were at court."

Charles nodded.

"Well, the king wants her back at court."

"But why does he want Philippe there too? I don't understand. And why don't they just leave?"

Jean shook his head. "It's complicated, Charles, but when you're older, you'll understand a little better." He started out of the barn with the harness. "Better get your chores done." Jean heard a horse approaching and looked toward the house. "Looks like we have company."

"*Bonjour*, Monsieur Clavell!" Pastor LeSeuer emerged from the small buggy, waving a piece of paper. "I have news from Madeleine!"

"Charles! A letter from your mother. Come!"

Charles dropped his shovel and ran headlong toward the pastor, beating Jean. He snatched the letter from the pastor's outstretched hand and gave it to his uncle, and Jean tore open the seal.

Dearest Ones,

I trust this finds you all well. Although our departure was sudden and unplanned, the trip to Versailles was pleasant enough. The musketeers were kind to us and treated us with respect. Philippe and I attempted to escape one night on the way, but to no avail. The captain caught us in the act.

Jean laughed. "That's our Madeleine."

I hope we will not be detained here long. This is a huge misunderstanding, and I'm sure once Louis realizes that, he will release us.

We have seen Pierre. He seems well, but I fear for his safety.

Please take care of each other. We love you all dearly and miss you terribly. I am certain we will be back soon.

Madeleine & Philippe

Jean folded the letter. "Let's go tell the others. Perhaps it will make Vangie feel better."

Charles ran ahead and burst through the doorway. "We've a letter from Maman!" He continued up the stairs to Vangie's room.

Claudine sat in a rocking chair next to the child's bed, her embroidery in her lap. "Shhh, she's asleep. What are you so excited about?"

"Pastor LeSeuer brought a letter from Maman. They are fine. She says the king might let them come back soon."

Vangie stirred and opened her eyes. Her milky-white skin appeared almost transparent against her dark hair. Dark circles surrounded her eyes that sunk down into her face. "Maman? A letter from Maman?" She sat up and pushed the covers back. "Where?"

Claudine stood. "Not so quickly, child. Here, let me help you."

"Hey, little one. Are you feeling better?" Jean tweaked her toes, and she giggled.

"When is Maman coming home?"

"I don't know, *mon chérie*. Come, sit on my lap while I read you the letter. Perhaps it won't be too long now. What you need to do is get better, so that when she does come home, we can take our trip." Jean read the letter again, then handed Vangie to Claudine. "We'll send a letter back to your maman." He kissed the little girl on the forehead. Her skin felt clammy.

"Tell Maman that I love her and to hurry home."

"I will. You get some rest. Come, Charles. Let's go back downstairs." Jean hesitated in the doorway.

Claudine looked at Jean as she tucked the child back in bed and shook her head. He closed the door and put his arm around Charles' shoulders as they descended the stairs into the kitchen, where the Du Puys and Pastor LeSeuer stood around the table.

"Pastor LeSeuer, can you get a letter back to Madeleine?"

"*Oui*, I told the courier to wait until I returned."

Madame Du Puy found paper and a quill, and Jean sat down at the table to write.

Madeleine and Philippe,

We miss you two as well. We pray for your safekeeping and that you will return to us soon. The agony of watching the musketeers kidnap you and take you away tortures our thoughts continually. We are pleased to hear that the trip did not proffer you undue harm.

Charles works hard with me and asks questions all day long. You know how inquisitive a mind he possesses. We miss Philippe and his strong back.

Jean looked up. "Should I tell her about Vangie? I don't want to worry her."

Gérard Du Puy and Pastor LeSeuer looked at each other.

Gérard spoke up. "I think speaking the truth is always the best policy, but choose your words carefully."

Jean resumed his writing.

We pray for your swift return. Vangie has not been feeling well, but we pray she is on the mend.

Jean looked up. "Read this. Is that sufficient? Too much?"

The two pastors looked over what Jean had written and nodded their approval. "Perfect."

Take care of each other and come back to us soon. We love you both very much.

Jean, Charles, and all

Jean folded and sealed the letter and handed it to Pastor LeSeuer. He clasped the pastor's shoulder. "Thank you."

"I cannot think of anything more important that I had to do today."

"No, I mean for everything, Pastor LeSeuer—not simply delivering a letter. You have been a true godsend to our family—a shelter in a storm when we first arrived in Geneva from France, then directing us to the Du Puys. Thank you."

"You'll have something to eat before returning." It was a statement, not a question from Madame Du Puy. "Sit down. Sit down."

Pastor LeSeuer seated his portly physique at the end of the trestle table. "Thank you, Madame Du Puy. My wife has only one rival, and that would be you—as far as setting a fine table is concerned, that is."

Madame Du Puy laughed and blushed as she gathered leftovers from breakfast and hurried the noon meal already cooking. The fragrance of bread baking and bubbling stew soon filled the house.

Jean headed back to the barn. A yellow barnyard dog loped up to him and licked his hand. The dog's tail wagged his whole body. Life comes and goes, and a pet always greets his master with joy. A spark of hope flickered in Jean's spirit. A subtle thread of hopelessness had begun to wind itself around his heart and take him captive. He vowed that he would no longer allow that. He would trust God's sovereignty in their lives and move forward. No more hopelessness.

He looked back toward the house. Henri was tending to the pastor's horse. Laughter came from the kitchen. Charles, in his usual exuberance, bounded out the door and headed toward Jean.

He looked up at Vangie's room. A pale, petite face peered out at him. He waved at her. She smiled, lifted her doll's hand, and waved back.

TWENTY-TWO

The guard led Madeleine and Philippe toward the king's quarters. At last they had been summoned. Philippe took his mother's elbow. She looked into his dark eyes but did not speak.

They entered into the royal wings of the chateau, then were ushered into a room with a table and upholstered chairs, a chaise, a large cabinet, and bookcases. A bed shrouded in a tufted ivory canopy and matching, heavy tapestry curtains stood in the corner. The guard closed the door and left without a word.

"Mère?"

Madeleine put her finger to her lips and shook her head. She looked around the room, went to the bookcase, stopped, and listened. Walking back to her son, she motioned with a nod of her head to the bookcase. "The king will come into the room that way. The bookcase is a secret entrance from his quarters."

"How do you know that?"

"Because this is one of the older wings of the chateau, and we used to . . . used to rendezvous in this room. He knows I would remember."

Philippe glanced at the bed.

Madeleine pretended not to notice. "Shhh. Someone is coming."

The secret enclosure scraped open, and the Sun King stepped through the opening alone. He wore one of his famous thick, brown wigs, but had taken his jacket off and appeared in gold breeches and an ivory lace shirt.

"Madeleine. My dear Madeleine." He went to her and grabbed both of her hands and kissed them. He turned toward Philippe. "And Philippe. I'm so glad you could come. I wanted us to spend some time together—just the three of us." His voice was deep, warm, and mellow.

As if we had a choice. Madeleine curtsied and turned to Philippe, who executed a proper bow.

Louis nodded. "Now, let us dispense with formalities and visit as old friends. Tell me, are you enjoying your visit at Versailles?"

Madeleine took the lead. "Certain aspects of it. We have enjoyed hunting in the afternoons. Thank you for including us."

The king sat down and motioned to the couch. "Sit, sit."

Mother and son sat on the edge of the chaise.

"The ball proved to be an invigorating experience for us last week." Madeleine smiled. "Although I'm afraid I was a bit out of practice, and it was Philippe's first time."

"You both did rather well."

"We did, didn't we?" Madeleine cocked her head. "But, of course, I learned from the best."

Louis chuckled. "Yes, I remember. Do you like the gowns I had made for you—except for the gold one, of course, which you returned."

"You know I don't wear yellow, Louis. You were testing me."

"Hmmm, yes, I suppose I was. I wanted to know if you were the same strong woman I knew years ago, and still"—he paused—"still dream about." He touched the skirt of her dress. "This is not one my tailors have made. But it's very nice. Jade becomes you."

"I love the gowns you commissioned for me. Your taste is exquisite as always, but the ermine is quite extravagant."

"It becomes you. Wear it for the next ball."

Madeleine tossed her hair and laughed. "Whatever you wish."

The king made a steeple with his fingers and pressed them back and forth, staring at Philippe. Finally he spoke. "How old are you, son?"

"Fifteen, Your Majesty."

"Hmmm. Same age as the Dauphin, my son."

"Yes, sire."

"What do you like to do?"

"As Mère said, I enjoy hunting—and riding. You have offered us fine mounts to ride." Philippe chuckled. "I don't know if dancing is going to be one of my favorite activities, but I did enjoy learning some steps the other evening."

Madeleine held her breath as her son answered Louis' questions. He was doing well.

"Have you made any friends?"

"One of the stableboys."

"None of the young courtiers or pages in the court?"

"No, Your Majesty."

"We shall have to remedy that." The king stood, and Madeleine and Philippe followed his lead. "Come with me, Philippe." Louis kissed Madeleine's hand again. "A guard will take you back to your apartment, Madeleine."

"But . . ." Madeleine grabbed hold of the king's arm as he released her hand. "I thought . . ." Her knees grew weak. "Louis, please."

He shook her hand off his arm. "I would like to get to know . . . *your* son. I shall send a servant for his things. You will be summoned later, my dear."

MADELEINE STAGGERED BEHIND THE GUARD BACK TO HER apartment, stunned at the turn of events. She collapsed on the chaise and began to weep. Her breathing came in gulps and convulsions.

Elise appeared in the doorway. "Madame! Oh my, what does Madame need?"

Madeleine sat up and wiped her eyes. "It's nothing, really," she said. "Simply the foolish tears of a mother who cannot bear to see her son becoming a man."

"Monsieur Philippe?" Elise looked around.

"He will be staying with the king for a few days. Please get his things ready. Someone will come for them—tomorrow, I suppose."

The servant curtsied. "*Oui,* madame." She disappeared into Philippe's room.

Madeleine held her handkerchief hard against her mouth to stifle her sobs. She could not even frame a prayer. Her spirit groaned. She went to the window and peered toward the king's quarters. What would the king say to her son? Would he persuade the boy to stay at Versailles? Would he convince him that he could be a king's son, a prince? Would the enticement of Versailles weave its sticky web around him?

Be wise, my precious boy. Be wise.

LOUIS LED PHILIPPE THROUGH A SHORT PASSAGEWAY AND then into the king's quarters. A bevy of servants turned to look at the king and the young man as they entered, and Philippe stared at the magnificence of the room.

The king spoke to an older valet, standing nearby. "This is Philippe Clavell, son of an old friend. I wish him to attend my *coucher* this evening. Then see that someone escorts him to one of the bedchambers in the royal quarters next to the Dauphin."

Louis motioned for Philippe to join the gentleman servitors. "I shall send for your things in the morning, and then you shall attend Mass with my party. Sleep well, son."

Philippe bowed. "Yes, Your Majesty."

The evening ceremony began, and Philippe followed as best he could, with an older servitor nudging him along. After the king retired, the servant showed Philippe to a chamber adjacent to the king's quarters. Although small, the room was luxuriously furnished. The servitor retrieved a nightshirt from the armoire and laid it out on the bed. "Does Monsieur require anything further?"

Numb with the procedures of the evening, Philippe shook his head.

The servant indicated the pitcher and basin on the table. "Water?"

"Oh yes, that would be nice. Thank you."

The servant picked up the pitcher and disappeared out the door on the opposing wall from where they had entered. Philippe noticed a Swiss Guard at the entrance. Philippe walked along the wall, touching the panels, looking for a secret passageway, but found none. Tears threatened to spring to his eyes, but he willed them away. What was he to do? Go along with the king, or try to escape?

Play the game. You must learn to play the game. His mother's words echoed in his ears. He needed to play a game in which he didn't know the rules. Perhaps the king would eventually acknowledge that royal blood did not course through his veins. In the meantime, he supposed he would have to go along with the façade and pretend to be an illegitimate son of the king.

The servitor returned with a pitcher of water and set it beside the basin. "Will Monsieur have need of anything else? Monsieur Bontemps gave instructions that you may have anything you desire."

"Who?"

"Monsieur Bontemps, the king's head valet."

"Oh. No, nothing else. Thank you."

The servant bowed and left the room.

Philippe turned around in a circle and looked at the strange surroundings; there were paintings on every wall of battle scenes and the Sun King. He splashed water on his face and lay down on the bed, ignoring the nightshirt. Then he sat up and pulled his knife from his boot that the king had ordered for him and set the weapon on the nightstand. He took off his boots and lay back down. Then he sat up and removed the knife from the nightstand and tucked it underneath the pillow. He finally fell asleep.

Philippe opened his eyes and realized he had slept in his clothes on top of the duvet. A servant entered with breakfast—fruit, cheese, bread, and porridge. The velvet fragrance of hot chocolate curled around him as he lifted the lid of the chocolate pot. After the servant left, Philippe thrust his hand underneath the pillow and retrieved the knife. He tossed it into his boot.

The servant reentered with two satchels and began to unpack Philippe's clothes. He stooped to pick up Philippe's boots beside the bed.

"No!"

The startled servant looked up.

"I mean . . . uh, I'm going to wear those again today."

"As you wish. Does Monsieur wish to perform his *toilette* now?"

"Uh . . . not yet. Return after I've eaten, please."

"Very well." The servant finished putting Philippe's things away and left the room once more.

That was close. He took off his clothes from yesterday and sat down to eat. Everything tasted delicious, or he was simply extra hungry. He selected one of his new outfits and put on the breeches. He pulled the knife out of his boot, then put the boots on, sticking the knife back in its hiding place. He looked at the boots. They didn't match his breeches.

At that moment, the servant reentered. "Is Monsieur finished?"

"My name is Philippe, and yes, I am finished. Thank you."

"Does Monsieur . . ."

"Philippe."

"Does Monsieur Philippe wish to wear this shirt? It would match nicely with the breeches you have chosen." The servant eyed the boots that Philippe had put on and held out a white lace shirt.

"Yes, that's fine. And the matching black jacket with the red trim."

"Ah, yes. Very good. And the black hat with the red and white plume?"

"Yes."

"Does Monsieur Philippe realize his brown boots do not match the black outfit?"

Philippe looked down. "Uh, actually, I did realize that. I will change in a minute. Did my mother send the black shoes?"

The servant almost glowed with approval. "Yes, Monsieur." He set out a pair of black shoes with oval buckles. "Very nice.

"Now, your hair?"

"It's fine. With the hat on, it will be fine." Philippe pushed his hair out of his eyes. "I cannot seem to keep this out of my eyes no matter what I do, short of tying it back, and even then it slips out and falls across my face—just like my father's."

The servant made no comment, but helped Philippe finish getting ready for Mass, except for changing his boots and putting on his hat. "Your boots, sir?"

"Yes, I need to change. You may take the breakfast tray out, please."

The servant picked up the tray and started out the door. Philippe began to pull off his boots.

The servant turned. "Anything else, Monsieur?"

Philippe hesitated, his foot held in midair, halfway out of his boot. He fingered the handle of the knife.

"No, thank you. You've been very helpful." His heart thudded.

The servant nodded and exited. Philippe exhaled a long breath and pulled his foot all the way out. He put on the tight black shoes with the elaborate buckles and stuck the knife in his cummerbund underneath his jacket. He tugged at the lace cravate on his shirt and buttoned the jacket.

Philippe looked in the mirror, pulled his hair back, and put on his hat. A young man he didn't recognize stared back at him. He fingered his budding moustache and smiled at himself in the mirror. Practicing a bow, he watched his reflection. He tipped his hat. "Good morning, mademoiselle. Very nice to see you." He turned around and looked at the back of his jacket to make sure the knife wasn't creating a bulge. *Humph!* With all the lace and ruffles, who could tell?

The door opened, and a courtier entered. "Monsieur Clavell?"

"*Oui.* I am he."

"The king wishes you to join his party for Mass."

Philippe followed the courtier out into the anteroom and fell in with the king's entourage as they promenaded to Mass. He tucked his gloves in his cummerbund, mimicking the courtier. The courtiers all had swords, and some wore riding boots. Philippe took his cue from the others and nodded to those on their right and their left as they made their way through the crowd.

As they approached the chapel, Philippe spotted Madeleine curtseying to the king's following. He watched her until she looked up. Her eyes glinted determination. No tears, no weakness. She pulled her fan away from her lips and mouthed, "Play the game." He could not stop, but nodded and entered the chapel with the king, turning his back on his mother.

TWENTY-THREE

Madeleine was a woman possessed. She glared straight ahead during the worship service, her thoughts far away from receiving God's Word or praying. She stared at the back of the king's head. *You've taken my home, my husband, my freedom, but you shall not have my son. I declare by all that is right and just that you shall not have my son!*

She bit her lip until she tasted blood. She knew of no one at Versailles now to turn to for help. *God, send someone.* Her prayer was not really even a conscious thought, but desperation hurled heavenward.

The Mass ended, and Madeleine caught a glimpse of Philippe as they exited. How handsome he was. Anyone would be proud to call him son.

She walked out with the crowd and aimlessly headed toward the gardens, her thoughts reeling. To a bystander, she simply appeared as another lady of the court—except for the Swiss Guard lingering nearby. She was alone, with nothing to do. She had no duties to perform. No summons had come for her to join the hunt.

She walked toward the Latona Fountain, hoping to find Pierre's friends, but saw no one that she recognized. Clusters of courtiers, courtesans, and diplomats gathered in groups, making boisterous conversation. Couples lingered here and there, gazing into each other's eyes. Servitors scurried about or hovered around their patrons.

The water began to spray, and Madeleine moved toward it and closed her eyes. The fine mist cooled her face.

"Most of the ladies shield their faces from the mist."

She recognized the voice and inwardly shuddered. Turning around, she nearly collided with her former nemesis. "Commander Boveé. What are you doing walking about leisurely in the gardens? Surely a dragoon commander has more important things to do." She offered her hand, puzzling again over the fact that this cruel dragoon was Pierre's father.

He bowed and kissed her hand. In reality, he could be quite charming when he put his mind to it, and as always, his smile disarmed her.

"We are not always such oafs. We do have a civilized side—when off duty."

Madeleine saw much of Pierre in the man's physical appearance, especially his smile, but certainly not in his demeanor or character.

"I am delighted to have run into you." He paused. "To tell the truth, I have been looking for you."

"Looking for me? Whatever for? I cannot imagine why—"

"Could we walk, please?" Commander Boveé took Madeleine's arm and began to walk around the fountain toward the Royal Paterre. "May I be completely honest with you?"

"Why does that remark make me uneasy?"

"No need to be. I have come with a pressing concern."

Madeleine did not respond, but opened her parasol against the rising sun.

"Madame Clavell, do you know the whereabouts of my son?"

"Why, Commander Boveé, it was my understanding that you two had a very distant relationship."

The façade of pretentious courtesies faded. He lowered his voice. "That was true in the past. But in recent days we have reconciled and determined to strengthen our bond. I have been . . ." He faltered. "I have been a miserable father. Now that I am growing older, I regret my indifference toward Pierre when he was growing up. Those years are never to be recovered, but I have vowed to make the remainder count."

Madeleine looked at the commander who had destroyed her home and kidnapped her daughter—the one who lit the torch and carried out the king's orders that devastated their lives. She wanted to hate him, and although she did not trust him, she found herself softening toward him. He appeared worn and tired. "Commander Boveé, I have found that sometimes it takes a lifetime to realize what a treasure we have in each other."

They stopped and faced each other.

"Well spoken." He stepped back and put his hand on his sword. "Madame, I ask you again, do you know what has happened to my son?"

"I do not. I wish I did. I . . . I need him desperately right now."

Paul Boveé waited for Madeleine to continue. A breeze picked up and blew her hair into her face. She closed her parasol and brushed the curls out of her eyes.

"Pierre is my only friend here. I have no one else to turn to. The king has . . . has taken my son."

"Taken him? What do you mean?"

"It is a long story, but we are being held as virtual prisoners here at Versailles." She looked over at the Swiss Guard. "And the king desires my son to be in the court in a more personal way. He has taken him away from me as a pawn, a bargaining piece."

"What is he bargaining for?"

"Me, for one thing."

"Madame Clavell, when I was sent to destroy your estate, I knew that the king had, shall we say, a special interest in your family. I'd heard the rumors about King Louis' first love—the beautiful young woman who ran from court and the arms of the young king, never to return. Are you telling me that you are that mysterious young woman?"

"*Oui.* But more than that, Louis thinks Philippe . . . thinks there is a possibility that Philippe could be his son."

"I see. May I be so bold as to ask? Is he?" He searched her eyes.

"*Non.*"

The two stood silent for a few moments. Then Commander Boveé broke the awkward moment. "It seems we both have a bit of a problem with our sons. I don't know where mine is, and you know where yours is but cannot claim him."

"At least I know that my son will come to no harm while he is in the company of the king. My fear is that his young mind and spirit will be captivated by the allure of the court." Madeleine shook her head. "I do not know where Pierre is, but I think I know why he has disappeared. I believe the king found out that Pierre helped bring my husband to us from the galleys. He knows Pierre betrayed him."

"Pierre did not tell me that he had helped you, but I suspected as much. He danced all around it. I instigated your . . . your sudden departure, and my son helped reunite your family. Fate is indeed strange, isn't it?"

Madeleine's heart began to pound. Had she revealed too much? Was Commander Boveé baiting her for information? She looked into his eyes.

He continued, "Pierre has changed, and perhaps I am changing as well. I don't care what he has done. I just want to find him and make sure he is well."

"I understand, but I would disagree that fate controls our lives. I believe God orchestrates it all."

"Perhaps." Commander Boveé stepped back and fingered his sword. "But if he does, he has orchestrated us into a mess at this point, hasn't he?"

Madeleine shook her head and spoke words filled with confidence, words that she indeed believed—but at this moment she didn't possess the confidence that she exuded to the commander. In spite of that, the words poured from her lips from some forgotten reservoir deep in her soul. "Sometimes it seems that life is a mess, but God always makes a way for his people."

"Ummm. I wish I shared your certainty that all will be well." Paul looked around and turned his back to the Swiss Guard. "Be that as it may, if it is for treason that Pierre has been 'detained,' then I know where they have taken him."

"The Bastille," Madeleine said, and the commander nodded. "I feared as much. But how can we find out for sure?"

Commander Boveé put on his gloves. "I will find out and let you know." He offered his arm. "May I escort you back to the chateau?"

"It would be my pleasure, Commander." She placed her hand on his arm.

The two former enemies, united now by a common pursuit, walked arm in arm past the fountain to the chateau.

God, send someone? The thought flickered across Madeleine's mind. Could it possibly be?

PIERRE PACED IN HIS CELL. HE HAD BECOME ACCUSTOMED to the dank odor, but periodically the musty stench pierced his nostrils and stung. He rubbed his nose. He sat down at the table with the left-overs from breakfast teetering on the corner, picked up a spoon, and tossed it into the bowl. Nothing tasted appetizing to him, although the cooks in the king's prison lived up to their reputation of providing unusually good dining for the prisoners.

He went through the books he had asked for. None of them appealed to him now. He poured water from the ewer into the basin and splashed some on his face. He pulled his hair back and tied it with a ribbon he had removed from his jacket. Soon the guards would come to get him for his daily hour of exercise—the one time of the day he looked forward to. He walked to the end of his cell and put another mark on the wall—two weeks. It seemed like two years.

Pierre thought about François and his time in the galleys. How had he survived for two years under those harsh conditions? It must have been his determination to get back to his family that gave him the strength to keep going. And God sustained him.

Will God sustain me as well? Pierre wondered. What was the larger scheme of things? All he wanted was out. How could his incarceration prove anything, except that if you cross the king, you will pay? But then there was the issue of the freedom of worship, and families who were being killed and tortured all over France for their beliefs. Wasn't that worth dying for?

Dying for? He wasn't even a Huguenot.

He sat on the bed and put his head in his hands. He was becoming disoriented, and he knew it. He rocked back and forth. *God, help me. Keep my mind clear so I can think. Make a way of escape for me.*

No answer. Nothing.

"Monsieur Boveé."

Pierre stood and grabbed his jacket.

The guard opened the cell door and escorted him to the open interior of the castle. Several other prisoners, including a few women, milled about. Pierre began to walk around the perimeter of the yard. Each lap he took faster than the last until his breath became labored. Then he slowed down. He bent over and rubbed his calves. Only two weeks a prisoner, and he could sense his strength leaving him. He must not let that happen. He needed to be strong when the time came for him to . . . to what? Escape? How was he going to do that with a twenty-five foot moat surrounding the castle and nobody to help him?

God would send someone.

God . . . do you see me here? Do you care?

What if this is my destiny? To grow old and die here without anybody knowing or caring . . . Wait, that's not true. Madeleine cares, and I know she's praying. Robert cares. Lisette cares. My father . . . does he care? I think maybe he does. And God will do something. I just need to keep praying and believing and maintaining my strength.

Pierre began to walk again with renewed vigor. *God, I trust you. God, I trust you. God, I trust you.* He set a pace and a rhythm as he walked. Was it really prayer if one prayed in rhythm as one walked? He knew it wasn't the normal stance of prayer, but somehow he didn't think God minded. He sensed that God heard his petitions. And what's more, that he would answer in his time.

THE SELECTED COURTIERS FOR THE DAY ENTERED THE king's chambers for the morning *lever*. The king searched the group for a certain courtier-to-be. At the signal from the gentleman servitors, Philippe entered the king's bedchamber and stood to the side. The wig carrier brought in the royal wigs, and the valets assisted in dressing the king.

The morning lever ended, and Louis spoke a word to Bontemps. "Ask young Philippe Clavell to join me in my office."

The king's valet walked over to Philippe and spoke to him in a whisper.

"Now?"

"Yes, follow me."

Philippe followed the older gentleman into the king's inner office, where Louis sat at a table, shuffling papers.

"Ah, Philippe! What do you think about the morning's activities so far?"

Philippe bowed. "I . . ."

"Speak up. You may speak freely here."

"It is a bit more complicated and formal than I imagined."

"You will get used to it."

"Is it the same every day?"

"*Oui*. The business at hand changes with the politics of the day, but the order is always the same."

"What happens next?"

"Mass, and then—hmmm, today is Thursday. I receive petitions from my subjects who have issues to discuss. Mainly that consists of courtiers wanting more money for this or that." He chuckled. "After that, the afternoon meal, then my favorite part of the day—the hunt."

"May I be included in the hunt today?"

"Of course, anytime you wish, son." The word rolled through the room like ripe fruit, to be either consumed or thrown away.

The boy averted his eyes.

"Philippe, are you afraid of me?"

"I am in awe of your presence, Your . . . Your Majesty. But, no, I am not afraid of you."

"Very good." Louis stood and with a wave of his hand dismissed his staff. After they cleared the room, he walked to Philippe and stood in front of him. He searched Philippe's face for what seemed an eternity. Finally he spoke. "Has your mother told you what my interest is in bringing you to Versailles?"

"Yes, Your Majesty. You and my mother were . . ."

"I loved your mother. I loved her very much. I still do." Louis turned and began to pace. "She was the one person who was honest and frank with me. I trusted her, but her parents snatched her away. She wouldn't answer my pleas. I suspect that she never got the messages." He stopped. "Then I got wrapped up in the politics of France. She met and married your father. You were born soon after that."

Philippe looked at the king and squared his shoulders. "I am Philippe Clavell, son of François and Madeleine Clavell." He brushed his hair back but did not turn his eyes away.

The king stared at the boy. In his memory he saw a slender man with a shock of dark hair that fell across his forehead as he stumbled to his knees, who refused to convert, even in the king's presence and upon threat of death.

The king's mouth settled in a grim slit. It was the son of François Clavell, not his own son, who stood before him. He knew that for certain now. Well, it didn't matter. He could still use the situation to his advantage—to persuade Madeleine to come to him at last. He continued to look at the young man. He liked him. He was a fine young man, one whom he would like to keep around.

"Perhaps, but I should like to enlist you into my court." Louis scribbled a name on a piece of paper. "Go find this courtier. He will take you under his wing and give you good training."

"I would prefer to work in the stables, Your Majesty."

"The stables! No son of . . ." He hesitated. "If you train as a courtier, you can have the best of both worlds. You will have plenty of time in the stables if you wish." He waved the boy off. "Now, go. I have work to do. I shall see you at the afternoon hunt."

PHILIPPE BACKED OUT OF THE ROOM, BOWING AS HE LEFT. Striding through the outer chamber, he looked at the unfamiliar faces staring back at him. A hand grabbed his shoulder, and he looked around. It was Robert Devereaux.

"You are in quite a hurry."

"I'm supposed to find this man and put myself under his tutelage."

"Let me see."

Philippe handed the note to Robert.

"Ah, Denis Greer, a good man. One of the king's favorites. I wish he had assigned you to me, but then he wouldn't do that, would he?

Knowing of your connection with Pierre, who is my best friend." Robert handed the name back to the boy. "No need to be frightened. Denis will take good care of you."

"But I don't want to be a courtier. I want to go home, or at the least, work in the stables. My mother . . ."

Robert took the boy by the arm and led him out of the anteroom to a bench underneath a large portrait by Mignard, encased in a heavy gold frame. He lowered his voice. "Sit with me a moment." Robert unbuttoned his jacket and rearranged his sword. "Play along with the king. Then when you see your chance, take it."

"That's what my mother keeps telling me, but I seem to be sinking deeper and moving farther away from getting out of Versailles."

"Your chance will come. In the meantime, would you like me to introduce you to Monsieur Greer? He's right over there." Robert pointed to a man with a medium build and long, dark-blond hair, wearing the coveted *justacorps a brevet*.

Philippe shuffled his feet. "Yes, please."

The two moved toward Monsieur Greer, who was in a heated discussion with two other courtiers, gesturing animatedly. Robert nudged Philippe along and pulled him into the circle of courtiers. When there came a pause in the conversation, he dived in. "Monsieur Greer, I have a note for you from the king."

The conversation halted.

"Ah, so? What does my sovereign desire of me?" He unfolded the short missive as he spoke.

"I believe he would like you to take this splendid young man under your tutelage and train him in the art of court life. May I present Philippe Clavell, from Grenoble, Dauphiné Provence."

Philippe executed his finest bow. "I am honored to be assigned to you, Monsieur Greer."

Robert smiled. "I shall bid you farewell now." Taking his leave, he whispered to the reluctant new courtier-in-training, "I will be around. Just a word or a nod from you, and I will be there. Play the game."

TWENTY-FOUR

Madeleine could not gain her footing, and she slid farther and farther down into a tunnel. She traveled at frightening speed, but she was not afraid. Beautiful colors swirled around her and reached out with fluid fingers to caress her. Her hair flowed behind her and melded into the colors, and she became one with the scene. She looked at her hands, and as she held them out, a cold fire poured from her fingertips.

She rushed to the bottom of the tunnel, and the faces of François, Philippe, Pierre, Vangie, Charles, and Jean loomed before her in a circle, smiling. They beckoned for her to join them. She stretched out her fire-emanating fingers for them as she rushed toward the bottom. But the moment she reached her loved ones, their faces transformed into one face—that of Louis.

"To set them free, you must come to me." He laughed and lunged toward her—and she woke up.

Madeleine's head had slid from her pillow, and her hair trailed down the multicolored duvet hanging off the bed. Her hands had fallen asleep—the cool fire from the dream. She sat up and rubbed them. She pulled her hair back and caught it up with a ribbon that had come loose during the night.

The grate in the fireplace scraped in the adjoining room. Elise must be up already, although Madeleine could tell it was early. She rearranged her pillows, lay back down, and mulled over the dream. It darted through her mind like a vapor and disappeared as she tried to recapture the details—except the sensation in her hands and Louis' words. *To set them free, you must come to me.*

She knew the meaning of the dream. Louis wanted to possess her as his maîstresse en titre. He had told her as much on her last visit to Versailles. He had not changed his mind, and now he had Philippe as leverage. She could not escape his clutches.

What does a mother do when her child is in danger? She sacrifices herself.

Even if it means compromising one's personal convictions? Isn't that what Queen Esther did in the Holy Scriptures? Madeleine asked herself. She sacrificed herself to save God's people. She allowed herself to be taken into the pagan king's harem to gain the ear of the king.

If that were the only way she could rescue Philippe, she would do it. If God wanted to rescue them, he could have already done so. Almost a month had passed since they had arrived at Versailles. Perhaps she would have to be a Queen Esther of sorts to rescue her "people," in this instance her son.

What about Pierre? Where could he be? She shook her head. She couldn't worry about him right now. Her heart ached at the thought of the handsome courtier, but Paul Boveé would have to find him. Madeleine had to liberate her own son.

She skirmished with God in her mind and thoughts. Her stomach churned. If God truly cared about her and her family, why did they continue to run into seemingly insurmountable obstacles? Maybe God was helpless, as impotent as the stone statues in the gardens outside her window. Perhaps what she had believed all of her life had plunged them into unnecessary danger and peril. After all, Louis was their God-ordained sovereign. Were they not instructed by God to obey the authority in the land?

Someone scratched at their door. Elise opened it, and Madeleine heard the courier greet her. "A letter for Madame Clavell."

"Yes, I'll give it to her. *Merci*."

Madeleine rushed to Elise and tore the letter from the servant. She read through it quickly. "Vangie! Vangie is ill?" She collapsed onto the hard parquet floor and began to rock back and forth. "Oh, God, oh, God. Not Vangie."

"Madame! What is wrong? Oh dear, let me help you." Elise helped Madeleine to her feet and then to a chair.

Madeleine blinked the tears away as she tried to read between the lines. *Vangie has not been feeling well, but we pray she is on the mend.* No hint what was wrong or how bad . . . *We pray she is on the mend.*

Madeleine's temples thudded, and her heartbeat raced. "How much more . . . how much more can I stand?" She twisted in her chair and looked out the window at the diplomats and court personnel going about their day. Then she stood and shook the wadded-up letter in her hand at the scene. "I hate you! I hate this place and all it stands for. I hate the decadence and the duplicity and the shallowness and the . . . the . . . even the beauty—the controlled, contrived beauty carved to meet Louis' lust. I hate you!"

She sat down again and melted into a sniveling mess, pounding her thighs with her fists. Elise stood by, wringing her hands, clearly not knowing what to do. After several minutes the sobs subsided. Madeleine took a deep breath and looked up at the astonished servant.

"I'm sorry. Please forgive me. I received some bad news from home. I am fine now."

"Does Madame need anything?"

"What day is it?"

"Thursday, madame."

She wiped her eyes and nose. "It's time. I've waited long enough. I'm going to see the king. He will have to see me if I go in with the open audience he receives in his quarters after Mass." She walked to the desk and picked up a quill. "Summon a courier, please, and send a message that I am coming. He cannot deny me in front of his subjects."

Madeleine scribbled a message, sealed it, and handed it to Elise. Then she pulled the ribbon out of her hair and tossed her head. "After you summon a courier, please prepare my toilette and—get out the red gown."

MADELEINE STARTED FOR THE CHAPEL WITH HER USUAL guard-escort close behind. Aware of the approving and jealous stares from the other members of the court, she held her head up and made her way to the front of the crowd gathering outside the chapel, awaiting the king's arrival. Across the aisle, she spotted Philippe

217

with an older courtier whom she did not recognize. His eyes widened when he saw her. A slight trace of a smile flitted across his face. She nodded.

The assembly quieted and bowed as the king's party approached. Madeleine remained upright until Louis saw her. He stopped in front of her as she curtsied. She looked up at him and smiled, then straightened up to her full posture. The queen, dressed in her usual conservative dark colors, turned her hooded eyes in Madeleine's direction. Following behind, Madame de Montespan, Louis' current official mistress, snapped her head around and surveyed Madeleine from head to toe, taking in the royal ermine trim. Louis chuckled and continued into the chapel.

Madeleine exhaled, and a bead of perspiration rolled down between her breasts. She didn't realize she had been holding her breath.

After Mass, she hurried to the king's quarters and queued up to await her turn to see Louis. The anteroom was full of courtiers and diplomats, and she saw that she was one of only two women in the room. One of the king's ministers emerged and looked around the room. "Madame Clavell?"

The heads of the men turned in unison to see who was being summoned. Madeleine did not shoulder her way through the men but waited for them to stand aside. She removed her cape with a flourish and carried it over her arm. The king's personal guards opened the door to his office, and she went in as the doors closed behind her.

Louis sat at his desk, signing documents.

"Madame Clavell, Your Majesty."

He did not look up.

Madeleine stood in front of his desk and waited. Several minutes passed in silence. Only the scratching of the king's pen could be heard.

Surely Louis could hear her heart thumping. At last he set the pen down, stood, walked around the desk, and approached her. She curtsied and offered her hand.

"Madeleine. How good of you to seek an audience." He looked around at his governmental officers. "We are rather busy. The Dutch continue to give us problems. But that's not your order of business, I'm sure. What brings you to my office?"

"Could we speak in private?"

"Anytime." Louis dismissed the cluster of men with a wave of his hand. "Now, what is it you need to see me about? Philippe? A fine young man. I am most impressed with him. I've assigned him to one of my best courtiers for training, Denis Greer. Do you know him?"

"*Non*, I do not believe I do. And, yes, I have come in regard to Philippe." She looked around for a place to put her cape. A chair sat in front of the desk, and she laid the cape across it. She turned back to the king, her skirt swaying.

Louis touched her sleeve. "That gown looks as ravishing on you as I thought it would. Red becomes you." He continued down her forearm and ended by kissing her hand.

Madeleine felt her cheeks flush. "You always preferred me in red."

"And the Dolebels managed a perfect fit on you." Louis took his time and let his eyes drift along the daring neckline.

Her heart skipped a beat. "Indeed, they are skilled. And ermine? The choice of royalty? Really now, Louis."

"You have always been royalty in my eyes."

"Hmmm." Madeleine looked at the king directly. "I came to appeal to you." She paused. "I received word today that my daughter is ill. Please, let us go back to our family. Philippe is not your son. Surely you have been able to see that by now." Madeleine moved close to him

219

and put her hand on his arm. She could see the color begin to rise in his face.

Louis put his hand over hers and waited for her to finish speaking.

"Philippe could have been your son, but he is not. I was not carrying your child when my parents forced me to leave Versailles. If I had been pregnant, I would have convinced my parents to bring me back to court. I would not have kept you from your own child."

Madeleine began to cry softly and went into Louis' arms. He drew a handkerchief from the sleeve of his jacket and handed it to her, and held her as she continued.

"Please let us go. This is a huge false impression—seeds of some truth and reality that have taken on a life of their own and produced a crop of tares. Philippe is a Clavell."

"Perhaps." Louis' countenance clouded. "But what have you to say about Pierre Boveé?"

Madeleine's breath quickened. "Who?"

"Don't play cat and mouse with me—the young courtier who escorted you to the Trianon when you were here last. Who—and I have this on good report—helped bring François to join you in Switzerland."

She pulled back from the king. "I remember the handsome courtier well because he was an excellent escort, but I'm sure I don't know what you are talking about beyond that. Switzerland? Why should one of your courtiers be interested in assisting a Huguenot family in escaping to Switzerland? You have received false information."

"Hmmm, maybe. Maybe not. Pierre Boveé does not have feelings for you?"

Madeleine chuckled. "Don't you think I would know if a gorgeous man like that had feelings for me?" She smiled. "He did have the most sultry eyes behind a mask I believe I've ever seen—an unusual gray, as I'm remembering."

"Humph! I'm sure I don't know about that. Only women notice such things."

"Why are we talking about some courtier who has nothing to do with us?"

"What *about* us? What about the life you and Philippe could have here—a life of luxury and grandeur?"

"I have two other children—two children who have already lost their father. Are they to lose their mother as well? I cannot simply abandon them."

"How old are they?"

"Charles is twelve, and Evangeline six. We call her Vangie." A sob caught in her throat. "I received word this morning that she is ill."

"Where are they?"

Madeleine hesitated.

"Don't trust me, eh?" Louis turned his back on her and walked to the window. He stroked his moustache. "Bring them here, Madeleine, and raise them at Versailles. They will have everything they need. Philippe will live the life of a courtier. We'll provide quarters for the others. And you . . ."

"What *of* me, Louis? What will be my position?"

He walked back to her and took her hands. "We will be together as we were always meant to be."

"As your mistress?"

"*Oui.* My official mistress, a privileged position in my court. Madeleine, I have been in love with you since I was a young man. Let's be happy. At long last, let's be together."

"I am officially still in the mourning period."

"Other than the mourning brooch, your appearance belies that fact."

Madeleine touched the jet brooch at the center of the neckline of her dress. "When one is ordered by the king that he wishes one to dress otherwise, one doesn't have much of a choice, does one?"

"Since when did you obey my every wish?"

Madeleine's thoughts were whirling. Was this their way of escape? "And we would need to convert?"

"We all worship the same God, do we not? Wouldn't God want us to be happy? And your daughter—what was her name again?"

"Vangie."

"Yes, Vangie. Bring her here, and I will see that she receives the best medical attention available. My own personal physicians will attend her."

"And my children would be safe? We would have to fear no reprisal of any kind?"

"*Non.*"

"May I have some time to think?"

"Do not take long, my dear." He cupped her chin in his hand and kissed her softly on the lips. "We have waited too many years already." He removed her cape from the chair and called for his ministers to return. "Please escort Madame Clavell to the door."

"I know my way out." Madeleine shrugged into her cape and walked out the door, leaving her pride and her convictions in the chambers of the king.

TWENTY-FIVE

Philippe stood on the fringe of the group of courtiers lingering in the anteroom adjacent to the king's apartment. He saw only a swish of red and ermine sweep around the corner and then down a darkened hall, but he recognized the cape and then saw the Swiss Guard. His mother had been in the king's chambers. He started after her, but by the time he reached the edge of the host of court officials and bystanders, she had disappeared.

Denis Greer turned toward Philippe as the boy returned to the knot of courtiers with whom they had been conversing. "Someone you know?"

"My mother. She . . . she is a close friend of King Louis."

"I see."

Philippe wanted to shout at the smug courtier, *No, you don't see! You only think you do.* But he remained silent.

"We might as well get started with your apprenticeship." Denis looked at Philippe from head to toe as he walked around him. "Good, very good. Your clothing is superb."

"The king had my clothes made for me special."

"Yes, his taste is always perfect. Does everything fit well? Your shoes—are they comfortable? You'll be doing much standing and dancing."

Philippe looked down at his feet encased in the elaborate shoes with the oval buckles. "They are comfortable. At least mine have buckles and not those ridiculous bows."

Greer chuckled. "Well, that's the fashion." He pointed to the bows on his shoes with his sword.

"Forgive me. I meant no offense. It is just that I prefer boots."

"No offense taken, but take a quick survey. None of the courtiers are wearing boots, unless they are assigned to duty or the hunt."

Philippe looked around the room at the shoes. Denis was correct. Except for one musketeer, none of the men wore boots. Philippe allowed his gaze to wander to the musketeer's face. Beady eyes stared back at him. Then they squinted closed as the man began to laugh at Philippe. It was Nicolas Maisson, standing next to Lisette.

Philippe turned his back on the musketeer. "Yes, you are right. I only saw one pair of boots, on a musketeer."

"The one staring at us and laughing?"

"That's the one."

"I shall teach him to laugh at me." Denis touched his sword.

"I believe he is laughing at me. He is the musketeer who 'escorted' my mother and me here."

The courtier relaxed. "I see. You are not at Versailles by choice?"

"*Non*. We were summoned here by the king."

"And is it the king's idea for you to be trained as a courtier?"

"Yes."

"You have no interest yourself?"

"I just want to go home."

"Where is home?"

"I . . . it's . . ." Philippe stammered and then stopped. "I guess I don't really have a home anymore." His maturing voice cracked, and he cleared his throat. "Our estate was in Dauphiné Provence, south of Grenoble, until"—he looked down at his feet sheathed in the fancy shoes that did not seem to belong to his body—"until it was destroyed by the dragoons. My father is dead. The rest of the family is in Switzerland."

"You are Huguenot."

"*Oui*."

"That's just wonderful. The king sends me a young Huguenot, who doesn't want to be a courtier, to train and educate in the ways of the court." Denis threw up his hands. "How am I always so lucky? It's complicated enough when you *want* to become a courtier. When one does not have the desire, it is almost impossible." He took Philippe by the arm and steered him to a corner of the room. "Where shall we begin? I suppose I need to find out what you already know. Are you going to be rebellious and resist?"

Philippe shook his head. "No, I will not be rebellious. My mother has asked me to . . ." His mother's words, *play the game*, almost slipped out of his mouth. "My mother has requested that I cooperate, and I will."

"Very well. Tell me what you know. The dance? Court etiquette? How to use a sword? Ride? Shoot?"

"My father taught me how to ride and shoot, and he taught me well. I have already been on a hunt with the king."

Denis nodded approval.

"We went to a ball, and I learned the menuet."

"Very good. Did you enjoy the ball?"

"Surprisingly, yes, I did enjoy it."

"Maybe this won't be so bad after all. What about the sword?"

"I do not know how to fence. I can use a knife, but my father never taught me about fencing. He was a *seigneur*, and a good one, but he didn't like coming to court or the intricacies of court life. That was my mother's world."

"We shall start with that, then—this morning, even. Fencing in the mornings and dance and etiquette in the afternoons."

"What about the hunt? May I go on the hunts?"

"Occasionally, but not every day. That is only by invitation of the king."

"I think he will invite me often."

"We shall see. Change into some more casual clothes, and we shall get started."

PHILIPPE FINISHED HIS FIRST FENCING LESSON UNDER Monsieur Greer's expertise at the *l Exercise des Armes*. After Denis dismissed him and left him standing in the yard, Philippe looked around and found himself alone, without the constant presence of a Swiss Guard. He figured he had a few hours before his afternoon classes began. A perfect time to go see his new friend at the stables.

Philippe had no idea where to look for the young groomsman, so he proceeded to the place where they had met a few days ago. He wandered inside and gawked at the sheer size of the facility. Coaches and horses as far to the left and right as one could see.

He saw an older man cleaning out a carriage and approached him. "I'm looking for Gabriel. Can you tell me where I could find him?"

"He's out in the yard—down at the far end."

"*Merci.*"

Philippe went back out into the sunlight and began to make his way around carriages and horses. He spotted Gabriel working on the front hoof of a black mare. "Hello!"

Gabriel looked up and grinned. "Hello, there." He dropped the horse's foot and gave her a pat. "What are you doing down here alone?"

"Looking for you. What're you up to this morning?"

"I'm checking the hooves on this new shipment of horses."

"May I help? I was taught by the best—our stable master, Henri." Philippe picked up the hoof pick and began to work on a chestnut standing by.

Gabriel shrugged and laughed. "If you insist."

The time passed quickly as the two young men worked side by side. Gabriel was quick to laugh and joke. The sun climbed in the sky and stood overhead, and Philippe wiped his brow.

"I suppose I should go get cleaned up. I have to go to . . . go to etiquette and dance classes."

"Really?" They finished with the last horse and started toward the stable. "Do you have time to eat something?"

Philippe nodded. "I have a few extra minutes."

Gabriel directed Philippe to an alcove between two stalls. "This is my personal space—my dining room, bedroom, and kitchen." He spread out bread and cheese, and they sat on bales of hay to eat.

"Do you live here in the stables?"

"*Non*, I live in town with my family, but I stay here at night sometimes. Especially when the king is in residence."

"Do you have brothers and sisters?"

Gabriel threw back his head and hooted. His mop of sun-bleached hair flopped back as his laughter filled the stall. "I'm the oldest of ten. Maman seems to have babies easier than she can cook dinner."

Philippe smiled, then grew somber. "I'm the oldest of three. My brother and sister are not with us. They are out of the country. My father passed away recently." He looked down at the bread that Gabriel was sharing. "I need to go. My tutor will be waiting for me."

"You don't seem very happy about that."

"I'm not. I don't belong here. We are only here for a few . . . well, I don't really know how long we will be here." Philippe looked at Gabriel. "May I ask you a question?"

Gabriel nodded. "Sure."

"Are you Catholic or Huguenot?"

Gabriel's jovial mood darkened, and he stared at Philippe. "Is that important?"

"It is to me. It is part of the reason we are here."

"My mother is Catholic, and my father is Huguenot. How about you?"

"Huguenot."

"Oh." Gabriel lowered his head and voice. "I am sympathetic with the plight of the Huguenots. My father has told me of atrocities taking place to force Huguenots to convert. I can hardly believe it. The Edict of Nantes was supposed to offer protection."

"Yes. We know firsthand of those atrocities. We escaped to Switzerland, but the king brought us back. My mother and he were childhood friends, and he is . . . well, I guess he still cares for her and wants her back at court."

"The king is in love with your mother?"

Philippe nodded and stood. "I need to go."

Gabriel stood with his new friend and grabbed his shoulder. "Please come again to see me. Perhaps one day we can go riding or something."

"I will."

"And, Philippe, if you ever need anything, I'm always here in the stable, usually in this area."

"Thank you."

"Anything."

Philippe nodded and walked out the entrance of the stable. He glanced back at his new friend, who stood with his hands on his hips, watching him as he started toward the chateau.

CAPTAIN MAISSON CORNERED LISETTE. HIS BREATH reeked of ale, even this early in the morning. "It looks as if young Monsieur Clavell has been assigned to Denis Greer."

She looked over Nicolas' shoulder. "He couldn't have a better mentor."

"Were you talking about me?" Robert Devereaux stepped up to the couple.

"Oh, Robert. Every conversation is not about you." Lisette giggled, opened her fan, and stepped around the musketeer to face the handsome courtier. She smiled at him, relieved that he had come to her rescue.

"Yes, well, may I escort you to dinner?"

Nicolas stepped to Lisette's side and cupped her elbow with his hand. "Excuse me, but I had planned on asking Mademoiselle Lereau for the pleasure of her company."

"Sorry, Captain. Looks like I beat you to it."

"Yes, Captain Maisson. Robert did ask first." Lisette moved away from Nicolas and took Robert's hand.

The musketeer glowered at the two. "Very well. I shall see you later then?"

"As you wish."

The musketeer slapped his gloves against his thigh and exited the room.

Robert motioned for Lisette to follow him to the staircase. "What have you found out? I know we agreed that you should be the one to ply him for information, but I don't like him fawning over you like that. I don't like him, period."

"He has told me nothing, except to say that Pierre is well, and that he would take me to him—for a price."

"That would be too high a price to pay." The pair moved down the stairs. "Let's go outside."

"You're a good man and a good friend, Robert."

"As are you—I mean a good friend, not a good man. And I for one am grateful that you are not a man." The two laughed.

"Robert, are you ever serious?"

"Not if I can help it." He winked at her. "I want to go over to the soldiers' yard and find Commander Boveé. Based on what Captain Maisson said to you, there is only one place Pierre could be."

"That's what I think as well. But trying to find him without a cell number will be next to impossible."

"That's no problem for someone like Commander Paul Boveé.

He will have ways of uncovering what we need. Just knowing that Pierre is alive and perhaps at the Bastille offers an avenue of optimism. Perhaps we can get him out."

"Then what?"

Robert looked over his shoulder and lowered his voice. "I fear he will not be able to stay in France. He will be a man on the run."

"Just like the Huguenots."

"I suppose."

The wind blew leaves across the courtyard. Threatening, gray clouds formed overhead, darkening the sun. Robert grabbed hold of his hat. "Those look like rain clouds."

Lisette buttoned the top of her cape, pulled the hood over her head, and snuggled closer to Robert as they walked. "Have you noticed a change in Pierre since his return? Has he talked to you about his . . . his relationship with Madame Clavell? And about his encounter with God?"

Robert stopped and looked at Lisette. His normally clear blue eyes clouded over like the gray skies above.

A lone raindrop fell and splattered on her shoulder. She brushed it away, held out her hand, and looked toward the sky. "I enjoy walking in the rain, don't you?"

"Rain only means our quarters are going to be cold and drafty, and I will have to find a new mademoiselle to keep me warm."

Lisette giggled. "You didn't answer me. Did you . . . have you sensed a change in Pierre?"

"Somewhat."

"Did he talk to you about God?"

Robert cleared his throat. "Not in so many words. He talked about wanting something more out of life, something . . . how did he word it? Something more substantial that would 'sustain our souls.' It made me nervous to hear him talk like that."

"You are nervous now."

Robert ignored her remark. "There's Commander Boveé. We will have to wait until he is finished."

The commander sat astride his horse, watching the dragoons proceed through their training exercises. He bellowed out commands and reprimands, never losing his authoritative posture.

Lisette nodded. "What about Madame Clavell?"

"What about her?"

"Did Pierre mention anything about her?"

"Only that he knew her because he escorted her to the Trianon for the king a few years ago."

"I suspect more involvement than that." Lisette's voice was just above a whisper. "I think he is in love with her."

"What? Lisette, your jealous imagination is running away with you. How could that happen? She's only been here a few weeks, and he's not been with her."

"No, and he's not been interested in me either since he got back. It happened while he was gone. He was with the Clavell family all during that time. And now that Monsieur Clavell is dead . . . I think . . ."

"But the king. He . . ."

"Doesn't it make sense? Not only did Pierre help the Clavells; he fell in love with a woman whom the king is in love with. Louis would be furious at him."

"All of this is speculation."

"Trust me. My woman's intuition is never wrong."

The light rain diminished, leaving a wet veil across the ground, which was chewed up quickly by the soldiers and horses. The commander finally dismissed his troops and rode toward Robert and Lisette. He reined in and dismounted. "Well, my young friends, what have you learned? Do you know what has happened to my son?"

Robert stepped forward. "I have not found out anything, but Lisette has plied enough information from Captain Maisson to give us an idea."

The formidable commander turned to look at Lisette, and he smiled. She found herself staring at his smile that mirrored Pierre's.

"You look so much . . . rather, Pierre's smile is exactly like yours. I never realized how much he looked like you before now."

"He *is* my son—whom I am eager to locate."

"Yes. Captain Maisson told me that Pierre is as well as could be expected, but has been 'detained.' Robert and I believe they have taken him to the Bastille. Nicolas told me he would take me to him—for a price."

"No need to sacrifice yourself to that lout. There's another way. I spoke with Madame Clavell, and her assumptions are the same—that Pierre has been incarcerated in the king's prison."

Lisette flinched at Madeleine's name. "What can we do?" She and Robert spoke nearly at the same time.

"I have a plan, and it involves both of you—if you are willing."

Robert did not hesitate. "Of course we are willing."

The commander looked at the delicate young woman shivering in the wet morning air.

"Anything. Pierre is dear to me. I am willing to do anything I can."

"It may be dangerous."

"All the better!" Robert pulled his sword out of the little-used sheath. "I have been bored with court life of late. I am ready for a little adventure."

"Methinks a courageous young man must be hiding under that persnickety court dandy." Commander Boveé grinned. "Put your sword away. You might hurt yourself."

"I have had the finest sword training available from King Louis' court." Robert returned his sword to its proper place.

The commander shook his head. "I do not think it will be that kind of danger. But you may be found out."

"What is your plan?" Lisette's soft voice calmed the moment.

"I need you, mademoiselle, to go to the Bastille and find out Pierre's cell number. The king is very generous in allowing visitors to prisoners. You need only to play the part of a jilted lover."

Lisette looked nervous, but she mustered a smile and said, "That won't be difficult."

"Yes, well . . . the guards will surely allow you to see him." Paul shifted his weight. "I will take you, but I do not think it would be wise to go in with you. My going to see my son would arouse suspicion."

"I'll do it. When will we go?"

"It's too late to go today. We shall ride to Paris first thing in the morning. Robert, bring her to the stables at dawn. Mademoiselle, you do ride?"

"Of course."

"Commander Boveé, I could take her to Paris."

"No. I do not want both of you missing from court at the same time. King Louis would notice."

Robert grumbled. "You're right, of course. He always notices when a courtier is missing." Robert's face registered his disappointment. "After you find out Pierre's cell number, then what?"

"Rumor in the soldiers' billets has it that the 'man in the iron mask' has been moved from the island of Saint-Marguerite to the Bastille for a few weeks. If we can locate Pierre, then perhaps we can ferret him out disguised as that unfortunate fellow."

"But that prisoner is under constant guard. I hear the assigned musketeers never let him out of their sight."

"We don't have to do anything about him. All we have to do is get Pierre out of his cell, disguise him as the man in the iron mask, and take him out. The famous prisoner does not always wear the iron mask. Sometimes they use a black velvet covering."

Robert scoffed. "All we have to do? What about the guards? How do we get into Pierre's cell?"

"Let me take care of that. We'll need some musketeer uniforms, but that's easy."

"Just the two of us?"

"I think it will be safer that way. Too many in on a secret mission only provides more opportunity for leak of information."

"You needn't worry about us, Commander Boveé." Lisette spoke for both of them.

"I still wish I were going with you in the morning." Robert's eagerness for excitement bubbled over in his voice.

"Patience, my boy. I promise there will be plenty of adventure for us all before we're through—more than enough."

TWENTY-SIX

"We have come for Madame Clavell's things."

Elise let the two gentleman servitors and an older female domestic into the dim light of the apartment. "Madame has not yet arisen."

"It is fine, Elise. I'm awake." Madeleine appeared at her bedroom door and pulled the sash of her robe tight. "I've not gathered my things together, but it will only take a few minutes. Come help with my toilette, please, and start packing my clothes."

The servant girl brought water in a golden-edged porcelain pitcher. "What gown would Madame wish to wear today?"

"My black silk."

"Black, madame?"

"Just to move to the new apartment." Black, dark, somber.

Madeleine's mood had plunged. She wondered if Louis would be moving her near Madame de Montespan's apartments.

A hazy recollection of François' face swam in and out of her thoughts. Focusing on his features only caused them to vanish into the mist of her memory—until she let the recollection sweep over her unbidden: his dark eyes when he gazed at her with love and passion; his slender hands; the unruly, straight hair that hung over his forehead, hiding the dragoon-inflicted scar.

Forgive me, François. You were so strong, and I am disgustingly weak. I sicken myself with my weakness, but I know no other way to save our children. She wiped the tears away from the edge of her eyelids.

Then the silent image of Pierre emerged in the background of her daydreams. Once again Madeleine's unspoken love for Pierre would remain undeclared. Where had he gone? Was Louis involved?

The servants bustled about the suite and had her belongings packed in no time. Madeleine upheld a cool exterior of control, but inside her stomach churned. She had expected Louis to send for her, but not so soon. She had not sent him her answer yet. As usual, Louis spoke his desires, and they came to be.

Agonizing over her family and Vangie's ill health, Madeleine vacillated between bringing her family to a place of safety versus her convictions as a Huguenot. Could she cling to both? She could still believe and be Catholic, couldn't she? The Mass had been comforting to her. Were *Sole Scriptura* and *Sole Fide* worth dying for and subjecting her family to any more suffering? Madeleine realized she was angry with God.

The servants left Madeleine behind in the empty room, taking all her belongings with them. She dropped into a chair and looked around the stiff, decorous room. Her soul felt empty. She would have to abandon the faith of her heritage to go to Louis. She would find the security she desperately wanted for her children—safety, shelter, luxury, provision, privilege, education—but not freedom. Her family had struggled all their lives, endured unbelievable suffering, to be able to worship God in freedom, and here she was, feeling she must sacrifice that freedom for security.

God, I am offended that you have allowed our family to go through all this heartache and misery. If you truly are our Father, then I . . . I don't think you are a very good papa. I am angry with you. I am angry with you! She paused, shocked at her own thoughts. *If misery and fear for our lives is what it means to be a Huguenot, I do not care to serve you as Huguenot anymore, or Catholic. I don't think I want to follow you at all. I'll go through the motions, but I am laying down any belief in you. I want my family to be safe, secure, and happy. You have not rescued us or kept us safe, and you took my husband from me.*

Sobbing uncontrollably, she clenched her fist toward heaven and shook it in the face of her Maker.

You took my husband from me, and now my Vangie is ill. If you are not going to take care of us, I will manage on my own. I don't trust you. Leave me be. Madeleine shook from the rage that surged through her veins. She raised a tearstained face to the gold paintings of cherubs on the ceilings and fell to her knees. *Just let us be.*

Eventually her sobs subsided. Madeleine rose and walked toward the king's chambers with the Swiss Guard following close behind.

ROBERT AND LISETTE MOVED SILENTLY THROUGH THE crisp dawn air. A slight yellow haze hung in the eastern sky, tingeing the chateau in increasing shimmers of gold. The dim figure of

Commander Boveé merged with that of two horses in a bizarre sil-
houette in front of the stables in the early morning light. The horses
pawed at the sticky, muddy ground.

Robert handed Lisette over to Commander Boveé, who immediately gave Lisette the reins and assisted her into the saddle astride a
rather large roan. "Can you handle him?"

"*Oui*, I can." With confidence Lisette took the reins and held out
her hand to Robert. "Go perform your court duties today. We don't
want the king to become suspicious."

Robert nodded, took her hand and kissed it, and turned toward
the commander. "When will you be back?"

"Two and a half hours each way, a couple of hours in Paris—
barring any complications. By nightfall, I hope."

"Lisette, I'll be eagerly awaiting word. Please send me a message
as soon as you return."

The pair turned and rode with the soft pinks of an early morning
sunrise coloring the horizon. Robert watched until they disappeared
from view.

MADELEINE STOOD IN THE MIDDLE OF THE ELEGANT
apartment and watched the assigned domestics unpack her belongings. A note rested on the vanity, nestled between a carved wooden
box holding a glass phial of lotion and a porcelain bottle of perfume,
and a small vase of orange liliums and carnations. She recognized
Louis' handwriting.

*I will send for you to attend appartement this evening. Then I shall
come to you later in the evening. Toi seule pour toujours. Louis.*

The inscription he had engraved on the poesy ring he gave her as a young girl. *You only, forever.* The ring she left at Versailles when they fled from Louis' wrath three years ago. Had he retrieved it?

He was introducing her rapidly to the court. They had already been seen dancing together at a ball. Now she would make an appearance at a gaming evening. Would Philippe be there? Of course, Louis would want Philippe to come.

The servants exited, all except Elise, and as they departed, Madeleine noticed that the Swiss Guard was no longer at his station outside her door. No longer needed. Clever. Now she was tethered with unseen chains.

COMMANDER BOVEÉ AND LISETTE RODE DOWN THE RUE Saint-Antoine and halted before the looming structure of the castle-prison. "I shall wait over there for you." He indicated a tavern, which appeared closed in the light of the midmorning.

Vendors and citizens of Paris bustled through the dirty streets, carrying baskets of wares. Beggars lurked near the doors of businesses, looking for a handout, or slept curled up in a dark alcove.

Commander Boveé dismounted and caught hold of the bridle of Lisette's horse. "Simply ride across the first bridge to the guard and tell him why you are there. Use your female charms to gain entrance, and then keep progressing over the bridges until you get inside. They should take you to Pierre's cell without any problem."

Lisette's delicate hands trembled on the reins.

"Can you do it?"

"*Oui,* I can."

"It would be expected that you would be frightened approaching the Bastille, so don't be concerned about that. But do keep your wits about you. Stay alert."

"I will." She took a deep breath. "I am ready."

"I'll await your return at the tavern. I will not leave."

"Very well." Lisette gripped the reins, steadied her hands, and urged her horse forward. "I hope to return with good news."

She rode toward the imposing structure and soon became dwarfed before the ominous eight towers. She turned and caught one last glance of Commander Boveé before she became lost in the mindless, wretched multitude moving into the prison.

It seemed that the maze through the outer courtyards and gatehouses went on forever. Finally she passed over the last drawbridge. Others rode or led their horses alongside her. At first she felt all eyes staring at her, but then it occurred to her that each person was walking in his or her own misery—unconcerned or even unaware of her. She was surprised to see the heavy, huge doors of the entrance standing open. A cluster of guards and musketeers milled about what seemed an official point of entry. She dismounted and led her horse to a short, slight musketeer with crooked teeth.

"Excuse me, monsieur." Her tremulous voice could barely be heard.

"Speak up, mademoiselle. What is your business at the king's prison today? Surely a beautiful lady such as yourself has not displeased his majesty." He leered at her and laughed.

Lisette blushed and spoke again, this time a bit louder. "I would like . . . A friend of mine has . . . has been taken prisoner and . . . I would like to see him."

"I'll bet he would like to see you as well." Again lecherous laughter. "Who is your 'friend'?"

"Monsieur Pierre Boveé."

The musketeer flipped through a large ledger of names. "Yes, he hasn't been here too long. A former courtier in the king's court. I see no instructions that he cannot have visitors." He pulled a ring of keys off his belt and turned to a guard standing nearby. "Escort Mademoiselle . . . ?"

"Lereau."

"Escort Mademoiselle Lereau to South Tower 110, Prisoner Boveé."

"Yes, sir. Right this way, mademoiselle."

Lisette took note and memorized the cell designation. Surprised at how easily she gained access to Pierre, she nonetheless shuddered as the dark interior of the prison closed in around her. She covered her nose against the stench of urine and mold. Men stared at her from their cells—some sitting at desks writing, some pacing, some napping.

They finally stopped in front of a fairly large cell door. Lisette's heart thudded so hard against her chest she thought she would faint.

The guard unlocked the door and ushered her inside the cell. "You have company, Monsieur Boveé. And lovely company it is."

Pierre leapt up from his bed, fully dressed, his eyes wide with anticipation. "Lisette!" He rushed to her and smothered her in his arms. "How did you find me? How did you know where I was? How did you get here?"

Lisette buried her head in his chest and began to cry.

The hinges creaked as the guard closed the cell door. "I shall come back and check on you in a half hour or so. That should give you enough time." He chuckled as he jangled the key in the lock and left. His steps echoed on the stone walkway and down the stairs.

"Come, sit down." Pierre led Lisette to a chair. Leftovers from breakfast remained on the table. "Are you hungry?" He handed her his handkerchief, and she wiped her eyes.

"Thirsty. Do you have anything to drink?"

"I have some wine left from dinner last night." He walked to one of the outcroppings in the stone wall and pulled down a flask.

She took a drink, coughed, and handed it back to Pierre. "So, what we hear of the king's prison is true. This is not your typical dreary dungeon."

"True. Aside from the fact that one is not free, it is tolerable. Would you like some bread? There is butter and jam."

She took the bread from him, but simply held it in one hand and caressed his cheek with the other. "Are you disappointed that I'm not Madame Clavell?"

"What?" He took her hand from his face and kissed it.

"Are you glad it is I? Would you have been happier if it were Madame Clavell who had come to see you?"

"Lisette, please . . . I am elated to see you. How did you get here? You didn't come by yourself, did you?"

"*Non*, your father rode with me."

"My father? You jest!"

"I do not. Robert wanted to come, but your father would not allow him. He was concerned that if Robert were not in court today, it would arouse suspicion. We have a plan to get you out."

Lisette related Commander Bovee's intention to disguise Pierre as the man in the iron mask and make an escape.

"I heard he was here. That sounds plausible, but how do we get me out of this cell?"

"That I do not know, but I am certain your father has thought all this out." Lisette brought her face close to Pierre's. "Do you miss me?"

She could feel his breath quicken. She held her face up to his, waiting for him to kiss her. "I've missed you. Oh, how I've missed you. Hold me, Pierre. Please hold me." She dropped the forgotten bread on the stone floor of the cell, and a rat darted away with it.

Pierre gathered the delicate young woman in his arms. The familiarity of his body aroused old emotions in Lisette. Surely he still cared for her.

She clung to him and began to shower his face with kisses. "I love you so much, Pierre. Please, please love me." Her hands began to explore his body.

Groaning, he pushed her away from him. "*Non*, Lisette. I cannot. Not that I'm not tempted. You are so beautiful, and I do care for you . . ."

"*Care* for me." Lisette pulled out of his arms. "Care for me, but love Madame Clavell."

"I will not lie to you. That is true. But it is also true that I care for you more than ever before."

"I don't want your 'caring'!" Lisette almost shouted. "I want your undying devotion. I want you to find me irresistible. I want you to adore me. I want your love."

The rattling of keys sounded down the tunnel.

"Shhh! Kiss me." He pulled her into his arms and began to kiss her passionately. She surrendered willingly to him.

A guard hurried to the cell door, then began to chortle. Pierre continued to hold Lisette in his embrace, but turned his face to the guard. "Simply a lovers' quarrel."

"Get on with it. You haven't much time."

"Yes, we would be glad to, if you would be so generous as to give us some privacy."

The guard leaned against the wall next to the cell door and continued to chuckle.

Pierre pleaded with him, "Please, sir, for the lady's sake."

Lisette sniffled.

The guard picked up his musket, which he had leaned against the stone wall, and twirled the keys. "Very well. I'll be back shortly. Enjoy yourself." He took one more look at the two and whistled as he left.

Lisette wiped her tears again with Pierre's handkerchief. "I apologize for my anger, but not for what I said. I meant it. I love you, and I want to be yours. Yours are the only arms where I feel I belong." She hesitated. "Your Madame Clavell has agreed to be the king's mistress."

"She would not!"

"She has. That is the court gossip."

"I do not believe it. You are just jealous. If it appears that she has become the king's mistress, there is something else behind it. I am certain."

Lisette began to cry uncontrollably, barely able to talk. "I . . . I am puzzled by your change of behavior—this standard of piety that you seem determined to uphold. On the one hand, I do not like it." She wiped her nose. "But on the other, there is something about you now that . . . that is strong. Something that is admirable."

Pierre looked at her and smoothed her hair. "Here, take your cape off. We need to at least appear to have . . . gotten comfortable." He helped her remove her outer garment and noticed the cameo necklace. He touched it lightly, then took both her hands. "I am sorry for the pain that I have caused you. Please forgive me." He kissed her hands.

Lisette began to cry again.

"Please don't." He wiped her flushed cheeks with his thumb. "I need you to be strong. I know you can do this. Tell my father that the best time to come for me would be when they bring the evening meal. There aren't as many guards then, as they are shutting down for the night. They leave the door ajar as the servants come in and out with the food. I've thought of attempting an escape then, but had no one to help me."

She nodded and sniffled. "What time do they bring your meal?"

"Usually around seven o'clock. Did my father say when he was planning this?"

"No, but I am certain it will be soon. How many servants bring the food?"

"Two usually. Sometimes only one."

"I'm sure Robert will come with your father."

"My faithful friend, Robert."

Approaching footsteps alerted Pierre and Lisette that the guard was returning. They hurried back to the bed and sat down. Pierre put his arm around the delicate shoulders of his onetime lover. "Pretend you are crying."

"I won't have to pretend very hard." She dabbled at her eyes once again.

The guard jammed the key into the lock of the cell door and slammed it open. "Time to go, mademoiselle."

The pair stood, and Pierre draped Lisette's cape around her shoulders. She flung herself into his arms. "Oh, Pierre, I love you so." He kissed her cheeks.

"How touching. Come, mademoiselle."

"Allow me, please, monsieur." Pierre walked Lisette to the door.

"That's far enough. I'll take her from here."

Pierre stopped and gave her another hug. "You'll come again soon? And bring Robert next time?"

"Of course. Expect us before long."

TWENTY-SEVEN

Lisette rode out of the prison into the sunlight toward the tavern. Commander Boveé strode out of the front door. "Here, let me take your horse." Paul assisted Lisette off the horse, took the reins, and tied the roan to a hitching rail. "Come on inside. Did you see Pierre?"

Lisette nodded. "Yes, and he is well." They walked into the dim interior of the tavern. All of the tables were empty, except the one where Commander Boveé's glass of ale sat. "He is in the South Tower, number 110."

"Excellent! Good work, my dear."

Lisette relayed the details of her visit and conversation with Pierre, and his instructions. "It appears that it may be simple to get Pierre out."

"The actual escape may seem to be simple, but nothing is easy when it comes to King Louis. He is clever, and he is tenacious. And he never gives up pursuing those who have opposed him. Come, we ride for home."

COMMANDER BOVEÉ DISMOUNTED AND HELPED LISETTE off her horse. "Get back to the chateau right away, and make sure you arrive at your assigned duties tonight on time. I have some investigating to do."

He gave the horses to a stableboy and strode through the soldiers' billets. Most of the men were at the evening meal or away on assignment, but none of those few loitering in the quarters greeted him, and he spoke to no one. A more intimidating figure would be hard to come by, and Paul Boveé enjoyed exploiting that aura. He came to the musketeer section and scanned the area. It appeared to be empty. That was good, but it also meant that two musketeer uniforms, especially hats, might not be easy to locate. Both Paul and Robert were tall. They could get by with their own breeches and boots, but they needed the blue musketeer tunics and hats. The commander found one tunic lying on the floor beside a bunk. He held it up to his shoulders. It would do. He stuffed it under his jacket.

"Ho, there!" A burly, tall musketeer came through a door on the side. "What is a dragoon doing in musketeer quarters?"

Paul whirled around. "I am Commander Boveé, looking for Captain Maisson. Do you know where I can find him?"

"He quarters in town, but he's been on assignment in Paris—the Bastille."

"*Ahhh, merci.*" Paul turned to leave.

"Commander."

"Yes?"

"You dropped this."

Paul's heart raced. The musketeer picked Paul's glove up off the ground.

"Thank you." He slapped the glove against his thigh. "Can't seem to keep this one secure." He tucked it into his belt.

"Know what you mean. I have the same problem." The musketeer sat on his bunk. He looked around. "Now, where is—?"

"Thank you again for the information. *Au revoir.*"

"Uh . . . you're welcome."

Commander Boveé hurried out the same door the musketeer had entered as the soldier lifted up his blanket to search under his bunk. But before exiting, the dragoon officer made note of the bunks around the doorway.

Paul smiled and walked to his quarters. He pulled the musketeer's blue tunic out from his jacket, folded it, and stored it in his trunk. One tunic down, one more tunic and two hats to go.

DENIS GREER OFFERED MADELEINE HIS ARM, AND THEY proceeded to the Diana Drawing Room. "I have the privilege of being the assigned mentor for your son. Fine young man."

Madeleine looked at the debonair courtier. He sported the coveted blue justacorps a brevet that only royalty and a few select courtiers were privileged to wear. He appeared to be mature and stable, unlike many of the flighty younger men in court.

"Yes, Philippe is a fine young man. Rather naïve in the ways of court. We've . . . we have been away for some time. But he learns quickly."

"I am fast becoming aware of that. You have robbed us of feasting upon your beauty by your absence. May I compliment you on your exquisite gown?"

"Thank you. You are very kind." Madeleine had chosen the ecru gown, and it provided a striking contrast to her dark coloring. She liked the garment more than she had expected. Her pearls accented the neckline perfectly.

"What has kept you from the court?"

"We've been living out of the country."

"I see."

"We have relatives in Spain. *Clavell* is actually a Spanish derivative meaning carnation." Madeleine threw out the evasive comment on purpose.

Walking through the Drawing Room of Plenty, she plucked a pear from the lavish pyramid of delicacies and bit into it. It was sweet and juicy. The rich, sultry colors of the larger-than-life paintings seemed to spill over the edge of the ceiling into the room. Peals of laughter and approving cheers punctuated the air.

Denis led her to the platform in the Diana Drawing Room, where the ladies of the court watched Louis play his excellent game of billiards. Every good shot resulted in applause and murmurs of admiration. Madeleine searched the room for Philippe and saw him standing against the far wall with other young courtiers. The others bantered back and forth with each other, but Philippe stood apart and watched the gaming. When he saw her enter with Monsieur Greer, his face broke into a wide smile. She longed to go to him and wrap him in her arms, but she simply smiled.

Athénaïs sat on an ornate, carved chair in the front, applauding the king. Madeleine took a second look at the king's official mistress.

The beautiful Madame de Montespan had grown heavy. A stout ankle peeked from underneath the lace of her skirt. Her blonde hair, still luxurious and shiny in the newly fashionable, towering *fontange*, nevertheless framed chubby cheeks. No wonder the king's eye had begun to wander.

Madeleine chose a seat near the back, to the side, behind Madame de Montespan. Louis glanced up as she came in and smiled. Athénaïs nodded at him and opened her fan.

She thinks the acknowledgment is for her. But Louis looked directly into Madeleine's eyes and then returned to his game.

Madeleine turned and noticed the dour Colbert enter at the far end of the room. He went to Louis' side and whispered in the king's ear. Louis put his cue down and clapped his chief administrator on the back. He laughed and picked up his walking stick, and the pair exited together.

The din in the room subsided as the courtiers and ladies of the court bowed and curtsied in the wake of the king's exit. Then the laughter and noise of the raucous crowd resumed. Madeleine stepped off the platform and made her way to Philippe. He walked quickly to her side, and they embraced.

"Mère, are you faring well?"

"Exactly my question to you." She stroked his cheek. "*Oui*, I am well."

"As am I . . . aside from this blasted cravate." He chuckled. "Where did the king go?"

"You will get used to it—the cravate. Since it was Colbert who came and got him, I would suppose that a pressing matter of state came up."

"I see. Well, I don't want to get used to it. I want to get out of here. I hate Versailles."

"I know, son. But . . . I received a letter yesterday from Uncle Jean."

"What did he say?"

Madeleine looked at her son. "Come out here." She led her son back into the Drawing Room of Plenty.

"What's wrong?" Philippe followed Madeleine through the crowd. The men jostled around them, cheering on one of the older courtiers for his good billiards shot.

She nodded to Monsieur Greer on the way. "Allow us to go somewhere quieter to chat." She smiled and cocked her head, flirting with him. He nodded and returned to his conversation with his colleagues. "Monsieur Greer will be a good mentor."

"I like him."

"I am pleased with that." They moved to a corner of the room away from the tables groaning under the heavy platters of food. "Philippe, Vangie is ill."

The big brother's eyes widened. "What's wrong? She's going to get better, isn't she? We must go to her."

"They are going to come to us."

"What do you mean?" Philippe searched his mother's eyes to comprehend her meaning. "I don't understand."

"It means, Son, that as your mother, I may have to put myself in a position that I would not voluntarily choose. It means that . . . that I may have to die to myself in order to give my children life."

Philippe stared at Madeleine for what seemed to be eternal moments. Finally he spoke, his voice hoarse. "You are succumbing to the king's demands?" He shook his head and walked away. When he turned back, tears brimmed on his lower lashes. "There has to be another way. Papa wouldn't—"

"No, Papa wouldn't, but Papa is gone. And I'm only a woman. I have to use what advantage I have as a woman." She reached up and took her son by his shoulders. "Please understand, my son, it's the only way. Louis has agreed to provide for us with no fear of reprisal. He will summon his physicians to take care of Vangie. What else can I do?"

"But, Maman, how can you . . . ?" The unfinished sentence spoke more clearly than anything Philippe could have said. *How could you go into the arms of the king? How could you allow yourself to be known as one of the king's mistresses? How could you bed with him?*

"Queen Esther allowed herself to be placed in the harem of a pagan king in order to save her people. Am I doing anything different? War and peace ride on the waves of the whims of the king. Our destiny does no less."

Philippe snapped at his mother, "You are not Queen Esther, and we are not the Jewish people. What about Uncle Jean? And Henri and Claudine? Will they come too?"

"Uncle Jean can live peaceably in Switzerland without us. Henri can as well. Perhaps Claudine will come to stay with Vangie. I don't know all the details yet, Philippe. I simply had to do something."

"And Pierre?"

"I . . . I don't know. I fear for him, because of his involvement with us."

Madeleine pulled her son into her arms and embraced him once again. "I must go now. Our apartments must be close together since we are both adjacent to the king's bedchambers. Will you walk me back?"

Philippe nodded. "Let me go tell Monsieur Greer."

"But, *non!*" The proper courtier would not hear of their returning to their apartments unescorted. He got between the two and made small talk as they made their way through the maze of Versailles to their quarters.

Madeleine indeed had been set up close to Philippe, but closer to the king's bedchamber than her son.

He clung to her as she gave him a good-night kiss. "Maman." He pulled back and searched her eyes.

"I'll be fine, son. Good night." She turned and went into her elegant bedchamber.

She removed her new gown and put on her nightclothes. Elise hung the gown in an enormous, ornately carved armoire along with her others. She set the matching shoes underneath the corresponding garments. Madeleine liked the maid's efficiency and organization.

"Help me get the pins out of my hair, please. Then you may go."

Elise quickly removed the pearl hairpins from the towering hairstyle.

"Thank you. It's been a long day. You may retire now."

Madeleine sat in front of the large vanity and brushed her hair. She took the fashionable black velvet stars from her forehead and breast and placed them in the wooden box. What should she do now? Wait for Louis? Go on to bed and go to sleep?

She picked a carnation out of the vase and sniffed the subtle, spicy-sweet scent—not overbearing like the tuberous roses Louis preferred. The heady fragrance of the roses hovered over Versailles all summer long and even sickened some. She returned the carnation to the vase, placed it on the table beside her bed, then she lay down and sank into the luxurious pillows. She looked up at the pleated canopy and then at the heavy brocade hangings around the bed. Not a cold, dank cell in the Bastille, as Pierre must be enduring, but every bit as confining. Perhaps more so.

TWENTY-EIGHT

That night a brilliant full moon showered an incandescent glimmer over the landscape. Early in the morning hours, a tall figure opened the side door of the musketeers' quarters. The bottom of the door scraped against the floor. Commander Boveé held his breath. One man turned over in his bunk. The others continued to snore. Paul left the door cracked open enough to allow the moonlight to usher in a ghostly glow.

He saw what he had hoped would be there—several musketeer hats dangling on the ends of the bunks. He slunk past the slumbering men and lifted two hats from the bedposts. Feeling his way along the floor at the end of the bunks with his foot, he found another tunic on the other side of the room. He inched toward the door and hit a beer stein with his foot. It went clattering across the room. A musketeer sat up and looked around. Paul squatted down behind the bunk of a soldier lifting the roof with his snoring.

The awakened musketeer noticed the open door, got up, and clanged the latch shut. Another soldier sat up. "What's going on?"

"Nothing. The door was open. Go back to sleep."

Both lay back down and in short order were snoring once again. Paul groaned. Now he would have to get out of the quarters by traversing the entire length of the room. He could not risk opening the side door again. After allowing several minutes to pass, he started down the aisle separating the bunks. Men stirred in their beds with each step he took.

Aha! He had an idea. He put on the tunic and hat and began to walk back to the side door. If anyone heard him, they would think he was one of them. He would think of something to say.

He lifted the latch, but the hardware caught on a bolt. He pulled it back toward himself, and it came free, but it clanged again as it did when the musketeer locked it earlier. The same musketeer sat up.

"Who goes there?"

Paul whispered, disguising his voice in a guttural tone, "Go back to sleep, my friend. Simply a rendezvous with a beautiful lady."

The musketeer laughed. "Must be a married one to meet this late at night. See that you latch the door when you go out."

Paul laughed. "Yes, to be sure." He exited and leaned against the outside of the door—and wiped the sweat off his brow.

MADELEINE ROLLED OVER AND HIT THE NIGHTSTAND WITH her hand. She sat up, not knowing for a moment where she was. She had fallen asleep on top of the covers. She was alone. Relief swept over her. She lay back down on the bed, curled up, and pulled the coverlet over her.

But why had Louis not come? The information that Colbert brought to him must have necessitated his being called away. He had seemed pleased. It must have been good news.

She dozed off and on until the sun forced its orange rays through the slits in the shutters. She sat up and looked around her new quarters at the numerous paintings, among them several of Louis himself. She smiled at the king's need to have his image at every turn in Versailles. She stretched and threw the covers back. Walking to the door of her bedroom, she traced her fingers along the gold carved moldings along the walls.

"Elise!" She could hear the young servant girl scurrying through the anteroom, dishes clanking.

"Madame." Elise entered with a tray of brioche, jam, cheese, wine, and hot chocolate. A note lay tucked underneath the plate.

"Thank you, Elise. You may prepare my toilette. I'll wear the green silk today."

"*Oui*, madame." The servant put the tray on the vanity and began to sort through the armoire.

Madeleine picked up the envelope and looked at it. There was no name on the outside. She slid her finger underneath the seal.

Dearest Madeleine,

The business of politics many times interferes with the pleasantries and passions of life. Spain has acquiesced and agreed to sign the Nijmegen Peace Treaty! We have had to dispense emissaries to Holland, and it took all night to set things in place. We are just this morning finishing up the details. I am elated, but it requires that I be away from you for a few more hours. Nothing shall keep me from your arms any longer than necessary. Toi seule pour toujours.

Louis

She picked up a piece of bread and lathered it with jam. The chocolate had gotten cold, but she poured a cupful from the chocolate pot and drank it anyway, pacing between the window and her bed. She finished the chocolate and put the cup back on the tray.

"Come, help me with my hair, please." Madeleine sat on the edge of the bed and then stood. "You may take the tray. I am finished." She opened her jewelry chest, which she'd placed on the floor beside her bed. Her favorite pearls lay on top. She reached underneath them and pulled out an emerald and diamond pendant and earrings to match. She opened the drawers in the vanity, intending to store the precious gems within them.

Elise returned just then, ready to help Madeleine with her hair. Madeleine handed the pearls to her servant. "Fasten these, please, Elise." The unpacking of the rest of the jewelry could wait.

MADELEINE EXITED HER APARTMENT, HOPING TO SEE Philippe in the hallway on his way to Mass. The Swiss Guard once again stood on duty in front of her door. Louis didn't trust her while he was away.

Nearing the chapel, she sighted Philippe with Monsieur Greer. Philippe's face appeared flushed. He broke into a grin upon seeing his mother, but his eyes held questions. He pushed through the multitude of worshippers to her.

"Mère, fencing is fun! Monsieur Greer is an expert instructor."

"I'm glad you are enjoying it." She brushed his hair out of his eyes. "Join me at Mass?"

He glanced over at Denis, who nodded his approval. Madeleine took her son's arm and fell in with the others. Denis Greer made it a trio. As the courtier joined them, the Swiss Guard backed off and lingered on the edge of the throng.

After Mass, Monsieur Greer never offered Madeleine and Philippe the opportunity for private conversation. Perhaps Philippe would be clever enough to catch veiled comments.

"Louis has been called away."

Denis answered her, "Yes. I hear that there is reason to be hopeful regarding the political situation with Spain."

"Word travels fast. I had a note from Louis this morning explaining his absence last night."

A slight flicker of understanding passed through Philippe's eyes. "When do you think he will return?"

Denis again. "It is hard to say. Negotiations sometimes take weeks." A fellow courtier clapped Denis on the back, diverting his attention.

"Maman, are you sure this is what you need to do? Is this the only way for us to survive?" They walked on ahead of Monsieur Greer.

"There is no other way."

"Well? What did you find out?" Robert and Lisette walked into the gardens after Mass apart from their usual gathering of colleagues. They walked toward the Water Parterre and then down the steps to the Latona Fountain.

"Pierre is well. They allowed me to see him. We know exactly where his cell is."

"That is great news." Robert's excitement bubbled over into his voice, and he laughed. "When does Commander Boveé intend to move?"

"Right away, I think. He fears that they will move him to a more remote facility, less accessible, if we don't get him out now."

"I agree."

"He said to tell you that he will let you know within a few days."

"That's wonderful. I'm ready." Robert kissed Lisette's hand and started to take his leave, but she held on to his hand. "Please be careful. I don't think . . . I don't know that I shall ever see Pierre again."

"What do you mean?"

"Surely you have suspected. He is in love with Madeleine Clavell. He will not ever come to me again." She shook her head and covered her mouth with her fan.

"But I hear that the king is prepared to announce that Madame Clavell is his new maîstresse en titre."

Lisette looked back up at Robert. "*Vraiment?* Are you sure? She has agreed to that?"

"That's the court gossip. She has been set up in one of the royal apartments."

"So I guess Pierre's lily-white Madeleine is not so lily-white anymore."

"You sound bitter. I see hurt obscuring those beautiful green eyes." Robert took Lisette's chin in his hand and kissed her on the cheek. "This is much too pretty a face to be creased with a frown and hardened with bitterness."

Lisette took Robert's hand in her own and stood on tiptoe to kiss him softly on the lips. "Faithful Robert. A friend to the end. Why has some young damsel never captured your heart?"

He laughed. "I'd rather have several young damsels at my beck and call. When one goes, I have another. I never want for someone to warm my bed at night."

"Do you never long for that one someone special to share your life with? Someone who would be with you forever and always, through every joy and adversity?" She stopped and smiled at him. "You are not getting any younger, you know. Don't you want a family?"

"Someday, maybe. But the kind of love you are talking about is not reality. That is a giddy young girl's idyllic dream. It doesn't happen in real life."

"I think it can happen."

"For you? With Pierre?"

Lisette shook her head. "I used to think it would be with Pierre. Now I know that is not possible, but I hope with someone, someday." She looked up at the tall, handsome man who loved Pierre as much as she did. For a moment she thought she detected a release of the courtier façade—a softening, a vulnerability. He looked like a little boy who needed reassurance. Then it was gone.

"Hold on to your dream, sweet lady. Maybe your knight in shining armor will show up one of these days. I am grieved that my dearest friend and brother will never be part of our lives again. But aside from that, I'm happy with my life the way it is."

Robert kissed her hand once more, and Lisette watched him walk away from her to join his court colleagues. Something about him stirred her sympathies.

He is pathetically alone, and he isn't aware of it. He believes he has the best of life, but in reality he is adrift—especially now with the certainty that Pierre will never return to Versailles. At least Lisette had family in Orleans. Robert had no one.

She walked back up the steps to the Water Parterre and noticed Madeleine Clavell and her son standing with Denis Greer beside the pond. The water was still today. No breeze at all. She started to turn and go the other way, but then changed her mind and walked toward the Clavells.

"*Bonjour*, Madame Clavell."

Madeleine looked at the young woman and seemed not to recognize her at first. Then she smiled. "*Bonjour!* Mademoiselle Lereau, is it not?"

"*Oui*, madame."

"Of course. We danced the menuet together one night at a ball. You were a most charming instructor for my son."

"Yes, the pleasure was mine entirely."

Philippe stepped forward and kissed Lisette's hand. "I am glad to see you again, Mademoiselle Lereau."

"As I am to see you."

Denis Greer bowed and acknowledged Lisette's presence. Looking to the Swiss Guard lurking nearby, Denis excused himself. "If you ladies will forgive me, I must take leave of you, although it pains me to have to abandon such exquisite company. I have business to take care of inside the chateau. Philippe, meet me at two o'clock in the Courtiers' Drawing Room."

"Yes, monsieur."

The courtier bowed and walked toward the chateau.

Lisette looked down and fumbled with her handkerchief. "I have news of Pierre."

Madeleine gasped. "Is he well? Where is he?"

Lisette looked at the woman who had stolen her lover's heart. "He is well. I saw him yesterday. He is in the Bastille."

"I guessed as much. The king is very angry with him."

"Yes." Lisette remained silent for a moment. "Is . . . is the king angry with him, because . . . because of . . . ?"

Madeleine sighed. "Me? I am afraid so."

"But now that you are . . ."

"The king's mistress?"

"*Oui*. Is that true?"

"I have been moved into the royal quarters, but this is more involved than simply being favored by the king. It involves my son and my deceased husband and my childhood friendship with Louis."

"Pierre said there would be more to the story."

"Pierre knows?" Madeleine turned away and then back again to face Lisette. "I did not want him to know."

"He knows, but he refuses to believe it."

"Dear Pierre. I . . ."

"Are you in love with him?" Lisette waited for Madeleine to reply, already knowing the answer, as did Philippe. Madeleine gazed at Lisette, but did not respond.

The young courtesan nodded. "You may not speak the words, but your eyes shout your answer." Lisette looked down and fidgeted with her handkerchief. "There is a plan afoot to break him out of the Bastille—soon."

"Who—how?"

"Commander Boveé and Robert."

Madeleine placed her hand over Lisette's. "Perhaps you and Pierre will be able to be together, to love each other."

Lisette pulled her hand away. "Pierre does not love me. He told me so. And I do not think I will ever see him again. He has been torn away from me by the cruelest of fates." She nodded slightly to Madeleine, then turned and walked away from the Clavells into the chateau.

TWENTY-NINE

Madeleine watched the slight figure of the young girl disappear into the throng of diplomats and cast of court players. That's what they were—all of them—a cast of players, acting out a role on the stage of Versailles. The only difference being that at the end of the play, they did not get to put on their own clothes and go home. They were playing dangerous roles for eternal destinies.

"Come, Philippe. Let us go to the dining hall to eat, and we shall make plans." Madeleine glanced over at the Swiss Guard, always ready, never appearing as if he were watching them, but she knew better. They started toward the communal dining hall, and Madeleine took her son's arm. "You will make a fine courtier, and one whom the ladies will seek out."

"The life of a courtier is . . . is shallow. Although I must say that I am enjoying learning some different things, like fencing and dancing."

"You are doing well. I am proud of you."

They entered the noisy communal kitchen and found a place to sit. The smoky, rich fragrance of *pot-a-oie* surrounded them as they helped themselves to platters of the succulent stuffed goose. "Only take the stuffing. The servants get the carcass."

Philippe nodded and took a hearty helping. Bowls of herb and pigeon soup sat on the table. Marzipan biscuits and jam rested in baskets at every hand. Madeleine looked at the plates of salads of marinated asparagus and cucumbers, and greens with vinegar dressing, alongside saltcellars. She took her deep plate, spooned up some soup, and watched Philippe eat with relish. She only toyed with her food.

"You are not eating." Philippe paused in midair, spreading jam on his biscuit.

"I'm not very hungry." She looked across the table. Lisette sat with Robert directly opposite of her at the next table. She stared at Madeleine, then lowered her eyes.

Madeleine studied Lisette's face. She reminded Madeleine of herself when she was a young woman at court—not in physical appearance, but in her hopes and dreams. Madeleine's heart went out to her, knowing that those dreams would turn to ashes.

Such a beautiful girl. I am sorry your heart has been broken. I'm so sorry.

LISETTE WATCHED MADELEINE CLAVELL AND HER SON at the next table.

Robert nudged her elbow. "What is going on in that exquisitely gorgeous head of yours?"

"It is all her fault."

"What? What are you talking about? Whose fault—for what?"

"Hers." She nodded toward Madeleine. "If Pierre had not gotten involved with the Clavells, he would be here with me now, not in the Bastille. He would still be in love . . . with me." She choked back a sob.

"You cannot think like that, chérie. What will be, will be. There are plenty of other handsome courtiers to choose from." He swept his hand around in a circle at the room full of dashing young men, ending by pointing at himself. "For example, *moi!*"

She wiped her eyes. "Oh, stop it, Robert. You would be the last one I would choose."

"Why is that? Am I not handsome enough, suave enough, debonair enough, brave enough to capture your heart?" He gestured with his hands and took his hat off.

"To be sure, you are all of those, but . . . I don't know. You have always been such a good friend, to me and Pierre. Someone to laugh and joke with. You are never serious."

"I'm serious now." He leaned toward her and looked directly at her. His clear blue eyes penetrated hers.

Lisette cocked her head and wrinkled up her brow. "What do you mean?"

"I mean that I was not completely honest with you—about finding someone to whom I could join my life. I think you are probably right. As you and Pierre have both reminded me recently, I am not getting any younger." He sat back in his chair. "Lisette, I have always been fond of you."

Lisette giggled and shook her head. "Why, Robert, are you proposing to me?"

"*Non!* Simply suggesting that we start doing things together and see how it works out."

"My friend, you are sweet, and you are kind. But I don't want somebody who is just fond of me. I want to fall madly, passionately in love with someone, and he with me."

"The way you feel about Pierre?"

"*Oui.*" Her voice could barely be heard above the din of the dinner crowd.

He leaned toward her again. "What if I said that I felt that way about you, but had hidden it all these years because of my good friend?" Robert's devil-may-care attitude slipped off him like a cloak, and he appeared to be more serious than Lisette had ever seen him.

"I-I'd say you were a liar. I'd say the gay Robert was simply trying to cheer me up."

"Perhaps the Robert you think you know is not the real Robert." He drew close to her face and touched her cheek with his fingers. "At least give me a chance."

She removed his hand from her face. "St-stop. You are confusing me. Don't talk to me of love. I still—"

"Ah, yes! You still love Pierre." Robert returned to his courtier character. "I do not blame you. He is a sterling fellow, that Pierre. The best man I ever knew—far better than myself." He stood. "Now, if you will excuse me. I have affairs of court to take care of." He put his hat back on. "*Au revoir.* I shall see you soon. At the ball tonight?"

"Robert—"

"Ah, there is Commander Boveé. Just the man I want to see." He bowed, turned on his heels, and wove his way through the tables to the dragoon officer.

MADELEINE ROSE FROM THE TABLE. SHE HAD OBSERVED Robert making his way through the servants with their platters and tureens of food and the chattering courtiers and ladies to Commander Boveé, who stood at the edge of the room. Their heads bowed down and leaning toward each other, they appeared deep in conversation.

"Come, Philippe. I want to see what this is about."

Approaching them, Madeleine snapped her fan and waited for their acknowledgment. They both bowed.

"Madame Clavell. How nice to see you again." Robert turned on the charm.

"Yes, indeed." Commander Boveé's less-than-enthusiastic response did not escape Madeleine. "You seem to have a rather persistent companion."

"Philippe?"

The commander nodded toward the Swiss Guard who had expertly inched his way along the wall, keeping Madeleine in his sights.

"Yes, however, he is really very unobtrusive. I forget he is even there."

"Don't underestimate him. They are highly trained and skilled—and completely loyal to the king."

"Well, there is nothing I can do about that, is there?"

"No, I suppose not—not at this moment anyway."

"Lisette tells me that you have a plan to break Pierre out of the Bastille."

Robert lowered his voice and looked around. "That is not exactly for public knowledge."

"That needn't be any concern of yours." Commander Boveé's eyes glinted through his steely exterior.

Philippe stepped up and took his mother's arm. She patted his hand.

"Commander Boveé, I feel responsible for your son's misfortune. It is because of his involvement with our family that he has become the object of Louis' wrath. I am truly sorry. He is . . . he . . ." Madeleine could not finish her sentence.

"He is . . . what, Madame Clavell? What *is* he to you? Why does it matter to you what happens to my son?"

Madeleine paused for several seconds, fluttering her fan. "This is not easy for me." She looked at the two men and her son waiting for her to continue, then back at Commander Boveé directly.

"Go on."

"As Pierre became more deeply involved with our family, feelings began to develop between the two of us." She glanced at Philippe, who averted his eyes. "However, I loved my husband and was committed to him. The affection that developed between Pierre and myself has never been acted upon. He has been a gallant gentleman."

Robert chortled.

"I . . . if . . . if things had turned out differently . . ."

"Has my son expressed how he feels to you?"

Madeleine lowered her head and nodded.

"Do you feel the same about him?"

"I think he knows." She raised her head. "But my feelings and Pierre's are not the issue, are they? Pierre is imprisoned at the Bastille, and I am equally imprisoned in the king's quarters here at Versailles. Do you indeed have a plan to rescue him?"

"We do, but . . ." Paul hesitated. "But I think it best you not know the details. Protection for both of us."

"I understand. When?"

"Soon."

"Very well. I pray Godspeed on your venture—for your safety, and Pierre's as well." Madeleine turned to leave, but then faced Commander Boveé again. "You know Pierre cannot return to Versailles. He may not even be able to remain in France."

"I am aware of that. We will deal with that unfortunate issue later."

KING LOUIS FINISHED SIGNING THE PAPERS AND SHOVED them across his desk to Colbert. "Is that the last of them?"

"*Oui*, Your Majesty. I will have these packed with your things. We can leave this afternoon."

"Tomorrow will be soon enough." Louis stood and stretched. "I am very tired. I need a good night's rest." He smiled. "I have plans for this evening after the ball."

"But, Your Majesty, surely the Peace Treaty is more important than—"

The king raised his voice an ominous notch. "I will decide what is important. Besides, we need more time to gather the court staff properly." He walked to the front of his desk and leaned against it. "Do we have the Dutch newspapers?"

"*Oui*, Your Majesty."

"Proceed."

The minister began to drone through the news from the Netherlands—nothing in it yet regarding the peace treaty with Spain. Louis walked to the window and looked out on the gardens. He spotted Madeleine walking down the South Parterre, alone but for the Swiss Guard to the side and behind her.

You will not have to walk alone much longer, cherie. You will be in your place officially at court, where you should have been all along. You will have official recognition and the entourage of the court. Finally, you will be by my side.

Madeleine looked up at the windows of the State Cabinet room and saw Louis standing at the window. She nodded and curtsied. He acknowledged her greeting with the slightest dip of his head.

"Sire?" The minister paused in his reading.

"I'm listening. Continue." Louis left the window and sat down at his desk. He turned his attention to the affairs of state and put affairs of the heart out of his head. He was, after all, the mighty Sun King of France.

THIRTY

Two musketeers stood on the Rue Saint-Antoine, holding the reins of their horses. The larger steed, a dappled Boulonnais, shook his head and pawed at the cobblestones. The other, a gray Breton, nuzzled his master's hand. The larger of the two men also held the reins of a black Percheron. He spoke. "It is time. Mount up."

The pair got on their horses and rode across the bridges toward the entrance of the Bastille.

Commander Boveé pointed to one of the imposing towers. "That is the South Tower."

Robert nodded, his usual flippant demeanor subdued. He touched the black velvet mask hidden in the pocket of the "borrowed" musketeer tunic.

They tipped their hats to the guards, who paid little attention to them, and hitched the horses to a rail in the central holding area. Barred windows lined the walls between looming, arched pillars. The two walked into the bowels of the prison, keeping their heads down but nodding at the other soldiers as they made their way to the South Tower. The smoky odor of roasted meat mingled with the ever-constant musty odor of the prison.

Paul stopped at a fork in the passageway. "What do you think? Which way?"

Robert shrugged his shoulders. "I do not know, but we had better hurry. They must be about ready to bring food to the prisoners. I can smell it."

Commander Boveé looked around and saw a prison kitchen attendant walking their way, carrying a basket of bread. "We have a prisoner transfer to make—number 110, South Tower?"

The man balanced the basket on his arm and pointed to the right. "Go straight up. We are taking supper into the cells momentarily."

"*Merci.*"

The two trudged up the stone stairs and found cell number 110 at the head of the steps. Paul could see his son hunched over a table. He whispered, "Pierre."

Startled, the prisoner looked at the musketeers, squinting his eyes. Then he stood, knocking his chair over. "Father!" He rushed to the cell door, gripped the bars, and peered at the two men. "Robert! Lisette said you were planning to get me out, but I didn't expect you this soon."

"Shhh! Had you rather we come back later?"

"*Non*, of course not." He eyed the two in their disguises. "Being musketeers becomes you both."

Robert smirked. "Not really."

"What is the plan?"

"Very simple. When they bring your meal, we will come in with the servants. We will disguise you with this—show him."

Robert held up the mask for Pierre to see.

"Then we will take you out."

"Just walk out with me?"

His father nodded.

"It sounds simple, but I don't know . . . the servants are watched closely when they bring the food in."

"We will face that obstacle when it comes. How many servants?"

"Sometimes two, sometimes only one." Pierre pointed into the dim passageway. "You can hide down there, under that arch, and watch for them."

Pierre watched Robert and Commander Boveé walk to the stone overhang. Paul gave his son a mock salute, then stepped into the shadows.

LED BY A GUARD JANGLING A LARGE RING OF KEYS, ONE kitchen servant—an older, heavyset, balding man—stood back while the guard opened the door. The creaking of the hinges echoed down the hall and joined the other cell doors clanging open throughout the tower. As soon as the jailer opened the door and the bearer of the evening meal entered the cell, Paul and Robert stepped up. "We'll take over here now. We have orders to transfer this prisoner."

The guard held on to the door and twisted his head around. "What's this? I have no knowledge of a transfer. Where are your orders?"

"I have them right here." Commander Boveé reached into his jacket, pulled out his dagger, and pressed it against the chest of the guard.

Robert stationed himself behind the commander with his sword drawn.

The servant threw the tray of food at Pierre and darted for the door, but Pierre dodged the scattered supper and grabbed the servant from behind, covering the man's mouth with his hand. In spite of Commander Boveé's well-placed dagger, the guard managed to slam the cell door shut and throw the keys down the dark stairs.

The commander sighed and shook his head. "You are not really in any position to resist, are you now?" He held the guard at bay with his dagger at the man's throat. "Robert, throw your knife to Pierre, and go retrieve the keys."

The courtier-turned-musketeer tossed Pierre a knife through the bars. It clanked and skidded along the stone floor and landed at Pierre's feet.

The old man struggled against Pierre's grip.

"Do not try to be a hero. I guarantee it will be futile." The servant uttered an expletive as Pierre tied his hands and put a gag around his mouth. He motioned to the bed. "Sit."

Pierre eyed the food slung all over the floor and speared the roast duck with the knife. "This may come in handy. You do an exemplary job in the king's kitchen."

The kitchen servant glared at him and pulled against the coarse rope binding his wrists.

Robert scurried back up the stairs with the keys and started to reopen the cell door. As he did, the guard knocked the dragoon officer's dagger away from his neck and out of his hand, giving him time to pull his own sword from its sheath. Commander Boveé stepped back as his weapon clattered down the passageway.

Robert left the keys dangling in the lock and prepared for action. The two stepped around each other like wolves circling in for the kill, then the guard lunged at the courtier. Robert dodged, but the blade of the guard's sword sliced into his upper arm. The sleeve of his shirt began to turn crimson.

Commander Boveé glanced around for something to use as a weapon. The guard's musket lay propped up against the bars of the cell. He grabbed it and swung the butt of the musket sideways, hitting the guard in the abdomen. The guard collapsed to his knees.

"Robert! Get my dagger." Paul hit the guard on the head with the butt of the gun, knocking him out.

Two more guards, alerted by the ruckus, appeared on the stone stairwell and ran to the cell, their swords drawn. Paul aimed the musket at them. "Looks like we have company. Drop your weapons, my friends."

The guards hesitated, then started toward the commander. Robert ran to Paul's side with a sword in each hand, and Pierre emerged from his cell with the knife. Robert tossed Pierre the commander's sword.

Paul cocked the musket. "I said, drop your weapons." Reluctantly, the guards dropped their swords. "Into the cell."

Robert and Pierre booted the other two guards into the cell, gagging and tying them around stone pillars in the back while Commander Boveé kept his musket trained on them. Robert moaned and grabbed his arm.

Pierre dragged the unconscious guard into the cell by his ankles, rolled him over onto his belly, and tied his hands behind his back.

Then he stuffed a napkin from the table into his mouth. He tied the man's feet and rolled him behind the bed.

Turning to the servant sitting on the bed, Paul ordered, "Lie down."

The servant didn't move.

"You heard what I said! Now! We don't have much time. Lie down on your side. Pierre, throw your blanket over him, so at first glance the guards will think it is you asleep. Now, let's get out of here. Get your things. Hurry!"

Pierre stuffed what few possessions he had into a knapsack and grabbed the roast duck and a flask of wine.

"Robert, put the mask on Pierre. Tie his hands as well."

"Sorry we have to do this, my friend."

"I understand. Get on with it."

Robert pulled the black velvet mask out of his pocket and groaned as he raised his arm to put it over Pierre's head.

Pierre touched Robert's sleeve, now wet with blood. "You are hurt."

"Only a nick." He aligned the openings in the mask for Pierre's eyes, nose, and mouth, and pulled the drawstring loosely around his neck.

"Let's go. Robert, get that musket." Commander Boveé opened the cell door, looking both ways, as Robert led Pierre out of the cell. They started down the stairs.

"Not so fast. I cannot see very well."

"Sorry."

"Keep quiet, you two." The commander slowed down as they reached the archway leading to the courtyard. He looked around and saw only guards lighting the lanterns hanging from stone pillars between them and their horses. "Walk slowly, with an air of confidence." The trio started across the yard.

The Percheron threw his head up and nickered as he caught a whiff of Pierre.

"You brought Tonnerre!"

"Shh! Help him mount up, Robert. And throw this cloak over him." The courtier helped his friend into the saddle with his good arm.

"Ho, there! What's going on here?" One of the guards started toward them.

Paul startled at the familiar voice. "Ach! It's Nicolas Maisson." Commander Boveé put his hand on his knife and turned to face the musketeer officer. "Orders from the king to transfer this prisoner back to the island."

"I have no knowledge of . . . what? What is going on here? Wait a minute, I know you. You're no musketeer; you're a dragoon officer."

The commander grabbed Captain Maisson's arm and wrenched it behind him, jabbing the knife in his back. "We are leaving, and you have the privilege of being our official escort." He looked around at the knot of musketeers, loitering throughout the interior yard. "Instruct one of your men to fetch your horse."

Nicolas hesitated only until the dragoon commander shoved the knife deeper into the folds of the captain's tunic. He arched his back under the point of the knife. "Uh." He peered down the muzzle of the musket in Robert's hands, then he called out, "Heber! Bring me my horse."

A young musketeer jumped to attention and ran around the corner of a stone wall, returning in a few moments with a saddled and bridled bay.

"Robert, mount up."

Robert balanced his musket across the saddle and mounted, grabbing the mane with one hand. His other arm hung limp at his side—the jacket sleeve now completely soaked with blood. The courtier winced as he threw his leg over the saddle.

Commander Boveé spoke to Nicolas in a hoarse whisper. "Tell them we are friends and that you are going to escort us out through the gatehouses."

"They won't believe that."

"We shall see. You and I will lead our horses until we get clear of the tower. By the way, the muzzle of Robert's musket is pointed right at your fashionable musketeer hat, and my knife is still at your back."

The two officers led their horses in front, followed by Robert and Pierre. An iron gate stood in front of them. A guard approached.

"Captain Maisson here. These . . . uh . . . gentlemen are personal friends. I shall escort them and their prisoner out myself."

"Yes, sir." The guard stared at the bizarre appearance of the hooded horseman.

"Close your mouth and open the gate."

The captain and Commander Boveé mounted. The entourage passed through and started across the first drawbridge. Only an occasional dim lantern lit the way.

Nicolas' horse began to step sideways.

"Get your horse under control, Captain."

"She's a new mount—doesn't like the bridges."

"If you don't get her settled down, she's going to have a new master."

Nicolas struggled with his horse and finally calmed the skittish mare. The horses neared the end of the first drawbridge and courtyard.

"Hey! Can we get this mask off of me?"

Commander Boveé clipped his words. "Not until we get past these confounded gatehouses and courtyards."

The four horsemen fell silent. Even those they passed along the drawbridges and in the yards spoke in muted tones, except for an occasional shout from a guard.

"Halt!" The guard at the final gatehouse drew his musket and stepped in front of the four. "State your business."

Commander Boveé muttered under his breath. "Make this good, Maisson."

"Captain Maisson here. I am personally escorting my . . . colleagues out. Transfer of a highly important prisoner."

The guard let his musket down and held it by his side. He eyed the party and walked around them. He stopped and gazed up at Pierre. "Ummm, I see."

Captain Maisson's horse began her sidestepping again. The captain swore at the guard. "It would behoove you to let your superiors pass, and quickly. My horse—"

At that moment his horse spooked and reared. The guard backed up and waved them through the gate. "Very well. Be on your way."

They spurred their horses and rode out of the last barrier leading from the Bastille.

"Untie me. Get me out of this." Pierre twisted in his saddle.

"Wait until we get on down the road, Son. Robert, ride in front with Pierre. Maisson, you ride in the middle, and I'll take up the rear. Just so I can watch you all the better."

The strange party proceeded out of the city and headed toward Versailles.

"Get me out of this contraption!"

"Very well. Pull over here. Robert, untie him while I watch our friend."

The wounded courtier dismounted and loosed Pierre's bindings around his wrists. Pierre ripped the hood and mask off the moment his hands were free, and sucked in a lungful of air. "I was suffocating in that ghastly contrivance. I don't know how the real man in the iron mask has stayed sane having to live in it every day."

"Maybe he isn't sane." Captain Maisson's cryptic tone reflected the atmosphere of the moment.

Pierre looked at the musketeer. "Perhaps not. We meet again, Captain, only under reverse circumstances this time, it seems. I only wish I had a cell to throw *you* into."

The musketeer captain glared at him and spat out his words. "You'll never be able to go back to court. You'll never be safe again in all of France. Traitor!"

Pierre spun Tonnerre around and stopped in front of the musketeer. "I am no traitor, but you speak the truth when you say that I will never return to King Louis' court." He turned to his father. "What are we going to do with him?"

Commander Boveé spoke in slow, measured words. "I'm not sure yet. Obviously, we cannot let him go. This is most unfortunate for Captain Maisson."

THIRTY-ONE

"Y ou do a good job with the fontange." Madeleine watched Elise pile the curls higher and higher, intertwined with the red ribbons that matched her dress. She pulled a curl down closer to her face. "Leave a few curls loose."

"*Oui*, madame, *merci*."

Elise finally finished the tower of ribbons. Madeleine stood and removed her dressing robe. She stepped into the skirt of the red gown and, with Elise's help, pulled it on. She saw in the mirror a lady of the court, one of King Louis' lovers. Her eyes glinted back at her, blue-green sparks of fire.

Put on the trappings of Versailles—take them off. As easy as putting on a gown. Wear the convictions of a woman of principle, or take them off at your own personal convenience. As simple as that. She didn't recognize the woman in the mirror.

Madeleine's own warnings regarding the subtlety of the decadence at Versailles had slipped by her as a duck glides in the water, forming soundless ripples around her.

Are one's lifelong principles really convictions if they are so easily sacrificed? Or are they simply mental assent to theological assertions? Her family's system of faith had been tested and tried many times through the years. Now she had thrown it all to the wind. She felt she must be the weakest Huguenot who ever lived. Her stomach felt tied in knots.

Maman, I'm sorry. François, please forgive me. I'm doing the only thing I know to do to save our family.

MADELEINE ENTERED THE BALLROOM AT THE APPOINTED time. The king and queen were just rising to signal the beginning of the ball by their solo dance, followed by the king's blood relatives. Then the beautiful players of the court followed in rank, joining the rise and fall of the dance. The metallic clanking of the harpsichord, filled in with flutes, hoitbois, and violins, pulled her into the room with the familiar strains of the menuet. She snapped her fan over her face and stepped into the crowd. Courtiers shot admiring glances her way and nodded to her as she passed by. She longed to see Pierre's dusky gray eyes seeking her out, but she would not find him there. She searched the crowd for Philippe, or any familiar face, but finding none, she backed against the wall and observed the dance.

"You look beautiful tonight, Maman."

The voice came from behind her. She whirled around. "Philippe! I was looking for you."

"We just arrived." He nodded toward Denis Greer, who approached Madeleine and bowed.

"Good evening, Madame Clavell. I agree. There is no more ravishing woman at the king's ball this evening." He extended his hand. "Red is delicious on you. Would you do me the honor of this dance?"

"Of course, Monsieur Greer. Philippe, would you excuse us?" She looked at Philippe, an impish expression flitting across her face.

"Enjoy the dance. I'll watch and see if you execute it correctly." His eyes twinkled at his little joke.

Monsieur Greer proved to be an excellent partner. Madeleine liked this veteran of the court who had been assigned as her son's mentor. He seemed stable somehow, and strong.

"How is my son faring? Is he learning quickly?"

"Oh, *oui*, madame. Of course, we have just begun, but you have every right to be proud of him. He takes instruction well." Monsieur Greer's nimble steps demonstrated his skill at the dance.

"He has an able instructor."

"Thank you." Denis put his arm comfortably around her waist for the promenade, not too tight, but not too loose—just right.

Madeleine followed the familiar steps of the dance that she had learned as a young woman. She stole glances at the faces of the other couples as she swept past them. Did they sense the shallowness of the lives they lived? Did they realize they lived among hunters and prey? Were they as miserable as she was underneath their smiling faces? Had the beautiful courtesans found fulfilling love in the arms of their respective chosen courtiers?

"What is this special interest that the king has in your son? He is more than mildly concerned about his training."

Madeleine stared at Monsieur Greer. The dance ended. The pair bowed to each other and walked to the edge of the crowd. Philippe stood with his back to them, conversing with another young courtier-in-training. Madeleine smiled. "It appears he is making friends."

"Yes. He is a personable young man. A bit reserved, but he'll learn. He has the natural grace and elegance needed to be an outstanding member of the court." Monsieur Greer looked at Madeleine. "You failed to answer my question. Why the king's special interest?"

Madeleine snapped open her fan. She fluttered it and cast her eyes up at him. "It is warm in here." Should she tell him? The court gossip would soon spread the word anyway. Perhaps if she did, Philippe would garner special favor from his mentor.

"Louis and I were friends years ago—intimate friends."

"Somewhere around fifteen years ago?"

"*Oui.*"

"I see. This all begins to make sense." He paused and executed a mock bow. "If a courtier-in-training is assigned to Denis Greer, he must have the special favor of the king."

"We are indeed bless—fortunate to have you as Philippe's personal instructor."

"And the king's attention to you, though veiled heretofore, is becoming quite obvious." Denis glanced in the direction of the king, who had resumed his place on the dais.

Louis' gaze fluttered over the crowd and lit upon Madeleine. He smiled and lowered his head in a barely perceptible nod.

"Not to mention the royal ermine." Denis fingered the ermine trim on the sleeve of her dress and looked toward the king. "I do believe the king has selected you for his next partner."

Louis rose from his chair and stepped down from the dais. The queen, engaged in conversation with the Dauphin, did not seem to notice that the king had left her side, until the assembly parted for him to come toward Madeleine. He looked from side to side as he made his way toward her, acknowledging one after another.

His eyes locked on Madeleine's, and she curtsied, low and with elegance, as he approached her. "Your Majesty."

"*Toi seule pour toujours.*"

"*Oui.*" Madeleine curtsied.

All eyes watched the king as he singled out the loveliest flower of the ball, but Madeleine kept her eyes on Louis. She put her hand in his extended one and rose to glide onto the floor. The music had ceased, and a hush fell over the room. Louis signaled the musicians to resume and the dancers to take their places. Strains of *La Courante* began, and Madeleine and Louis performed the undulating steps with ease. The music ceased, and Louis took Madeleine's hand and started back toward Monsieur Greer.

"Thank you for wearing the red gown, *petite amie.*"

"It was fitting, I thought—for the occasion."

Louis paused. "I must go away in the morning, but not before I see you later tonight. Unfortunately, I shall be gone for several days. At last we will be together again—as it should have been all along."

Madeleine looked Louis directly in his almost-black eyes and saw traces of the young boy that she had loved so long ago. She smiled at him.

He took her hand in both of his and kissed it. "Too many years have gone by. I have missed you." The king seemed to be unaware that they were in the middle of a crowded room. "I have missed the way the sun glints titian in your dark hair." He brushed a lock of her hair with the back of his fingers. "I have missed your laughter in the wind as we rode in the mornings. I have even missed the way you dare to challenge me." He chuckled.

"Things won't be the same as they were all those years ago, Louis."

"Perhaps not, but at least you are here once again."

She bowed her head and curtsied. Louis turned to walk back to the dais. With a wave of his hand, he instructed the dancers and musicians, "Continue."

The queen turned a grim expression in his direction, but he ignored her and chatted easily with a court official to his right.

Madeleine rejoined Denis Greer and her son.

"Mère? Is all well?" Philippe asked.

"Yes, all is well." She laughed. "At least in the tiny kingdom of Versailles. My François is gone; Pierre is being held in the Bastille because of us; we are prisoners at Versailles—but God is in his heaven, and the king is on his throne. Why would it be anything else other than *well*?"

Philippe stared at his mother.

"Would Madame excuse me for a moment?" Monsieur Greer covered a nervous cough and turned away.

"Forgive me, Philippe. I sound cynical, don't I?"

Philippe shrugged his shoulders. "I suppose you have a right to be bitter, but I have never seen you this way. I suppose I shall have to get used to seeing you in many different ways from now on, shan't I?"

Madeleine grabbed Philippe's arm. "Please try to understand, Son."

He pulled his arm away. The din of the music and the chatter of the crowd made it difficult to hear. But Philippe raised his voice to make certain his mother heard. "I am trying to understand, but I don't. What has happened to my maman who brought us through the persecution of the dragoons—who believed in spite of all the odds that Papa would return to us, and got us safely to Switzerland without him? Where is the faith of our Huguenot heritage? Are you tossing it all aside? Haven't we come too far to compromise now?"

A courtier with his lady standing close by turned their heads at the word *Huguenot*.

"Keep your voice down."

Philippe shook his head. "I will not abandon you, but I don't understand. I still believe God will make a way for us."

"It's too late. Our lives are too shattered and broken. I've sought for God in all this, and he is not there. Where is the power of God to fix what is broken? If he is there, his power is not evident to me. No, Philippe, this is the only way."

A BRIGHT MOON ILLUMINATED THE RUTS IN THE ROAD as Paul and Pierre Boveé, Robert Devereaux, and Nicolas Maisson, now tied to his saddle, came to a fork—one headed west, the other back to the east toward Versailles. "I am afraid this is where I must leave you, Son."

"Wha-what do you mean?"

"I mean you must leave the country, and Robert and I must ride hard to get back to Versailles tonight. Our absence will be noticed if we are gone any longer." He motioned toward the musketeer. "And then I need to decide what to do with our unexpected traveling companion." He pulled the musketeer tunic off and stuck it in his pack.

"I'm not leaving France without Madeleine."

Nicolas sneered.

Paul startled visibly. "Are you insane? You cannot go anywhere close to Versailles, ever again. The king will have you hanged."

"I will not leave without her." Pierre pulled his horse around and came face-to-face with his father. "So decide what to do with me as well, because I am going after her. Staying at Versailles with King Louis will kill her just as surely as being hanged by the king would have killed me. It will kill her spirit. She will dwindle away."

A breeze picked up and ruffled the plumes in the musketeer hats. "She has given herself to the king."

Pierre didn't answer for a moment. He held the reins in one hand and rubbed his thigh with the other. "If she has indeed surrendered to Louis, it has been against her wishes. He is blackmailing her with Philippe. She would never go to him willingly." He sat up straight in the saddle. "We're wasting time."

The commander got off his horse. "Robert, watch our prisoner."

Robert sat slumped over his saddle, cradling his wounded arm in front of him. He sat up and nodded.

Paul led his horse to a stand of trees. "Come here, Son." In the shadows of the night, father and son appeared much the same—both muscular in build, with a formidable profile, although Paul stood taller than his son. The shoulders of each were broad, and both men stood straight and erect.

Pierre hesitated, but dismounted and walked over to his father. The commander took his dragoon jacket out of his saddlebag and began to put it on. "Be sensible, son. You are wanted by the king, charged with treason. The moment you are spotted at the palace, you are a dead man. Then you will do Madeleine no good at all, ever. I will get her out eventually, but not now, not tonight."

Pierre turned his back on his father and looked toward Versailles. Then he faced Paul. "I cannot explain it, but I know I need to rescue her now. If I don't get her out of Versailles tonight, she will be lost to me forever."

"Halt! Stop!" Robert shouted as Nicolas Maisson's horse tossed dirt and rocks amidst hooves churning in the air.

The musketeer captain bent low in the saddle and spurred his horse away from his captors. Commander Boveé swore, removed his musket from his saddle, planted his feet, took aim, and fired. Nicolas screamed and fell sideways from his horse, his shoulder and most of his left side blown away. The spooked horse reared and streaked off into the woods, his master's body dangling from the saddle.

The three men stared at the macabre sight. Paul reholstered his rifle. "Unfortunate, but one less problem to solve."

Pierre grabbed the reins of his horse, mounted in one motion, and spurred his horse to an immediate gallop. He entered the woods and followed the crashing through the forest of Nicolas' horse. The panicked musketeer's horse darted through the trees with no pattern.

Behind Pierre rode the dragoon commander, whipping his horse to overtake his son. "Stop! Pierre, stop!"

Pierre pulled Tonnerre up and spun around.

Paul's horse reared in front of the black Percheron, snorting and wheezing. "Son, we'll never catch him. Captain Maisson's body is probably shredded to pieces by the trees the horse has banged against by now anyway. Whoever finds him will have no idea what happened to him. There's nothing we can do. I suspect that horse will wander for a bit, then who knows where she will go? Not back over the bridges to the Bastille, that's for sure. Let things be." He reached over and took hold of Tonnerre's bridle. "Come. If you are determined to go after

Madame Clavell tonight, let's be on our way. The ball will be coming to a close about the time we get back. Robert needs to put in an appearance, eh?"

Pierre looked back and forth between his father and the direction in which Captain Maisson's horse rode. They could no longer hear hoofbeats. Paul held Pierre's horse steady.

"Let's go, Son. The man is dead. There is nothing we can do."

"What kind of men are we?"

"Men who had a narrow escape and need to get on their way. Men who have to make a hard decision."

Pierre sighed and allowed himself to be led back to the edge of the forest, where Robert waited for them. As they approached, the courtier collapsed over his saddle and began to slip sideways. He grabbed the mane of his horse with his good hand.

Pierre bounded off his horse and ran to Robert's side, easing him to the ground. "You've lost a lot of blood."

"Let me look at your arm." The commander got off his horse once more and removed the musketeer tunic from the courtier. The right side of Robert's shirt was drenched with blood, some of it dried and stiff. Paul tore the sleeve to expose a gash on Robert's upper bicep that continued to ooze. "Give me that wine flask."

He poured wine into the gash, then gave the flask to Robert. "Drink as much as you can. It will help some." He tore a strip of cloth from the sleeve and tied it above the gash. "Why didn't you tell us it was still bleeding?"

"Didn't want you to think I wasn't up to the task."

"*Bête!* Can you ride?"

"I think so."

"We must get you back. Once we get to the palace, you can feign illness or make up some sort of story, but we need to get you some help." Paul looked at Pierre. "I still think you're crazy to risk showing your face at Versailles, but if you cannot be dissuaded, let's get on with it."

Commander Boveé took a brisk lead, and the trio headed toward Versailles.

THIRTY-TWO

The stables sat as silent sentinels against the outline of the chateau. The two Boveés and Robert approached the Place d'Armes.
Pierre and his father dismounted and helped Robert off his horse.
Paul spoke in a low, hoarse whisper. "We need to get Madeleine out as
quickly as possible."

"And Philippe."

Paul swore. "Is there anybody else you would like to join our little
late-night tryst?"

Robert chuckled, then groaned and gripped his arm.

"We will need horses," the commander grumbled under his
breath. "Pierre, take Robert to his apartment and get him settled in.
Do you know where Madeleine's apartment is?"

"I know where it *was*, but I doubt she is still in that room." Pierre hesitated. "It's not yet midnight. Madeleine and the king will still be at the ball. Perhaps . . ."

Robert spoke up, his voice weak. "If the rumors are true that she has agreed to become the king's mistress, she would be in one of the king's apartments, close to his bedchamber. I would suggest you chance it, go to that wing, and try to find her. If you can find it and wait for her, that would certainly make things simpler. One thing you need to know, however—she has a Swiss Guard with her at all times, night and day."

"That is not simple, my friend." Paul's terse observation hushed the two younger men.

Finally Pierre said, "God will show us the way. We knew this was not going to be easy."

"Expecting God to show us the way is a bit unbelievable, don't you think? If God exists, he is not concerned with our mission tonight. We are on our own. This is no time for religion."

"This has nothing to do with religion. It has to do with faith, with trusting God. You'll see. God will lead us."

"You two quit arguing. Let's go find her." Robert held his arm and began to walk toward the chateau.

"Can you make it, my friend?" Pierre put his arm around Robert's shoulder.

"I'll be fine."

Paul trotted toward the stables, leading the other two horses, and Robert, leaning on Pierre, hobbled across the grounds. They avoided the courtyard and swung around to the side, entering from the south wing. A dozing guard roused. Pierre pulled his hat down and ducked his head. The guard waved the two courtiers through.

The dimly lit halls gave them enough cover to ease along the sides of the walls. A courtier lifting the skirt of a courtesan and kissing her passionately paid them no mind. Couples of the court leaving the ball were beginning to fill the hallway.

Robert stumbled on a step and went to his knees. "I'm fine."

"Hmmm, yes, you are just fine."

"A little weak, maybe."

"Act like you are drunk."

"That won't take much acting."

The two courtiers finally reached Robert's apartment. Pierre eased his friend onto the bed and removed his boots. He lit a candle. "Is there any wine left?"

Robert held up the flask and shook it. "A bit."

"Finish it off. Sleep as long as you can, then send for Lisette."

"Sleep, glorious, numbing sleep. That's what sounds good to me."

Pierre felt Robert's arm and removed the bandage. "The bleeding has stopped. Take it easy, though. You don't want it to start up again." He washed the wound and tore the towel into strips to bind up the cut. "You are going to have another battle scar to add to your collection."

Robert grinned and leaned up on his good elbow. His smile faded as he looked at his lifelong comrade. "We will not see each other again, will we?"

"I fear not. This is where we say good-bye, my dear friend."

"I find it incredulous that this is how it comes to an end. I wish . . ."

Pierre paused as images of boyhood days in the stables, laughter and adventure, raced through his head—days when both were alone and only had each other—days of triumph, of defeat and bewilderment. How could he leave Robert behind? "Would you consider coming with us?"

Robert stared at this man who knew him better than anybody in the world, who loved him more than anyone else, who knew all his secrets.

"Would you?"

Robert shook his head. "I belong at Versailles. She gave me a home when I had none. She has been the mother I never had. I . . . I wouldn't know how to get along . . . I wouldn't know how to live my life outside of Versailles."

"You could learn."

Robert continued to shake his head. "I cannot." He grinned. "And then there is Lisette. Someone needs to take care of Lisette."

"That is true. And who better than you?"

"If she will have me."

"You care for her?"

Robert repeated. "If she will have me."

Pierre sat on the bed and grabbed his friend in a tight embrace.

"Ow! My arm."

Pierre released him and chuckled. "Sorry."

"*Au revoir*, my friend. I wish you well." Robert lay back on his bed.

"*Au revoir.*" Pierre started out the door, then turned back. "You have been like a brother to me." His voice caught. "You have *been* my brother."

Robert looked at Pierre, gave him a wave, then turned toward the wall—but not before Pierre saw a tear on his friend's cheek glisten in the candlelight.

Pierre closed the door and stepped out into the hallway. Looking both ways before venturing out, he made his way toward the king's chambers. He did not know if he could find Madeleine's apartment, or whether she would be there or at the ball with the king. He simply had to trust that things would work.

Father God in heaven, I need your help. Guide me to Madeleine. Orchestrate this and protect us. Help me find her.

PIERRE PICKED HIS WAY TOWARD THE KING'S QUARTERS. He evaded a servant here and there replacing candles in the chandeliers for the next day of court, and hid his face from courtiers and courtesans leaving the ball. The number of guards increased the closer he got to the king's apartments. Pierre assumed a posture of authority but kept his hat pulled over his face. He rounded a corner, stopped, and backed into the shadows—a Swiss Guard stood at attention in front of an apartment adjacent to the king's bedchamber.

What should he do? Walk boldly up to the door and demand to be granted entrance? What if Madeleine was not in her room? Or what if the king was there with her? He could see a faint glow coming from underneath the door, but that could mean the chambermaid was present. There was no other entrance to the room except a balcony window.

From his hiding place, Pierre watched for a few moments. Presently he heard footsteps from down the way. His heart raced. Someone was coming from the opposite direction.

Three figures emerged from the shadows—Madeleine, Philippe, and another Swiss Guard. As they approached the apartment, the guard escort clicked his heels and turned Madeleine over to the guard at the door. Madeleine gave Philippe a brief embrace. Philippe shook his head and walked away.

Pierre flattened himself against the wall. Philippe pulled a key out of his tunic and walked in front of Pierre, nearly brushing against him as he passed by.

"Psst."

The boy whirled around. Pierre pulled him into the shadows.

"Pierre! What are you doing here? We thought you were in the Bastille."

The Swiss Guard took two steps forward and turned in the direction of the two.

Pierre brought his finger up to his mouth and held his breath. Philippe's eyes grew large as they waited. The guard walked toward them. Pierre pulled his hat down over his face and slumped down. Philippe tucked his key in his tunic and pretended to be helping a drunken courtier rise to his feet.

The guard towered over the two. Philippe looked up. "This man has passed out nearly on my doorstep. He is a friend of mine. I'll take him to my room until he comes around."

The guard frowned. He said nothing, but nodded, turned, and went back to his duty station.

Philippe held up his key and motioned to a door a few feet from them. Pierre nodded, and they shuffled into Philippe's room.

"My heart is pounding out of my chest." The young man fell on his couch. "Pierre, were you in the Bastille? How did you get out?"

"Robert and my father executed a brilliant escape. I've come for you and your mother. We need to get both of you out of here."

Philippe's eyes grew wide. "*Bien!* But . . ."

"But what? We can do it."

"I have no doubt that we can, but . . . she . . ."

"What is it, son? Tell me." He sat down beside Philippe. "Talk to me."

"The king is coming to her room momentarily."

"Oh, I see." Pierre remained silent for a few moments.

Philippe leaned forward. "Maman would not have agreed to it if she believed she had any other choice. We received word that Vangie is ill. The king offered to bring the rest of the family here and have his personal physicians to treat her, if Maman would consent."

"We have no time to waste. Can you go into your mother's room without being stopped?"

"Yes."

"Then let her know I am here. Tell her to give you enough time to get back to your suite, then she is to open her door and call out to the guard. When he turns to go into the apartment, we will rush him. Tell your mother to have a goblet of wine in her hand and to toss it in his face as we charge him. I will ram him, and you go for his lance."

Philippe exhaled a slow "Ohhh."

"Can you do that?"

The boy nodded.

"Good boy. We will have to knock him out, or . . . kill him. A Swiss Guard will not relinquish his station any other way. Go on now. I'll be right behind you."

MADELEINE BACKED OUT OF THE HEAVY GOWN. "LAY IT on the bench at the end of the bed for now, Elise, and then fetch my robe."

The servant laid the garment out with care. The mounds of fabric covered the bench. She placed the red brocade shoes beneath the gown. "Will there be anything else, madame?"

"I think I would like some wine, please."

"*Oui*, madame."

Madeleine sat at her dressing table and fingered her pearl neck-lace. She took the pins out of her hair and let it tumble around her shoulders. Elise returned with a silver goblet of wine and sat it on the vanity.

Madeleine placed a candle in a brass holder. She sat down and took a sip of wine. She finished brushing her hair in the dim light, picked up the goblet, and placed it on the nightstand. Plumping up the pillows, she sat down on the bed. She reached for the goblet and trailed her fingers over the ornate filigree—then downed the remainder of the liquid.

She got up and went to the armoire. Looking through her gowns, she pulled out the black mourning dress. She laid it on the bench alongside the ermine-trimmed red gown. Then, like a little girl play-ing dress-up, she got the shoes to match and placed them beneath the edge of the black dress, together with the cloak, bonnet, gloves, and parasol. She looked at the ermine cape and muff in the armoire, but left them. She still wore her pearl necklace.

She picked up the candle and looked at the contrasting outfits—both beautiful, but one conservative and dark, befitting a widow; the other daring and provocative. She opened her jewelry chest. Taking off the necklace, she placed it on top of the tangled pile of expensive pieces. The black mourning brooch peeked through the glittering stones.

"Elise?"

"Madame?" The servant girl scurried into the room, wearing her nightclothes.

"I'm sorry. You had already retired. I'd like more wine, please."

"*Oui*, madame." She returned with the flask. "Perhaps Madame would like me to leave this?"

"Yes, thank you."

Elise poured another goblet for Madeleine and turned to go.

"Elise, I know nothing about you. Tell me about your family. Where did you grow up?"

"Madame?"

"Your family. Where are you from?"

"Nobody I have attended before has asked me personal questions."

"Do you mind? Does it make you uncomfortable?"

"*Non* . . . er, *oui*." The maid gave a slight curtsy.

"Which is it, yes or no?"

"It . . . it makes me uncomfortable, but I do not mind." Elise shuffled her feet and gave Madeleine a slight smile.

"A young girl whom I loved dearly attended me at our estate in Grenoble. Her name was Suzanne. Before her there was Thèrése, who nursed me as a baby and cared for me like her own, until . . ." Madeleine paused. Memories of holding Thèrése's limp body after the dragoons had ravaged their estate swung through her mind like a sticky cobweb and stuck on the edge of her consciousness. She shuddered. "She is gone now. I miss both of them more than I care to think about." Madeleine motioned toward the jewelry chest. "Suzanne always had to untangle my jewelry for me."

"I would be happy to do that for you."

She looked at the girl. She was rather plain looking, but her demeanor appealed to Madeleine. "Are you married? Have children? How old are you?"

Elise tugged nervously at the long braid that she always wore. "I . . . I'm not married, but . . ."

"But you have a sweetheart?"

"*Oui*, one of the stableboys." Her dark eyes lit up, and she smiled.

"What is his name?"

"Gabriel."

"I know him. He has helped us with our horses on occasion."

Elise blushed and looked down again.

"How old are you, Elise?"

"Sixteen."

"Oh. I thought . . . I presumed you were older. Are you from around here?"

"*Oui*, my mother lives in town with my brothers. I am the oldest, the only girl. My father is dead."

"And your mother brought you here to the palace to find a place so you could survive?"

"*Oui.*"

"What does your mother do . . . to feed your brothers? How many brothers do you have?"

"She is a cook in the kitchen. There are five boys."

Madeleine sat on the bed. Several seconds passed.

"Is there anything else Madame needs?"

Madeleine shook her head and smiled at the girl. She envied the simple life of the young servant—work, love, laughter. Why did life have to be so complicated? "Would you put the candle on the nightstand, please, before you go? Perhaps in the morning I shall have you untangle my jewelry." She hesitated. "I shall have a . . . the king will come to my room later tonight."

Elise ducked her head and curtsied. "*Oui*, madame."

"I shall see you in the morning when you bring breakfast."

In the morning, when my whole life will have been altered.

THIRTY-THREE

Philippe peeked out his door, and finding no one in the hall other than the Swiss Guard, walked toward his mother's apartment. Pierre slipped out behind him. The guard seemed not to notice. Philippe reached out and scratched on the door.

A beam of soft light sliced through the darkness as Elise, with a candle in her hand, opened the door. The chambermaid nodded and let Philippe in.

Madeleine sat up in the bed. "Philippe! What are you doing here? Is there anything wrong?" She still wore her robe.

The young man went to his mother as she got up and put on her slippers. "Dismiss Elise."

Madeleine looked at her son with questions in her eyes; nevertheless, she followed his bidding. "It's fine, Elise. You may go back to bed."

The maid set the candle down and returned to her cubicle.

Philippe took Madeleine's hands and whispered, "I told you God would rescue us."

Madeleine's eyes grew wide. "What do you mean? What has happened?"

"Pierre is outside my room at this very moment. Gather some clothes. You don't have time to change, but put your things into a bag. After I leave, go to the door and distract the guard. Call him into the room. Have a goblet of wine in your hand, and when Pierre comes in, throw the wine in the guard's face. Pierre and I will do the rest."

"Pierre is really here?"

"Yes. Now, go! We have no time to spare. Isn't the king due here soon?"

"Any moment." Madeleine ran to the armoire and pulled out her hunting jacket, skirt, and boots, and thrust them into a tapestry bag. She picked up the wine goblet and nodded to her son.

"Wait until I get back to my room, then call to the guard." Philippe exited, and Madeleine waited.

As soon as she felt Philippe had time to get to his apartment, Madeleine walked to the door, opened it, and called to the guard, "Sir, I heard someone at the window. Come quickly!"

The Swiss Guard turned and rushed into the room. In an explosion of energy, Pierre and Philippe burst through the door and charged the guard, hitting him from behind. At the same time, Madeleine splashed the wine in his face. Philippe lunged for his lance. The guard, knocked off balance, nevertheless managed to swing the lance around. It glanced off Pierre's head, knocking his hat off. Philippe grabbed the lance as the guard brought it up to strike again, and Pierre hit the guard low with his shoulder. The man's knees crumpled beneath him.

Pierre took the lance from Philippe and hit the guard over the head, knocking him out. The guard groaned and fell back against the wall. A rivulet of blood trickled down his forehead where the courtier had struck him.

Madeleine and Pierre stood frozen for a moment, staring at each other as if each were an apparition, then rushed into each other's arms. Madeleine caressed his face over and over. "Pierre, it's you. It's really you."

"I am here, chérie, I am here." He held her face and kissed her.

Philippe broke in. "We must hurry. That guard is not going to stay out forever. And the king . . ."

"Of course, you are right. Put the guard in there." Pierre pointed to the corner of the anteroom.

All three of them pulled and tugged the man into the anteroom. Philippe tore a cord from a drapery and quickly tied his hands. Madeleine handed him a handkerchief. "Gag him with this."

"My father is waiting for us with horses, but we must hurry!"

Elise appeared in the doorway, her face drained of color. She looked around at the chaos and started to run, but Philippe caught her arm. "What about her?"

Madeleine looked at the young servant. "Let her be."

"But . . . she may . . . she'll sound the alarm." Philippe walked to the anteroom and glanced at the Swiss Guard. "He's stirring."

Elise lowered her eyes. "You've been kind to me. I won't betray you. But you must tie me up."

"What?"

"Tie me up, so that the king will not question where my loyalties lie."

Philippe pulled his knife out of his boot and grinned. "I knew this would come in handy again sometime." He cut a drapery cord off a heavy tapestry and sat the chambermaid down in a chair, binding her wrists together. "I am sorry."

She shook her head. "Go ahead. You must hurry."

Pierre took a stocking lying on the floor, tied it around her mouth, and patted her on the shoulder. "*Merci*, dear one." He turned to Madeleine.

A loud thud interrupted them. Then another.

"The guard!" Pierre ran to the anteroom to find the guard awake, but still tied up and hitting the wall with his feet. Pierre shook his head. "I hate to do this, but . . ." He picked up the guard's lance and swung it at his head. But the guard doubled up his legs and kicked Pierre in the groin, shoving him against the wall. He dropped the lance and fell on his knees. The guard staggered to his feet.

"Pierre!" Madeleine ran to his side and picked up the lance.

The guard hesitated for a moment—a moment too long. Madeleine swung the lance with all the force she could muster. Months of pent-up emotion, anger, and frustration fed her momentum as she hit the guard in the face. He fell back, stumbling over a bench, and collapsed between the bench and the wall. Philippe dashed to her side and with his foot pushed the bench, pinning the guard against the wall. Madeleine dropped the lance and stared at the bloody destruction she had caused. She covered her mouth and lurched out of the anteroom.

Pierre pushed himself up, holding his stomach. "Tie his feet. He won't give us any more trouble with his face split open like that." Pierre picked up the guard's plumed helmet and unbuttoned his red jacket, peeling it off the bleeding man.

Philippe tied the guard's feet, and Madeleine gathered her things.

Pierre folded his hat and stuck it in his tunic. He donned the guard's helmet and put the Swiss Guard's jacket on over his own. "This will be perfect for getting us out of here without being stopped." He nodded toward the door. "Let's go."

"Wait." Madeleine ran back and picked up her jewelry chest. She gave Elise a quick hug. The terrified maid's eyes shone above the gag. Madeleine patted her shoulder. "You'll be fine. I'm so sorry we have to leave you in this condition. Thank you, Elise."

Madeleine stopped at the bed and ran her fingers along the ermine trim on the red gown. She touched the collar on her black widow's weeds. Then, with Philippe and Pierre on either side, she turned her back on Versailles and walked out the door.

COMMANDER PAUL BOVEÉ WALKED INTO THE DIM INTE-rior of the stables, having left his horse tied up outside with Robert's gray and Tonnerre. Philippe could take the courtier's horse. *Sorry, my friend. I owe you one.*

He made his way down the stalls undetected, the familiar odor of the place a comfort amidst the tension of the past few days. Bursts of snoring from both horses and stableboys punctuated the air. An occasional steed stood in the stall, munching on hay, and watched the soldier with vacant eyes.

A beautiful palomino mare roused from her slumber at his approaching footsteps. She poked her head over the gate and nickered.

"Ah, perfect. You'll do fine for Madame Clavell." He spied the horse's saddle and bridle at the back of the stall and readied the mare, then walked the horse outside.

Crunching footsteps startled him, and a familiar voice called out,

"Oh, Commander Boveé, it's you. I saw someone leading a horse out, and at this hour I thought—"

"Gabriel, you are up early. I have . . . have to be down the road before dawn on assignment."

"Hey, isn't that your son's horse?"

From the chateau three figures emerged and began to run toward the commander. Paul pointed toward the stable. "Gabriel, I need another saddlebag. Would you go back into the stable and get it for me?"

"But . . ." Gabriel's attention was diverted to the three running toward them. "Philippe!"

Commander Boveé grabbed Gabriel by the ruff of his neck. "Keep your tongue, boy, if you value your life. Get back in the stable."

"But . . ."

Philippe stepped between the intimidating figure of the dragoon officer and his friend. "Leave him alone. We are friends. He won't betray us."

Paul released the boy. "If he knows what's good for him, he won't."

Gabriel shook his head while rubbing the back of his neck. "I won't."

Paul looked at his son in the Swiss Guard's uniform. "Good work, Son."

Pierre laughed, threw off the helmet, and pulled the jacket from his shoulders. "No one even gave us a second glance." He took Tonnerre's reins and mounted.

"Hurry! Madame Clavell, take the palomino." The commander assisted Madeleine into the saddle, her nightclothes tangling in the stirrups. "I would suggest you change as soon as you get out of range."

"Yes, I will." She pulled the gown loose. She had wrapped the hunting jacket around her shoulders, and now she thrust her arms through the sleeves.

"Commander Boveé, who but God would have known that you would finish your business with the Clavell family as our rescuer? We will be forever indebted to you."

"Fate indeed has dealt us a strange hand."

"This has nothing to do with fate, Father," Pierre interjected. "God arranged it."

"You are entitled to your opinion, Son. But isn't that what started this whole affair—differing opinions concerning religion? Well, we certainly don't have time to discuss our beliefs at the moment. You must go."

Pierre dropped Tonnerre's reins and flung his arms around his father. "I wish . . . I wish . . . we . . ."

The commander returned the embrace. "I do, as well. Perhaps someday, in a better time." Commander Boveé shoved his musket toward Philippe. "Take this. You'll need it."

"*Merci.*"

Pierre mounted. "Let's go." He held Tonnerre steady and grabbed his father's arm. "I . . . I am proud to be your son." Then he tipped his hat and gave a salute to his father.

Paul's throat caught in a surprise surge of emotion.

Whirling Tonnerre around, Pierre took off, and Madeleine and Philippe spurred their mounts and followed him toward the southeast.

Commander Boveé leaned on the railing and watched the three

horsemen disappear into the darkness. The hardened dragoon soldier swallowed hard. "Good-bye, Pierre, my son. I . . . I do love you."

THE HINGES OF THE HEAVY MIRROR GROANED AS THE king stepped into Madeleine's dark bedroom. "Madeleine? Your lover is here." He tiptoed to the bed and sat down. He took off his wig and reached to the opposite side of the bed. Feeling nothing but covers, he stood.

"Madeleine? Where are you? Are you playing coy with me?" Muffled sounds came from the other side of the vanity. He peered through the darkness as his eyes adjusted. Someone appeared to be tied up in a chair. "Madeleine!" He dashed to her side.

But it wasn't Madeleine. Elise rocked the chair back and forth as she struggled, twisting her head and pulling at the drapery cord that bound her hands. The king loosened her gag and untied her. "What has happened here?"

"They've escaped . . . the guard . . . in the anteroom . . . hurt." Elise stared at the king's bald head.

"Sound the alarm!" The king ran back to the nightstand and put on his wig.

The severely injured Swiss Guard moaned as Elise loosened his bonds and tried in vain to soothe his wounds. Blood had pooled around his head, making a sticky mess of the floor.

The king dashed back through the bedroom and halted at the end of the bed. He picked up the red gown and let himself back through the secret passageway to his quarters as the alarm sounded and Madeleine's apartment filled with personnel. He raged back and forth in his room. He lit a fire in the fireplace and began to slowly rip the gown apart. Then he leaned against the mantel with both hands, stared into the flames, and watched the fabric melt and smolder into ashes.

"Never again, Madeleine. You will never make a fool of me again. But neither will I exercise mercy toward you. Next time, I will bring justice on your head."

The ermine trim lay on a table. Louis folded it and placed it in a trunk. *Ermine belongs to royalty—only royalty.*

THE THREE ESCAPEES, ONE FROM THE BASTILLE AND THE other two from a prison of luxury and decadence, spurred their horses on as fast as they dared. They continued putting distance between them and the palace until it disappeared from sight. Eventually Pierre signaled for them to slow down.

"We need to let the horses catch their breath. Pull in over there."

They rode into a grove of oak trees that descended to a small stream. The sky, beginning to turn gray, gave them enough light to guide the horses down the sloping knoll out of sight of the road.

Madeleine eyed thick underbrush. "This would be a good place to change my clothes." Her voice was uncharacteristically soft. The enormity of the last few hours threatened to crash on her, and she did not know if she could control her emotions. She felt dirty and shameful.

Pierre looked at Madeleine, his eyes tender. "Go ahead. I'll take the horses and water them in the stream." He took the reins of Madeleine's horse and helped her down.

As he lifted her down, Madeleine collapsed in his arms. She began to cry so hard that she could hardly speak. "P-Pierre, I don't . . . don't know what to say. You have once again risked your own life to rescue me, but I am unworthy of your devotion." She paused and took a broken breath. "The king . . . I agreed to become . . . Oh, God, I am a disgrace, an abysmal failure—as a woman, a Huguenot, and a m-mother." She looked at Philippe and reached out to him.

Philippe dismounted and went to her side and embraced her. "Maman, you did what you felt you had to do to save us." His chin quivered. "I . . . I am proud you are my mother."

Madeleine took his hand and held it against her tearstained face. "And I am proud to call you my son. You are a fine son. I should have trusted our God to make a way for us, but instead I thought I had to do it myself. I took things into my own hands and made a mess of our lives." She fell to her knees, still holding Philippe's hand. She looked up into his eyes, hot tears coursing down her cheeks. "Can you ever forgive me? I am so sorry. What an embarrassment I must be to you."

Philippe knelt beside her and gathered her in his arms. "You never would be an embarrassment to me. You are already forgiven."

Pierre helped Madeleine get to her feet. She faced him and looked him directly in the eyes. "I need to ask your forgiveness as well. I would understand if you no longer felt the same about me."

Pierre cupped her face in his hands. "It doesn't matter, Madeleine." He kissed her, first on one cheek, then the other, then softly on the lips. "Yes, you are forgiven. Now and for always."

The three of them stood in a three-way embrace for a brief moment, and then Pierre broke the silence. "We must move out quickly."

Madeleine nodded and reluctantly pulled away. She gathered her clothes from her saddle and pulled a handkerchief from her jacket pocket and blew her nose.

Pierre picked up the reins to Madeleine's horse. "As soon as Louis finds out we are missing, he will send his soldiers after us. We could zigzag and try to throw the king's soldiers off, but that would cost us valuable time. I think we need to head straight for Geneva, gather the family, and get out of Switzerland as quickly as possible. We have a bit of a head start, but not much. Go change, and I'll be back with the horses shortly. Come help me, Philippe. Watch that mare. She's bucking a bit."

"Maman can handle her."

"I'm coming to realize that your mother can handle whatever comes her way. She's an amazing woman."

"I want to thank you as well." Philippe waited while the horses drank. The quiet burbling from the stream accompanied the chirping of birds in the trees as the sun began to rise.

Pierre smiled at Philippe and clapped him on the back. "Let's go. We have miles to cover."

Madeleine rejoined them, and the strangely attired three—Pierre in his dirty courtier clothing, Philippe in his new courtier outfit befitting attending a ball, and Madeleine in hunting garments—mounted and rode toward the sunrise.

THIRTY-FOUR

Commander Boveé led his Boulonnais toward the interior of the stables and heard the commotion. A dozen soldiers ran toward him, officers shouting commands over their shoulders to the men. Paul halted one of them. "Whoa, there! What's going on at this hour of the morning?"

The man saluted the dragoon commander and gave a quick answer. "The king has ordered us to follow a lady he highly favors and her son, who have departed Versailles without permission."

"A mademoiselle and a boy? Shouldn't be hard to overtake them."

"They have a former courtier, a traitor, leading them, but we will catch them." The man ran into the stables.

A rush of lava-hot emotion rose into Paul Boveé's throat. His son was not a traitor. Or was he? Pierre had defied direct orders from the king by aiding the Clavells in their escape. He claimed to have a relationship with God that Commander Boveé could not understand. Perhaps by the king's definition Pierre was a traitor. But he was still his son, and tonight Paul Boveé would supply the protection for his son that he never provided for the boy in his childhood.

Commander Boveé mounted his horse and watched as the men began leading their horses out of the stables. They stopped to speak to a groom—Gabriel, just leaving the stable. Paul held his breath. He watched Gabriel raise his hand, then point in the opposite direction in which Pierre, Madeleine, and Philippe had ridden only moments before.

Well done, my boy.

Gabriel stopped and looked in Paul's direction. The Boulonnais reared. Paul pointed toward the young boy and shouted, "Good job!" He gouged his horse with his spurs and galloped off in the direction that the escapees had traveled.

The soldiers would not get far down the road before they realized they had been led astray. The trackers would see no fresh hoofprints and would turn around. Paul had thirty minutes at the most to formulate a plan. Racing around a curve, he brought his steed to an abrupt halt. This was the perfect spot. Thick trees lined the road, arching overhead. He pulled on the reins, causing the horse to rear and pace backward. He guided the horse into a gully. Reaching for his musket, he remembered with alarm that he had given it to Philippe. He patted his sword. "You'll have to do."

He slipped off his horse and yanked a rope from his gear, tying one end to the trunk of a tree. He ran across the road and anchored the rope around the trunk of a second tree. Returning to his horse, he pulled on the bit of the bridle to make him lie down. He took up cover behind the bulk of the horse's belly. The dew of the early morning soaked through his gloves.

Not even twenty minutes passed before the rumble of hoofbeats shook the ground. Paul checked the tautness of the rope and waited. In the early light of dawn, he could see the forms of horses leaning around the curve, running headlong toward the invisible barrier across the road. The guards' horses hit the rope full force, stumbling and crashing into each other amid whinnies and snorts of the horses and shouts of the men.

Commander Boveé stood and, with the roar of a man possessed, charged the chaotic contingent of men, with his sword drawn. Slashing and thrusting, he pierced the trunks of two men and sliced the hand off another before a blast from a musket hurled him backward. He tried to get up, but his right leg had been blown away. He clasped his sword and pushed himself up on his good knee. Blood gushed from the wound. The face of a palace guard loomed over him. The guard's mouth was moving. Paul thought he must be speaking to him, but his voice faded into the din. Paul raised his sword, and instead of the sure, steady blade threatening from his strong hand, he watched it shake and tremble. The guard kicked it away and sent it spinning on the ground. The dragoon commander toppled over as the guard sliced through Paul's heart with his sword.

The world appeared sideways to him. He felt his cheek grind into the rocks on the road. He could not keep his eyes open, and they formed slits through which he could see only misty shadows and forms of men and horses.

So this is what death is like. It's not so bad. I . . . feel . . . peaceful. He heard himself draw one last raspy breath. *I pray your God is real and that he is merciful—Pierre, my son.*

Pierre pulled sharply on the reins. Tonnerre reared and whirled around. "That was a gunshot."

Madeleine and Philippe halted their horses and listened. Silence.

"Go! They are not far behind us! Get off the road and into the cover of the forest." The three spurred their horses and galloped toward the darkness of the trees. Tree branches slapped against them as they plunged into the forest. They rode into the morning at a steady jog, dodging trees and boulders, wading across streams. Every so often, Pierre signaled for them to stop, and he listened. Finally he said, "I cannot tell that anyone is following us. Perhaps that gunshot was simply a farmer shooting at a fox in his henhouse."

Madeleine and Philippe peered through the trees. Pierre rode to the edge of the forest line and looked up and down the road. "I think it will be safe now to travel on the road." The sun had risen and cast beams of light through the clouds in an overcast sky.

"Could we rest for a moment?" Madeleine dismounted and tied her horse to a tree.

Pierre took one more glance again toward the road and slipped off Tonnerre. "That's probably a good idea. The horses could use a rest as well." He checked the saddles and loosened the girths, and let the horses graze. "Too bad we don't know the palomino's name. I guess she belongs to us now." He looked at Philippe on Robert's gray Breton. "You know, you have Robert's horse. His name is *Aigle*." Pierre laughed. "Robert's not going to be happy about this."

"Eagle." Philippe rubbed the Breton's face. "Well, Eagle, are you going to carry us above the clouds and away from here?"

The horse nickered.

Madeleine brushed the forelock away from a white star on the mare's face. "Interesting that your father made away with a palomino for me. My father bought me one for my sixth birthday. I named her *Cheveux Dorés*, because of her golden mane."

The mare turned and looked at her new mistress.

"I'll bet you are wondering what is going on and where your former master is."

The horse turned her head away, pulled on the bridle, and continued to graze.

"No, I would wager that you belonged to a woman. I'm going to call you Goldie. That is what I ended up calling Cheveux Dorés most of the time."

Philippe smiled at his mother. "Do we have anything to eat? I'm hungry."

Pierre went to his gear. "I grabbed a flask of wine and roast duck as we left the Bastille, but I'm afraid Robert and my father and I ate most of it already." He unwrapped a greasy kerchief filled with pieces of bone and meat from the duck, and handed Madeleine the flask of wine. Philippe picked at the bones in the kerchief.

Pierre pulled Tonnerre's head up and prepared to mount. "We need to keep moving. And that's something we hadn't thought about. We will need to buy food, or hunt for it, on the way. We don't have any money, do we?"

Madeleine smiled. "We don't?"

"Not that I know of." Pierre looked at Philippe and Madeleine. "Do we?"

Philippe went to his horse and pulled Madeleine's small jewelry chest down from behind his saddle where he had lashed a rope around it. He handed it to his mother. She opened it and dug down to the bottom of the container, through tangled pieces of jewelry. She chuckled. "I never was very good about keeping my jewelry straight."

She pulled out some coins. "There are not riches here, but there is more than enough to get us to Switzerland." Madeleine looked toward the east. "But Switzerland is not safe for us either. We found out how far Louis will send his spies to get what he desires when he sent his musketeers after us. He will stop at nothing."

Pierre helped Madeleine mount. He held the horse steady and looked into Madeleine's eyes. "We will make it. I may not have riches to offer you, but I vow to you that I will get us safely out of France." He mounted his horse and touched his hand to his heart. "I promise you."

THIRTY-FIVE

The soldiers limped back to Versailles with their dead and wounded slung over their horses. Gabriel gaped at a dappled Boulonnais that carried the bloody body of a dragoon commander. He ran up to the soldiers. "Wh-what happened? Who . . . ?"

A tall soldier who seemed to be in charge slid off his horse and pointed toward the Boulonnais. "One dragoon officer. *That* is what happened. One lone dragoon officer caused this havoc. But there'll be no more interference from him. Get some help and take care of the horses. Some of them are injured. Feed and water them and curry them down. We had to shoot a couple that broke their legs stumbling over the rope the blasted dragoon strung across the road."

Gabriel lifted the blanket that had been thrown over the body of Commander Paul Boveé. He shuddered. "What do I do with . . . ?" He looked around at two other bodies and at the injured.

"My men will take care of the dead and wounded. Just take care of the horses."

"Yes, sir." Gabriel's legs began to tremble beneath him, and his hands shook as he loosened the saddles. But it wasn't from the blood or the wounded soldiers, or even the dead ones. It was the sight of Commander Boveé's body, and the fact that Gabriel had played a part in the carnage. His muscles turned to water, and he could hardly lift the saddle off the horse.

The soldier began to laugh. "Can't take it, eh?"

Gabriel looked at the man and felt the bile begin to rise in his throat. "It's not that. I . . . I knew this man." He threw the saddle to the ground, ran to the railing, and vomited into an empty feed pail.

The soldier turned and began to walk away. "Just be sure you get the horses taken care of."

Gabriel wiped his mouth on his sleeve and glared at the guard. He stepped to the watering trough, dipped his hands into its chilly contents, and splashed it on his face. Elise! Had she been harmed in the escape? The young groomsman began to walk toward the chateau, then started to run, leaving the horses milling around in the stable grounds.

"Hey! Come back here!" the soldier shouted and then swore at the stableboy.

Gabriel looked back and saw other stableboys emerging to help with the horses. The soldier threw his arms up in disgust.

Gabriel ran to one of the doors on the south side of the chateau. It was unlocked, and he stepped inside. A Swiss Guard blocked his way.

"What is your business in the palace?"

Gabriel looked down at his clothes, looked back up at the guard, and spread his arms out. "What is my business? I am a servant of the king's in the stables, and I have been sent on an errand by soldiers gathered on the grounds. They just returned from a mission and need medical attention."

The Swiss Guard eyed him. "Very well. Strange goings-on in the palace last night. Be on your way."

Gabriel made his way to the area of the king's apartments to find Elise. The palace was just waking up, and servants scurried through the halls, lighting the chandeliers and carrying water to their patrons. The closer he got to the royal apartments, the more activity he encountered and the more guards he saw. He hurried to the apartment where Elise worked. It was cordoned off. He ducked under the velvet rope and walked through the open door. Pools of blood puddled on the floor of the anteroom. His heart skipped a beat. Where was Elise?

He stopped a maid who was mopping up the blood on the floor. "Do you know what happened here? Where is the chambermaid?"

"Elise? I don't know what happened, but she went down to the servants' quarters."

Gabriel turned and ran out of the door and down the stairs. Weaving his way through the servants coming and going, he found his sweetheart in the kitchen, sitting in a chair in front of the huge fireplace, rubbing ointment on her wrists. He knelt in front of her. She turned a tearstained, reddened face toward him, her eyes full of terror.

"Are you injured? Did they harm you?" He took her wrists in his hands and turned them over.

"Take me away from here, Gabriel. I don't want to work here anymore. This is an evil place. Let's leave. Let's get married and leave."

He tilted her chin toward him and kissed her cheeks. "We'll see, mon chérie. We shall see."

THE KING HURRIED THROUGH HIS MORNING LEVER AND moved to his office. An underlying hum filtered through the palace as the royal staff began the massive preparations necessary to transfer the royal personnel to the Netherlands for the signing of the peace treaty. The king paced in front of his desk and pounded the floor with his gold walking stick. "Full staff! I want the entire royal entourage to accompany me."

Colbert approached Louis with his usual reserved expression; however, a slight hint of excitement shone in his eyes. "Sire, this trip is of the highest importance. I agree that the court of the Sun King needs to display the magnificence that truly belongs to Your Majesty."

Louis sat behind his desk and straightened the capacious lace on his sleeves. He stroked his moustache. "I detect a bit of enthusiasm for this venture. That is unusual for you."

Colbert gave a slight bow. "I discern that this is a monumental moment for our country."

"You have always been obsessed with Holland." Louis stood. "And I agree. It is a rich and beautiful country. But this is not a pleasure trip. To finally access the jurisdiction of Franche-Comté back to France will show Spain who is the superior nation." The king walked to a couch and sat down. "Let's see what is going on in the fair country of Holland."

Colbert nodded, picked up a Dutch newspaper, and prepared to do the reading. One of the gentleman servitors entered and whispered to Colbert. The chief advisor's head shot up, and he looked at the king, who was staring out the window deep in thought. Colbert nodded. The servant left, and an officer of the guards entered the room.

Colbert put up his hand to signal the soldier to wait. He folded the newspaper and approached the king. "Your Majesty, I believe one of your officers has a message for you—pertaining to an incident early this morning."

The king acknowledged the guard and stood. Papers from his lap fluttered to the floor. "Yes? What word do you have for me?"

The soldier snapped to attention, then bowed. "Your Majesty, I am afraid we have failed in our mission."

"You what? You failed? How is that possible? I sent you after a woman and a mere boy, and you failed?" Louis walked to the front of his desk.

"There was a third person with the woman and her son. We were ambushed by . . . by . . ." The soldier hesitated.

"Spit it out, soldier! Who ambushed you?"

"A dragoon officer, one of our own. He somehow perceived what we were doing and rode out ahead of us. He strung a rope across the road and ambushed us."

"Who else was with him?"

"As far as we could tell, he was alone."

"One man? One man ambushed you and aborted the mission?"

"Yes, Your Majesty."

"Where is he? Who was it?"

"We took care of him. His body is in the stables. It was—"

Louis held up his hand. "Never mind. It was Commander Paul Boveé, was it not?"

"Yes, Your Majesty."

"That third person with the woman . . . it has to be Pierre Boveé, the commander's son. That must be why he went after your unit. But Pierre was sentenced to the Bastille." The king motioned to Colbert. "Find out if Pierre Boveé is still there in his cell, or has he escaped?"

"Yes, Your Majesty."

The guard remained at attention. Louis stared at him, but seemed to be looking through the soldier. His voice lowered and darkened with intensity. "Regroup your unit and leave as soon as you can for Switzerland—Geneva. We have a reliable contact there. I will not allow my subjects to toy with me and defy my authority." His voice rose with each sentence until he was fairly shouting. "My subjects will not betray me and get away with it! Bring Pierre Boveé and Madeleine Clavell back to court."

He walked behind his desk and sat down. He steepled his fingers and lowered his voice. "Leave the boy. I care no longer about him, but I will deal with these two who have defied me—for the last time." He waved his hand. "You are dismissed. You need not report to me again until you have the former courtier and Madame Clavell in tow. If you fail this time . . . You will *not* fail this time. If you do, you will pay with your lives. Is that understood?"

The officer clicked his heels together and saluted the king. "*Oui*, Your Majesty. We will not fail again."

The king glared at the soldier as he backed out of the room.

THE CAMPFIRE BURNED LOW. PIERRE THRUST A STICK into the flames and watched it burn toward him until he could no longer hold it. He threw it into the fire, along with a couple of small logs. Madeleine and Philippe sat huddled together, mesmerized by the fire. Madeleine smiled and looked at the two men, who in turn gazed at her in the dim light of the campfire. No one spoke.

Pierre stood. "I will stand guard for the first part of the night, then I will wake you, Philippe, and you can finish out until dawn. Let us plan to be on the way early, as soon as we can see. After we get across the border, we won't have to be as furtive as we are now—alert, of course, but we will be able to travel more openly once we are in Switzerland."

"We were captured in Switzerland."

"I know." Pierre paused. "But for now, we are a bit ahead of our pursuers. No one is looking for us in Switzerland—yet."

Images of the previous few weeks played across Madeleine's mind. She had pushed them aside in their dash from Versailles, but now they demanded her attention. She stood up abruptly. "I need some time alone. I'm going to walk down here a ways."

Both Pierre and Philippe jumped up as if to protest.

She smiled. "No need to worry, my brave protectors." The tears began to spring to her eyes. "I need time to . . . to pray. Please allow me to . . ." Madeleine ran past the horses into a clearing. She glanced back and saw Pierre stop Philippe from following her.

She fell to her knees, and convulsive sobs erupted from her throat as she rocked back and forth. "Oh, God. Oh, God! I'm sorry, I'm sorry, I'm sorry." She could not think of anything else to say. Her sobbing subsided after a bit, and she sat back on her heels. Night air sounds floated through the forest—the hoot of an owl, the rustle of an unknown animal, the nicker of the horses, the crackle of the fire.

"I beg your forgiveness, Father, for doubting your love for us; for railing against you and . . . and . . . oh, God . . . I even shook my fist at you." Madeleine covered her face with her hands as sobs shuddered through her body. "B-but most of all for not trusting you. Even if you had not rescued us, I should have believed in you, in who you are, and remained steady, like Job: 'Though you slay me, yet will I trust you.' But I was incredibly weak and chose to think my way was the better choice. What a fool I am. You are always good, no matter what the circumstances may appear to be. I should have trusted you. Forgive me." She paused and felt a peace settle over her.

"I thank you for rescuing us from the clutches of the king. I thank you for Pierre. I thank you for . . . for Captain Boveé. Please bring him to yourself and protect him. And for my precious son who remained steady and true, thank you. He's much like his father, isn't he?" She smiled and wiped her eyes.

She looked through the legs of the horses at Philippe, staring at the fire and talking with Pierre. He looked so much like a young François. She began to cry softly. "And thank you for allowing us to have François for the time we did," she went on. "You didn't have to bring him back from the galleys. But you did. Thank you. Forgive my ungratefulness. Even when I let go of your hand, you would not let me go. I am caught in your grace, surrounded by your mercy. When I turned my back on you, your Spirit wouldn't let me go from you. Where can I go from your Spirit? As David wrote in the Psalms, if I ascend to the heavens, you are there. If I plummet to the depths of hell, you are there. You are with me at my rising up and my lying down. I am bound to you with cords of everlasting love. How can I ever thank you enough?"

She rose from her knees. "Take us swiftly back to our family. Please heal Vangie. She's just a little girl. Please, God . . . make a way for us as we travel. And we will give you the glory, forever and ever. Amen." Madeleine looked to the night sky and began to sing a familiar Huguenot hymn. "God be merciful and gracious to us and bless us and cause His face to shine upon us."

Philippe stood and joined his mother as her voice rose. Pierre stood, too, and removed his hat, listening to the mother and son declare their faith in song.

THE ROYAL ENTOURAGE GATHERED AT THE STABLES, awaiting the arrival of the king's official party. Ladies of the court chattered excitedly in anticipation of the adventure of the journey to the Netherlands with the king. Madame de Montespan's luxurious carriage, drawn by six horses, pulled in front to await the plump maîstresse en titre, who had given birth three months ago to a baby boy, Louis Alexandre. Mere childbirth would not prevent the colorful Athénaïs from going on the trip with her lover. The king tolerated no absence from court for childbearing. Her servants cleared a place in the carriage for the king in the event he decided to honor her with his presence.

The queen's carriage, equally elegant, rolled up beside Madame de Montespan's. A place in this carriage also awaited the king. Shouts from the stable hands and footmen permeated the damp early morning air.

The king, already astride his chestnut steed, rode with his ministers and accompanying guards up to the waiting party. "I shall ride for a bit, Colbert."

"Very well, Your Majesty."

"Let's be underway. We have the business of the kingdom of France to take care of."

The royal party mounted and rode out of Versailles, leaving the magnificent chateau and the events of the past few days to take care of themselves. On the other side of the stables, a small contingent of soldiers mounted and headed for Switzerland.

THIRTY-SIX

Madeleine, Philippe, and Pierre veered off the road that led to the Du Puys' property and entered the forest surrounding it. They watched the early evening activities of the small farm as the shadows lengthened over the farm. Soon darkness would envelop them.

Nobody seemed to be around except the Clavells and the Du Puys. Henri, Jean, and Charles emerged from the barn and walked toward the house, stopping to wash up in the water trough.

Philippe gave a whistle, and Charles' head shot up. Philippe sounded the whistle once again. This time Jean and Henri heard it.

"It's Philippe!" Charles began to run in the direction of the whistle. The two men followed behind at a trot.

Jean overtook Charles and burst into the forest ahead of him. Spotting Madeleine, he rushed to her, picked her up, and swung her around. Philippe ran to Charles and clenched him in a bear hug. Henri clapped Pierre on the back and watched the reunion.

Jean turned to the former courtier, grabbed his arm, and embraced him as well. "Do we have you to thank once again for rescuing the Clavell family?"

"I guess my destiny is forever tied to yours."

Madeleine hugged Charles and cupped his face in her hands, smothering his cheeks with kisses. "Are you well, Son? Have you been a good boy?" She tousled his red locks.

Charles nodded his head up and down and clung to his mother. "Yes, Maman." He wiped a tear away. "I was afraid that . . . that . . ." His chin quivered.

"What, Charles? What were you afraid of?"

"I was afraid that you wouldn't ever come back." He broke down. "I thought the king would make you stay at Versailles, and we would never see you again." His breath caught as he tried to stop the tears.

Madeleine embraced him again. "He tried, but . . . well, he didn't succeed." Madeleine looked around the group. "Vangie? She is ill? What is wrong with my little girl?" She grabbed the reins of her horse and began to walk to the house.

Candlelight flickered through the windows. Smoke curled up toward the navy blue sky, and the fragrance of meat roasting beckoned them indoors.

Henri and Jean caught up to her, and Henri, stepping into his role as head servant, took her horse. "Allow me, madame, to resume my job."

"Thank you, Henri."

Jean walked alongside her toward the house as Henri took the horses to the barn." The doctor doesn't know what's wrong with Vangie. She's frail and lethargic. She won't eat. Has no interest in anything."

Madeleine broke into a run, the rest of the party following her. She burst into the house.

Madame Du Puy, holding a basket of bread, looked toward the door and gasped. The bread toppled out of the basket onto the floor as she ran toward Madeleine, embracing her in one of her characteristic smothering hugs. "Oh! Oh my! You're back. You're here. You're well. Are you well? Let me look at you." She held Madeleine at arm's length, then embraced her again. "Praise God! You are back!"

The Du Puy girls gaped at Madeleine, and at Philippe and Pierre as they followed her in.

"We indeed are back. Where is my Vangie?"

"She is upstairs with Claudine."

Charles started toward the stairs. "I'll go get her."

"No, Son. Let me go." Madeleine took off her cloak and hung it on a peg next to the door. She started up the stairs and motioned for Philippe and Pierre to come after her.

Claudine appeared at the top of the stairs. She covered her mouth in shock and started to speak, but Madeleine touched her finger to the front of her lips and patted the governess on the shoulder as she hurried past.

She approached the bedroom where François' spirit had left the earth only a few months before. Unbidden emotions clamped around Madeleine's heart, and she paused. She swallowed and blinked back tears.

The door to the bedroom stood slightly ajar. Tiptoeing to the doorway, she peeked in at her daughter, seated among the several pillows, playing with her doll. Madeleine turned her head with her ear to the opening to hear what the child was saying.

"We have to have faith that Maman and Philippe are going to come back to us." Vangie sat the doll down beside her. "And Prince too. He will come too. He will rescue them, like he always has."

Madeleine stepped back and leaned against the doorjamb. Tears filled her eyes. Even though she knew Vangie was ill, the pallor of the little girl's face and thin arms shocked her. And this child, in her innocence, exhibited more faith than any of the adults. Madeleine peered into the room once more.

A board creaked, and Vangie looked up. *"Maman!"* The child struggled to throw the covers back and get down from the bed. "You're back!"

Madeleine gathered the little girl in her arms and swayed back and forth with her, cooing words of comfort, crying and caressing the child. "Yes, I'm back, mon petite chérie, and we will never be separated again. As long as I have breath, we will never be separated again."

Vangie sniffled and looked over her mother's shoulder. When she saw her brother in the open doorway, observing the scene, Philippe bounded into the room and embraced Vangie around his mother's arms. "Hey there, little sister."

Vangie reached out and patted his cheek. "You're all dressed up."

"Yes, but not for long. As soon as I can change, I am rid of these clothes."

Then Vangie spotted Pierre. "Prince! I knew you would come."

The former courtier gently lifted the fragile child from her mother's arms. "You did? How did you know that?"

"I just knew. I prayed."

The three looked at one another, and Pierre tweaked her chin. "You just knew, and you prayed?"

"Uh-huh."

"Pretty simple, huh?"

"Uh-huh."

Vangie pointed at Philippe. "Where did you get those clothes?"

Madeleine took her daughter from Pierre. "It's a long story. We left rather unexpectedly and didn't have time to pack anything."

"And you smell funny." Vangie wrinkled up her nose.

Madeleine laughed and kissed her daughter's fingers. "I'm sure we do. We'll go wash up, and then let's eat dinner together. How does that sound?"

"Good." Vangie twisted around in her mother's arms and reached for her doll. "May I bring my dolly?"

"Of course, chérie. Anything your heart desires. As long as we are together."

The party went downstairs and caught up on the story of Madeleine and Philippe's abduction as Madame Du Puy finished preparing the evening meal. Madeleine held Vangie in her lap and caressed her hair. "Have you all been well? Catch us up on your news."

"Nothing exciting. We purchased a new milk cow, and more chickens. Pastor Veron from the Cathedrale came out one day. He asked about you." Pastor Du Puy set out goblets of ale and bread on the table.

"Why would he be looking for us?" Madeleine shot a look at Pierre.

Jean shrugged his shoulders. "I don't know. Concerned about us, I suppose."

"Concerned about us? That weasel, I am certain, is the one who betrayed us to the king. We have no time to waste. We must gather the family together and be on our way quickly. He could show up again at any minute and put the king's men on our trail once more."

Pierre said, "I agree that we need to move with haste, but in spite of the fact that the king's soldiers know exactly where to look for us, it will take them some time to piece together what has happened. Captain Maisson is no longer available to share that with the king." He paused. "It will take us most of the night to gather our things and be ready to leave first thing in the morning. Even a couple of hours in a bed sounds awfully good." He rubbed his back. "We've been sleeping on the ground all of the way from Versailles."

"We have no clothes except what we are wearing." Madeleine waved her hand in front of her face. "I'm sure you can tell that." She looked at Philippe. "And look at the clothes he traveled in. Fancy, eh?"

Philippe grinned and performed his best court bow for his uncle, coming up with the knife in his hand. "I kept it. You were correct, Henri. It came in handy."

Jean leaned down and slid his hand over the top of Philippe's boots. "Nice boots, son."

Philippe laughed. "I figured the king didn't need them, so I kept them."

Pierre looked at Madeleine with obvious tenderness and affection. "As for Madame Clavell, she looks stunning no matter what she is wearing or how many days she has been riding." He took her hand and kissed it.

"Come, come, everybody! Let's eat. You can fill in details while we have dinner." Madame Du Puy instructed all to sit around the large table and began setting food in front of them, with help from

Suzanne. Henri carried in another load of wood, huffing and puffing as he lowered the logs into the wood box.

Laughter bounced its way around the table and off the walls of the mountain cabin during the meal. The Du Puys and Charles and Jean fired question after question to Madeleine, Philippe, and Pierre. Madeleine looked around at her little family, allowing herself to enjoy the jocular moment, but overshadowing the lighthearted conversation loomed the dark cloud that this illusion of safety was just that—an illusion. France was not a safe place for them, nor was Switzerland. She longed to simply have a home again and enjoy her family. But as the illusion of safety slipped through her fingers, her thoughts tumbled to a halt. She had no husband. François was gone. She was a widow with three children, one of them ill. She looked around the table at her children—Philippe now in his usual casual, comfortable clothing, answered Charles' questions; Vangie sat on Pierre's lap.

Pierre looked up and smiled at her. Faithful, loyal Pierre. Where would they be if this man had not sacrificed his life for theirs? Her heart swelled with love for him. He raised his eyebrows at her, and she felt herself blushing.

Madame Du Puy and the girls began to clear the table, and Madeleine rose to help. Pierre stood and, giving Vangie to Philippe, walked to Madeleine's side. She felt his touch through her sleeve. The dishes in her hands clanked as her hand began to tremble. "Careful, Pierre, you're going to make me drop these dishes." She set them down on the sideboard.

"Leave them and come into the other room with me. I want to talk to you."

"Very well." She looked around the room. "Would you please

excuse us for a moment? We have . . . uh . . . business to discuss. I mean . . . arrangements, plans . . ."

Pastor Du Puy bellowed, "Why, of course you do. If you are to leave in the morning, you must discuss your plans. Do you need any advice?" Gérard laughed and rose from the table.

Jean joined in, "Yes, we would be glad to add our comments."

Pierre shook his head. "I can handle this." He led Madeleine to the front room and indicated that she sit down on the only upholstered chair in the room. Late-summer flowers stood upright in a porcelain vase beside a lantern.

He knelt down beside her, in order to look straight into her eyes. "Madeleine, can you not see that I am a man in anguish? During our journey from Versailles, I longed to hold you and comfort you. I wanted to lie down beside you and go to sleep with you, and then greet the sunrise in the morning with you. But once again, out of respect for you, I put my affection aside. But I cannot stem the tide of love that I feel for you any longer. I adore you. I am hopelessly and eternally in love with you." He stood. "This is a turning point in our destiny. Yes, we are fleeing for our lives, but let us do it together. We must do it together."

Madeleine looked down at her hands and clasped her fingers into the folds of her skirt. Her hands were rough and red. Holding her reins in the wind and the rain, washing in cold rivers and streams, having none of her creams and lotions—they were no longer the soft, white hands of a lady. Her nails were broken and grimy.

"Officially together—as one." Pierre unfolded her hands and kissed them. "You are beautiful." He looked into her eyes and drew a long, deep breath. "Would you consider spending the rest of your life with this man who has had many lovers, but only one love; one who did not know or understand the true meaning of life until I met your family; one who has much to learn about God and his mysterious ways, but is willing—eager—to learn? I know I could never take François' place, but would you do me the honor of being my wife? Would you marry me?"

Madeleine's eyes shimmered. "You still want to marry me?"

"I told you in the forest that your past with the king didn't matter to me, and I meant it. It is in the past. The Lord forgives you. I forgive you."

Madeleine wiped her eyes and smiled at Pierre.

"Well? What is your answer? Will you marry me—now, tonight? Pastor Du Puy could perform the ceremony. All of our family is here—everyone except my father."

Madeleine looked into the eyes that captured her from the first moment she gazed into them behind a mask at Versailles. "If you truly want me."

"*Want* you? I want no other. From the first night I met you at the ball, you have been the air that I breathe and the reason that I have for living. You have been the object of my dreams. The one I think of at first morning's light, and at the rising of the moon at night. I love you, Madeleine."

Madeleine stood and went into Pierre's arms. "I would be honored to be your wife. How could it be any more obvious that God has brought us together?"

Pierre tilted her head and kissed her gently on her lips. A kiss that had lingered only in fantasy in both of their minds for years, now finally consummated in all the ardor that had accumulated through the denial of that affection.

Applause and laughter erupted from the hallway. The entire Clavell and Du Puy clan had gathered to peer in at the couple.

Madeleine pulled away, but Pierre drew her back to him. "Is that a yes?"

Pierre first looked toward Philippe, then Charles and Vangie. "Children, do I have your permission to marry your mother?" The boys nodded their heads, and Vangie clapped her hands.

"I knew we would get married. I knew it. Didn't I tell you so, Maman?"

"Yes, you did, ma petite chérie. You surely did." She caressed Pierre's goatee with the backs of her fingers, then touched his cheek. "That is a yes. Now—tonight—from this moment forward, until God calls us to himself."

Pastor Du Puy broke through the huddle in the hallway. "Sounds like you need a preacher here!"

"Can we do it right now?" Pierre clasped Madeleine around her waist.

"We can."

"And it would be official?"

"It would be. We'll record it in our family Bible, or yours, if you have one, and it's official."

Madeleine shook her head. "The dragoons burned our Bibles. I have none of our books left."

"No matter." Madame Du Puy took their heavy family Bible from the bookcase. "We shall record this extraordinary occasion in our Bible, then, when you get another, you can put it in yours."

"What about the mourning period? François has been gone only a few months."

"Oh, my dearest." Gérard stepped up and took Madeleine's hands in his own. "We Huguenots are living in perilous times. Often necessity must take precedence over tradition and social customs. I would declare that this is one of those times." He chuckled. "I'm sure our heavenly Father would agree."

Madeleine smiled. "Very well. If you are certain that it will be legal and that . . . it is permissible under these circumstances." She pulled her hair back. "Let me go arrange my hair and—"

"No." Pierre held on to her. "You have never looked more beautiful to me than you do at this moment. I want to marry you just as you are right now."

She fussed a bit more with a stubborn curl and finally let it fall across her shoulder. "Very well." She reached over and plucked a bronze lily out of the vase and nestled it in her hair above her ear. "At least let me do this." She beckoned to the children. "Come here, my precious children. I want you all to surround us."

Philippe and Charles stood behind the couple, and Vangie came beside her mother and hung on to her skirt. Madeleine patted Vangie on her shoulders, then took both of Pierre's hand in her own and faced him. "Pastor Du Puy, are you ready? I believe you have a wedding to perform."

THIRTY-SEVEN

Pierre shook Madeleine's shoulder. "Wake up, my love."

Madeleine snuggled back into the feather mattress and pulled the quilt up under her chin. "Ummm. I don't want to get up."

Pierre sat on the bed and pulled her into his arms. "I know." He held her face in his hands and stared at her, caressing first her hair and then her cheeks. "I cannot believe that I am married to the most beautiful woman in all of Europe, the only woman I have ever truly loved. I cannot believe that the agony of the past three years of yearning to hold you but thinking I never could are over. We are married. Married!" Pierre laughed and fell back on the bed. "Am I not the luckiest man in the whole world?"

Madeleine gathered the bedclothes around her and smiled at her new husband. "I do not think I would use the word *lucky* to describe your association with the Clavell family."

"Maybe not. But I *feel* lucky." He stood and reached for his pants. "We need to gather our things and get on the road."

Madeleine nodded. "I agree." She sat on the edge of the bed, still wrapped in the quilt. She hesitated.

Pierre sat in the chair and pulled on his boots. He stood and smiled at her modesty. "I'll go check on the children."

Madeleine rose from the bed and went into his arms, letting the quilt fall to the floor. She kissed him with fervor. "I want to begin our married lives with no walls between us, physically or otherwise. I want to stand unashamed before you in every way."

Pierre, the experienced and jaded courtier, blushed.

"What is this? The worldly courtier, the much sought-after Pierre Boveé, is embarrassed?"

"I . . . I feel young and innocent again with you. I do not understand how that can be, but that is how I feel."

Madeleine reached up and smoothed his hair. "God is restoring that to both of us. He truly makes all things new."

Pierre grew quiet. "I do not want to think about those days. In spite of the excitement of the court, a river of darkness and loneliness wound its way through the halls of the palace and touched us all."

"How very well I know." Madeleine kissed him on the cheek and pulled the quilt around her again. "Now, go gather everybody. I'll get dressed and collect my things." She looked around the room. "It won't take long. Look, my trunks are there, doubtless still packed from the first time we tried to leave. Jean and Henri must have brought them in after the kidnapping."

Pierre started for the door. "I'm going to go down and eat something, then I'll get the horses ready." He took hold of the doorknob and turned. "You'll not be long?"

"*Non*, I'll not be long."

Pierre went out the door, whistling as he went down the stairs.

She had never heard Pierre whistle. There was much to learn about her new husband. They had experienced trauma and crisis together from the beginning, but the mundane, daily routines of life would be an entirely new adventure. Madeleine smiled. They were a long way from settling into a daily routine, but she looked forward to the time when they could.

She opened one of the trunks and took out some undergarments and a dark green traveling dress and bonnet. She rummaged to the bottom for shoes. She was glad to have her own clothing back. She poured water from the pitcher into a basin, washed up quickly, and got into her chemise. Pulling her hair back in a ribbon, she walked to a large armoire near the window and looked into the oval mirror. She leaned in and pinched her cheeks.

Madeleine reached for the small brass key and opened the cabinet. The doors creaked open. François' shirts hung on one side of the interior, Charles' and Vangie's things on the other. She took a shirt off the hook and buried her face in it. The masculine fragrance of her deceased husband lingered in the fabric. She let out a deep sigh.

"My precious François. How I miss you. I'm so sorry. I'm so sorry." She folded the shirt and placed it in the trunk with her things. François would want Pierre to have his clothes. "We are following your wishes, my love. We are going to the New World, leaving Europe to escape Louis' clutches."

A soft knock interrupted her thoughts. "Enter."

"Madame?" Claudine cracked the door open and looked around the room. "Were you talking to someone?"

Madeleine shook her head and wiped the moisture from her eyes.

"Just myself. Come in. How is Vangie this morning? Did she sleep well?"

"*Oui*, madame. She is still asleep."

Madeleine pulled three more of François' shirts and two pairs of breeches out of the armoire. "I need help with my stays and getting packed." She held the pants up. François had been taller than Pierre. She would need to take them up, but the shirts would suffice.

Claudine helped Madeleine with the stays and into her dress. She began to fold the clothing and place it in the trunk.

Madeleine put the rest of Charles' and Vangie's things in a bag and started out the door. "Claudine, would you please finish packing the trunk, then join me downstairs?"

Claudine curtsied. "Madame."

Madeleine hurried down the stairs into the kitchen. Before she could speak, Madame Du Puy stopped her with a finger to her mouth. "Shhh." She pointed outside.

Madeleine set the bags down and looked out the window to see Pastor Du Puy by the water trough, talking to a thin man on horseback. Jacob Veron! Her heart began to pound. "Where's Pierre?"

Madame Du Puy pointed to the barn where Tonnerre stood tied to the hitching rail and the modest black coach had been rolled, awaiting its pair of horses.

Madeleine stood immobile. The two women watched, horrified, as Jean and Pierre strode out of the barn, leading the team of horses for the coach. Philippe and Charles followed close on their heels, carrying tack, ropes, and horse blankets for their journey. All four froze as they recognized the Judas on horseback.

The barnyard dogs circled around the unwelcome intruder. Some wagged their tails and yipped at the horse's hooves. The hum of a low growl rumbled in the throat of a large yellow mutt. The chickens pecked away at their feed, oblivious. A just-milked cow in the barn mooed her protest at being left in the stall.

Madeleine watched Pastor Du Puy shush the wary mutt with a pat on the dog's head and engage Jacob in conversation. The dog remained at the pastor's side, snarling at Jacob.

JEAN RECOGNIZED PASTOR VERON FIRST. HE HALTED the horses and tried to hide Pierre behind them, but it was too late.

Jacob spotted Pierre and reined his horse back a few steps. He tapped his hat brim. "Ahhh, Monsieur Boveé. Looks like you have company, Pastor Du Puy. Or perchance you didn't know this traitor was in your barn?" He guided his horse around to face Jean and Pierre. "Or perhaps you *did* know and did not want to disclose his presence. Most fortunate, is it not, that I happened to swing by here on my way back to Geneva?"

Pierre walked in front of the horses to face Jacob Veron. "I am no traitor. Unless you believe that coming to know the God you claim to serve is being a traitor."

Jacob's face reddened. He spoke through tight lips. "You have no idea what it means to serve God, you heathen courtier." He started inching his horse away. "King Louis is France's sovereign ruler, set in place by God. You defy him, and you are defying God himself. You will not get away with this." He spurred his horse.

Henri and Armond, emerging from the corner of the barn, halted. The pastor's horse was mere inches away from the two as he attempted to leave. Henri reached out and caught hold of the horse's bridle. The horse reared, and its hooves, pawing the air, kicked the old gentleman in the chest. Henri fell to the ground, holding his side and gasping for breath. Armond pulled on the horse's bridle and brought him down.

Pierre broke in a run toward the action, and with a burst of strength that seemed almost supernatural, leapt on the horse and wrestled the wretched pastor off his mount. He pulled Jacob up by his less-than-holy collar and said, "I don't believe you'll be going anywhere for the time being."

Jean ran to Henri, and Madeleine burst through the door of the house at the same time. Jean took the old man's shoulders and attempted to lift him up. "Henri! Henri, we're here." Henri groaned as he struggled to breathe.

Madeleine grabbed the hem of her skirt and wiped blood and foam from his mouth. "Henri, it's me, Madeleine. Can you hear me?"

Henri blinked his eyes open for a moment. Then they fluttered shut, and he lapsed into semiconsciousness.

Jean instructed Philippe, "Let's get him into the house." They lifted the old man and carried him up the steps of the porch.

Madame Du Puy held the door open and motioned to them. "Bring him in here." Goblets and bowls clattered to the floor as Rachel swept them from the long table. Claudine gathered Vangie in her arms, along with her porridge. Madame Du Puy tore off her apron, wadded it in a ball, and stuck it underneath Henri's head as Jean and Philippe lifted him onto the table.

Pierre shoved Jacob Veron onto the porch, gripping the pastor's wrists behind his back. "Charles, hand me one of those."

The boy, who was still holding the rope that he had carried out of the barn, sprang into action.

Pierre pushed the informant down in a rocking chair. "Tie his feet. Hurry. I'll get his hands." Pierre looked at Charles. "Do you know how to do that?"

"*Oui*, monsieur. My papa taught me."

A flash of a thought—barely discernible—rushed into his head and then disappeared. *I have big shoes to fill to be a father to these boys.*

Pierre tightened the rough lash around the pastor's slender white wrists. Jacob grimaced. "Ach!"

"Too tight?" Pierre tightened it further. "Just to make certain." He shook his head. "Got his feet?"

"Yes, monsieur."

Pierre checked the knots. "Good job, Charles." They started toward the door. Pierre put his hand on Charles' shoulder. "It's Pierre. You don't have to call me monsieur."

Charles smiled up at him.

Pierre went to Madeleine, who stood with Pastor Du Puy at Henri's head. The pastor put his ear to the old man's chest, raised his eyes, and shook his head. "We shall send for the doctor in the village, but I don't think there is anything he can do." He bent down to listen again. "I hear much gurgling in his chest. He probably has broken ribs that have punctured his lungs." He motioned to his wife. "Get a blanket for him."

Madeleine took the old man's leathery hand and caressed it. "Not you, Henri. Stay with us. Don't leave us now."

Henri opened his eyes and looked around at the family. He grabbed his side and moaned. "Sit me up. I can't breathe." His face reddened, and he struggled to come to a sitting position.

Jean and Pastor Du Puy got him under his arms and pulled him up. "Is that better, my friend?"

Henri shook his head. "I feel like a boulder is on my chest." He looked at Madeleine. "Go, madame. Leave now. Don't delay for my . . ." A gasp, wrung out of his chest through the agony of the pain, cut him off. He fell back on one elbow and looked at the woman he had protected and served since she was a baby. "I am ready to see Jesus—and Thèrése, and your mother, and François. I'm too old to make the trip anyway." He collapsed on the hard surface. "Only harm can come if you delay leaving. Go! Go now. Pierre, take good care of my . . . my . . ."

Madeleine patted his hand. "Your family, Henri." She placed it on top of the blanket and looked around the circle.

Jean spoke up. "He's right, Madeleine. The Du Puys will take care of him—either way. There is no profit in delaying our departure. Time is critical."

Pastor Du Puy nodded. "Finish gathering your things. We will take care of Henri—and Jacob Veron."

"What will you do with him?" Madeleine nodded toward the figure tied in the rocking chair on the porch.

"Keep him here for a few days. Then escort him back to the Cathedrale and let Pastor LeSeuer know what a sniveling conniver he has had in his service. I don't believe he will be any more trouble to you." Gérard rubbed his beard. "But just to make sure, as you pass by him on the porch, why don't you do this?" The pastor whispered to Charles and Vangie. "Can you do that?"

They bobbed their heads up and down in agreement.

"Carry Henri into the downstairs bedroom. Then, Armond, would you ride to the village to get the doctor, please?" He clapped his hands as he finished issuing his orders. "Now, everybody be about your tasks. And may the Lord make his face to shine upon you and give you peace. Go!"

The room remained quiet as Jean and Pierre carried Henri to the next room. The only sounds that could be heard were the shuffle of feet and the thuds of trunks and luggage on the stairs.

Madeleine brought the children to the door of the room and motioned to Pierre. "Let's say our good-byes quickly."

The Clavells, the children unusually quiet, peeked into the bedroom where Henri lay on a small rope bed. His eyes were closed. Madeleine whispered, "Good-bye, faithful and loyal servant. Until we meet again."

Vangie patted the old man's cheek. They lingered for a moment, then backed out of the room. A board creaked underneath their feet as they turned and left.

Henri opened his eyes. "Farewell, beloved ones."

Armond ran to saddle his horse, and Madeleine and Philippe began carrying their bags to the coach. Suzanne stood in front of their small cottage, holding their toddler on her hip and shielding her eyes from the sun. She picked up her skirts and ran toward the coach to help Madeleine and Philippe. "I guess we must say good-bye again, madame."

"So it seems, Suzanne," Madeleine said. "Perhaps we shall see you again one day. But if not on this earth, we shall meet again when we all get on the other side."

Pierre and Jean had finished hitching up and saddling the horses. Pierre called to Madeleine, and she gave Suzanne a quick hug. "You and Armond take care of each other, and that precious little boy."

Claudine and Charles, with Vangie in tow, came out of the house, their hands full of belongings. Madeleine beckoned to them.

Vangie giggled as they passed Pastor Veron, still tied in the rocking chair on the porch. "I am so excited to go see our cousins in Spain. Is Spain as beautiful as France?"

Charles shushed her and hurried her along. Claudine cut her eyes over at Jacob Veron and saw his eyes widen at the child's words.

Madeleine shooed Vangie into the cab. "Well?"

"He heard it, and I think he believed it." Claudine smiled.

"Good job, children."

Charles grinned. "Maman, may I ride with Jean and help him drive?"

Madeleine looked at her younger son. He, too, was becoming a young man.

"Yes, you may. Keep your cap on those red curls." She gave him a hug and felt something sharp in the pocket of his shirt. "What's this?"

Charles pulled out the metal box of little wooden soldiers that François had recovered from the burned-out estate. "May I please keep these?"

Madeleine frowned as she recalled the day Commander Boveé invaded their home. "Of course, Son. Of course you may."

He shoved them back in his pocket and climbed onto the driver's perch.

Pastor Du Puy hurried outside, joined the group around the coach, and took the lead. "We have not time to say long good-byes. I pray godspeed and his blessings over you. Amen."

Jacob Veron, still tied up in the rocking chair on the porch, grimaced at his bindings. His hat had fallen to the floor and crumpled under the swaying chair.

Jean climbed up beside Charles and gathered the reins, and Madeleine and Claudine entered the coach and settled in. Pierre and Philippe mounted up. The three men planned to switch out driving the coach and riding horseback.

Jean turned the coach west, and they left the little farmhouse and the Du Puy family, who had opened their arms and home as a shelter in a storm for the Clavells for the last time.

THE CAPTAIN OF THE GUARD CALLED HIS UNIT TO ATTEN-
tion. The dead had been buried, including Commander Paul Boveé,
and new troops added. "We failed in our mission to capture Madame
Clavell and Monsieur Boveé once. We shall not fail again." The captain's plumed hat ruffled in the breeze. "We will ride fast and we will
ride hard to reach Geneva as quickly as we can. Our informant is
there. Where we will go from that point is anybody's guess. If you feel
you cannot ride on this mission and be gone for an indefinite period
of time, step out of rank now."

No one moved.

"Very well. Mouu-uunt uupp!"

The soldiers mounted as one and followed the captain as he rode
out of the stables.

A stableboy walked into the arena, holding a saddle. Gabriel swallowed hard at the lump in his throat and watched the soldiers head
for Geneva.

THE KING'S ROYAL PARTY HALTED AT A STREAM TO WATER
the horses. The king slipped off his horse and handed the reins to his
groomsman. "I shall ride in Madame de Montespan's coach for a bit."

The groomsman bowed. "Your Majesty."

Louis approached Madame de Montespan's grand coach and patted the new team of six spotted horses that the maîstresse en titre had
purchased recently. A footman opened the door, set with ornate carv-
ings and swirls. The king stopped as Athénaïs returned to her carriage
after having gone with her chambermaids to relieve herself.

"Am I to be honored with the king's company this afternoon?" she
inquired with a smile.

The king stared at his mistress of over a decade. She truly was a beautiful woman—her blonde hair still full and lush, her skin smooth and creamy. He gave a slight nod and motioned for her to enter the carriage. The glamorous Madame de Montespan seated her once-slender body on the soft upholstered cushion. She arranged plump pillows of rich-colored tapestry and silk around her and leaned toward the king. "I have been waiting for you to join me."

Louis smiled at her teasing and stepped onto the footplate. As he stuck his head into the cab, a frown creased his brows, and he pulled out his kerchief. Lifting the cloth to his nose, he retreated. "Must you insist on lavishing the entire coach with that infernal perfume?" He waved the hanky in front of his face. "I shall join the queen instead. Leave your windows open and air out the interior. Then perhaps I shall join you."

The king strode to the queen's carriage and settled himself across from his wife. He pulled off his riding gloves, unbuttoned his heavy brocade jacket, and greeted the queen, already seated in the royal carriage.

"I'm happy to see you, Louis."

The king gave her a cursory nod and patted her hand. He narrowed his eyes at her. She reminded him of a little brown wren—plain, quiet, drab, nothing exciting or flamboyant about her. Athénaïs was like the parrots the king had imported—colorful, loud, dashing about, squawking.

And then there was Madeleine—Madeleine was like a peacock—regal, rich in color and hue, only showing her colors when necessary.

"Has something upset the king?" The queen looked out the window at Athénaïs' carriage.

"*Non.* I simply prefer to ride with you for the time being. That would be pleasing to you, my dear?"

The queen smiled and hid her black teeth behind her fan. "I always prefer the king's company to anyone else's."

The king tapped the back of the driver's perch. "Let's be on our way."

The carriages lurched forward, and Louis sat rigid in his seat, gazing into space. Images of Madeleine in the red gown, dancing with him at the ball, raced across his mind as the colors of the landscape raced by the open windows of the carriage. He could almost smell the faint fragrance of jasmine that whispered in her hair. He was sure she had fled back to Geneva. She would want to reunite with her children as soon as possible. But then where? Blast Commander Boveé! Blood ties to his son had preempted loyalty to his king.

Perhaps it was time to forgo his dalliances with his mistresses and focus on his wife and children. He truly did care for them. He was tiring of Madame de Montespan anyway. She was getting fat and too demanding. He would deal with Madeleine de Vaudois Clavell and Pierre Boveé upon his return. He was certain his guards would not fail again in retrieving the two.

However, for now, he needed to concentrate on the peace treaty to be negotiated at Nijmegen. The magnificent Sun King of the French Empire sped northeast in his royal carriage toward the little country of Holland.

Jean halted the coach. Pierre and Philippe rode up beside him.

Madeleine descended from the cab and paused on the foot iron. "Is anything wrong?"

Jean peered down at her. "*Non.* I think we can safely turn around now."

Pierre swiveled in his saddle and looked around. "I think so too. Lead the way." He motioned to Madeleine. "Ride with me for a few miles?"

She nodded. Pierre slipped off his beloved Percheron and lifted Madeleine into the saddle. Tonnerre nickered. "See, even my horse approves."

Madeleine chuckled and leaned back into Pierre's chest as he settled himself behind her. Vangie, color returning to her pale cheeks, leaned out of the window and begged, "Me too!"

Pierre guided Tonnerre closer to the coach and took the little girl's hand. "You may ride with me next." He kissed her hand. "I want your mother close by my side right now."

Vangie pouted, pulled her head back inside, and flopped on Claudine's lap. Charles laughed at his little sister and teased her through the window from the driver's bench.

Pierre swung his arm around in a circle. "Let's go, Jean!"

Jean whooped, turned the team of horses around, and headed the coach north toward Holland.

Pierre pulled Madeleine close to him. "This is the turning point of our lives."

Madeleine swiveled around in the saddle and looked at her new husband. "A new beginning."

Pierre took her hand and kissed it. Then he touched his heart, with her hand in his. "New beginnings in a New World."

ACKNOWLEDGMENTS

Writing a book is a monumental team effort, and I am indebted to so many people:

The fabulous fiction team at Thomas Nelson, particularly my editor, Natalie Hanemann, and Allen Arnold, Katie Bond, and Jennifer Deshler, who believed in me and this project, and kept pushing me in the right direction.

My agent, Mary Beth Chappell, Zachary Shuster Harmsworth Literary & Entertainment Agency, without whom this series probably still would not be published.

My family, especially my husband, for their continued support and encouragement.

My personal horse expert, Richard Clifton, who e-mailed answers to my questions promptly, accurately, and with kindness.

And, finally, but most importantly, to the Lover of My Soul, who captured my heart at the age of fourteen, and I never got over it.

READING GROUP GUIDE

1. It is a matter of history that King Louis XIV literally sent spies into Switzerland to ferret out the Huguenots who had fled there to escape religious persecution. What would you have done if you had sought refuge from the tyranny of religious persecution and you knew that soldiers could arrest you at any moment and take you back? Would you give up, hide, flee to another country?

2. Madeleine and her family had financial reserves. But what if you had no means to flee any farther? What would you do? Where would you turn?

3. What were your thoughts concerning François' death? Would you have given him the laudanum? Did that offend you?

4. Madeleine was forced to return to a place that put her in a confused and conflicted position. As a young girl, she loved Versailles and King Louis, but as an adult, she could see the seducing, subtle evil behind the lifestyle. Have you ever been in a position to return to a lifestyle that, though tempting, you knew would

hold you prisoner and ultimately cause your demise? Perhaps it was a person or maybe even an addiction. What did you do? Did you give in? Did you flee? Did you return only to find what you remembered as glamorous and fun was now empty and hollow?

5. Look up 1 Corinthians 10:13. What does God promise to do for us when we are tempted? How did he make a way of escape for Madeleine?

6. Commander Paul Boveé turns out to be a hero of sorts. What were your feelings about that? Has there ever been anyone in your life that you started out disliking, but then eventually befriended?

7. What scene did you feel was the most tense? When Madeleine and Pierre try to escape from the musketeers? When Pierre reports to King Louis? When Pierre is thrown into prison? When Madeleine and Pierre and Philippe escape? When Commander Boveé is fighting the soldiers? Or some other scene? Why?

8. Have you ever been angry at God? Before you answer too quickly, every major character in Scripture was offended by God: Moses, Abraham, David, even Jesus ("My God, my God, why have you forsaken me?"). At times they questioned God, asking why he hadn't come to the rescue. And all except Jesus tried to work out their situations by their own schemes. Moses ran away into the desert to escape God's call on his life; Abraham tried to "help" God out by having a child by his wife's handmaiden instead of by Sarah, his wife; David had been anointed king, but had to run for his life for years, finally crying out to the Lord, "Wilt thou forget me forever?"

   Madeleine was offended that God had allowed her family to go through trial after trial; the oppressions were unending. She could not understand why God was not rescuing her from what seemed to be the destruction of her life. Could you relate to her? Would it have been so bad in the "honored" position of the king's *maîtresse en titre*?

9. Discuss the conclusion. Was it a satisfying conclusion to you?

Thank you for reading *A Prisoner of Versailles*. Contact me through my Web site www.goldenkeyesparsons.com or e-mail me at GPar0719@aol.com. I love hearing from my readers!